WESTPORT

WESTPORT

JAMES COMEY

THE MYSTERIOUS PRESS
NEW YORK

WESTPORT

Mysterious Press
An Imprint of Penzler Publishers
58 Warren Street
New York, N.Y. 10007

Library of Congress Control Number: 2023922348

ISBN: 978-1-61316-524-9
eBook ISBN: 978-1-61316-525-6

10 9 8 7 6 5 4 3 2 1

Printed in the United States of America
Distributed by W. W. Norton & Company

To my grandchildren,
an endless source of joy and optimism

AUTHOR'S NOTE

I once worked served as the General Counsel of a large investment manager in Westport, Connecticut, where I worked with extraordinary people. Like all lawyers for private clients, though, my duty to protect client confidences never ends.

That obligation, however, does not preclude me from using my imagination in writing a novel. In other words, *Westport* is a work of fiction. It's made up. For that reason, my former colleagues are not in the book, but I will always be grateful for their friendship and all they taught me.

PROLOGUE

The sun was now fully above the horizon and Ernie Sosa could see the outline of Long Island across the Sound, which meant the best part of his day was finished. He had squeezed in almost two hours of fishing by starting while it was still dark. His family would eat fresh flounder for dinner, and now it was time to get to his real job.

The route in and out was tricky for a midsize motorboat like Ernie's *Pride and Joy*—the name stenciled on the back. Seymour Rock could eat your boat. And it was hard to spot that small pile of stone early in the morning, especially in late October, so Ernie Sosa cut his engine to a crawl as he headed for the Connecticut side. The water near shore, still warm from baking all summer, was giving off morning mist like a steam iron. That, plus the fact that Seymour Rock sat low and directly in the path to the Saugatuck River harbor, made it a dangerous hazard for a boat like his.

Not today, rock, Sosa thought. He would just barely have enough time to dock his boat, change, and make it to his job at Newman's Own, the charitable food company based in Westport. But he still wasn't going to hurry past "the rock" and risk the boat it took him twenty years to buy. So he watched carefully as Seymour Rock slid by the left side—and, yes, he knew it was called *port*, but he still couldn't get used to saying fancy boating stuff.

He saw it, even with the mist. There was something long and red on the rock—a kayak, canoe maybe. *Who the hell would leave their boat out here?* He quickly looked around. There were no other boats or people. He squeezed his hand on the throttle handle, trying to force himself to motor past and make it to work on time. *Goddammit.* Ernie eased the throttle back and gently steered toward the rock. He could use a boat pole to grab and tow. It was the right thing to do. *Five minutes late isn't a disaster.*

Ernie paused his boat a few feet from Seymour Rock, throwing two fenders over the side in case a swell carried him against the rock face. He reached out with his pole and hooked the back end of the canoe. It was entirely up on the rock, about a foot above the waterline. He began to pull the canoe toward the water so it could slalom onto the Sound without flipping over. It didn't move. *Wow, a lot heavier than it looks.*

Ernie's second pull on the pole only moved his boat closer to the rock. He made sure his third yank was short and sharp, pulling so forcefully that his boat swayed. That did it. One end of the canoe slid toward him and slapped the water. Suddenly he couldn't breathe.

Ernie was looking down at a fully dressed middle-aged woman with short brown hair. She was lying on her back, with her head toward him, under the rear crossbeam. Her legs stretched out toward the front of the canoe, which was still stuck on Seymour Rock. He started to shout, "Lady!" but stopped. There was no lady here anymore. Her eyes were closed and her throat was cut wide open. Around her head, the canoe was filled with partially congealed blood. Ernie dropped the pole and grappled for his radio, his heartbeat pounding in his ears.

CHAPTER ONE

Nora Carleton took a drink from her travel mug and stared out at the Long Island Sound, which was like yellow glass in the morning sun. She really should be getting to work, but the same thing that made her turn right instead of left from her driveway was keeping her from getting off this bench at Southport Beach. She lifted the steel gray mug toward her mouth again, but stopped short this time to study the faded gold and blue circular logo. The eagle in the middle was almost gone. As was the red, white, and blue shield. *God, I miss that work.*

It had been two years since Nora left her job at the United States Attorney's Office for the Southern District of New York. She moved only fifty miles away, but it seemed like another planet—Westport, Connecticut, and a job at the world's largest hedge fund. She liked the people at Saugatuck Associates. They were brilliant, honest, and sometimes funny, but most of them had never known what it was like to have a job where you were supposed to do good, to rescue the taken or stop evil people from harming the weak. They had never been the organized crime prosecutor she once was. They worked ridiculous hours, as she had in the government, but it was to make money for the firm's clients, and for themselves. Sure, many of the assets were retirement funds for teachers or firefighters, and making money for those folks was good, but even that moral bank shot required squinting past clients like Middle Eastern oligarchs and genocidal authoritarian governments.

Nora was careful how she talked about this at work—it wouldn't do for the firm's general counsel to be badmouthing the business—but some of her friends there knew what was eating at her. Her mentor and boss, Chief Operating Officer Helen Carmichael, urged her to try to find meaning through the "kibbutz theory." There was a moral purpose, Helen argued, in the collection of people who had come together to work at Saugatuck. They cared for one another, shared a goal of excellence, and promised to tell one another the truth at all times. Whether they made shoes or invested money, she said, the community itself was a source of meaning. And in a world where lying seemed to be epidemic, a culture based on truth above all else intrigued Nora. She took the job mostly for the money and the location, but it was a benefit that the place apparently despised liars as much as she did.

Nora liked and trusted Helen, who was kind and protective of "her people," but she wasn't persuaded by the kibbutz argument. Of course, even with Helen she didn't say so. But she didn't have to. After all, the company's founder, legendary investor David Jepson, had explained the shared commitment to honesty this way: *You don't need to say everything that's on your mind, but if it's on your lips, it better be what's on your mind.* So Nora couldn't lie about it, but she kept quiet about her growing doubts, the ache that kept her staring out at the Sound when she should be making the short drive to her office. It wasn't on her lips, but it was eating a hole in her heart.

Still, the money *was* damn good. She ran her fingers through her hair and smiled. With Nora's starting bonus and the money her mother made from selling the family town house in Hoboken, New Jersey, they had purchased a big house in Westport. Sure, it was close enough to

Interstate 95 that the dull roar of traffic was a constant feature. But it was a "*water* feature," Teresa Carleton routinely insisted, with a smile. "Our waterfall." Nora didn't find it so charming, but the third generation of Carleton women in the house—eight-year-old Sophie—did. "Nana's waterfall," she called the noise, which grew louder on her short drive to school, then somehow disappeared as they passed under I-95 to the lush campus of Greens Farms Academy on a former Vanderbilt estate overlooking the Sound. Nora liked to joke that rich people had found a way to pay the highway noise to move only inland, so as not to mar the sparkling vistas along Beachside Avenue.

She took another sip from her aging Department of Justice mug and laughed at her own moping. There was no disputing that life on Connecticut's "Gold Coast" had been good to them. Sophie was thriving in the second grade at GFA, with small classes and deeply committed teachers. Sophie's father, Nick, lived nearby with his new wife, Vicki, and had the good grace not to mention that Vicki's extremely wealthy father had helped Nora get her job at Saugatuck Associates and paid Sophie's tuition at her fancy private school. But Nora knew it, and was grateful, both for the help and that it went unspoken.

She and Nick had never been a great couple, even when they were dating in Hoboken and created Sophie by accident. But they agreed Sophie was a gift and easily cooperated to move her between their Westport homes on alternating weeks. She missed the "nesting" days in Hoboken—before Nick got married—when Sophie lived with Nora's mom, leaving Nora and Nick to take turns staying in the "nest" with Sophie. Teresa continued to be a huge help with Sophie, while also volunteering in Bridgeport, a less wealthy, very diverse city nestled up against the rich, predominantly White towns that gave the Gold Coast its name. Her family was happy and thriving. Things were good.

Nora imagined her mother's voice. *C'mon Debbie Downer, time to get to work.* Smiling, she levered her six-foot frame off the bench and stepped to the sidewalk, stomping her feet to get the sand off her shoes. She backed the car out and steered down Beachside. She would drive past Greens Farms Academy—Sophie was at Nick's this week, so he had taken her to school—and parallel to I-95 until she reached the Saugatuck, and the firm's modern fieldstone and glass offices on the bank of the river.

CHAPTER TWO

Nora grinned as she pulled her Honda CRV into the Saugatuck Associates parking garage, with its rows of moderately priced cars. David Jepson was seventy now and determined to transition out of running the company he built, but his presence was everywhere in its culture, including the parking lot. Every employee knew that the billionaire Jepson drove a beat-up Ford Explorer. They had also heard the story about his visit to the office of an investment firm interested in a merger, where he looked with disgust at the fancy cars parked outside and loudly asked the Saugatuck employees with him, "Are these the cars of people you want to make a life with? I sure don't." There was no merger. And there were still no fancy cars in the Saugatuck lot. Many of Nora's colleagues owned expensive sports cars, but those were for weekends.

The garage walls were studded with cameras. Saugatuck was as serious about security as it was about truth and transparency. The company made millions—billions, really—for itself and its clients because, over decades, it had deciphered connections among world events and used those connections to automate its investment decisions. Drought in central Asia? That meant the stock price of American big-box retailers was destined to go down. Why? Because the ships that weren't needed to move grain drove down the cost of shipping electronics from

Asia and forced competing retailers to lower their prices. Most people didn't know that, or the hundreds of other connections that made up Saugatuck's "secret sauce." This complex recipe of causes and effects could never get out or the company would lose its edge.

That explained the cameras and the fingerprint scanner Nora pressed to open the door from the garage. More cameras in the ceiling watched her walk down the long hallway past chrome and glass walls toward Abe, who was waiting for her outside her office door.

"Morning, boss," he said with a smile.

"Boss? You know we have no hierarchies here at the Saugatuck meritocracy."

"Oh yeah, then why am I called your 'assistant' and I sit in a cubicle while you get a private office with a big desk and a view?"

"Fair point," Nora answered. "And how are truth and transparency this fine morning?"

Abe followed her into her office, which, like all Saugatuck workspaces, was designed to have a microphone in the ceiling to record meetings. Saugatuck's default was that all work-related conversations should be recorded so any person interested in the topic could review them—and to enforce the company rule against gossip: No absent person should be talked about unless the conversation was recorded and the subject notified. Not long after she started at the company, Nora stood on a chair and yanked the microphone out of the ceiling. She also unplugged the one connected to her desk phone.

Abe had watched her on the chair that day, wide-eyed. He came to Saugatuck straight out of Harvard and was attracted, like dozens of other young graduates of elite schools, by the company's determination to root out the twin poisons of hierarchy and gossip. And also by the money, although that was something one didn't admit at Saugatuck.

Abe Evans had lasted two years so far, all of which he had spent as Nora's assistant. As she stepped off the chair that morning two years ago, she noticed Abe's thick rust-colored mustache had drooped along with his mouth. He looked sad and confused watching Nora destroy transparency.

"Oh, I should have explained," she said. "No way the general counsel's conversations can be recorded. Too much risk to the company that the taping and dissemination will blow the attorney–client privilege. But if there's some meeting that doesn't relate to my role as a lawyer, we can plug it back in."

The mustache went back up. "Got it."

With her right pointer finger, Nora mimed a mustache on her own face. "So you a redhead?"

Abe smiled and ran one hand over his shaved head. "Would be if I had enough hair to cover. Premature baldness is a big thing in my family. I'm way ahead of it."

"Looks great," she answered, immediately regretting that she asked about the man's hair. After a half beat of awkward silence, she pressed on. "What does it mean for you to be my assistant?"

"Not really sure," Abe replied. "One of those undefined Saugatuck things. All they told me was: Do what makes sense."

Nora chuckled. "I'm from the federal government, where every job comes with a two-page, single-spaced definition. I kinda like 'do what makes sense.' Let's go with that."

And they had, for two years and counting. Abe didn't know anything about the law, but he was extraordinarily bright, hardworking, and interested in learning. He did secretarial chores like making copies, but slowly grew into what Saugatuck called a "thought partner," someone Nora could kick ideas around with. He also quickly became the younger brother Nora never had. As close as they were, though, she couldn't quite bring herself to talk to him about her sense that things at Saugatuck were not always what they seemed.

Now, as she dropped her bag on the desk, he answered her usual morning question. "The search for truth at the weekly Management Committee meeting is delayed this morning. Not sure why, but I think they're having trouble rounding up the members. We'll get a five-minute warning before they start."

The Management Committee, or "MC," was made up of the eight most senior leaders of the company and met once a week in the large glass-walled conference room. The MC members sat at a big rectangular table, with assorted assistants and invited guests sitting behind in chairs along the walls. As the firm's chief lawyer, Nora was always invited and liked to sit facing the Saugatuck River, which was only inches below the glass walls. This close to the Long Island Sound, the river was really an estuary, reversing direction with the tide in a mesmerizing water dance, which made things challenging for the frequent paddleboarders headed down to the Sound or up to the center of Westport. Nora found those distractions indispensable to enduring the endless MC meetings, which often went on for hours. She could only listen so long to brilliant people challenging each other's thinking without refreshing herself by rooting for a paddleboarder. And now she had some extra time before the MC began its weekly marathon.

"Good," Nora answered with a smile, "that gives me time for free food. Can I buy you something?"

Catered meals were provided to all company employees in break rooms spread throughout the sprawling three-story building. Abe had his plate covered with fresh fruit carefully arrayed around a bowl of granola on a bed of Greek yogurt. He set it on the counter to look at his buzzing phone. "They pushed the start back to eleven with lunch served at noon. I'll come get you a few minutes before."

"Sounds good," Nora said. "I'll be in my awesome office eating and drinking free stuff."

"And *I* will be in my completely equal nonhierarchical cubicle, ready to provide assistance at a moment's notice."

Their laughter filled the hallway.

CHAPTER THREE

The door to the office next to Nora's was closed, which was just as well because laughter tended to irritate Louis Lambert. It also seemed to Nora that he kept it closed because her very existence pissed him off. Lambert was a formal man—she once addressed him as "Lou" and was met with an icy "My name is Louis." It didn't help that he thought she stole his job. Lambert was twenty years older and had been the deputy general counsel at Saugatuck since Nora was in high school. He'd repeatedly demonstrated his mastery of all legal aspects of the financial management business and his devotion to the company. He should've been promoted to general counsel when Nora's predecessor was hired—also from outside the firm—but at least that guy came from the finance industry and knew the actual work. Nora had put mobsters in jail—certainly worthwhile, but she hadn't demonstrated competence in the business they were actually engaged in, something he found frustrating. He believed he'd been passed over because he was a White man and she had been hired because she was a woman and the firm was attempting to show more diversity to its institutional clients.

Nora knew all this because Lambert came into her office on her first day and told her these things, in precisely those words. He explained that he believed strongly in the culture of truth and felt duty bound to tell her she was an unqualified token hire. It wasn't personal, he assured her, but he didn't want to be less than fully candid with her.

Nora remembered the waves of anger, embarrassment, and fear that took turns washing over her as this balding middle-aged man with a flannel shirt tucked into his belted jeans stood in her doorway and delivered his "truth." She was actually quite proud that she showed no reaction. In the awkward silence that followed, she could think of nothing to do except tell the first lie of her Saugatuck career. "I look forward to working with you," she said as he turned to enter his office next door. *And you can stick your transparency up your petty little butt.*

Of course, what Louis Lambert didn't know was that Nora actually got the job through family connections. Sophie's new stepmom, Vicki, was the daughter of one of David Jepson's oldest friends and earliest investors. That's what got Nora in the door, where she met Helen Carmichael, who knew she needed a talented prosecutor to take over a sensitive internal investigation. Lambert didn't know any of that.

The real reasons behind her hiring did nothing to reduce Nora's imposter complex. So she treated that disease herself by reading *Investing for Dummies* and listening to hours of company meeting tapes. She quickly became fluent in the language of finance and the Saugatuck culture. Nora had devoted her early legal career to a government-run system designed to find truth through the collision of viewpoints in an adversarial environment. Could a company really strip away all the usual hierarchies of money, power, age, gender, or race and arrive at the best answer entirely through logic, persuasion, and consensus? She didn't know, but was excited to find out, despite Louis Lambert icing her on her first day.

CHAPTER FOUR

A fter Labor Day, the cops only patrolled the beaches part-time, and it took a while for Westport PD marine officers to arrive at Seymour Rock, even though it sat just off Compo Beach. The department's ten-meter Naiad Marine Patrol Vessel was docked less than a quarter mile away, but it was a half hour before the boat pulled up next to Ernie Sosa's. He had stayed, as the dispatcher asked, letting his boat drift a bit so he didn't have to look at the canoe. When the police boat arrived, he was met by a petite detective with short black hair. She instructed him to meet another detective at the Compo dock to take his statement and he slowly motored off.

Detective Demitria "Demi" Kofatos had seen a lot of dead bodies in her fifteen years with the Westport PD. But through all the car crashes, strokes, suicides, and overdoses, there had never been a body that looked like the woman in the canoe, her head nearly cut off and resting on a gelatinous pillow of blood. After photographing the scene carefully, she and the other officers used gloved hands to lift the canoe—with the body still inside—into the police boat and headed for the dock. There, they waited another half hour for an Associate Medical Examiner to arrive from the chief coroner's offices in Farmington, just outside Hartford. There was no phone or other personal possession visible in the canoe but they didn't search the pockets of the dead woman's slacks or look beneath her. Crime scene protocol dictated that the Associate ME should be the one to first touch the victim. So they put the time to good use, taking more photographs, including of the twelve-digit Hull Identification Number on the bow of the canoe, from which Demi learned it was a Westport-registered canoe, assigned to a slot on the storage racks fifty yards from where she was standing.

She walked over to the sprawling wooden skeleton of the kayak and canoe racks, mostly empty as the October 31 town deadline approached for residents to remove their boats for the winter. It felt strange to be here on a case. This wasn't where people died; it was where she brought her dog to play in off-season months. There were no signs of unusual activity in the sandy grass by the racks, but she photographed the ground anyway. A chain and open four-digit padlock dangled from the assigned slot. She photographed them and, using rubber gloves, removed and bagged the chain and lock as evidence.

When she got back to the dock, the Associate ME had arrived and was supervising the removal of the body from the canoe. The vessel would be wrapped in plastic and taken to the state police lab for processing. She recognized Martin Mortenson, who was assigned to cover southern Fairfield County, from other unattended-death scenes in Westport. She knew him well enough to know he had a good sense of humor, like most people in the death business, but hated the nickname "Morty the Mortician" that gave so many cops the chuckles. She called him Martin.

There was no identification on the body, which Martin processed for transportation to the Chief Medical Examiner's office on the campus of the University of Connecticut Medical School. He bagged her hands, but there was no apparent sign of trauma on her hands or fingers. Her clothing, including the bra and underwear, appeared undisturbed, although detailed examination would come later. There was no sign of a weapon. In fact, the only thing inconsistent with being a well-dressed woman napping in the bottom of a canoe was the smoothly cut opening just above her thyroid cartilage, slicing her from one ear to the other.

On her cell phone, Demi made calls to nearby police departments, checking for any missing persons reports. She used her laptop to query the LInX system, looking for reports that might match their victim. The Law Enforcement Information Exchange was the cop version of Google, knitting together the many local departments of Connecticut and the other states. But nobody in Connecticut or neighboring states had a missing middle-aged, five-foot-three-inch White woman with short brown hair.

"Really strange, Martin," she said, tapping the laptop screen with one of her black-painted fingernails.

"What is?"

Demi couldn't shake the feeling that she should know the woman. Westport cops didn't belong to the clubs or attend the cocktail parties of the residents they served and protected—in fact, it was a miracle they could afford to live here—but she still knew the look.

"This lady looks Westport-fancy. Nice pants, silk blouse, expensive shoes, salon-looking haircut. But nothing on LInX. Maybe too fresh for something to be there, but I also called all the adjoining departments. Nothing. Could it be that only the killer knows she's missing?"

"That *is* odd," Martin replied. "Rich people usually don't go missing without ripples."

"Yup, and we got lots of them around here—rich people, I mean. I'm gonna start with the canoe's owner. Maybe it'll end there. Safe drive to Farmington."

"I'll let you know as soon as we have anything. You do the same, Demi?"

"Will do."

CHAPTER FIVE

A be leaned into Nora's office. "They're gonna get started, even without a full complement. David's assistant says he's pissed, thinks people don't care about the MC or the culture anymore."

"He always says that," Nora said, taking her last sip of Illy coffee. "Who's not here yet?"

"Thing 2 isn't in yet. Helen neither. Oh, and Artemis says he's here but has to do a client call."

Nora smiled at the culturally dangerous reference to Thing 2. In another company, calling one of the founder's twin sons by that Seuss-derived name would be as natural as breathing. But this was Saugatuck and nobody would call the mercurial brat that to his face, so it really shouldn't be said. She worried she had corrupted Abe, but she let it go.

"Artemis is full of shit and will do anything to avoid painfully long meetings. Rob in?"

"Yes," Abe said, "I saw him rolling toward the conference room."

"Good. Maybe if I hurry I can get my seat next to him so we can pass funny notes."

Nora hurried from her office and down the hall to the conference room. A man in a wheelchair with close-cropped black hair and muscular arms was just reaching to push the door assist pad. She stepped in front and slapped the little square. "Ironside," she said with a smile, "allow me."

Rob Arslan looked up at her and grinned broadly. "You know nobody gets that reference, right? Sixties television about the disabled? And it's probably inappropriate anyway. Especially from our general counsel."

"Make a report," Nora answered, holding the door. "In this place, that's not gonna make the top fifty."

"Probably right," Arslan said. "How's my girl?"

Nora chortled. "Of course, calling grown women 'girl' might be higher on the list."

"Not you, woman. Sophie. How's the new year at GFA?"

Nora beamed. "Ah, she's doing great. Thriving, really. This move has been so good for her, as you predicted. You know she still talks about you? 'That man who can play basketball in the chair.' You're Sophie-famous."

"My goal in life," he answered with a smile.

Robert "Rob" Arslan was one of the best things about Saugatuck, in Nora's opinion. His story never failed to move her. The child of Turkish immigrants to the United States—their last name was a common one in Turkey, meaning "lion"—he went to West Point, graduated at the top of his class, became a member of the elite Delta Team, and deployed to Iraq in the First Gulf War. During a special forces night HALO (high-altitude, low-opening) mission, his chute became tangled and he landed hard, damaging his lower spinal cord.

After a grueling recovery in military hospitals, Arslan left the Army and worked at several tech start-ups before joining Saugatuck. David Jepson had long been fascinated by the American military's special forces (although he never served himself). In fact, Jepson frequently referred to Saugatuck's employees as "the intellectual Delta Team." In Arslan, he found both a real Delta member and a powerful brain. Arslan worked his way up to one of the firm's most important positions—overseeing the company's IT systems. In addition to managing tech, Arslan used his former military connections to develop long relationships with the firm's important clients in the South Pacific, and Saugatuck counted on him to regularly make the grueling flights to oversee Australia's Future Fund and New Zealand's NZ Super Fund.

But Nora liked him most for his sense of humor and his commitment to helping disabled veterans. Rob liked to say he made more money than he knew what to do with and so he wanted to do good with it. He contributed large sums to veterans charities, including his own, ran a wheelchair basketball league, and visited wounded vets, many of whom he helped get jobs. In fact, his assistant, Sally Lynch, was a former Army helicopter pilot who lost an arm when her Blackhawk was shot down during the invasion of Iraq in 2003.

Sally was devoted to Rob and to Saugatuck's way of operating. Watching them together, Nora had sometimes wondered if the divorced Rob was attracted to more than Sally's commitment to truth and transparency—after all, she was a striking beauty with huge warm eyes and a natural Afro of soft curls. So Nora once gently asked him, explaining that the GC had to know about key personnel conflicts of interest. But he denied it and she believed him.

Nora liked to sit next to Rob at MC meetings because he was fond of turning his wheelchair and solemnly extending one of his thickly muscled arms to hand her a note, as if he urgently needed legal guidance. What he really needed was to poke fun at what he called the "intellectual Escher stairs" of the MC meetings—"neither up nor down, just endlessly around and around." If David Jepson ever demanded to see his notes, they might all be in trouble, but David thought too much of Rob to push him and, in an emergency, she could always play the attorney–client privilege card.

Nora and Rob were working closely together—along with Chief Operating Officer Helen Carmichael—on Nora's most sensitive work assignment, investigating something subtle and troubling that had been going on with respect to the firm's trades.

Three years ago, her predecessor had conducted a series of audits that first detected tiny, unexpected moves in the financial instruments Saugatuck used when buying or selling for its clients, resulting in what experts called "poor execution pricing." This was a signal that someone might be "front running" Saugatuck, selling or buying just before Saugatuck did to take advantage of the way Saugatuck's trades, even seconds later, would move the price. The differences on any particular trade were small, but, in aggregate, somebody could make a lot of money by knowing where Saugatuck was going and, by getting there first, costing Saugatuck's clients a great deal of money in total.

Figuring out who was doing it and how—corrupt broker, systems breach, or bad Saugatuck employee—was a difficult task. The previous GC left abruptly for reasons unrelated to the investigation and after his departure Helen wanted to focus on solving the case. So she pushed to hire Nora, despite her inexperience in the investment management world. Nora knew how to chase down criminals, and, in Helen's view, somebody was stealing from Saugatuck's clients. If they didn't stop it, the firm would be ruined; institutional investors would not place billions of dollars in pensions with a hedge fund that couldn't safeguard their money from slimy Wall Street practices.

CHAPTER SIX

With Helen and Artemis "Arty" Falcone, the head of client relations, absent, half the seats at the MC table were occupied by Jepson family members. So when she wasn't looking for paddleboarders or answering Rob's hilarious notes, Nora liked to pass the time trying to imagine what was going on inside those Jepson heads.

Sitting closest to David at the head of the table was his oldest, Miranda—bright, hardworking, and his heir apparent. She was married to her job and liked it that way. The better twin, Charles—Thing 1, in Abe's heretical formulation—was less talented than Miranda, but believed the company should be his someday as the eldest male heir. Charles, who went by Chip, was married, had a steady family life, and believed his sister—like all women—was too emotional to run the logic-based company, although he was careful not to say so.

Thing 2—who, to be clear, was never called that—was Jeffey, given name Jefferson. If Jeffey were as honest as Saugatuck's training said he should be, he would admit he would rather be a TikTok and Instagram influencer, and not what Nora knew him to be—a constant drunken issue at Saugatuck's employee parties. Jeffey's problem, as Nora also knew, was that his father refused to bankroll his lifestyle and he had been unable to make it big on his own.

In fact, that was true of all three kids. Their father severely limited their access to his billions, reasoning that he wanted them to have enough money so they could choose to do anything, but not so much that they could do nothing. The result was that both sons continued to work at Saugatuck while deeply resenting their treatment, although for different reasons. Miranda Jepson was aware of the family drama but worked hard to grow the business that she hoped to run when her father retired, something he had been talking about for ten years. Many people believed he would never leave, because Saugatuck was David Jepson's life—he had no passions besides investing—and it gave him tremendous power over his own children and over everyone who worked for him.

Rounding out the MC members in attendance, and sitting on the other side of David Jepson from Miranda, was Marcus Baum, who shared the Chief Investment Officer role with David. He was a boy genius now approaching forty, affable and kind with a slightly off-putting affect. His trademark was sitting in wrinkled jeans and an untucked shirt, with one of his feet folded under him, staring off into the middle distance as he conversed with people sitting close to him. Nora liked him, in spite of—or maybe because of—his eccentricities. She also often wondered whether his oddness and bright red hair had made him a target for childhood bullies, a part of the human experience she hated—and something that made being a Mafia prosecutor deeply satisfying. "I put the biggest bullies in jail," she once explained to Sophie.

Baum had once given Nora her most memorable Saugatuck performance review, detailing in a flat voice all the ways in which she was short of excellent, before adding, "Oh, and you do the humor thing. That's good." Like many senior people at Saugatuck, Baum really didn't understand the humor thing, but he was a deeply honest, decent person.

The meeting began with a discussion of whether the real-time employee evaluation system—under which employees used iPads to give ten-point-scale numerical reviews to their colleagues as they spoke in a meeting—should be changed in any way. Nora thought the system was idiotic. In company meetings, someone would make a statement and get an instant rating from listeners, who were looking down at their iPads; when someone responded, the response would be rated, and around and around, with everyone rating and nobody looking at each other—a kind of heaven for those who disliked eye contact, which were many of the employees. She was following the discussion closely—noticing that MC members didn't give the instant ratings to one another—until Saugatuck's chief security officer, Laslo Reiner, slipped into the room and leaned down to her.

"You got a minute?" he asked quietly, leaning his head toward the door.

"Sure," Nora whispered and got up to follow him out of the conference room.

CHAPTER SEVEN

Demitria Kofatos didn't know anything about art, but there was nothing else to look at from where she was sitting. The two-story-tall canvas in the Saugatuck visitors lobby looked expensive. Sure, it also looked like a bomb had gone off inside a paint store, but she had seen similar paint-bomb art in the palatial homes that dotted Westport and in Manhattan at MoMA. *Fancy stuff.* Before she ran out of things to think about art, Saugatuck's security guy returned with a pleasant-looking woman walking beside him.

Nora Carleton was tall—five foot twelve, she liked to say—with a chin-length auburn bob that framed large brown eyes. She was wearing a tan quarter-zip sweater over green corduroy pants and hiking shoes, which was not what the detective expected from the chief lawyer of the world's largest hedge fund, but then Demi didn't really know what a hedge fund was beyond the more-money-than-God thing.

The detective was shorter, with a friendly, heart-shaped face. She wore her thick dark hair in a low bun, from which escaped a few curls, no matter how much hairspray she used. Demi couldn't shake the feeling that in another time and place Nora was someone she would like. But this wasn't some other time and place. She stood and presented her badge. "Ms. Carleton, I'm sorry to interrupt you, but I need to ask you about your canoe."

"Of course," Nora answered with a polite smile, "but I'm surprised you make these visits personally. I promise I'm going to get it out of there before the thirty-first."

"It's not that," Demi replied. "Is there somewhere we can chat, privately?"

"Sure," Nora answered, gesturing to the glass-enclosed conference room connected to the lobby. "In there."

Turning to the security chief, she added, "Thanks, Laslo, you don't need to hang around. I'm guessing somebody stole it. And, yes, I know how many times you told me to actually use the lock."

He smiled and stepped aside as the two women walked to the conference room. "Let me know if you need anything."

Once they were seated, Demi confirmed Nora owned a red canoe that she stored on the racks at Compo Beach. "That looks like it," she said when the detective produced a photo of it sitting on the dock. "I have no idea what the serial number is but that looks like mine. I also have no idea why it's on the dock."

"Well, I do," Demi said. "It was found this morning."

Nora shook her head and smiled. "I don't want to rat out my coworkers, but everybody uses it. We were out there yesterday for the Compo sunset, but I can't remember who had it. Still, I'm glad you found it. Is there some kind of fine because it was loose?"

Demi reached into her bag for a folder. "No, no, that's not what this is. We're trying to identify somebody in connection with the canoe."

"I'm not tracking," Nora said, tilting her head and noticing for the first time that the detective's short fingernails were painted black.

Demi slid the folder toward Nora. "We're hoping maybe you recognize this woman." She pinched the top edge of the closed folder with her fingers and paused to look at Nora. Still watching Nora's face, Demi flipped the folder open, revealing an eight-by-ten color photo of the dead woman in the bottom of the canoe.

Nora squinted at the picture for several seconds before it hit.

Then her vision narrowed for an instant to a single dot before widening to a cloudy haze. Her ears thumped, and the sensation radiated down her arms. It was hard to breathe, but she brought a hand to her mouth, loudly pulling air between her fingers.

Control yourself Nora, you've seen worse than this. Goddammit, control yourself.

She closed her eyes, took one more deep breath, and dropped her hand. When she looked up and spoke, her voice was flat and professional, like the prosecutor she had once been.

"I can identify the woman in the photo as Helen Carmichael, the Chief Operating Officer of this company. When did this happen? Have you made arrests? Where does the investigation stand?"

Demi jerked back in her chair, retracting her chin to signal her surprise and then leaned in with a raised voice, punching words for emphasis.

"Wait just a minute. This woman was found *murdered* in *your* canoe and her body was discovered this morning and *you're* asking *me* for investigative updates? Nope, that's not how this goes. How about you give *me* an update? Where were you last night, Ms. Carleton, and what was your relationship with the victim? Did you or anyone you know have reason to want her dead?"

Nora missed Demi's intensity because she was lost in her own thoughts. *I moved here to get away from this kind of violence. How the hell did Helen end up dead in my canoe?*

CHAPTER EIGHT

Almost three years earlier, she had towered over Helen in the restaurant, even after Helen stood to greet her as she approached the table. She seemed so different in person—smaller than the New York–accented voice on the phone, but also softer, cooler. Her smile went all the way to her hazel eyes, spreading out from the corners into friendly wrinkles. She wore her dark hair short, with simple gold earrings and a gold chain over her black mock turtleneck, which she wore under a black leather jacket with dark gray slacks.

Helen's look was Manhattan, where for years she worked running the unglamorous back-office operations of big Wall Street banks, before moving to Westport and Saugatuck Associates. She knew the guts of the investment management business better than most. David Jepson brought her to Saugatuck to run stuff. He had enough people who could think deep thoughts about the connections between world events. He needed someone who could manage an actual business. And that was Helen Carmichael.

When Nora sat, Helen swept her arm across the broad patio dining area of Artisan, a farm-to-table restaurant in the neighboring village of Southport, a spot Nora would learn was a popular Saugatuck hangout. "I love this place, and not just because there are no tape recorders. I thought we should get together for a bite before your job interviews at our office tomorrow."

Nora smiled tightly.

"Hey, don't be nervous," Helen continued. "I think you're exactly what we're looking for. I figured we could use this time to talk about a few land mines you might not want to step on."

After the waiter took their menus, Helen lifted her wine glass and toasted Nora. "To a successful day tomorrow at crazy-land."

Nora touched her glass to Helen's and offered another half smile, unsure what to make of the derogatory reference to what might be her future employer.

Helen took a drink and exhaled before continuing. "Okay, so you signed the nondisclosure agreement and then read the pile of stuff we sent you and listened to all the tapes, right?"

Nora nodded. "Until my ears hurt from the headphones."

Helen laughed. "That's our way. And what you read and heard is real. We really, *really* are committed to telling each other the truth, to transparency, to logic and death-to-hierarchy and yada yada. And I probably shouldn't say it that way, because I do believe in it."

Helen exhaled audibly again and took another drink of wine. "Here's the thing: It's just that it's the most real at the bottom and gets successively less real the farther up the chain you go. The kids believe it, and live it, which is wonderful and also a bit tiring, to be honest. At the Management Committee level, not so much."

She took another drink, glanced over Nora's shoulder, and lowered her voice. "Sure, we all speak the language of the culture but there's a bit of an underground economy. There's what goes on in the meetings, the endless plumbing—I'm sure you know by now that's our charming term for questioning someone—and you can hear it all on tape. Then there's what goes on that's not on tape, including at places like this. Alliances, secrets, backstabbing. That game goes on at Saugatuck, same as all companies. But what makes it so challenging here is that everyone in the game must always and at all times deny that there is a game. Because there is no game, right? We really do fire people who're caught gossiping, after all. So no game. And also the hardest game you've ever played."

Nora couldn't hide her surprise. "Does David Jepson know?"

Helen shrugged her shoulders. "Honestly, I don't know. I've worked with the man for fifteen years and never had a countercultural conversation with him. He's never mofo'd someone when it wasn't on tape and then shared with that person. Yet it goes on all around him."

"He's a genius, right?"

"He is, but in a narrow kind of way. What I mean is, he can see patterns in data like nobody I've ever known. But he can't read faces, or tone. He thinks emotion is some kind of weakness, when it's actually the oldest form of human cognition. Sarcasm makes no sense to him, so he mostly misses it. He's Spock from *Star Trek*. Honest, transparent, logical, decent. And he assumes everyone else is as well, which is why I'm not sure he sees the game."

Nora chuckled softly. "Okay; other land mines?"

"Just rich people in general," Helen answered. "You spent a lot of time around folks with a ton of dough?"

"Can't say I have," Nora answered with a smile. "Hoboken didn't offer many opportunities."

"Well, here's the deal. Really rich people know, on some level, that chance—pure luck—played a big role in their success. And they deal with that in one of two ways: Some hold on to a sense of guilt and compensate by trying to help other people; most submerge it by convincing themselves they are uniquely talented and deserve the money. Jepson is the first type. Most of the others aren't."

Nora shook her head. "So why, exactly, is this a good place to work?"

Helen laughed. "Oh, that's easy. Because it's better than any-place else. The ratio of honest people to weasels is far higher than at any other company, especially in the world of finance, *especially* at the big dumb banks. What's aboveground here is really pretty amazing—smart people being honest with one another. And what's belowground doesn't ruin it and is actually kind of interesting. I just wanted you to know about that part of us because I need your help in protecting this wonderful and screwed-up place. You can't do that if you can't see it fully."

Nora's full day of interviews went well, once she adjusted to the exhausting beers-in-a-dorm-room-after-midnight interview style. In her first session, ninety minutes with MC member Marcus Baum, he looked toward the corner of the room and asked her to "explain the difference between justice and mercy." The rest of her interviews were no less strange, including a session with an industrial psychologist, who said he was an expert at determining her conceptual thinking ability.

At the end of the long day, she met company founder Jepson, whom she instantly liked. He was open and vulnerable, talking of his love for the culture and his hope that it would long outlive him and provide a lasting source of "purposeful relationships" for talented, honest people. It was also clear that he really liked Nora, and he offered her the job at the end of the interview.

"I want people to come here for the culture, but let's talk about money," he said, going to a whiteboard. He explained she would be paid a salary and also a bonus. If the company did better, the bonus could go up; if it was a bad year, it could go down. He wrote numbers for the salary and bonus target on the board. It was more money than Nora had made in her entire career as a federal prosecutor. She squinted to be sure she wasn't misreading the number of digits.

"Seems fair," she said, trying not to sound out of breath.

Jepson turned back to the board and erased the numbers, replacing them with two larger figures. "How about this?" he asked, his face a mask.

Nora stayed under control, not sure what was happening. "Fair, for sure," she said flatly.

Jepson turned again, erased again, and wrote new, higher numbers before turning back to her. "This?"

Nora lost her grip. "Wow! Are you serious?"

Jepson smiled. "Yes, entirely. So are we done here?"

All Nora could do was nod.

When Nora joined, Helen had been true to her word, guiding and coaching every step of the way. The patio at Artisan became their regular spot, and they could each walk home from there, allowing them to explore the restaurant's extensive wine list. They talked and laughed for hours. Nora's story of her salary "negotiation" with David Jepson became one of Helen's favorites. She explained that Jepson always wanted Saugatuck's compensation to be the best in the industry—"beyond fair" was the expression he used—so he had taken her muttering of "seems fair" as a rejection. "If you had just stifled the 'wow' for a bit," Helen laughed, "you might own the place."

About six months into her tenure at Saugatuck, Nora seemed unusually quiet at their regular dinner.

"What's eating you?" Helen asked, taking a long drink of wine.

"Finally had a one-on-one in my office with Arty Falcone," Nora replied, "and it was really unnerving. He—"

"Wait, don't tell me," Helen interjected, lifting her palm. "He stared at your tits the whole time he spoke to you."

Nora nodded. "I was just going to say 'he didn't meet my eye,' but yes, he did exactly that."

Helen laughed. "Total dirtbag. And don't let it go to your head. That scumbag'd stare at your mother's tits. And your grandmother's, for that matter."

"That's quite a relief," Nora said, squinting. "And he kept combing his greaseball hair back with his hand the whole time and reeked of cologne. I'm never gonna get that smell out of my office."

"Yep, that's classic Arty." Helen laughed, clearly enjoying this. "What else?"

"That's it. He just totally grossed me out. That'll be our last one-on-one meeting."

Helen searched Nora's face. "He touch your butt?"

"What?"

"Like in an inadvertent way? Brush against your rear? Maybe you hardly noticed, while he was trying to pick up a pencil or some keys he dropped by your feet?"

"When's the last time you 'hardly noticed' a colleague touch your butt? He did not."

"Okay, that's progress because creepy Arty has been known to butt-touch," Helen said with a tight smile. "Maybe he passed because you're the general counsel. Again, it's not about your butt, either good or bad. He would—"

"Touch my grandmother's butt," Nora finished, shaking her head. "So gross. And not really a helpful thing to say, if I'm being honest."

"Hey, just giving it to you straight. But that's our boy. Clients love him. Especially the oil money types, which should not shock you. Your grandmother would not be safe with them."

Nora just shook her head and reached for her wine glass.

After dinner, they strolled down Pequot Avenue together, pausing to say good night at the corner of Westway Road, where their paths home diverged.

Without thinking, Nora bent down and kissed Helen, who responded by leaning in and lifting her hands to Nora's head, fingers touching her auburn hair. Nora gently lifted her own hands onto Helen's shoulders as their mouths moved together.

After a long moment, Helen shaped her lips into a smile and slid her hands to Nora's face, softly moving her head back.

"Mmmm, that was nice," she said, holding Nora's cheeks for another beat before slowly withdrawing her hands. "But you know we can't, right? Me being your boss and all, despite the total lack of hierarchy?"

Nora's face flushed and she took a step back. "I'm sorry, I don't know what came over me."

"Hey, hey," Helen said quickly, "don't get me wrong; in another life, I'd be dragging you into those bushes right there. I wish we could, but we just can't."

"You're right, you're right," Nora answered, still mortified. "I hope I haven't ruined things."

Helen laughed gently. "Uh, let's see. Me getting kissed by a beautiful woman? You ruined nothing. You changed nothing. And let's mark that place, in case we both get fired someday. In the meantime, I deny it ever happened. And if it did, it was pretty great."

"Thanks," Nora said, her cheeks beginning to return to their natural color.

"I had no idea you were into chicks. You know, with Sophie and all."

Nora nodded. "Been a bit of a journey for me, honestly. Figured out who I am later than most."

"Doesn't matter," Helen answered. "Who you are is pretty great."

She smiled and waved as she turned toward home. "See you tomorrow, Nora."

Nora nodded and smiled as they separated. "Thanks, boss. Good night."

CHAPTER NINE

Demi was still talking. "I'm sorry, I'm sorry," Nora interrupted. "I zoned out for a minute. This is so fucking overwhelming. Can you start again? What can I do to help you?"

"Okay, let's start over. Why don't you start by telling me what her job was here and what your connection to her was."

After Nora explained Helen's role at the company and as her direct supervisor, the detective turned to the personal.

"She have a family?"

"No, never married, lived alone. Don't know about her extended family. I actually think she considered a lot of us here as her family."

The detective paused. "And what about you? Where were you last night?"

"We had a get-together of people from here at Compo Beach to watch the sunset—something we do a lot on Sunday nights when the weather is good. Lot of Saugatuck people live here only during the week, so we get together when everybody is back at the end of the weekend. This was the last of the season."

"Can you get me the names of those people?"

"Sure. It was a big group—company-wide invite—but I'll try."

"And then what did you do?"

"I packed up and drove home and stayed there for the night."

"Anybody take your canoe out?"

"Not that I remember. Anybody can, which is why I leave it unlocked with the paddles in it. But I think most of them thought the water was too cold. They have to get their feet wet to get the canoe started and they're not up for that."

"You say you were home last night. Can anybody confirm that?"

Nora didn't intend to, but she laughed. "Do I have an alibi for Helen's murder? Is that what you're asking?"

"I suppose it is. Gonna ask a lot of people the same thing."

Nora shook her head. "I suppose I don't. My daughter Sophie is with her father this week—his regular week; we alternate—and my mother, who lives with me, is in Cape Cod visiting friends. So no, I have no alibi. Although my phone was at home with me, so if you really care, you could get the location data on it."

Demi didn't answer that. "Speaking of your phone, you have any communications with the deceased over the weekend?"

Nora pulled her phone from her pocket, shaking her head.

"Why are you shaking your head," the detective asked.

"The deceased. Word you used. Makes no sense that it's Helen."

She looked through her phone. "No calls with Helen; we usually only spoke in person or over text or email. One text from last night. *Need to talk,* she wrote, which is what she always said when she wanted to remind me to talk to her about something."

"Any idea what it was about?"

"No, it's the kind of thing that I would ask her about the next time we saw each other. But I don't know what it was."

"Can I have your phone?"

Nora paused before answering. "Actually, you can't. I don't mean to break your chops, but there's a lot of work stuff on there and I have to protect Saugatuck's information, especially given my role here. So if you want it, we'll need legal process and then we'll work through the privilege and attorney work-product issues."

Demi dropped it. "Do you know any reason anybody would want to hurt Helen Carmichael?"

"No," Nora answered, sounding louder than she intended to. "Everybody respected her, loved her really. That's what makes this seem like a bad dream." Nora hesitated, but didn't mention the investigation she was conducting for Helen. *No way that's connected to this.*

"Okay, and we're going to need access to the deceased's office and her car. Is it here, do you know?"

"Is what here?"

"Her car."

"I don't know. Didn't notice on my way in. I can show you where she usually parks."

"That'd be great. And her office?"

"That I need to talk to our management about. I'll have Laslo seal it off, but we need to think through any issues related to you accessing her office or systems. Security is a big deal here and I'm not saying we won't, but we need to discuss it internally. They don't even know this has happened. You okay if I tell them all?"

Demi handed her card to Nora. "Sure, you can spread the word. And you'll send me the names of the people at the beach party last night?"

"Will do, but hard to call it a party. People sit around in beach chairs drinking wine and eating pizza until it gets dark. But I'll get you the names."

Nora led Demi to the garage and gestured toward an empty space. "We don't have assigned spaces, except we kinda do, informally. That's where Helen usually parked. Red Volkswagen Jetta. Not here."

"Where do you park?"

Nora turned back toward the rear of a parked white Honda they had walked past. "Right there. That piece of crap CRV is me."

"Woulda thought the cars would be fancier in here."

"It's a thing. Don't get me started."

As the two women retraced their steps, the detective paused behind Nora's car gesturing toward a dark stain above the rear hatch handle, just below the license plate. "Can I ask what that is?"

"No idea. Looks like paint or something."

"Honestly, Ms. Carleton, it looks like dried blood."

"Can't be. No way."

The detective pulled out her phone and took pictures of the mark. "I'd strongly advise you not to touch that until we can sample it."

Nora's face flushed. "Do I look stupid? I'm not going to touch anything and you can sample all you want. I don't know what it is."

"Actually, Ms. Carleton, I'm going to stay here until one of my colleagues can come over and sample that. Just to be careful."

"Be as careful as you like," Nora answered. "I'll tell Laslo you're still here, although I'm guessing he sees us on the cameras. Now I have to go tell Helen's friends what happened."

CHAPTER TEN

Nora's return to the conference room drew little attention; people were always coming and going during the endless MC meetings. But when she stopped and stood just inside the door, all heads turned to her. Even David Jepson knew there was something odd about her and the way she was standing.

"What is it, Nora?" he asked.

The prosecutorial calm that Nora felt after seeing the photo of Helen's body vanished and waves of emotion washed over her in this room filled with people who were like family to Helen. Her eyes were moist and her stomach was churning. She blurted it out, her voice growing louder with each word. "The police were just here. Helen's dead. Someone killed her. They found her body down at Compo. They showed me a photo."

Nora stood alone at the front. In a room full of people who normally struggled to process emotion, this was entirely too much. They simply didn't know what to do or say. Only Rob Arslan moved, quickly wheeling himself to Nora's side, where he reached and pulled her down into a hug. The former special forces warrior was crying. "I'm so sorry, Nora, I'm so sorry. Oh my God."

They were in Nora's office waiting for the MC to reconvene in thirty minutes. Abe sat bent over with his knees apart, talking down to the carpet. "Mighty nice of them to adjourn for an entire half hour. Don't want to go overboard when one of your colleagues is murdered. A full sixty minutes would be wildly excessive."

"No, that's not it, Abe," Nora said gently. "They're just trying to process this. It's not something that comes naturally to most of them. I'm sure David wants to talk about what we can do or should do now. For example, he has to tell all our employees, and fast, before they hear it someplace else."

"I'm sorry. I guess you're right."

"And one thing the MC's going to want to know from me, in my lawyer role, is how we work with the investigators to help them solve this while protecting the firm's information. And, personally, I need to figure out what's up with my car and whether the cops are really going to want to take it."

Abe sat up straight. "Why on earth would they take your car?"

"Some Westport detective thinks there's blood on the back, which makes no sense, but if there is, they'll definitely want to take it. I would, in their shoes."

Abe was shaking his head. "That's nuts. So what should we do first?"

"You draft something for David to send around telling all employees. Then get to Laslo and have security lock down all of Helen's stuff, both her office and all her system accesses, and we should probably have someone from security lock down Helen's office at her house. I'm going to go talk to Tracey. She wasn't in the MC because Helen wasn't there, so she probably doesn't know. Needs to hear it from me. Oh, and ask Rob to come see me when I get back. Thanks."

Tracey Stein had no idea. She was sitting facing her computer in her assistant cubicle when Nora walked up. Her face was inches from the screen, which is the way she worked. Although "legally blind" from the blast of an Iraqi roadside bomb, Tracey could read, with the right accommodations. She had been Helen's assistant since Saugatuck began using that odd word a decade earlier, joining the firm as one of the wounded vets Rob Arslan sponsored. Tracey and Helen were thought partners and close friends. This was going to be awful.

"Tracey?"

She spun in her chair. "Nora, what's wrong?"

Tracey couldn't have read her face because she couldn't see it clearly, but she picked up something about the way Nora said her name.

Nora dropped to her knees next to Tracey and spoke in an urgent whisper. "Something terrible has happened. Helen's dead. They found her down at Compo. They think somebody killed her."

Tracey was frozen. She had been in these horrible conversations many times, but that was long ago and in a country far away, where she lost squad mates, colleagues, and friends to IEDs, snipers, suicide bombers. But this was Westport. It wasn't possible here. Nora pulled her close, feeling Tracey collapse into her, crying. "No, no, that can't be," Tracey said, again and again.

"I'm so sorry, I'm so sorry," was all Nora could whisper back.

When Tracey had recovered from the initial shock, Nora leaned back from the embrace and told her that security would be coming to secure Helen's office and her computer and that Tracey should not allow anyone access until then.

Tracey nodded and added, "Yes, the files will be important. Need to protect the files."

"I know," Nora said quietly. "All her stuff will need to be kept safe. The police will want to know that nobody messed with it."

"No," Tracey sniffled, "her personal files. She would want them safe."

Nora wasn't following this, but it didn't matter. "Of course, we can figure that out later," she said. "Laslo's team will make sure everything is protected and I'll have to go through it all before the police have access."

Nora left Tracey crying quietly in her cubicle and walked back to her office. Just before she entered, her neighbor's door opened and Louis Lambert was standing there. Nora paused briefly and he offered what might be called a condolence. "I'm sorry," he said in a monotone. "I know she favored you." Then he closed his door.

⸺∞∞⸺

Rob Arslan was already in her office. "What the fuck was that?" he asked, nodding toward the office next door.

"Another Vulcan trying to figure out how we humans are feeling. Just forget it."

"How're you holding up?" Rob asked as Nora shut the door.

"Numb. But thanks for coming over." Looking up, she added, "I wanted to connect with you in a place without microphones. I'm worried this could have something to do with our investigation."

"Why do you say that?"

"Because I feel like we've been making progress. Somebody could have been feeling the heat and done something desperate."

Rob paused to consider that before continuing. "Maybe, but—not to get too dark—then why wouldn't they come after you? It's your investigation. Helen and I are just your internal clients on it. How does getting rid of her, or me for that matter, stop what you're doing?"

"Good question and I don't know the answer. But I can't think of any other reason somebody would kill Helen. Hell, maybe you and I *are* in some kind of danger. I don't want to brush that off. If somebody knows we're close to nailing the front runner and that it's coming from inside the house—they may get pretty desperate. There's a shitload of money at stake and they have to know David would ruin whoever it is."

"I know all that, believe me, I do. But killing someone like Helen? Over a financial crime? I'm as dark as they come, but that's even hard for me to imagine."

Nora nodded. "Yeah, yeah, that's gotta be right. I'm sorry, I'm seeing shadows everywhere today."

"For good reason," Rob said. "And nothing wrong with that. Those instincts kept me alive for a long time." He slapped both sides of his wheelchair. "Until the ground snuck up on me at about a hundred twenty miles per hour."

Nora smiled tightly. "I'm not sure how you manage to make me feel better by talking about awful things, but you do."

"It's my gift," Rob said, returning the smile. "Also, I've been through hard times before and this situation is terrible, but remember: Stay strong, and stay close. Let's watch each other's backs. And if you see a shadow, don't ignore it. That hair on the back of your neck is what allowed your ancestors to live long enough to pass their DNA on to you."

He spun his chair, leaned forward, and opened the door. "See you at the MC in five," he said, wheeling away.

"Will do, Ironside," Nora called after him.

Without stopping, Rob shouted to the ceiling. "Seriously, nobody gets that."

CHAPTER ELEVEN

The reconvened MC meeting was awkward, even by Saugatuck standards. The group discussed internal and external communications, deciding to leave for another day the question of whether clients needed to be notified that the Chief Operating Officer had been killed. Marcus Baum, sitting on his foot, suggested that the murder of a Chief Investment Officer would be significantly more important to clients than the death of someone in operations. He began to explain his logic, when Rob Arslan interrupted.

"Stop, just stop," he barked. "What the fuck is wrong with you people? A wonderful woman is dead. Who gives a shit what the clients think at this point? And they'll all hear it on news reports soon anyway. We'll sort it out later."

David Jepson was nodding as Rob spoke, so the conversation ended there.

Nora then took the floor and explained the steps she had taken to have security seal Helen's office and lock down her home office and all her system accesses. She explained the likely law enforcement requests for Helen's emails, texts, and files. David Jepson said it was his desire to both assist in the capture of Helen's killer and protect any appropriate firm confidences. Nora said she assumed that would be Saugatuck's approach and she would return to the MC to confer before giving law enforcement access to anything related to Helen's Saugatuck work.

Nora didn't mention her suspicions about a connection to her front-running investigation, because so few knew about the investigation. She also didn't mention that Helen was dead in her canoe. Or that someone's blood might be on the back of her car.

—◦◦◦—

With the mercifully brief meeting finished, Nora went to her office and closed her door after telling Abe she needed some time alone.

She picked up her phone several times, but there was nobody to call. She wasn't going to tell an eight-year-old about a murder over the phone. And her mother would just worry needlessly from Cape Cod. So she sat, trying to process what had happened. As she did, a voice kept coming to her, a deep Brooklyn-accented baritone. It kept saying, "You remember to call me, you ever get in a crack. You don't, I'll never forgive your dumb ass."

The voice in her head belonged to Benny Dugan, a mountain of a man and legendary Mafia investigator whose office was once next to Nora's at the United States Attorney's Office in Manhattan. Although Benny and Nora were twenty years apart, they'd "been through it together," as Benny liked to say, and their time in the crucible of high-stakes investigations had made them family.

Benny was fond of calling Nora "Ms. Smooth," because she was good on her feet in court. In return, Nora called Benny "Mr. Rough"—a nod to his complete lack of diplomatic skills—frequently adding in a tone of mock apology, "Just messing with you. Don't mean anything bad about you."

Benny would invariably give her a sideways look, adding, "I'm not as good a person as you think I am."

Nora's practiced reply was the final piece of this shtick: "Did I say you were a good person?"

The phone rang one time before the booming voice answered on speaker. "Ms. Smooth, my Connecticut sister, to what do I owe the pleasure?"

"Mr. Rough, are you busy? I hear cars in the background."

"Out on surveillance, as usual. Watching some mopes in the Bronx stand around thinking criminal thoughts. But I can talk. They don't think that fast. What's up, hedge fund queen?"

Nora paused and Benny instantly heard it. "Hey, hey, silence ain't golden," he said. "What's up?"

"Remember when you told me to call if I ever got in a crack? I don't think I'm in one, but I kept hearing your voice in my head, so I called."

"Hearing voices. That's never good. So give me your evidence."

Nora told the story of her day, including the part she didn't tell Detective Kofatos—about the investigation she was conducting. She knew that was a breach of her confidentiality agreement at Saugatuck, but she trusted Benny more than anyone alive. When she was finished, he took his phone off speaker. It was as if all six-foot-five and two hundred fifty pounds of him just stepped into her office.

"Okay, you know I love you, but this is the definition of a motherfucking crack. Kills me that you didn't see it, although maybe you did on some level, which is why you called. To state the obvious: Somebody is setting you up. Dollars to doughnuts that's blood on your car and it belongs to the dead woman. Shit, *your* canoe? And that's probably not the end of it. Undoubtedly gonna be other shit connecting you as well. They're coming for you, Nora. Don't say another goddamn word to anybody about this. I'm on my way now. And I'm gonna grab Carmen. Go home, stay there, wait for us. Not another goddamn word. We clear?"

Nora was embarrassed. Years as a fed and she had missed it. "Crystal," she answered. "I'll be at my house."

She paused before adding, "And Benny, I want you to know I didn't kill her."

"Yeah, no shit, Sherlock. But somebody's workin' hard to lay it on you. Now go, hide. And don't answer the door for anybody but us. No exceptions, capisce?"

"Got it. No exceptions."

Nora hung up and walked out to Abe's cubicle, looking over the top of the "privacy wall," as she typically did. "Hey, need you to assist me with a ride home, now."

He jumped up with his keys. On the way to Abe's car, they saw police tape surrounding her CRV and a police tow truck backing into the garage.

"Don't talk. Just keep walking," Nora said. He nodded and pushed the unlock button on his key fob.

CHAPTER TWELVE

"Hey Demi, I wanted to check in quickly. Can you talk?"

"Sure, Martin, let me just move over to the side. We've identified the victim. Helen Carmichael is her name, age fifty-three, bigwig at a hedge fund here in town. I'm actually standing in their parking garage. Techs are pulling what looks like blood off the back of a car belonging to one of her colleagues. What've you got?"

"Really just the obvious," Associate ME Mortenson said. "We're putting time of death between nine P.M. and midnight last night. She was killed with a very sharp, nonserrated knife pulled in a single stroke from under her right ear to under her left. From the blood evidence, I'd say she was killed while lying in the canoe. I stopped at the state lab on the way back to my office to look at the boat again. No blood spatter anywhere above the level of her head, lying prone in the canoe. All the blood appears to have flowed toward the canoe bottom, under and around the back of her head. Of course, what wasn't congealed by morning sloshed a bit when that poor fisherman tried to save the canoe. But that doesn't change how I see it."

"Killed while lying in the canoe?" Demi asked. "How does that make any sense?"

"Whether it does or not, that's what the blood indicates. And the incision is so clean as to be almost surgical, like there was no movement at all while the blade was pulled across. Nothing under her fingernails, no defensive wounds or marks anywhere on her body, and no torn clothing. In fact, nothing to indicate any kind of struggle, which may make sense given that she wouldn't be hard to hold down. We have her at five-foot-three and a hundred eight pounds."

"Or maybe she was unconscious already," Demi added. "Any toxicology yet?"

"Not back yet. But we pulled some dark, straight hairs from her jacket that look too long to be hers. No root on any of them so I sent them for mitochondrial DNA workup."

"Thanks. State police get anything on the canoe?"

"I talked to the examiner while I was there. All kinds of prints on the boat—I understand a lot of people used it—but none appear to belong to the victim. We're going to need to do a ton of printing to see if the bad guy is among all the borrowers, but I'm starting to doubt it."

"DNA?" Demi asked.

"That's why I doubt we'll find bad-guy prints. So far all swabs that return anything are only showing the victim's. I'm guessing the killer wore gloves."

"And our people processed the lock and chain from the canoe storage rack. Nothing, but not surprising. Apparently, the lock was never used and somebody borrowing the boat could slide it off without touching the rack."

"Okay, thanks," he said. "I'll let you know when tox comes back and anything on the hairs. May want to run them against whoever owns that bloody car."

Demi couldn't resist sarcasm. "Oh, wow, thanks Martin. What a great idea."

A little snort sound came from Mortenson's end. "Yeah, I deserve that. Sorry, Demi. I'm Captain Obvious today."

"No worries, Martin. Sorry to be an ass. I'm about to go see my boss, who'll be worked up, as usual. All suggestions are welcome. Talk soon."

The Westport Police Department occupied a two-story brick building within sight of the Saugatuck River, just diagonally across the water from the offices of Saugatuck Associates. After talking to Nora Carleton and impounding her car, Demi could have walked back to brief her boss. And as she stood in front of Captain Dunham's desk getting peppered with questions, she almost wished she had. Would have given her more time to think.

Tom Dunham grew up in the Nutmeg State, although in the less tony environs upstate around Hartford. After college, he joined the NYPD, seeking excitement. He found plenty, too much really. So when he could retire at the age of forty-one, he came to the Westport PD seeking a healthier suburban life. To his wife's delight, the move was extremely good for his blood pressure, which, when elevated, transformed his pasty white face into a Google map at rush hour—mostly red lines, with a few blue and yellow running in odd directions. The work in Westport focused on traffic accidents and drunk driving, along with the occasional burglary and constant misbehavior by pampered youth. Dunham liked to say that Westporters didn't know the police existed, unless they needed them, and then the response was inadequate. Or unless a family member was speeding, driving drunk, or breaking something at school. Then the police needed to be defunded.

Historically, there were few murders in Westport and those were almost always marital disputes gone bad or the rampage of a disturbed young person against family. In the last decade, there had been a robbery in which a merchant was shot and killed, but no slashed senior executives in canoes. Dunham's face was already starting to show traffic backups as he stared at Detective Demi Kofatos.

"So how did a rich lady get her throat cut while lying fully clothed in a damn canoe from Compo Beach? And how did she get dumped out on Seymour Rock in the fucking dark? How does an outdoor crime scene end up as clean as a hospital OR? And why the fuck aren't there cameras down at Compo Beach? And you're out there towing shit out of Saugatuck's garage without checking with me first? Do you have any idea how much of this town's tax base comes from those eggheads? What the actual fuck, Kofatos? Whose team are you on here?"

The only questions she could actually answer were the ones about teams and the blood from Nora Carleton's CRV. "I'm on your team, sir, and the quick test says it's A-positive, like the victim's, and we just sent it for DNA. We'll know in a couple hours. Look, I'm trying to solve a murder here."

"Okay, okay," Captain Dunham said, his voice dropping. "So the victim's work colleague is shaping up as a good suspect?"

Demi made a sour face.

"What?" Dunham asked. "Now you're tellin' me you don't like her for this, even if the dead woman's blood is on her goddamn car?"

"I don't know, sir. Are we supposed to believe the general counsel of the world's largest hedge fund murdered her boss by slitting her throat in a canoe registered in her own name, then left the canoe and the body on Seymour Rock, but wiped the scene down except, oops, she forgot the big splash of blood on the back of her own car, which she drove to work the morning after the murder? Is she a master criminal or a complete idiot?"

"Well, stranger things have happened, Demi. Seen a lot of wacky shit in my day. Criminals get caught because they sometimes do both smart and dumb stuff."

"I guess, sir, but she also seemed pretty damn surprised when I showed her the crime scene photo. Normal as could be up to that point, then looked like she lost her shit for a minute before she got it together and went all robotic on me like a prosecutor would. I admit I haven't questioned many murder suspects, but this one doesn't really scream 'guilty.'"

Dunham sniffed dismissively. "But lots more work to do, I assume. Gotta get into the dead woman's house and her devices. And if that's her blood on what's-her-name's car—"

"Nora Carleton."

"Right. If that's the victim's blood, we sure as hell need to get into ol' Nora's house and her devices."

"Agree, sir, although getting anything out of Saugatuck Associates, even with a search warrant, is going to be a battle. That's a secretive crowd across the river there, and both the dead woman and Carleton dealt with a lot of their most sensitive stuff, including legal. So they're gonna play the privilege card on us. But we'll get after it. I'll keep you posted."

"Roger that," Dunham answered. "And link up with someone from the State's Attorney's office. If they're gonna break our balls on access, we're gonna need our own legal support."

"Got it. Thank you, sir." Demi turned and walked down the hall to her office.

CHAPTER THIRTEEN

It was starting to get dark when Abe dropped Nora at home. "Want me to stick around?" he asked.

"No, no, giving me a lift is enough. I'll be fine. Appreciate you."

She stepped from Abe's Subaru and waved as the car tires crunched away on the pebble driveway. Turning back toward the darkened house, she noticed Nana's waterfall was quiet. *Must be bumper-to-bumper traffic in both directions on 95.* She shook her head at the idea that her peace and quiet meant hundreds of people were going to be late for something. *What a world.*

Nora didn't often use the front because she usually parked in the garage. But the front door always brought a smile. Sophie and Nana had insisted they paint it bright red. "Makes it a happy house, Mommy," was all the explanation she needed. She pulled out the big key that opened the red door. But in the dim light, she missed the keyhole and the point of the key gently tapped the lock surface. The door swung slowly inward. Nora lifted her phone to the lock. In the screen's light, she could see a piece of black tape holding the latch flat. A chill shot up her neck. *Those hairs Rob talks about.*

Nora stepped into the dark entryway. "Hello?" she called, inching her way into the silent house, leaving the door open behind her. She flicked on lights and slowly walked through the kitchen, her heart thumping in her chest. She stopped in the kitchen and listened. It was quiet. She turned quickly and rushed out the patio door and onto the back lawn, where she called Benny. He answered on the first ring, again on speaker.

"Hey, we're supposed to be fifteen minutes out, but all we see is brake lights ahead—I got Carmen here—"

Carmen Garcia's voice came over the phone. "Hey girl, can't wait to see you."

"—we are stuck in some really shitty traffic. What's up? You home?"

Nora told him.

"Son of a bitch," he answered, spitting the words. "I'm gonna go lights and siren and drive on the goddamn shoulder but I still can't be there quick enough. Call 911, and do not, under any circumstances, go back in that house. Sit on your front porch until the cops get there and clear the house. Do it now."

He hung up. Nora called 911, walking rapidly around the house toward the front. A marked Westport PD unit was in her driveway two minutes later. Nora was talking to the officer when an unmarked unit crunched to a stop and Demi Kofatos stepped from the car.

"Can't get enough of us today, huh?" Demi called, immediately regretting the humor.

Nora looked stricken as she gestured toward front door. "Somebody broke in," she said.

Demi joined the two of them. "I'm sorry about that," she said. "Been a long day. But for you, too, I'm guessing. Seems unlikely somebody is still here, but let us clear the house, okay? Stay here."

Demi and the uniformed officer walked up the front steps and disappeared into the house. Five minutes later, they were back.

"All clear," Demi called from the front porch. "Can we go inside and talk? And don't touch the door. We're gonna want to print it."

Nora didn't answer, but stepped up the stairs and through the open door. She walked through the house to the kitchen, dropping onto a wooden chair. The detective went to the sink, running the faucet and reaching into the cabinet. "I'm gonna get you some water." She put the filled glass on the table in front of Nora and sat across, watching Nora take a long drink.

"Thank you," Nora said, setting the glass on the table.

"You're welcome," Demi said gently. "You okay to talk for a minute?"

Nora nodded.

"I don't know what's going on here," Demi said. "But I'm pretty sure the dead lady's blood is all over the back of your car."

Nora didn't react.

"So you have no idea how that got there?"

Nora shook her head. "I don't."

"Or about what she was doing in your canoe?"

"Nope."

"Forensic people pulled a couple long reddish brown hairs off her jacket. Those going to be yours?"

"I have no idea," Nora said. "Probably, the way this is going."

"You and Helen have any kind of beef?"

Nora widened her eyes. "Are you joking? None."

"Fights over work or money or love? That's the usual stuff, as I'm guessing you know from your past life."

Nora shook her head again. "I know. And no. None of the usual stuff, or unusual stuff."

"So somebody wanted to kill Helen and frame you? Why would they want to do that?"

Nora paused, then shrugged her shoulders.

Before Demi could respond, Benny's voice filled the house. "Hey, where you at in this McMansion?"

"In the kitchen!" Nora called. "Just keep walking."

Demi turned to see a human form nearly filling the doorway, its blond crew cut passing just beneath the frame. Benny strode across the kitchen floor, swiping a wooden chair with one huge paw and putting it next to Nora, who had turned in her chair with a broad smile.

"Benny," she said.

"Hey kid," he answered, dropping into his transported chair with a thud, putting one hand on her shoulder. "The cavalry's here."

Demi was so distracted by this mountain of a person—who was entirely ignoring her—that she nearly missed a short, dark-haired woman who seemed pulled into the kitchen by his wake. But the trailing woman noticed her and leaned over the corner of the table, extending her hand.

"Hi, I'm Carmen Garcia, Nora's lawyer. And you are?"

"Demi Kofatos, Westport PD."

"Can I ask what you two were talking about?"

"We were chatting while the uniforms checked around."

Carmen arched her eyebrows. "Chatting about?"

"The case, the dead woman."

"Yeah," Carmen said sharply, "no offense, but the chatting has to stop. Appreciate you checking around but if you want to chat about the case, you should talk to me. Okay?"

Demi shrugged and stood. "Fine by me, but I think some chatting might make sense the way this one is shaping up." Looking at Nora, she added, "Hope you feel better," and walked through the house to her car.

When the detective was gone, Nora stood and leaned over to embrace Carmen. Through her tears, Nora chuckled and said, "So you're my lawyer now?"

"You bet your ass," Carmen said, her hands reaching up to hold Nora's shoulders as her face broadened into a smile. "We Puerto Ricans are a generous people, but I'm pretty sure you can't afford my fancy law firm rate."

"You never know," Nora answered. "I'm a private sector person now, just like you. But I'm also pretty sure you aren't licensed to practice in Connecticut."

Benny interrupted. "Hey, don't mean to stop the lawyer stuff, but I need two things before we continue: a chair that don't hurt my butt and some whiskey."

When Nora finished her story, Carmen and Benny looked at each other across the living room. "You first, by all means," Carmen said, gesturing with one hand.

"Okay," Benny said, cupping his whiskey glass in his gigantic hands and crossing his feet on the living room ottoman. "So no doubt the Westport cops are coming for you. The blood on the car, the hairs on the body—which are definitely gonna be yours—and it being your canoe put too much pressure on them. And they're gonna think you staged this little break-in here at the house. They probably haven't charged you yet because all the lab work isn't done. And maybe because they need some piece of motive proof. Soon as they get that, you're in the shit. And before I forget, you gotta go through every inch of this place to see if anything's missing or been messed with."

Benny gestured back to Carmen with exaggerated formality. "Counsel?"

Carmen grimaced. "Well, that was your usual ray of sunshine, Benny, now wasn't it?"

Turning to Nora, she added, "And I know our beloved colleague doesn't like—what was his charming phrase?—oh yeah, 'lawyer stuff,' but I want to be clear that all our conversations are in connection with my potential representation of you. I'm not licensed here, but that just means I need special permission to appear in a Connecticut courtroom; I'm still an attorney and these are privileged conversations. Okay?"

Nora nodded. "Got it."

"And I no longer work for the federal government, as you know, but Benny still does. For these purposes, though, he is here not as a special agent with the United States Department of Justice, but on his own time, volunteering to assist me. We talked on the ride up here. Should this go any further, he intends to take a longer leave of absence from his day job and work for me, on your behalf, full-time. But here's hoping it doesn't come to that."

Benny rapped two of his knuckles on his own forehead. "Knock on wood."

"Questions?" Carmen asked.

Nora felt a wave of emotion so strong that she could only shake her head no. Carmen had been the chief of Violent and Organized Crime in the Manhattan US Attorney's office for almost a decade, and Nora's immediate supervisor for five hard years. As with Benny, she and Carmen had developed a connection formed by great stress, and she felt guilty that she had not been in regular touch after they both left government, Nora for Westport and Carmen for a big Manhattan law firm. Yet here these people were, dropping everything to help her, literally on a moment's notice.

She gathered herself. "I'm very grateful you are my friends. And my legal team."

Benny cleared his throat. "And here's the thing. Given you got assholes breaking into your house, my leave starts now. I ain't goin' anywhere until you're safe and this is sorted out. You know I got no life anyway. You got a guest bedroom in this fancy place?"

Nora smiled. "Of course. This is Westport, we aren't savages. It's downstairs with its own private bathroom. And its own fridge."

"Perfect," Benny said. "On at least two counts. And are you too fancy to have an alarm and cameras? What, you move to the suburbs and think crime doesn't exist? Seriously? That's top of my list."

Nora was grinning broadly. "Will be good to have you around."

CHAPTER FOURTEEN

The next morning, Benny was already sitting in the kitchen when Nora came down. He was at the table scrolling on his phone with his legs crossed, one penny loafer resting atop the opposite knee, exposing on his bare leg the ankle holster with the Smith & Wesson revolver he always wore.

"A gun in the kitchen," Nora said as she entered.

"And good morning to you too," Benny replied. "You know I always have it, and it's gonna stay there, as long as you got creeps breaking into your house and whatnot."

Nora smiled tightly as she walked to the coffee maker. "See you figured this thing out," she said, pouring herself a cup. "Thanks. How'd you sleep downstairs?"

"Like a baby. In the sense that I woke up every few hours and wanted to cry—'cause you don't have an alarm system. But that changes today. I got people coming to wire you up."

"Wow," Nora answered, "that's fast."

"I know some people," Benny said. "Even some who will drive out to the suburbs. I'll hang here to wait for them. Just leave me a set of keys. You see anything going through the house last night?"

"Nothing. Everything seems the same."

"Okay, good. Maybe you interrupted the creep before he could do—whatever. What's on your dance card today?"

"To work," Nora said. "I have to talk to them about handling the PD's requests."

"What'd Carmen say about that? And let me add that I'm sorry I went downstairs last night and missed all the lawyer talk, but I really needed some shut-eye."

"Not a problem, Benny. She said I should stay away from anything having to do with the company responding to the cops, so I don't set myself up for some obstruction of justice claim if they think anything is missing or has been messed with. Makes sense, but it also means I have to tell my bosses I'm a suspect, which is going to be bizarre."

"I get that," Benny said, "but didn't you tell me you came here because they're all about truth and stuff?" When Nora nodded while sipping coffee, he went on. "And the truth is you didn't kill the lady, so that should mean something to them."

"It will," Nora said, "but hard to predict how it'll go. None of Saugatuck's leaders ever got killed before."

"Ain't that the truth," Benny said, picking up his coffee. "When're your mom and Sophie back?"

"I talked to my mom last night and convinced her to stay up at the Cape. Sophie isn't back until this weekend and you're here, so I got company. I also called Nick so he knows, in case Sophie hears something about it. But that seems unlikely. And Sophie and my mom didn't know Helen very well, so it's not like they'll be at the funeral, which I'm guessing will be sometime this week."

Benny nodded. "Makes sense." He paused, and then added, "After I get the alarm guys squared away, I'm going to stop by Westport PD, just to say 'hey.' Never hurts to have a channel."

Nora turned and put her coffee cup in the sink. "Okay, I'll let you and Carmen know how it goes at work. Thanks for doing the alarm thing. I'll leave my credit card on the counter to pay them."

"No problem," Benny answered. "You gonna eat something? Most important meal of the day, and all?"

Nora smiled. "Jeez, and I thought my mother was still away. Not to worry, Mr. Mom, we get free breakfast at work. Actually, free food all day and night. I'm good."

"Wow," Benny said. "Free food and the truth. Who can believe it? May have found my next career."

Nora chuckled. "Be fun to see you mix with this crowd. They're, uh, 'different' from your normal cup of tea, fair to say."

Benny laughed. "For free food and less bullshit, I can put up with a lot. And I don't drink tea, as you know."

CHAPTER FIFTEEN

D avid Jepson's office always made her slightly uncomfortable. As usual, he was sitting behind his enormous driftwood desk in the corner above the river, the black floor-to-ceiling shelves cluttered with the memorabilia of a billionaire world traveler and amateur anthropologist. His version of snow globes seemed to be carved fertility totems, a source of amusement for Helen Carmichael and of stress for Nora.

"What if some of those things are stolen from some indigenous people someplace?" she once asked Helen after a meeting in the office.

"Yeah, well maybe those tribes shouldn't have been making shit out of banned material," Helen answered in a serious voice.

"Wait, you think that's ivory or something?"

"Don't know," Helen answered, her tone growing lighter. "Anyway, it's all been on those shelves since before the import ban went into effect, and it's not against the law in Connecticut to possess ivory—I shudder to imagine the devastating impact that would have on WASP clubs—so it's all good."

As usual with Helen, Nora couldn't tell what was shtick and what was real. But they both hated the chairs. Of that, Nora was sure. She imagined Helen was at her side as Jepson gestured to one of the brown leather, sloped lounge chairs facing the gigantic driftwood desk. Helen had always enjoyed watching Nora try to keep her six-foot-tall self from sliding off the chairs, which seemed to slope forward. "Jesus," Helen would say as they walked out of recording range, "we have to drive piece-of-shit cars but he can have fifty-thousand-dollar chairs that you can't keep your butt on. How does that make any sense? And I'll bet that's the skin of some poor endangered creature."

As Nora made her practiced move to dig her heels into the floor to stay on the chair, Jepson leaned forward to activate the recording device on the glossy surface of the desk. Nora quickly lifted her palm and David stopped, mid-lean, and stared at her. "This is a legal conversation," she explained, "so we shouldn't tape it."

David paused, likely recalling their many battles over recording—including his wish to record auditors from the Securities and Exchange Commission, a request that was emphatically rejected by the government—before leaning back without pressing the button.

"What is it, Nora?" he asked, turning to the credenza behind him. There was the faintest scraping noise followed by a tearing sound as he pulled a two-inch piece of Scotch tape from a desktop dispenser, something he would do regularly during all conversations in the office—pinching and rolling the tape between his fingers before getting a fresh piece.

As was also his habit, Jepson only stole quick glances at Nora while looking out the window or down at the finger tape. And although she had rarely seen him smile, Nora felt warmth in those glances. He could be abrupt and brutal in his directness, but David Jepson was a kind man who cared about the people who worked for him—even if, from time to time, he felt obligated to tell them they were idiots and needed to be fired.

"Should we wait for Marcus?" Nora asked. She had told Jepson's assistant that Baum should be invited for this meeting. He was "co-Chief Investment Officer," which wouldn't seem like a role required for this discussion, but Nora had been at Saugatuck long enough to know that titles at the firm were like points in the TV show *Whose Line Is It Anyway?*—they were made up and meant nothing. Whatever he was called, Baum was Jepson's alter ego. He had joined Saugatuck out of college twenty years ago and would never leave. And Nora knew what few others did—that Jepson had given his protégé a large ownership stake in the firm, second only to Jepson's own. If you wanted to speak to Saugatuck, you needed David and Marcus.

Before Jepson could answer, Baum entered, wearing his usual uniform—rumpled white shirt untucked over loose-fitting blue jeans and Birkenstock sandals with white tube socks. His hair looked like one side had very recently been pressed against a bed pillow.

"Hey Nora," he said as he walked behind her, "you doing okay?"

"I am. Thanks for asking, Marcus."

Baum stood to Nora's left, by the window, leaning against a bookshelf with his back to the river. The two men did not acknowledge each other, something Nora might once have mistaken for tension, but there was none between them.

"Okay," Jepson said, "what's this about?"

Nora explained that the police would likely seek access to company records relating to Helen—emails, texts, personnel files, and so forth—and that it was important Saugatuck cooperate, but in a way that reduced the risk that sensitive company information would accidentally become public.

"Okay," Jepson interrupted, "what you're saying makes sense, but you are the responsible party here for these matters. That's why we hired you as general counsel. I don't see why—"

Nora interrupted back, an essential skill at Saugatuck. "I can't be the one to make those decisions. I believe the police might think I killed Helen and so it puts me in a position of conflict to make those decisions."

Neither man showed any reaction. Jepson continued speaking, his voice level. "I see. And why do they think you killed Helen?"

"Is she allowed to answer that?" Baum asked in the same level tone.

"I think so," Jepson answered, reaching for a new piece of tape. "Our general counsel is telling us she can't act as our lawyer in this situation and I think we're entitled to know why."

"I think you're right," Baum replied. "We should know the answer." Looking toward Nora, he added, "What's the answer?"

Nora had been at Saugatuck long enough to be comfortable speaking with a flat tone no matter the subject of conversation. "Because she was found with her throat cut in the bottom of my canoe and her blood was found on the back of my car."

"Oh, I see," Jepson said. "It makes sense that they would think you killed her. Did you kill her?"

"I did not," Nora answered, her voice still flat despite the fact that she could feel her heart beating.

"Okay, I believe you," Jepson answered, "but I also understand the conflict thing. How do you propose to handle it?"

<hr />

After clearing her plan with Jepson and Baum, Nora had next done the hard part by knocking on Louis Lambert's office door.

"Enter."

"Louis," Nora said, stepping into the small office, "I need you to handle something."

As she explained why she could not represent the company in dealing with the police, Nora swore she saw the skin of his cheeks rise in just the slightest hint of a smile. God how she wished Helen were here. *Bet he can't stand up because he's got a woody,* Helen would say. *Vulcan's blood just all rushed to his dick,* she would add.

"And so I should communicate directly with the MC on this?" he asked.

"Yes," Nora answered. "I would lean on David and Marcus, in particular, but that's your call. They're aware you'll be handling this."

"Very well," Lambert replied.

After an awkward silence, Nora turned to leave, adding, "I'll direct the police to you as soon as they make contact." *Prick,* Helen would say.

———

All prosecutions in Connecticut were handled by the appointed State's Attorney assigned to each judicial district. Nora was on the phone with Aileen Shapiro, the State's Attorney for the Stamford/Norwalk district, which included Westport, trying unsuccessfully to interrupt Shapiro's description of the access investigators wanted to Helen Carmichael's records at Saugatuck. Shapiro finally took a breath and Nora cut in. "I don't mean to be abrupt, but the firm has decided your contact on this should be with my deputy, Louis Lambert, so I'm going to transfer you right now. Please hold on."

"Louis," Nora said into the phone. "I have the State's Attorney for you. She'll be on as soon as I hang up."

After disconnecting the line, Nora sat at her desk. She could hear Lambert's voice through the wall. *In a world of transparency,* she reminded herself, *soundproofing is not a big priority.*

CHAPTER SIXTEEN

Benny stood facing the bulletproof glass, bending down to speak through the voice port. "Benny Dugan, here to see Detective Kofatos."

The sergeant on duty behind the barrier lifted two fingers and used them to bend one ear forward in the universal gesture meaning he couldn't hear.

Why do the safest places have all this shit? Benny thought. But he didn't say that. Instead, he raised his voice and repeated the message. The sergeant asked for his license, examined and returned it, then pantomimed that Benny should take a seat. *Unbelievable. Fort Knox on the damn Gold Coast of the Long Island Sound.*

Moments later, a heavy door opened with a loud buzz, and Demi Kofatos leaned through it, motioning to Benny. As he walked toward her, he nodded his head to the wall of plexiglass. "You get a lot of armed attacks on Westport police headquarters?"

Demi smiled. "Not yet. I think we must've had some extra money one year."

"That's a relief," Benny said, reaching to meet the hand Demi extended. "I think I'm just jealous of how nice your world is. I came by because I didn't think we got off on the right foot last night."

"Glad you came," she answered. "Come on in."

When Benny was squeezed into a small wooden chair in Demi's tiny office, she started.

"Can you tell me first what your connection to this case is?"

"Sure. Me and Nora go back a ways. We've 'been through it,' as they say. We did mob cases together at the US Attorney's office. She's the best. When I heard she was in a spot, I dropped everything. I'm now officially on leave from the government. Just a civilian here to help a friend by workin' on her legal team should she need one as things develop."

"Must be nice to have friends like you."

"I don't know about that. But for sure it's nice to have friends like Nora. You know she didn't kill nobody, right?"

"Well, that's what we're trying to figure out. There's some bad facts, you know that, right?"

"Yeah, I do. I spent years on the job with NYPD and then lots more chasing mob killers for the Department of Justice. So I've been around the block a few times. My experience? Some facts are so bad you can't trust them. Maybe you feel that?"

"I don't know what I feel, at the moment," Demi answered. "You were NYPD? My boss came from there. Lemme see if he's in. Maybe you know people in common."

With that, Demi squeezed past Benny, returning a moment later. "He's in. Said he'd be happy to say hello. This way."

Benny followed her down the hall and into a much larger office. Captain Dunham rose from behind his desk with a broad smile. "Tom Dunham," he said, extending his hand. "Always happy to meet someone who wore the bag," he added, using NYPD slang for a police uniform. Gesturing to an empty chair, he added, "Sit, sit."

"Benny Dugan. Great to meet you. How long were you on the job?"

"I did my twenty and retired to come here."

"This seems like a sweet gig."

"It is, excluding dead ladies in canoes," Dunham said. "But we don't get a lot of that. So where were you assigned, back in the day?"

"Outta the academy I went south Brooklyn to the Six-Oh," Benny said, adopting the NYPD practice of pronouncing each number of a two- or three-digit precinct's designation. "I had some good rabbis so I made detective pretty early and they sent me to the Brooklyn DA's office, workin' mob stuff. But was only there a hot second and got recruited to be a fed, moved to the US Attorney in Manhattan. Been workin' organized crime ever since. Course I'm on leave now to help my friend. How 'bout yourself?"

Something about Dunham had changed. "I bounced around," he said in a clipped tone. "Here and there."

"What's that mean?" Benny asked, reflecting the change in tone.

"What I said," Dunham answered coldly. "I did a bunch of stuff and now I'm here. You writin' a book?"

Benny paused. *Not gonna smack some asshole who has power over Nora.* "Nope, just makin' conversation," he said, standing. "Which seems about over. Take care and thanks for your time."

Benny turned and followed Demi down the hall to her office.

She closed the door and squeezed past, sitting behind her desk. "You got some kind of history with the captain?"

Benny exhaled. "I didn't think so, but I'm startin' to think maybe I do. Dunham is the name, right?"

Demi nodded. "Thomas. He didn't say so, but he once told me he worked in a special mob homicide unit."

Benny paused and looked at the ceiling before speaking. "Son of a bitch. That's where I know him from. He doesn't know me, personally, but I spent a lot of time staring at the guys in that unit. I suspect he knows that, which is why he looked like he saw a ghost."

"I don't get it. What do you mean?" Demi said.

"It was called the OC Homicide Unit and it included two detectives who were honest-to-God on the mob's payroll. Doin' hits themselves and also tipping informants who then got whacked. They even misread a report once and got a mobster named Bruno Facciolo killed for being a rat when he wasn't a rat. Real pieces of shit. They both got life in federal prison for murder and conspiracy to murder for Cosa Nostra. I testified at their trial 'cause I spotted both of them when I was out on surveillance at mob clubs. I think your boss was one of the guys who knew what was goin' on and decided to just look the other way. I'm not sayin' he whacked guys, but he got the stink all over him just by being so close to them. So when the cases came down, he musta put in his papers and beat feet to Westport. What a small fuckin' world."

Demi suddenly looked very uncomfortable. "Look," she said, rising, "I don't know anything about that. I'm just trying to do my job. I appreciate you coming by."

Benny stood. "Yeah, I get that, and I'm not trying to cause you any kind of problem, but I know how these things can go to shit. Nora is good people and she ain't no killer. I just hope you do your job and don't let yourself get pushed into anything, when we both know Nora didn't do it. Because some of the people doing the pushing may not be the best kind of people."

Demi stiffened. "Again, thanks for stopping by. Let me show you out."

They walked in silence to the lobby.

CHAPTER SEVENTEEN

The door from the garage into the house chimed when Nora walked in. Benny was standing in the kitchen, wearing a wide smile and speaking rapid-fire. "You like? My guys busted their asses. Every door and every window on the ground floor alarmed, glass-breaks and motion detectors all over the place—including the driveway—and they threw up a few cameras. I was tracking you from the moment you turned in. You can run it all from the wall monitor or your phone. Lemme show you."

"My day was fine, and yours?" Nora answered. "Jeez, let me catch my breath."

Noticing his deflated look, she added, "But the chime is really nice. Thanks. I don't mean to be a jerk."

"You're not a jerk," Benny answered. "Sorry to jump on you the minute you walk in. Just excited, is all. And wait till you hear what I learned about our Westport PD friends."

Nora put her bag on the table and pulled a White Claw from the fridge. She knew Benny hated them so she didn't bother offering and handed him a beer instead. "You wanna sit?" she asked.

"Sure," Benny answered as he twisted the top off his beer and took a swig. "Then I wanna show you something in the basement."

Nora updated him on her conversations with David Jepson and Marcus Baum and the handoff to her deputy, Louis Lambert. "Spent the rest of the day reaching out to Helen's family to see what they want in terms of a funeral. She wasn't religious, but she always loved the Southport Congregational Church. If the ME releases her body, they want to do it there on Thursday."

Benny nodded. "Good, good. I'm gonna cover that, just like in the old days."

Nora raised her eyebrows. "Like a mob funeral surveillance? Seriously?"

"Definitely," Benny answered. "Unless *you* know who killed her, I wanna use every tool in the box to see what we can see. And ya never know what you'll see until you look."

Nora decided not to try to untangle that one. "So tell me about the cops."

When Benny finished the story of his visit to Westport PD, Nora exhaled loudly. "So Detective Kofatos seems straight, but her boss might have a few kinks in him, and maybe a hard-on for you."

"That about sums it up," Benny said. "Now let me show you the war room."

"I don't have a war room," Nora replied.

"Uh, you do now," Benny said with a smile, leading the way to the basement stairs. He continued talking over his shoulder as he walked down. "I found this great room down here, just past my bedroom."

At the bottom of the stairs, he turned and walked across the open–floor-plan basement, stopping in front of a heavy, ornate wood door. "Behind this funny door—" he began.

"Is what is supposed to be a wine cellar," Nora interrupted, "which we have not made a high priority."

"Which is just as well," Benny said, pushing the heavy door open, "because it's our war room."

He flicked the light switch and swept a huge hand across the space. Nora took in a large whiteboard covered with photos of Saugatuck executives. At the top was Helen Carmichael, with pictures arrayed below of David Jepson and his three children, along with Marcus Baum, Rob Arslan, and Arty Falcone of client relations.

"The whole MC," Nora said. "Where'd you get the pictures?"

"Ye olde internet," Benny answered, rapping on the board with his knuckles. "I didn't put you up there 'cause I know you aren't a suspect, but every one of these mugs has to be. And I'm sure we're missing others. We gotta go up the asses of each of these with a microscope. Because the cops aren't gonna do the work to get you out of this. We gotta do it."

Nora paused, studying the board. "Tell me again why you are so focused on Saugatuck people?"

"Easy," Benny said. "Whoever killed her is trying to set *you* up for it. Who would do that except someone in Saugatuck's world? Some serial killer or pissed-off lover might kill Helen, but set you up? Use your canoe, which all the Saugatuck people borrow, and put blood on your car?"

He slapped his hand against the board. "No way. It's somebody up here or somebody who's gonna be up here as we dig deeper into this little stew of rich brainiacs. Which is why I gotta cover Helen's funeral."

CHAPTER EIGHTEEN

The bells of the Southport Congregational Church were smooth and friendly, which struck Benny as strangely nice for a funeral morning. The gray stone church had been on Pequot Avenue in the little village next to Westport since 1875. The old road was narrow, but Benny found the perfect spot, backing his rental panel van into a little side street that offered a perfect view of the church's front door. Inside the van, he perched his enormous frame on an upside-down five-gallon paint bucket and took photos through the tinted back window, his elbows forming a tripod on his thighs. He had done this work dozens of times at funeral homes and churches all around New York, capturing images of those paying respects to dead organized crime members. He had also jammed himself into hotel ballroom crawl spaces to photograph mob weddings. But he had never covered the funeral of a hedge fund executive. *This has gotta be the geekiest funeral I ever worked.*

He snapped pictures of every mourner who came to the church, including the eight whose pictures he already had on the whiteboard in the "wine room"—Nora's new name for his basement workspace. He rested his arms when everyone was inside for the service; he would snap them all again when they came out, to be sure he didn't miss anyone. Just then, a solitary figure walked quickly past the van and cut diagonally up the church's sloping front lawn toward the door, removing his cap as he approached the entrance. Benny got a couple pictures of the side of the man's head before he slipped into the church. *Maybe just late, but strange that he's wearing a baseball hat.*

Benny was ready when the guy hurried out of the church before the service ended. He got one good picture as the man lifted his hand to put his cap back on, and several more as he walked directly toward Benny, retracing his route. *Who the fuck comes late to a funeral and then leaves early, and in a goddamn baseball hat?*

—·—

The alarm was off when Nora got back to her house, so she paused in the doorway from the garage. "Benny?" she shouted.

The sound of a reassuring Brooklyn baritone made its way up the basement stairs. "Down in the war room!"

She turned the alarm system back on and went downstairs to find him standing in front of the whiteboard. "Scared me a little," Nora said. "The alarm was off and I thought you were out on surveillance."

"I was," he said, "which is why I'm here now. Saw an odd one and wanted to print some copies of his picture."

He turned and stabbed a finger at a new photo on the whiteboard. "Who's the dude in the hat?"

Nora squinted and took a step closer to the board. "No idea. He was at the service?"

"Yeah, slipped in late and out early. Probably went up to the balcony. Not normal behavior, eh?"

"Let me send it to Laslo at work," Nora said. "He knows everybody who's been around Saugatuck the last ten years."

Benny pulled the picture off the board. "You can use this. I got others."

Nora smiled, holding her palms up. "Seriously? *Text* me the picture and I'll *text* it to Laslo. You know the nineties are over, right?"

"Everyone's a comedian," Benny said, taping the picture back to the board. Turning back to Nora, he added, "Let me *text* it to him myself, you being the subject of a murder investigation and all."

Nora winced. "Yeah, that's right. Strange and painful, but right."

Benny sat at the little table he had moved into his war room and opened his laptop.

"What're you doing?" Nora asked.

"The pictures are on here, off my camera's SD card. You think I'm stuck in the nineties but there's a reason I don't use my phone for surveillance, despite all the bullshit about the amazing iPhone camera."

"Yeah, I actually get that," Nora said. "Phones can be hacked and they're the first thing cops grab. We should know who our mystery man is soon enough. Laslo's pretty good about answering texts."

Benny looked up after sending the message. "How was the funeral? I should have asked when you came in. Sorry."

"Thanks. It was sad, but also weird. She never had a family, except it turns out she had this big extended family—I'm sure you saw them from the van—two sisters and a brother and lots of nephews and nieces. They really loved her. So sad to hear the ones who spoke during the service. Evidently, she was the fun sibling and the cool aunt and she helped them in all kinds of ways—tuition, house down payments, any kind of emergency—none of which surprised me. And her mom seemed broken, honestly. I can't imagine what it's like to be at the funeral of one of your kids. And when somebody took that child's life."

Nora paused and shook her head. "The unbelievable part, of course, is that somebody in that church may have killed her, or gotten somebody to kill her."

Benny's phone buzzed.

"Laslo," Benny said. "He says it's Brad Holtzer, who had your job before you. What the hell's he doin' sneakin' around?"

"That's weird," Nora said. "I never met him, but Helen told me his story. He was in the GC job for nine months. They worked to steal him from one of Saugatuck's big hedge fund rivals. He was nervous about the move because he knew how many people didn't make it long at Saugatuck before running or getting fired, so they gave him a strange clause in his contract. If he got fired for any reason in his first year, they would pay him a ten-million-dollar lump sum."

"Holy shit," Benny said. "And?"

"Jepson fired him after nine months. Helen thought Holtzer figured out early that he wasn't a good fit and wouldn't be happy long term, so he played the whole thing, working harder and harder to get under Jepson's skin. She said she tried to warn David, but he said, 'If that's the kind of person he is, we definitely don't want him, and ten million is a small price to pay for our mistake.'"

Benny made a whistling sound. "Whoa. Small price? We're not in Kansas anymore, Dorothy."

"But in a sense he's right," Nora answered. "If you're worth billions, ten million doesn't seem very big, now does it?" She laughed before adding, "You and I could live forever on the money guys like Jepson lose in their couch cushions."

"Remind me to find that couch," Benny said, shaking his head. "And so what happened to Holtzer?—who I gotta admire a little for being a player, based on what you just told me."

"Helen said he took his money and disappeared. She said nobody'd seen him and he wasn't available for me to consult. So I didn't try."

"Well, we're gonna consult the hell out of him now. Trackin' him will be top of my list for tomorrow."

CHAPTER NINETEEN

"Thanks for calling me back, Nora," Carmen said. "Benny with you?"

"Happy Friday, chief," he said looking at the phone sitting between him and Nora. "All hands are on deck. Well, in the kitchen, actually. What's up?"

"Just got off the phone with Demi Kofatos from Westport. She called to tell me that the blood on Nora's car is a DNA match to Helen Carmichael's."

"There's a shocker," Benny said, glancing across the table at Nora, who was looking down at her hands.

"And they got mitochondrial DNA from the hairs found on the body. They aren't Helen's and they want to know if Nora will submit a sample. They also want to know if Nora will sit for an interview."

There was silence in the kitchen. Benny broke it. "Remind me what the mito whatever is?"

Nora looked up, the light coming back in her eyes. "Mitochondrial DNA is from a different part of the cell than the normal DNA you read about, which is called 'nuclear.' Unless a hair is found with the root attached, it's hard to get normal nuclear DNA out of it. But you can get mitochondrial DNA and compare it to a suspect's hair. It doesn't identify the person for sure but it tells you the hair came from someone with the same mother or grandmother."

Benny looked confused. "Grandmother? And how are you some kinda hair expert?"

Carmen's voice came through the phone. "Mitochondrial DNA is passed down by females so the lab could only say it belongs to Nora or her mom or to her grandmother. And she knows a lot about it because we had postconviction challenges to old cases in SDNY where FBI lab people said stuff about microscopic hair comparisons that wasn't accurate."

Nora picked it up, smiling at Benny. "In the nineties—where people sometimes get stuck, as you know—they didn't have mitochondrial DNA testing, so the FBI lab would look at hairs and try to compare them using a microscope. It was bullshit, like reading the bumps on your head, and led to a lot of bad testimony. That's how I know."

"Okay, now *my* head hurts," Benny said. "So where are we on Nora giving them a hair?"

"She could refuse," Carmen said, "but they'll easily get a warrant. My vote would be to give it to them. And politely decline the interview."

Nora began to speak, but Carmen cut her off. "But, I don't think we should decide today. I told Kofatos I needed time to think about it. I think we should use that time to line up Connecticut counsel. I want to make sure there isn't some local practice angle we're missing, even on something like this, which seems straightforward.

"And, look," Carmen continued, "she didn't say it, but I'm sure she's going to be coming to your house with a search warrant. She'll probably do the same for your spaces at Saugatuck. They'll look for the murder weapon, seize your phones and computer. They have to at this point."

Nora was nodding as she stared at the phone in the middle of the table. "Yup, it's what I would do. And I agree on hiring local counsel. At least I can afford it for the first time in my life. You have any ideas?"

"I do," Carmen said. "I think I found the perfect person—Porter Raleigh, out of Hartford."

"The name's familiar," Nora said. "Where do I know him from?"

"Longtime AUSA in the District of Connecticut. Did a bunch of mob stuff, so maybe that's where you heard the name. Or maybe from his last federal job. He was a special prosecutor in DC, supposed to look into allegations of corruption at the Department of Homeland Security. Became a total clusterfuck. His operation fell in love with some political conspiracy theory, leaked like the Titanic, and then he charged a few people, using speaking indictments to make it sound like he'd solved the Kennedy assassination."

Nora chuckled. "I remember now. Total shitshow."

"Yup," Carmen went on, "the cases ended with door-slamming acquittals on everything and he was chased out of town, although he remained a saint in some conspiracy-nut circles."

Nora looked up at Benny, her eyes wide. "I can't wait to hear how this story ends with him being the answer to our problem."

"See, that's just it," Carmen answered. "I'll give him some credit. He was always a little grouchy and gung ho for my taste, but the DC experience turned him into a scorched earth defense lawyer when he left the government. Seems he found out—maybe from the mirror?— that there are overzealous prosecutors and wrongly accused defendants. Better late than never, I suppose."

"I suppose," Nora echoed.

"But I think he's our guy. He's not just a flamethrower. He also knows everyone in Connecticut. I'm going to reach out and see if he can meet us at your place this weekend, ideally tomorrow."

"Okay," Nora said tiredly, "but it's got to be before noon tomorrow. My mom and Sophie will be back after lunch."

"Got it," Carmen answered. "Be back to you soon."

CHAPTER TWENTY

The next morning, Benny was standing by the kitchen sink looking out the window to the back patio. "What's the ramp to the back door for?"

"It's for Rob Arslan. I ordered it so he'd feel welcome," Nora answered as she straightened the chairs at the table.

"That's a nice thing you did. Hey, this here's a huge house, right?" Benny said as he turned to watch her. "So why we gotta have all the meetings in the kitchen?"

"You'd prefer the wine room?" Nora whispered.

"You gotta stop calling it that—show some respect for my war room," Benny whispered back, just as Carmen entered the kitchen, leading a medium-height, bald man with a gray Vandyke-style goatee. He wore rimless glasses that were sliding down his nose and a perpetual angry look, as if always squeezing his eyebrows together to move the glasses higher.

"Nora, Benny, I'd like you to meet Porter Raleigh."

Nora extended her hand. "Nice to meet you, Porter. Thanks for coming on a Saturday."

"Likewise," Benny said, shaking hands.

"My pleasure," Raleigh answered, pulling out a chair. It came out *pleh-zha*.

"Where you from?" Benny asked as they moved to the table. "I know you're Mr. Connecticut and all, but I'm pickin' up some Beantown."

He smoothed his goatee with one hand. "Born and raised in Boston"—*Bahh-stun*—"so you're picking up something real. And let me say it's an honor to meet you, Benny. I've heard great things about you."

Benny didn't return the compliment. "So you Sox or Yankees? I hear Connecticut is split."

"You're right," Raleigh said, "and you're standing on the line. It actually goes through Westport. Any farther up and your accent might be a problem. Any closer to Gotham City and mine might be."

"I'm sorry," Benny said in a tone of exaggerated seriousness, "what accent are you referring to?"

Carmen laughed. "Okay, okay, enough with the rivalries nonsense. We're here to talk about Nora and the Westport cops. Why don't we start by Nora giving Porter the lay of the land, how she ended up here, Helen's story, her interaction with the cops."

⸺

Raleigh sat for a long moment when they finished the briefing, pulling a white cloth handkerchief from his pocket before removing his glasses and slowly cleaning the lenses. After hooking the glasses behind each ear, he returned the handkerchief to his pocket, did his ritual one-hand goatee smoothing, and then spoke.

"I would say, based on my forty years of service as a federal prosecutor and now as a private practitioner, that the key here is going to be firing across the bow of the State's Attorney before they charge. From the sound of things, the cops are going to push because that's what they do. It's what they have to do. A wealthy businesswoman was killed in their town and it's a major problem to have it uncleared. But the State's Attorneys are different animals. They have a lot more than one town to worry about and they also don't want to be embarrassed."

He paused and turned toward Nora. "So, with your permission, assuming you want me to be your lawyer, I'd like to do two things. First, call your deputy at Saugatuck who's dealing with the investigators and make sure he's insisting they do it right. And, second, call the prosecutor—I've known Aileen Shapiro for years—to make sure she isn't letting herself get stampeded by the cops into doing something that will blow up in her face. There will be no interview right now, but I'll tell her you'll voluntarily provide hair and DNA samples—I agree we don't want it to get out that you're stonewalling somehow. Our posture is that you're innocent and we'll work to prove that to them."

Glancing at Carmen, who was nodding, Nora said, "Yes, I'd like you to be on the team. And, yes, it makes sense for you to do those things. I'll give them the sample whenever they want. And if they show up with the warrant—*when* they show up—we'll stay out of their way and give you both a call." She gestured to Benny. "And meantime, he'll keep working to understand the universe of possible suspects."

Benny nodded and turned to Raleigh. "And just so we're clear. It isn't just our 'posture' that she's innocent. She's actually innocent."

Raleigh's bald head reddened. "Of course," he said stiffly. "I didn't mean to suggest otherwise. Our client is innocent. I'll be in touch and my firm will be sending a retainer letter."

As Raleigh rose and followed Carmen to the front door, Benny lifted his right hand and flicked under his chin with the backs of his fingers, before whispering to Nora, "Well, ain't he a fancy piece a work, Mr. Forty Years, and if he don't stop grabbing that little beard of his I'm gonna shave it for him."

She smiled. "Behave. We need that obnoxiousness."

CHAPTER TWENTY-ONE

Nora was standing on the front porch watching her lawyers drive away when Nick's familiar car turned into the pebble driveway, eight-year-old Sophie's face pressed against the rear passenger window. As soon as the car stopped, the back door jerked open and Sophie came flying across the little stones toward her mother, who was running down the front walk. Sweeping the little girl into her arms, Nora let their collision become a series of spins as she squeezed Sophie, one hand behind her head, the other on her back. When they stopped turning, Sophie leaned her head back beaming, but quickly dropped the smile. "Why're you crying, Mommy?" she asked.

Nora sniffled as she gently pulled Sophie back into the hug. "Oh, I'm just so happy to see you, ladybug. It seemed like you were gone forever."

Nora could see that Nick was now out of the car, looking concerned. He lifted and dropped his chin, as if to ask, "You okay?"

Her face still streaked with tears, Nora nodded to him and gently set Sophie down.

Nick's eyes darted quickly toward the front door. Nora turned to see Benny emerging from the house.

"You remember my friend Benny," she said, addressing Sophie in a voice loud enough for Nick to hear. "He used to work with Mommy putting bad guys away. Now he's going to be staying with us for a while." Looking at Nick, she lifted one hand to mime a phone call before adding, "Give Daddy a hug and a thank-you for a great week. We'll see you next week, Daddy."

Sophie ran across the pebbles to hug her father, then skipped back. "Is Nana home?" she asked as she headed toward the front door.

"Any minute, bug. She'll be so excited to see you."

"Bye!" Nick hollered. "Talk soon, I hope!" As he turned the car, Nora could see him mouth *call me* before steering out of the driveway.

Inside the house, Nora got Sophie settled with a snack in front of her favorite movie, *Frozen*. Benny slid into a comfortable side chair, explaining that he didn't want to miss the show, which he had never seen. When the movie started, Nora leaned toward Sophie. "Mommy will be right back. I just need to go to the other room and make a call. Two seconds."

Nick picked up immediately. He was still driving, even though he and Vicki lived only ten minutes away. "What the hell, Nora? What's going on? Why is Benny here? And I know he always carries a gun and that is not a good thing."

Nora took a breath. *In through the nose, out through the mouth.* She ignored his questions. "I'm sorry we couldn't talk at the house. It just seemed best not to do it in front of Sophie."

"Well, it just seems—"

She cut him off. Sophie was the best thing that ever happened to her, but how that magical little girl had half this dolt's chromosomes was an enduring mystery. "Nick, just listen. I'll tell you everything that's going on. Then you can ask me anything you want."

He was silent, so she went on, explaining where things stood with the police, the intruder, Benny and the new alarm system, everything. When she was finished, Nick's end was quiet. He must have pulled off the road to listen before he got too close to home.

Finally, he spoke in a serious voice. "Thanks for telling me all that. I can't imagine the stress you're dealing with. I'm so sorry."

Wow, that's a pretty mature response. Maybe I'm too tough on the guy sometimes.

"But I've got stress of my own," Nick added, then stopped talking.

Okay, there he is. Now, I've gotta ask him about his stress?

After a long pause, Nora asked, "What's going on?"

Nick answered rapid-fire. "Vicki's pregnant and we've been trying for a while before this, so the doctor says this could be a difficult pregnancy. I don't want her stressed about stuff like this. And you know how protective her dad gets. He's over the moon about a grandchild and he would lose his shit if he thought we were making things hard for her."

Got it. So you don't want her burdened by me being wrongly accused of murder? Jesus H. Christ.

Nora failed to fully conceal her sarcasm. "Okay, well, first, congratulations to both of you, and of course to her father. Second, I'll do everything possible not to be a source of stress for Vicki. Third, I know you meant to ask about *our* actual living child whose name is Sophie, but my mom and I will keep things completely normal and safe for her. She'll be fine. If anything changes, I'll let you know. Again, congratulations."

Nora hung up, her face flushed, her fists balled tightly. She took a deep breath, then walked back to the den and snuggled up against Sophie to watch Anna climb mountains in a blizzard. Benny turned toward her with a concerned look but said nothing.

They were interrupted a short time later by the sound of a chime from the driveway motion sensor, although Sophie missed it among the movie's music. Nora reached for the remote. "Bug, I think Nana may be coming in. Let's surprise her." They hurried to the garage door as Benny headed for the basement to give them some privacy.

Teresa Carleton opened the door from the garage, pulling her suitcase behind her. "Surprise!" shouted Sophie, launching herself at her grandmother's legs. Teresa let go of her suitcase and dropped to her knees in the doorway, wrapping her arms around her granddaughter, but looking up at Nora standing behind. "I'm so happy to see you, my two favorite girls in the world. Nobody can stop us now!"

Sophie stole her grandmother's catchphrase: "Because Super Nana is home!"

"Yes she is," Teresa answered, getting to her feet and brushing away long strands of her straight silver hair. "Would you pull Super Nana's suitcase? Her powers are not what they should be right now."

In the kitchen, Teresa lifted Sophie onto the center island and stood facing her, leaning against the sink with Nora so Sophie could report on her week at school. As the little girl finished, the basement stairs creaked as Benny came up to the kitchen.

"Oh, Mom," Nora said, looking up, "you remember my friend Benny, who's come to help for a while. I told you about him on the phone. He's been sentenced to the basement guest room."

Benny crossed the kitchen and extended his hand. "It's not exactly hard time down there. It's so nice to see you again, Mrs. Carleton. Been too long."

"Please," she said, taking his hand, "It's 'Teresa' and it's a pleasure to see you again. Nora has told me a lot of amazing Benny stories over the years, so I'm a big fan."

Something in her voice made both Nora and Sophie look at her. Nora said nothing. Sophie asked, "Should *I* call you 'Teresa'?"

"'Super Nana' to you, my girl," Teresa answered, before looking at Benny and adding, "I know Nora feels lucky to have you here. So do I."

"Well," Benny began, just a hint of red appearing on his cheeks, "it's the least I could do. I think the world of your daughter. And I answer to 'Benny,' or whatever else you may want to call me."

"'Benny' is a very nice name. I'll stick with that," Teresa replied, smiling, her grin highlighting the laugh lines framing her brown eyes.

After a brief awkward silence, Nora spoke. "Bug, why don't you help Nana put her things away, 'kay? I need to chat with Benny for a minute."

When Sophie and her grandmother were upstairs, Nora turned and gently punched Benny on the arm. "Something going on with you and my mother?"

"Whataya talkin' about?" Benny answered with a laugh. "We barely talked and you witnessed the entire thing. What's wrong with you?"

"Nothing. Just checking," Nora said with a smile.

"But ya know your mother is a very attractive woman, right?" Benny asked.

"Hah! I knew it." Nora almost shouted. "I knew it. And I'm not saying it would be wrong. She's single, you're single. I'm just saying it would be weird, so cut it out."

"You know nothin'," Benny replied. "All this stress is messin' with your head. Can we gather in the war room to talk about the mysterious Mr. Holtzer? Been workin' it and got some leads to show you."

"Sure," Nora said, gesturing to the basement stairs. "Lead the way."

As she followed his broad back down the stairs, she added, "And to be clear, I'm never going to call you 'Dad.'"

Benny shook his head and answered without turning around. "Somethin' seriously wrong with you."

CHAPTER TWENTY-TWO

Even after two years, Nora still found the drop-off line at Greens Farms Academy intimidating. It was like a Range Rover convention, with the long line of Carpathian gray, Santorini matte black, or Belgravia green cars—hundred grand a pop—occasionally broken by a huge shiny black American SUV, which meant a hired car some families used to deliver their children to the small private school with the gorgeous view of the Long Island Sound. GFA offered a great education, and worked hard to attract low income students on scholarships, but Nora often wondered whether the motto, *Quisque Pro Omnibus*—"each for all"—meant that everyone got a fancy car.

"Love you, Mommy!" Sophie shouted as the school staff member at the head of the line opened the rear door of Nora's rented Honda Accord.

"Love you, bug! Have a great day!"

"Have a lovely day," the woman said in a British accent before gently closing the door.

Really from the UK or is that just a thing here? Nora didn't have time to answer her own question because her cell rang. It was Abe.

"Hey, assistant," Nora answered, "I'm just leaving GFA. Be to you in ten. What's up?"

Abe was whispering. "You should know people here are talking about you. And it's not good."

"Say more," Nora answered quietly. "Who's saying what?"

"Well, everyone, near as I can tell, is talking about Helen being found in your canoe and her blood being found on your car. You're the prime suspect, is the word."

"How . . ." Nora began, but she stopped.

"You there?" Abe asked.

"Yeah, just thinking. That son of a bitch Louis must've told people. David and Marcus are the only other people who knew those two facts and they wouldn't talk about it. And I thought the one thing we weren't supposed to do at this place was gossip about shit like this."

"Yup," Abe said. "But I heard it in the break room, at the gym, and two guys from trading were talking about it while playing Ping-Pong in the lounge. Like high school, for God's sake, except Mr. High-and-Mighty would probably say he's just being transparent."

"Okay, thanks for the heads-up. See you in a few."

"Hey Nora?" Abe asked. "You gonna be okay?"

Nora exhaled. "I sure hope so, Abe. One thing's for sure: I didn't kill Helen, but the way things are going I'm gonna have to figure out who did—before I get arrested or I lose my job."

"I know you didn't. Anything you need, I'm here. See you soon."

—·—

By the time she had driven the four miles to Saugatuck, Nora was hot. She walked quickly to her office, closed the door, and dropped her bag on the desk. She wasn't going to talk to him in his office because he might tape her, so she looked directly at the wall and shouted. "Louis! Please come in here, now!"

In about ten seconds her door opened and a surprised looking Louis Lambert appeared, in his usual tucked-in flannel shirt and belted blue jeans.

"Yes, Nora, what is it?"

"Please come in, and shut the door."

She paused and touched a hand to her mouth, then dropped the hand and looked at Lambert. "I only need you to listen. It's a firing offense to gossip at Saugatuck, an offense made worse when the information is confidential and obtained in the course of employment. If I can prove you have done that by spreading malicious gossip about me, I'll burn you to the ground. Am I clear?"

He looked almost hurt, but his answer came out in a Saugatuck-style monotone. "Yes, you are, but may I ask you a clarifying question?"

"Of course," Nora answered.

"If it is true that Helen was found in your canoe and that her blood was found on your car, how can saying that be inconsistent with our values? People are saying what is true, as I understand it."

"I don't blame those people," Nora said.

"Well, I suppose that will be a relief to them."

She couldn't tell from his tone whether he meant to be sarcastic. She pointed at him. "I blame *you*. I know you fucking told people. I know you are spreading information to make me look bad. You've wanted to get me since the moment I set foot in this place."

Louis didn't respond. After two beats, he simply turned and left the office, quietly pulling the door closed as he left.

Dick, Helen would have said. *At least he didn't lie,* Nora thought. Seconds later, there was a quiet knock on the door. *Maybe he's come back to offer transparency about what a prick he is.*

"Come in," Nora said angrily.

The door moved slowly, guided by two slender hands gripping the moving edge. The pleasant face of Tracey Stein, Helen's assistant, came into view. She was squinting and moving cautiously.

"Nora?"

Nora moved toward her. "Oh Tracey. Come in, come in."

Nora extended a hand and guided Tracey to a chair in front of the desk. She pulled the other guest chair close and sat next to her.

"What is it, Tracey? You should have called and I would have come to you."

"No, no," Tracey said, "I wanted to talk privately."

Nora looked at the wall to Lambert's office. "Okay, but we need to keep our voices down because these walls are so thin. What is it?"

"First of all," Tracey said quietly, "I don't believe you would ever hurt Helen. She thought the world of you and I know what you thought of her. I've heard what they're saying this morning and I know someone else did it."

Nora sighed and leaned back in her chair. "Thank you for that."

Tracey was speaking in a barely audible whisper now. "I know there are people here at Saugatuck who really didn't like Helen. And I know there were things about some of those people that Helen really didn't like."

"Why do you say that?" Nora whispered. "Did Helen tell you that?"

"No, no," Tracey answered, "because of the files."

"What files?"

"I think I mentioned them last Monday. Helen kept personal files with things she learned about people here. She told me they were confidential and sensitive and it was important to protect them. She said they didn't belong to Saugatuck, that they were hers. It was all hard copies—nothing electronic—and she kept them in a locked drawer in her credenza, where she also had her workout stuff and a change of clothes. She kept that key taped to the underside of her middle desk drawer."

Nora wasn't sure what to say. "What was in them, do you know?"

Tracey shook her head. "I don't. I never looked. And not because of my sight. I can actually read text if I hold it very close, or I could have used the magnifier, but I didn't, because Helen said they were private and her personal property."

"And where are they now?"

"Monday when we all learned about Helen, I put them in my backpack and took them with me when one of the drivers took me home. You know Rob and Helen got the company to pay for my transportation to and from work, every day. Anyway, I took Helen's files to my place. And they're still there."

Nora paused and exhaled before whispering, "Why are you telling me this?"

"Because I think she would want you to have them. Especially given what people are saying about you. I know you didn't kill her. Helen knows. I can feel her. You wouldn't, you couldn't. Maybe there's something in those files to help you figure out who really did."

Tracey paused before adding, "And to be honest, I'm telling you because Rob said I should. I went to him first about the files. He said he wanted no part of them, but that I should definitely tell you. So this is me doing that."

"Okay Tracey," Nora said, "I'm really glad you did. I've got a few things to finish up here, then maybe we could go to your place so I can get them?"

"Sure," Tracey replied. "Just come by my cubicle when you're ready."

CHAPTER TWENTY-THREE

Nora's phone started playing "Don't Stop Believing" by Journey, her mother's favorite song.

"Hey, Mom," Nora said, pressing the phone to her ear.

"The police are here, as you predicted, with a warrant. Anything I should do?"

"Nope, just let them in and stay out of their way. Hey, is the detective there? Woman? Demi Kofatos? Could you give her the phone?"

"Yes, here she is."

Demi's voice came through the earpiece. "Hello, Ms. Carleton?"

"Yes, thanks for getting on," Nora said. "You do what you need to do and my mom will stay out of your way. You'll leave her the inventory?"

"Of course. And we also need to get hold of your phone."

"Sure," Nora replied. "You coming to Saugatuck?"

"Not today," Demi said. "Legal issues. Above my pay grade."

"Okay, I have a few things to do. If you're done at my house, I'll drop it by your office, but you'll probably be a while."

"Yeah, we'll be here a couple more hours," Demi answered, before adding, "Oh, and the State's Attorney told us to stay out of the wine room. Attorney work product or something."

"Yeah, I appreciate that. So I'll bring the phone to the house. Thanks for your courtesy."

"No problem. And, Ms. Carleton?"

"Yeah?" Nora replied.

"Please don't think this means we've decided this thing. 'Cause we haven't. Least I haven't."

"I appreciate that," Nora said. "Can you put my mom back on?"

"Nora?" Teresa asked.

"Hey, Mom. You don't have to leave the house, but just steer clear of them. If they finish before I get there, they'll leave you a written list of everything they take, but I'm guessing it will be a bunch of our knives and my desktop computer. Don't read too much into it all; it's what they have to do and it's gonna be fine."

"Okay," Teresa replied, "I'll handle it. But they need to finish before Sophie is done with school."

"They should be out of there long before Sophie gets home, but if they're not, I'm sure Benny can swing by while you get Sophie and you can take her out for ice cream or something. Thanks for all your help, Mom. Love you."

"I love you too."

—◦—

They drove in silence for a long time before Tracey spoke. "You know this is the only part of Helen that was walled off from me."

"I didn't," Nora answered, steering her rental car into the parking lot of Tracey's apartment complex. "How'd you feel about that?"

"Unsure, honestly. She was such an open person, or seemed to be. This black box—almost literally—was the only thing about Helen that ever gave me a bad feeling. But she did so much for me, and was so fun to work with, that it wasn't a big deal. Until what happened last week, and since then I haven't been able to stop thinking about the files."

Nora stopped the car in a parking space. "And you still haven't looked at them?"

"Not beyond what she wrote on the file label tabs. I looked at those when I put them in my backpack."

Nora waited and Tracey went on. "Each file had a name on the label, the names of nearly all the bigwigs at Saugatuck. Almost all of them had a lot of stuff in them. In fact, they all did, except I think yours was almost empty."

Driving away from Tracey's, Nora dialed Benny.

"Hey, Mr. Rough."

"Ms. Smooth, what's up?"

"Busy day. I got some stuff you gotta see. And the cops are at my house doing the search we expected. My mom's holding down the fort but I don't want to roll up there with this stuff in my car. Meet me at the Sherwood Diner?"

"Sure, I'm ten minutes away. Where are you?"

"About twenty from the diner. See you there."

"Copy," Benny said, ending the call.

After meeting at the diner and transferring Helen's files to Benny's car, Nora and Benny drove separately to Nora's house, where they parked on the street. The driveway was still crowded with police vehicles, although officers seemed to be packing up. Teresa was sitting on the front porch, reading on her Kindle. She heard their feet crunch on the little stones and looked up with a tired smile. "I think they took everything in the house that resembles a sharp knife."

"Not surprising," Nora said.

"You doin' okay?" Benny asked Teresa. "They didn't harass ya or anything right? 'Cause I could set 'em straight if need be."

"Thanks Benny, I'm okay, although this is a whole new world for me."

"Understandable," Benny said. "Not sure having your house searched should ever feel normal."

Demi Kofatos appeared in the doorway. "We're all set," she said, handing Nora the two-page list of what they had seized. "I put your cell phone on the list," Demi added, gesturing with an empty plastic bag and pulling it open with two hands.

Nora dropped her phone into the bag. "We'll image it and get it back to you tomorrow," Demi said.

"My mom says we'll be cutting our steak with a spoon for a while."

Demi smiled tightly. "Yeah, sorry about that. You know how it works."

"Yup," Nora said. "And who needs steak, anyway?"

"I do," came Benny's voice from behind her.

"Take care," Demi said. "Thanks for being so cooperative," she added, extending her hand to shake Nora's. "We'll get out of your hair now." Then she turned to Teresa, saying, "I'm sorry for the inconvenience ma'am. Thanks for your patience."

Benny shook his head as he walked inside. "What's she sucking up for? That shi—excuse me, Teresa—that *behavior* makes me suspicious."

As the two women stood on the front porch watching the police drive out, Teresa turned to Nora.

"That detective seems really nice," she said.

"She's okay," Nora answered as the last car pulled away.

"And she's cute," Teresa added.

"Mom."

"And she seems to like you."

"Oh my Lord, Ma, stop, stop. She just searched our house for God's sake."

CHAPTER TWENTY-FOUR

"Ho-ly shit," Benny said, drawing out the syllables. He reached into the cardboard box sitting on the wine room table and grabbed a file. "Artemis Falcone," he read, flipping the file open. "Ol' Arty sure has a fat one."

"Not surprising with that creepster," Nora said as Benny skimmed through pages.

"Wow. He's been a bad, bad boy. And a lot of these are reports from a private investigator. Seems Arty was not only grabbing, kissing, and—what?—*biting* young female Saugatuck colleagues. He was into some sick shit off campus as well. This PI was doing all kinds of surveillance, which I gotta admire."

"Yup, from the reports, it's some guy named Jatinder Singh. Do they still call them 'private dicks'?" Nora asked.

"Hope not," Benny said, not looking up from the file. "In fact let's agree to never."

After a moment, he held up the thick file on Arty Falcone, using it to gesture at the box. "So Helen fucking Carmichael was spying on all of you? The plot just thickened, as they say. Did you look at the one on you yet?"

"Of course. Like three pages," Nora said. "Just a credit report and copy of a couple news articles from when the defense accused me of withholding exculpatory evidence in the D'Amico case five years ago."

Benny chortled. "Complete bullshit. Nothing in the world was exculpatory for a mobster like 'The Nose,' may he rest in peace."

"I know, and the judge said so, but the *New York Post*, scrupulous journalists that they are, forgot to run articles saying that, so there aren't any in there clearing me."

"It's a great country," Benny said, shaking his head. "Who else has thin ones?"

"Rob Arslan's is almost nothing as well."

"Makes sense for you and Captain America not to have much," Benny said. "Anyone else?"

"Nope," Nora said. "She had a lot of stuff for all the other MC members. Also a pretty good amount for Louis Lambert, which is where I want to start."

"Okay," Benny answered. "And lemme ask something that I can't believe I'm the one asking, but, are we cool to read this stuff? I mean, should we check with Carmen or pain-in-the-ass Raleigh?"

"I thought about that," Nora replied. "I think we're okay to go through it once and then talk to them. These aren't Saugatuck records and so far as I know they aren't covered by any kind of subpoena at this point. They are Helen's personal property that her assistant gave me. And you and I are going to preserve them so there's no obstruction of justice issue."

Benny nodded. "And here's another one I should have asked before putting my mitts all over these, but fingerprints? Should we stop touching the originals? Just in case the murderer was pawing through these before going after Helen?"

"In an office with glass walls and a hidden key? Don't think so. So no, I don't think fingerprints are an issue," Nora said. "And, honestly, it's too late anyway."

"Okay," Benny said, "I've done my due diligence. Now let's read the dirt on the Saugatuck mopes."

Benny paused, studying Nora. "Why the sad look?"

Nora shook her head. "Honestly, I'm not sure. I think it's a combination of finding out a lot of bad stuff about the people I work with and finding out that Helen was a bit of a snake."

"I get the first part. But why a snake?"

"Well, she clearly wasn't collecting this stuff so Saugatuck could make informed personnel or security decisions. A piece of this I knew about because the complaints—like some of the stuff with Arty and the women at company parties—came through official channels and we investigated it. Helen has that information in here, but she also has all kinds of stuff I didn't know about and issues outside work that she was digging into and not sharing. And I'll bet Laslo knows nothing about it either. So she wasn't doing this to protect Saugatuck. She must have been doing it to protect herself *from* Saugatuck in some way—somehow get control over her peers. Why else would she have it and keep it like this?"

"I don't know," Benny answered. "But I do know that those files may tell us why somebody killed her."

Benny stood, walked to the whiteboard, and grabbed a marker. "So let's pull out the big stuff on each of these creeps. Who you wanna start with?"

"I already told you—that prick Lambert," Nora said, grabbing the file for Louis Lambert. "Helen's PI documents that he lives far, far beyond his means and works hard to hide that. He buys expensive art that he never displays and blows huge money on travel, which he does alone. Weird as hell."

"Got it," Benny said as he turned from the board. "Who's next?"

"Well, Arty, whose file seems the thickest. The off-campus stuff Helen's guy dug up goes way beyond the nastiness at company events: dungeons, snuff-film cosplay, dark-web chats, really sick shit. And I'm guessing none of it known to the lovely Mrs. Falcone and their three kids."

"Okay," Benny said as he wrote. *"Bad sex stuff, on and off the clock.* Next."

"Marcus Baum," Nora said, opening the file. "Loves David Jepson and also hates him because this was supposed to be Marcus's company years ago. Looks like it was Marcus who leaked all the bad stuff to *The Wall Street Journal* about Saugatuck and David a couple years back—wild parties, David supposedly being ill, employees unhappy with evil clients."

Nora kept reading. "Whoa. It also looks like Helen helped him do the leaking."

Benny filled the silence, narrating his own work at the board. "Okay, *pissed, leaking to hurt Jepson.* Next."

"Rob," Nora said, opening Arslan's slim file. "He was addicted to painkillers when he first got here. Got divorced, no kids. He did therapy, got off the pain pills, and went on antidepressants. Set up a charity, which is legit. Helen helped him through all of it. Nobody besides her knew anything about it."

"So *painkillers, divorce, depression, treatment,*" Benny said as he wrote. "Not the end of the world, but not nothin'. Who's next? What about the Jepson family? Start with the boss."

"She has lots of stuff on David's wife. Seems the marriage is a fiction. She mostly lives in the British Virgin Islands, has attractive young men escorting her wherever she goes. Claims they're assistants."

"Bet I know what they assist with," Benny said as he wrote on the board.

Nora looked up. "Kinda sad, actually. David talks so much about his wife. Yikes."

She grabbed the next file. "Miranda Jepson. She hates her father for not leaving and giving her the company. Apparently, Miranda found out her father was spending big money on strange life-extension treatments, planning to be in charge forever. And Helen found out, too, of course."

She continued reading. "Oh wow. Also seems she was secretly banging Marcus Baum at some point—another person who thought the company should be his. All kinds of hotel records and photos here."

"Whoa, messing with the boss's daughter? That shit'll get a guy killed where I come from. Gonna add *adulterer* under Baum too." Benny said. "Next Jepson?"

"The good one," Nora replied, lifting a file. "Chip."

She read for a minute. "Okay, not so good, apparently. Seems he date-raped a poor drunk girl who passed out in his college dorm bed. Victim went to the campus cops. They interviewed him. He was all, 'She wanted it, she was into me, we were on a date and I bought her a nice dinner and she came to my dorm room and got naked in my bed' and all the stuff frat boys tell themselves to justify their behavior. Of course, that was not consistent with any of the evidence, including vaginal bruising and her contemporaneous past statements to friends about not wanting to have sex with the guy. Chip's mother paid the girl's family off with a *lot* of money to keep her quiet. She transferred to another school. David never knew. Chip met his wife in grad school, so she has no idea this ever happened. Police reports, NDA with the victim, everything's here."

"*Rapist*," Benny wrote. "Lovely family. And I'm adding his mother up here—*Liar* and *Briber*. One more?"

"Yup," Nora said, "Jeffey the jet-setter." She read for a bit before looking up. "Oh, I really thought his would be sex, drugs, rock and roll, and being pissed at daddy. Turns out it's Chinese intelligence. Somehow Helen got onto the fact that the Ministry of State Security—their CIA—ran an op against Jeffey. Sent a pretty young thing in on him and she got into all his devices, then exfilled a ton of company data and implanted malicious code to spy on Saugatuck. After being the love of his life for a few months, the woman vanished back to Beijing. Saugatuck found the spyware and booted the Chinese off their systems, but never figured out what was taken. And it turns out that nobody but Helen knew it was Jeffey who let the bad guys inside the castle. Her notes say he begged her to protect him from his father. And she did."

"*Chinese spy*," Benny wrote beneath Jeffey's picture, before stepping back to look at the full board. "Wow, what a crowd you got here. Truth and transparency, my ass."

He turned to Nora. "I gotta be honest: Your mentor Helen doesn't seem like such a gentle soul. Cost her a lot of money to get all this shit. Musta been a reason. Blackmail?"

Nora shook her head. "I don't know. Clearly there was a side to her I didn't see, but I still don't think she was some kind of evil blackmailer. My guess? It was somehow about protecting her people, which was always her thing. You mess with one of hers, she'll hurt you."

"Maybe," Benny said, "but it doesn't exactly explain why she had one on you and Rob, who were clearly in the 'her people' category."

He turned back to point at the board. "Either way, in this pile of bad behavior is our killer. Gotta be. We just gotta figure out which one."

Benny turned back to see Nora tilting her head. "What? I know that look."

"Should have hit me earlier," Nora said, "but I'm pretty sure Tracey told me there was only one file that was nearly empty—mine. All the others were loaded."

"And so?" Benny asked.

"Probably nothing, but we've got *two* folders that have almost nothing."

"Right, you and Rob. You thinkin' the blind girl is messing with you somehow?"

"No, couldn't be. It's just that she's a really precise person—very Saugatuck that way. So is she misremembering or am I? Or is it something else? Or maybe nothing."

"Easy enough," Benny said. "I'll have a chat with her. Done. What else is buggin' you?"

She gestured toward the board. "Nothing, except this crowd is making me miss Helen, even with everything we've learned about her. What a world."

"What a world, indeed," Benny said, "filled with motherless fucks, as you may have heard."

CHAPTER TWENTY-FIVE

Porter Raleigh was scowling and cleaning his glasses. Carmen was nearly shouting, her face red.

"How far up your butt is your head, Nora? The point is not that this isn't potentially important evidence. The point is that you are now in the goddamn custody chain. If we ever want to use these files to defend you, we will probably need you to testify that you got them from Tracey what's-her-name and brought them here to review with Benny. You will be forced to testify at your own trial, if it comes to that, God forbid. That's why I'm so upset. I just wish Benny had gone to Tracey's apartment to get them to establish a chain of custody without you in the middle of it."

Nora studied the kitchen table. "You're right, Carmen. I should've talked to you before going to Tracey's place—Tracey Stein, by the way—but there was no chance she was going to give them to anyone but me. So I made the decision in the moment. And if I'm charged and if these files are useful evidence and if the prosecution won't stipulate they were Helen's, then I'll have to testify."

Raleigh cleared his throat. "And then there's the not-so-small issue of whether the State's Attorney is going to see this as some kind of obstruction because we removed evidence—"

"We didn't remove evidence, Porter," Nora interrupted, lifting her head. "Tracey Stein did."

"—*accepted* evidence that had been removed from the victim's office," Raleigh amended.

Carmen seemed less angry now. "Although the evidence is likely exculpatory, Porter, and we'll definitely figure out a way to share it with the state at some point."

Raleigh cleared his throat in reply. "Fair, fair," he said. "I just hate to be vulnerable to procedural claims like this, especially when I'm going to roll boulders down the hill at the State's Attorney to keep her from moving against Nora. Through forty years of practice, I've tried to avoid putting myself in that kind of position and don't like the idea of being professionally tarnished by a client's poor judgment."

The kitchen was awkwardly quiet before Carmen finally spoke. "Okay, I think we've flogged Nora, and this topic, enough for now. She understands that she's the client and should not be investigating, at least not without a member of this team with her at all times."

There were nods all around the table before Carmen continued. "And are we clear on next steps? Benny, you're going to interview Tracey and lock down the movement of these files. And you're also going to track down this private investigator Jatinder Singh and the mysterious funeral visitor, Brad Holtzer. You're also going to see if you can catch up with the chief security officer, Laslo Reiner, off campus to see what he knows. Porter's paralegal is taking Helen's files to his office, where they will stay for now, and he'll return a copy of the files for use here. Meantime, tomorrow morning, Porter and I are taking Nora down to donate hair and blood to the Westport PD."

For reasons he couldn't explain, blind people made Benny uncomfortable. "Don't like it when I can't tell what somebody facing me is seeing," he told Nora before leaving for his interview with Tracey. "That's why I always make shitheads take off their sunglasses during an interview."

Nora smiled. "Well, for starters, she's no shithead. And Tracey's what they call 'legally blind'—she can see shapes and, if she holds a text up to her face, she can make out letters and read. She uses a magnifying screen at work."

"Then I guess she ain't actually blind," Benny responded. "So is there a thing like 'hard of seeing'—like what they say about people who don't hear so good?"

"I don't know, actually, Benny," Nora had said, "and I hope to God you manage not to talk about this with her."

Now Benny was sitting on Tracey's couch after following her gesture toward the living room furniture and declining her offer of a glass of water. Tracey stepped smoothly around an ottoman and settled gracefully in an armchair facing him. There was an awkward pause before Benny broke the silence. "So you full-on blind, or what?"

Tracey smiled. "I'm not sure that's even a thing, but it's not what I am. I was born with twenty-twenty, but got too close to a bomb in Iraq. Shrapnel damaged my eyes. The docs say I'm lucky they could save them, but my vision's been severely impaired ever since. Although I can see enough to do my job."

"Right. Thanks for that and for your service. No offense intended," Benny mumbled.

"Absolutely none taken," Tracey said pleasantly. "I don't mind your directness. So tell me how I can help."

"Can you walk me through how you got the files you gave Nora and how you handled them?"

"Of course."

When Tracey finished repeating the story she told Nora, Benny followed up. "Tell me more about the thickness of these files. You said one was a lot thinner than the others?"

"Yes, the one with Nora's name on it. As I said, I lifted each one so I could get up close to the file tab—that's how I read text—and I remember hers was skinny in a way none of the others were."

"See that's the thing, Tracey, all but *two* of them are really thick files, and those two are noticeably thinner than the others, at least they are now. What do you make of that?"

"Well, I suppose I could have missed it. If a second one was thin, I suppose I could have accidentally lifted it together with a thick file. I don't remember doing that, but I wouldn't have noticed if I lifted them at the same time. So I guess my answer is that I didn't see a second thin file, but there could have been another. I didn't notice any names missing, but you have to understand that this was a bad time—right after Helen."

The room was quiet before Tracey spoke again. "Did I make a mistake? Is that a problem?"

"No, no, not at all. Really doesn't matter much, but the lawyers wanted me to follow up. Lemme ask you this: anybody have access to the files between the time you got them out of Helen's office and when you gave them to Nora?"

"Only Rob, although I don't know if he actually went through them. I left the backpack with the files in his office when I told him about them. He said he would think about it. Not more than an hour later, he came to my cubicle and returned the backpack. He said they should go to Nora and I should make sure nobody else sees them. That's when I took them home. So 'maybe' is my best answer. But I can't say for sure."

"Okay, Tracey," Benny said, "that's really helpful."

"Hopefully I didn't screw something up."

"Not even a little bit. I appreciate your time. And, again, I meant no offense about the blind stuff. I'm sorry that happened to you. Really sucks."

Tracey rose with him and extended her hand. "No offense at all, as I said. And three people in my squad didn't come home from that day, so I'm actually pretty lucky, if you think about it."

Benny shook her hand. "Honor to meet somebody like you and I'll show myself out."

Tracey laughed at his awkwardness as she stepped in front to lead him to the door. "Nice of you, but I can navigate my own house with my eyes closed, as they say."

When Benny didn't answer, Tracey added, "Sight humor never gets old, no matter how many times you don't see it."

Benny rushed through the door, calling over his shoulder. "Again, grateful for your time. Lemme know if you need anything."

CHAPTER TWENTY-SIX

Teresa's voice echoed down the stairs to the basement. "Hi Benny if you're down there! Don't mean to frighten you but I'm coming down with fresh towels."

As she reached the bottom of the stairs, Benny stepped out of the war room and answered across the basement. "Nothing about you frightens me, Mrs. Carleton. And you don't have to do that. I'm used to puttin' a lot more miles on my towels."

"Teresa, please," she answered. "I thought we covered that. And you're the easiest houseguest ever. The least we could do is spoil you with a couple towels once a week."

"Many thanks, Teresa," Benny said, taking the towels. With a smile, he added, "I'd invite you to sit, but as you can see, not big on chairs down here."

"Or anything else," Teresa added, smiling back at him. "We just haven't gotten around to it. The house is so big to begin with, and we didn't expect guests."

"Well—" Benny began.

Teresa interrupted, speaking rapidly. "And I'm not trying to suggest you aren't welcome here. Of course you are. All three of us Carleton girls are glad you're here and I am very grateful for you helping Nora during this difficult time."

She looked around before adding, "I really do wish there was *someplace* to sit here. Even a beanbag chair. I'm going to HomeGoods tomorrow."

"Hey," Benny said, gesturing behind him, "why don't you come in the war room—which your wiseass daughter calls the 'wine room.' We got two chairs *and* a table and there's nothing secret, least not from you."

"I'd like that," she said.

Nora called out from the bottom of the stairs toward the open war room door. "Hey, Mr. Rough, I'm heading out to pick up Soph. I'm not sure where my mom is. Do you need anything?"

Teresa's voice came from the little room. "Oh, I'm in here, dear. Just chatting with Benny."

Gently shaking her head, Nora crossed the basement and stood in the war room doorway. "What are you two doing down here?"

"Just talking," Teresa said. "Getting to know each other better. Did you know that Benny and I both love Elton John's music? We grew up with it and it's still on the radio."

Nora arched her eyebrows and looked at Benny, whose face had flashed pink. "Wow, Elton, who knew?" she said. "He comes back stronger than a nineties trend." They both looked confused, so Nora dropped it rather than explain her reference to a Taylor Swift lyric. "Glad there's bonding going on in the wine room, but I'm getting Sophie. Anybody need anything?"

Teresa stood. "Why don't I come with you? Then I can run into the cleaners on the way home."

"You wanna drive? Nora asked.

"Love to," her mother said, "but I can't find my keys."

Nora exhaled loudly. "Mom, if you'd put the AirTag Aunt Sue gave you on the key chain you'd always be able to find them."

"Fancy," Teresa said. "Now I just need to find *that*. You drive. I'll take care of the tag thingy later."

"Sounds good," Nora said. "Let's roll."

As the two women walked to the stairs, Nora said, "Oh, wait, I forgot to check one thing with Benny. Meet you in the garage."

She walked back to the war room and leaned through the doorway with a raised hand, pointing her first two fingers at her own eyes before turning them to point at Benny. He lifted his hands, palms up, and raised his shoulders toward his ears, whispering, "Hey, she came to see *me*. What am I supposed to do?"

Nora repeated the *I have my eyes on you* gesture and hurried to join her mother.

<hr />

"Oh, I forgot to ask you about tonight," Nora said as she steered onto Greens Farms Road headed for Sophie's school. "Soph was really counting on going to Rob's basketball game, but I feel like I'd be a distraction with the company people who will be there and all the drama around Helen and my fricking canoe. Would you mind going with her?"

"Of course not," Teresa said. "Just give me the address."

"Oh, no need," Nora replied. "It's at the middle school right by my office, but Rob'll pick you up. He insists and Sophie thinks his car is the coolest thing in the world. He'll be in the driveway at six so let's have an early dinner. The game will be over by eight. She'll be in bed before nine."

"Sounds great," Teresa said. "I've never been to a wheelchair game."

"They're amazing athletes and it's really fun to watch."

They drove for a few minutes in silence before Nora changed the subject. "So what's going on with you and Benny?"

Teresa turned to look at the side of Nora's head. "What do you mean, what's going on?"

"I mean: What's going on? You seem pretty chummy."

"Can't I be friendly with people, Nora?" Teresa asked. "I like him. I like talking to him. He makes me laugh. And it feels like we have so much in common. Honestly, it almost feels meant to be."

"Mom," Nora said, her mouth tight.

"No," Teresa answered, sounding slightly irritated. "I mean it. The big stuff. Like we're at the same stage of life, and we both married our first loves and then we both lost them way too early. We've dealt with a lot of the same hard things and pushed through. That man hasn't taken a day of vacation since his wife died twelve years ago. He's taking some now, to help you, but still, wow."

Nora paused before saying, "You're good people."

"I love being with you and Sophie, but talking with him reminds me of something I didn't even know I missed."

"I didn't realize you were lonely, Ma."

"I'm not, except I think talking with Benny shows me I actually am a little bit, in a way I'd lost touch with. That's all. We're not running off to Vegas, but I like talking to him."

Nora didn't answer.

"Please don't be mad," Teresa said.

They drove in silence for several beats.

"Ma, you know I love Benny, but there's a reason I call him Mr. Rough. He's a complicated guy, been in tough places, done hard stuff, a lot of which he doesn't talk about. Honestly, I worry you don't really know him. He's not Dad."

Teresa was hot now. "Nora, for heaven's sake, we are all complicated people. I know more about Benny than you realize. And I sure as heck know more about your father than you do. He was a good man, but there are no perfect people, there never have been. Benny is another good man."

The car was quiet for a full minute before they stopped at a traffic light and Teresa added quietly, "He's a good person and we have a lot in common. That's it. And we aren't 'hooking up'—or whatever they say."

"Ma! Ick."

"What 'ick'?" Teresa asked. "He's a fine-looking man. And you've got to get over this business about me being older. The whole world dismisses us, but I'm a real woman with real human feelings. My hair is starting to go gray, but I'm alive and attracted to Benny Dugan in ways that surprise even me. And he makes me laugh and that feels so good. Also Nora, don't you always tell me I'm hot?"

Nora laughed. "Okay, you are hot—beautiful—and I absolutely want you to be happy Mom, but I cannot engage on the fine-looking-man thing. So can this conversation be over, before I need therapy?"

"Well he is a fine-looking man," Teresa added.

"Done. Over," Nora said, reaching to turn up the radio.

CHAPTER TWENTY-SEVEN

The Horseshoe Café had been in tiny downtown Southport for almost a hundred years and took its name from the blacksmith shop it replaced. The moment Benny stepped inside the Shoe—as locals called it—he was transported to the great dive bars of his youth—dark, cluttered, filled with random wall hangings, including, in this one, many, many horseshoes. As he paused and took a connoisseur's deep breath, he recognized Laslo Reiner watching the door from a high-top table in one of the Shoe's vintage Windsor swivel spindle stools. Laslo stepped off the stool to greet him and appeared to shrink. He was a squat, muscular block of a man, handsome, with thick dark hair kept short and parted on the left side of his head. He looked as if one or both of his parents were Asian. "First one's on me," he said, gesturing to the bar. "They got the usual suspects on draft. What'll you have?"

"Somethin' dark and meaty," Benny answered, taking the empty chair.

Laslo returned with two pints of Guinness and mounted the stool, which raised him almost to eye-level with Benny, who lifted his glass. "Slainte."

"Here's mud in your eye," Laslo replied as they clinked glasses.

"So you're former law enforcement?"

"Yup," Laslo answered. "How'd you know?"

"This bar, your seat facing the door, that toast," Benny said, before adding with a smile, "Plus Nora told me you did your twenty with the Bureau before coming to Saugatuck."

"Your detective skills are impressive," Laslo said, grinning. "Out of Quantico I got sent to New York and escaped to New Haven Division five years later and stayed until retirement, which I took as soon as I hit fifty."

"What'd you work?" Benny asked.

"New York runs everybody through the applicant squad first—doing backgrounds, as you probably know—then I got sent to a major theft squad. Was fun chasing thieves and fences. But my wife was up here in graduate school at Yale and no way she was moving into the city. I actually got a hardship transfer to New Haven. Really did save me a lot of hardship, including a divorce."

"So what'd you work up here?"

"Public corruption, mostly. This seems like a nice little state, but we have a proud tradition of crooked state and local pols, and some bad cops. We were busy."

"Then why'd you jump when you hit your twenty?"

"Money," Laslo said. "Saugatuck was looking to build a real security operation for the first time and I heard through a buddy of mine that they would pay a ridiculous amount for the right guy. Put my hat in. Turned out I was the right guy—I'm still not sure why—and my friend was right about the money. Now I got a place on the water just above New Haven and a boat, so I'm a happy camper—boater, actually. And still married."

"Sweet," Benny said. "Hey, let me ask you a question. You ever run across a thief in New York named Daniel Albert Joseph, nickname 'Frenchie'? Did some big jobs on the Upper East Side, including a monster heist at the Valnaghi. Also had a hard-on for Persian rugs."

"Huh. Name actually rings a bell, but that's about all. I do remember the Valnaghi job, though. Bunch of Old Masters taken from a place that thought it was burglarproof. We had all kinds of people on that, along with NYPD. Why do you ask?"

"Just curious is all. He became a witness for me, flipped on some really bad mob people. So how was New Haven FBI compared to New York?"

"Less arrogant, honestly. Only an hour away, but we were so small up here—I think we were the FBI's second smallest field office, after Anchorage—that we needed to get along with the locals and the other feds. The New York office is so big it has a tendency to tell everyone to go fuck themselves—which New Yorkers like to do anyway. We played better with others up here, is the bottom line."

"Good to hear," Benny said, "'cause I've had my bumps with the New York office's attitude, to be honest."

"I heard," Laslo said. "Hope you don't mind; I put out some feelers. Word back was that you know your job and don't bullshit, which may explain why you didn't get invited to a lot of FBI Secret-Santa parties."

"Fair enough," Benny said, lifting his glass. After taking a long drink of Guinness, he set the glass down and changed the subject.

"Okay, lemme level with you. I'm worried somebody is settin' Nora up to take the fall on Helen and I'm gonna try to figure out who that is and stop it. I need to know where you are on the whole thing, whether you'll help. Normally—and I'm sure you're the same—I take my time to get a fix on whether someone is a standup guy. I don't have that time here. So where are you?"

Laslo didn't answer right away. He lifted his own glass, took a drink, then set it down and looked at Benny. "I thought very highly of Helen. I feel the same about Nora. No way she did this. That's the easy part."

As Laslo paused to take another drink, Benny said, "Good to hear."

"Yeah," Laslo sighed, "but the answer to your 'where are you?' is harder. Saugatuck, our little bastion of truth and transparency, is a dangerous place. Old man Jepson is strange in all kinds of ways, but he's a good guy, and straight as an arrow. He really believes all the stuff he preaches. His problem is he thinks everybody else believes it. Now don't get me wrong—the young people eat it up and live it, wearing my ass out with their endless pursuit of truth and whatever. But they're good kids, in the main. The people at the MC level? Not a single one of them believes it the way Jepson does, including his own children. But they're also a complicated bunch, different mixtures of good and bad, like all people. I trust—well, trusted—Helen. I trust Nora. I trust Rob Arslan, the guy in the wheelchair. The rest, I can't say I trust any of them in that way and some of them I wouldn't let behind me, if you take my meaning."

Benny nodded. "I do. And I appreciate you being straight with me. I promise you the same."

Laslo exhaled. "Honestly, with what I just said, you're already holding the keys to my boat. Jepson ever found out I talked to you this way, I'm done. I wanted to meet here because Saugatuck people never come here; too blue collar."

Laslo paused and Benny let the silence be, staring into his glass, waiting. *C'mon bud. Do the right thing.*

Finally Laslo spoke. "But for Nora, for Helen, and 'cause of what I've heard about you, I'll help you the best I can. I can't promise I'll light myself on fire in front of the MC for you, but I'll help."

Benny lifted his nearly empty glass and tapped the bottom edge against Laslo's. "Appreciate it. And I won't burn you. You have my word."

Laslo pulled his lips into a tight smile. "Counting on it. Okay, so what do you need?"

"First," Benny said, "more Guinness, which I'm takin' care of. And you good with wings?"

They were settled with the next round and a plate of spicy chicken wings. Benny wiped his mouth. "So what's it like working security stuff inside Saugatuck?"

"I think most of it is what you would deal with at any company. Thefts, fraud, harassment, that kind of stuff. The big difference here is that the culture is my partner, in a way. What I mean is that, whenever I do an internal investigation—trying to find out who stole supplies or some shit like that, or who might be talking about company stuff in places they shouldn't be—the whole truth and transparency thing is a major advantage. First of all, they're used to being taped, so I get to record my interviews if I want. And I've also got tapes of nearly all their meetings and phone calls, and cameras everywhere, which makes it easier to make a case."

Laslo took a bite and washed it down before continuing. "But the best thing is that people here don't lie, or most of them don't, for a couple reasons. They know that if they bullshit me—even a little bit—their ass is out the door. And on top of that, most of them really believe it's a major betrayal of the culture to lie. It runs through their veins."

"Amazing," Benny said.

"So, for people who do what we do? Pretty great. Imagine how many more cases would be made on the outside if the real world worked that way."

Benny laughed. "Don't know how I would handle it if everybody I interviewed didn't lie at least a little."

Laslo ate another wing before continuing. "I think we could work this thing for Nora together, if we do it right."

"Whataya thinkin'?" Benny asked through a full mouth.

"I mean we partner on this, but on the down-low. When you have to speak to someone at the company, I set it up, and be there when you do it. I got enough background on the place and the people that I think I can be useful to you, and to Nora. 'Course we need David Jepson's blessing to do it, but I think if he sees it as a search for truth, he'll be up for it."

He took a drink before adding, "Although I gotta be the good cop. I can't be breaking balls if I'm going to keep riding this sweet gig."

Benny laughed. "I hear ya, I hear ya. No worries. I got the bad cop thing covered, don't you worry. Let me pitch my legal team on the idea."

Laslo grinned tightly. "And I suppose we should get the height jokes out of the way at the start."

Benny kept a poker face. "Don't know what you mean."

Now Laslo smiled widely. "You fucker. You know exactly what I mean. You're a giant. I'm"—he swept one hand up and down his torso—"less so."

Benny couldn't hide his smile any longer. "Hey, worked in all those movies for Kevin Hart and The Rock."

Laslo chortled. "Yeah, keep that in your pocket, big man. Last I checked, neither of us resembles either of those guys and nothin' but problems lie down the comparison road."

Benny began to speak, but Laslo help up a finger to silence him. "Nope, nope, don't. I know the next words out of your mouth are gonna be some Jackie Chan shit and I'm gonna have to go to HR. Let's just agree you aren't Chris Tucker or The Rock and no sense ruining this partnership at the jump. You be Benny. I'll be Laslo."

"Got it," Benny laughed, "but the *Rush Hour* movies were pretty great, am I right?"

"No comment," Laslo said, stepping down off the stool. "Thanks for the wings."

CHAPTER TWENTY-EIGHT

Nora was sitting in the dark on the front steps when Rob's customized black Cadillac Escalade crunched into the driveway and made a wide swing so its rear came to rest just in front of her. Like something out of *Star Wars*, the entire back of the vehicle opened, the mouth of the great beast making electrical whirring sounds as a long black ramp extended out onto the sidewalk. Sophie came running down the ramp and into her mother's arms.

"That. Was. So. Awesome!" she shouted. "Our team won and Rob was the hero. I wish you could have been there, Mom!"

Behind Sophie, Nora could see Rob grinning and waving from the driver's seat. Teresa chose the less dramatic exit, opening the front passenger door to step onto the driveway.

"Thanks again, Rob," she said. "That was a great game and so fun to watch! I just wish the Knicks had someone who could shoot like you."

He laughed. "With maybe a slightly higher launch point."

The three Carleton women stood and watched the spaceship close up again before Rob turned the car until his open window faced them. "Okay, big girl," he said to Sophie, "thanks for carrying us to victory. Now straight to bed, like you promised. I don't want your mom thinking I'm keeping you out too late."

"Bye, Rob!" Sophie shouted as Nora mouthed, *Thank you.*

"See you at work tomorrow," Nora added out loud. "More opportunities for excellence."

"Yup," Rob said with a sweaty smile. "The journey never ends; the joy is in the striving or something."

"Whatever," Nora answered. "Thanks again. See you tomorrow, although I'll be late because I have to go donate blood to the Westport police."

"Ugh," Rob said. "Hang in there." He rolled up the window and honked his horn twice for Sophie as he drove away.

Nora turned when the car was out of sight. "Okay, wheelchair basketball fans, time for bed. We're gonna skip the bath tonight."

Sophie didn't protest. "Can I go again to see Rob play? It's so fun. They crash into each other and move around so fast, just using their arms. And Rob is the strongest."

"Of course you can," Nora said, lifting her into her arms. "I think he's going out of town, but when he comes back, I'm sure there'll be another game. Maybe I can go to that one with you."

Nora came down the stairs and dropped heavily on the couch next to her mother. "She's out like a light. Tonight's one of those memories that'll stay with Sophie forever. Thanks again for doing it, Mom."

"Oh, it's a memory I'll have forever, too. I didn't realize it was a fundraiser for his Dustoff Home charity, but the gym was packed. And Rob's talk before the game. Wow. Just thinking about it gets me emotional."

"What'd he say?"

"I'm sure you've heard him talk about his dream for wounded vets."

"I probably have, but tell me."

"So eloquent. And passionate. He talked about the importance of helping vets get jobs and housing. But he said that's about changing their *days*. What we really need, he said, is to change their *lives*. And that's only going to come through investment in the science of what he called 'human engineering.' He ticked off things that were already here or close to reality, things like eye transplants, prosthetic hands and feet actually wired into the brain. Amazing. He talked about the research he funds to regrow spinal cords by implanting these amazing proteins called 'dancing molecules.' He didn't say why they called them that."

"No idea."

"And he finished by going back to the jobs and housing. He said those things are great but the wounded and broken need something more important; they need hope and a path to recovering themselves as whole persons. 'Even I need that,' he said. Had me crying like a baby. I don't know how they played basketball after that. But they did. He's quite a person, Nora, and those people in that gym love him."

"For good reason," Nora answered. "For good reason."

CHAPTER TWENTY-NINE

Carmen and Porter left Nora with the lab technician and followed Demi Kofatos upstairs to her tiny office, where they took the two chairs facing her desk.

"Are we clear that she's not going to be asked any questions down there?" Porter asked.

"By the lab guy?" Demi replied. "I can assure you she will not. And that he could not. He's gonna pull out her hair and take her blood. That's it."

"So what's the big mystery?" Porter said, smoothing his goatee. "What do you need to show us that our client can't see?"

"Oh," Demi answered, "I'm fine if your client sees what I'm going to show you. I just didn't want to do it in front of her and get accused of trying to get her to say something. There are two things."

Demi passed a sheet of paper across the desk. "This is the only communication we have found so far between your client and Helen Carmichael on the day of the murder. It's a text Helen sent Sunday evening at 8:25, not long before the ME says she was killed."

Carmen and Porter looked down at the paper. *Need to talk,* Helen had texted Nora.

"Any answer?" Carmen asked.

"No," Demi said, sliding a clear plastic envelope across the desk. "Here's your client's cell phone that we took with the warrant. The State's Attorney is still working out a process to avoid any privileged stuff but she said we can return this now that we have a complete image. And we're waiting on the results from your client's cell carrier to see where her phone was that evening and whether there are relevant communications on the device. We're also wrestling with Saugatuck to get all relevant emails or texts. Which is like pulling teeth."

There was an awkward pause before Carmen asked, "And the second item?"

Demi opened her laptop and slid it across the desk so it faced the two attorneys. "This came in as an anonymous tip," she said, pressing the space bar.

It appeared to be a cell phone video, taken at night, depicting two women standing talking on a street corner sidewalk. A few seconds into the video, the taller of the two leaned down and kissed the shorter woman, who responded by leaning into her and bringing her hands to the taller woman's face shortly before the kiss ended. The video stopped there.

Porter's brow grew more furrowed than usual. "Why are you showing us this?" he asked sharply.

"Because I think the taller woman is your client and the other is the dead woman, Helen Carmichael."

"So the fuck what?" Porter said. "Surely you aren't trying to say that's a nonconsensual encounter."

"Oh, no, no," Demi answered. "Seems very much consensual to me. But the point is that your client and the dead woman seemed to have some sort of secret extracurricular relationship."

"And?" Carmen asked.

"And nothing," Demi said, "except that most murder victims are killed by someone close to them and, as you know, romantic relationships often go sideways, with bad results. So maybe that's what happened here."

"Stop, just stop," Porter said angrily. "We're not even going to dignify that with a response. And I'm grateful you didn't try to show this silliness to our client. Honestly, in my forty years of practice—"

Carmen cut him off. "And I'm hoping you're considering that whoever made that video and then sent it to you is the one with the bad motive in this situation."

When Demi didn't respond, Carmen asked, "Do you know when that was taken?"

"We do not," Demi answered, "and it's even hard to tell the time of year in the dark. And no metadata on it."

After a few beats, Porter asked, "We done here?"

"Given that your client is not willing to be interviewed," Demi said, "we are."

As they stood to leave, Carmen turned to Demi. "Would you be so kind as to send us a copy of that video?"

Demi leaned down to her computer. "Just did," she said and squeezed past to lead them out.

CHAPTER THIRTY

"I remember exactly where that was," Nora said, pointing at the computer on her kitchen table. "About six months after I got here, Helen and I had dinner, and wine, at Artisan in Southport and walked home. Before we went our separate ways, I kissed her, which I shouldn't have, but she was great about it, telling me it was nice but we couldn't, given our roles. She was right, of course, and I was a little embarrassed, but that was the end of it." Nora stopped and shook her head.

"What?" Carmen asked.

"The deeply weird part is that someone was following us that night and waited two years to do something with the video they took? How does that make any sense?"

"It doesn't," Porter answered.

From behind them, Benny's voice boomed. "Somebody's been trying to fuck with Helen or you or both for a long time. I'm guessing whoever took that also whacked Helen and is the same piece a shit wiping her blood on your car."

"Yup," Carmen added. "And I'm guessing there may be more on this romance angle as your motive."

Benny exhaled loudly and gestured at Nora. "So the spurned lover here waits two years to kill Helen in her own canoe, then uses her hatchback as a napkin? Give me a fucking break."

"First of all, there's no date stamp on that video and the detective said there's no metadata," Carmen said, "so I don't know whether we'll be able to show how long ago that kiss happened. But, in a way, it doesn't matter, because if you're really going to set Nora up, you need more than that to get it done. Nothing about that video suggests Nora was some kind of spurned lover doing wild shit. I'm not worried about it."

Nora shook her head again. "So glad not to be wild, spurned, or stupid. But I'll do my best to figure out the exact date it must have been. Then you can pass that to the cops."

"Agreed," Carmen said. After a pause, she turned to Benny. "So how'd it go last night with Laslo?"

"He's on team Nora," Benny said. "Good guy. We just gotta figure out the best way for him to help. For starters, I'm thinking it's using Saugatuck info to track down this Holtzer character from the funeral."

"Can he help us on Helen's PI, Singh?" Nora asked.

"Nah," Benny said, "he never heard of the guy or of Helen using a PI. He also never heard anything about Helen havin' any private files, so I didn't show him any leg on that at the start, but I'm gonna take him through the files. I figure for sure I use him on the Holtzer piece and ask him to give us a heads-up if he sees any squirrelly behavior by the Saugatuck crowd."

Nora and the two attorneys all nodded. "Is there something else?" Carmen asked.

"Yeah," Benny said. "I already ran this by Nora and we're convinced the killer is on the inside at Saugatuck and the motive is in Helen's files. As strange as it sounds, I think Laslo and I could run an internal at Saugatuck—with David Jepson's blessing, of course—to see what we could see. Laslo's up for it, although he wants the good cop role, which is fine by me. He thinks Nora could pitch it to Jepson as a search for truth—which it would be, by the way—and we'd promise full transparency to the MC, at the appropriate point."

Carmen turned to Nora. "That seems completely bizarre. And why would they go for that, exactly?"

"Because he built this whole place around the idea that truth is what he calls 'the paramount value.' It's all that matters and David believes Saugatuck finds it better than anywhere else, including the criminal justice system."

"Okay," Carmen replied, "I think I get that, maybe, but why would he go for Benny being part of it?"

"Because Benny is my proxy," Nora replied. "I can't do the questioning—what Saugatuck calls 'the plumbing'—because I'm conflicted and have the cops coming after me. But I can ask that Benny stand in for me, working with Laslo to find the truth. I think if I ask, David will agree. I already talked to Rob Arslan about the idea. He likes it. Said he'll push David to do it. 'Consistent with our values,' Rob will tell him."

Porter had his glasses off, cleaning furiously with his handkerchief. Without looking up, he said, "Craziest thing I ever heard of. But it *would* get us ahead of the cops, that's for sure. Worst case it gives us stuff to get them off Nora."

Carmen grimaced and turned to Nora. "I can't believe I'm saying this, but I think you should pitch Jepson on it."

As Nora nodded, Carmen turned to Porter and changed the topic. "So what's likely to be our next touch with the cops?"

"They'll get back to us once they compare Nora's hairs to the ones found on Helen. And I'm gonna poke the State's Attorney to see where they are with getting records from Saugatuck. If you're right about other stuff coming, that's likely where it will come from."

"And have you spoken to Louis Lambert about what help we'll get on the company's end?" Nora asked.

"I did, on the phone," Porter replied. "Honestly, the guy was a bit of a dick to me, so I'm going to go see him in person."

Nora shook her head. "Won't be any less of a dick, I'm sorry to report. But let me know, so I can go over his head to Jepson or Baum if need be. I'm headed over there now for an MC meeting."

"He looks to be more than just a dick," Benny added. "The shit in Helen's file has to put Louie boy at the top of our list." He looked up at Porter. "So, good luck. And you might mention to him that you've been practicing for forty years."

Porter looked confused.

"Just a thought," Benny shrugged before walking out of the kitchen.

CHAPTER THIRTY-ONE

When Nora walked into the conference room, the Management Committee meeting was under way. Louis Lambert was sitting at the table next to Rob Arslan, in the seat Nora normally occupied. She slipped into a chair along the wall just as Rob was addressing David Jepson, who was in his usual spot at the head of the table.

"I'd like to start by understanding why Louis is here," Rob said, gesturing with his head toward the deputy general counsel.

David lifted his chin in thought, looking toward the windows and then back to Rob. "It's your prerogative to plumb anyone at this table," he said, using the Saugatuck term for questioning, one that always struck Nora as a strange mixture of home repair and sex. It was another Saugatuck-ism that gave Helen the giggles. Suddenly she was in Nora's ear. *Plumb, like they want to push something into your rear. Similar feeling, really.*

Rob turned his wheelchair slightly to address Louis. "Why are you here?"

"Because I am acting general counsel for all matters touching on the death of our former colleague, Helen," he said flatly. "In light of Nora's entanglement with the investigation, the MC decided I should take that role. And I needed to provide an update to this body this morning. That's why I'm here."

Rob's face reddened. "And speaking of Nora and her alleged entanglement, who the fuck is responsible for the gossip about that all over this place?"

David spoke before Louis could answer. "First, Rob, I'd ask you to keep emotion out of this. Second, what is this about gossip?" He was always the last to hear gossip, for good reason.

When Rob spoke again, his voice was noticeably calmer. "I apologize for the emotion. I find it difficult, given my affection for Helen, and for Nora. I will do better. As to your second question, the entire place is talking about Helen being found in Nora's canoe and her blood being found on the back of Nora's car."

David squinted. "How can that be?" he asked. "First, very few of us know that and, second, there shouldn't be anyone at Saugatuck who doesn't know how we feel about gossip. Tell me, why do you direct your question to Louis?"

"Because I suspect he is the source of the gossip," Rob said evenly.

"That's a serious accusation," David said, without inflection. "You may plumb."

Rob turned back to Louis. "Did you tell people about this?"

"What do you mean by 'people'?" Louis answered.

"Did you discuss those facts with anyone?"

"Of course."

"Who?"

"Well I'm not sure it makes sense for me to describe my work as counsel for this company in an open forum like this, but I discussed the facts around Helen's death with those necessary for me to discharge my duties as acting general counsel."

"So maybe you start with a list—" Rob began before David interrupted.

"This has quickly reached the point of diminishing returns," he said, using Saugatuck code for a conversation the boss wanted to end. "Is there other business that relates to this?"

Louis cleared his throat. "Yes. I'd like to suggest that Nora be suspended from her employment at this point. The company cannot credibly interact with the authorities while she remains on campus. I also see the prospect of severe reputational damage if these adverse facts reach the public and she is still employed here."

Rob turned his wheelchair again to face Louis. "And, by complete coincidence, that would make you the general counsel, am I right there, Louie?"

"Louis," he responded calmly. "And, yes, were Nora suspended, it would make sense for her deputy to act in her stead across her portfolio."

Rob now spun to face David, his voice rising. "It's just not right to do that to Nora without due process. It would get out and it would destroy her reputation. We don't do that to people without pursuing the truth."

Nora blushed but didn't speak. *Now I know how Bruce Willis felt in that movie where he doesn't know he's dead.*

Arty Falcone had been facing the water, but now turned back to the table so quickly that his long auburn hair—normally carefully coiffed in a slicked-back style—fell out of position and swept across his face. He combed it back with the fingers of one hand as he spoke. "Look, no offense to Nora, or our culture, but the truth in a murder case has to be found by the *government*. It's just not our job. Our job—mine in particular—is to make sure the clients are happy. And I'm not sure they'll love the idea of our chief lawyer being a murder suspect."

He rocked back in the chair and folded his hands across his flat stomach—the product of many Pilates hours—then quickly realized that move was making his white V-neck sweater bunch up on his chest, in which he had made a similar investment, so he lifted his hands and quickly pulled the sweater down tight.

Rob looked across the table at the handsome Falcone. "Two things, Arty, one practical, one principled. I don't know all our clients the way you do, but I know the Aussies and the Kiwis like I know myself."

For years, Rob had handled the Australian and New Zealand public pension funds that invested with Saugatuck, mostly because in his military career he had fought side by side with their special forces, but also because he was willing to make the grueling trips to go see the clients regularly.

"They would have a problem," he continued, "if we kicked a senior employee to the curb based on a mere accusation, even in a case like this. And I suspect a lot of our clients would feel the same way. And as a matter of principle, we've always conducted ourselves in the way we believe best and left it to the outside world to decide whether they want to give us their money to invest. It's not right to do this without knowing the facts."

Chip Jepson spoke next, from his usual seat next to Arty Falcone—Helen liked to call them "the lax bros" behind their backs. Nora assumed that was because, although fifteen years apart in age, they looked like teammates on a college lacrosse team. Over dinners at Artisan, Nora would always laugh off the label, but Helen would defend it.

"Seriously, at the next meeting, look at them over there, thick as thieves, and tell me I'm wrong. Same high forehead, same slicked-back douchebag hair, same I-took-a-lot-of-hits-to-the-head gaze. Same cruelty vibe. Lax bros. I'm telling you. I nailed this one."

"I'm afraid I have to agree with Arty," Chip was saying. "This isn't about *firing* Nora. I wouldn't support that without the facts being established. This is about protecting the future of this firm. I acknowl-edge there is marginal risk to her reputation from a suspension, but there is a larger risk to the entire company. And although I recognize and appreciate Rob's work in the South Pacific, Arty has the more complete view of our clients."

"I'm not so sure," David Jepson said, "but let me wait to offer my view. Who else wants to be heard? Marcus, Miranda, Jeffey?"

"I'll go," Miranda Jepson said. "I'm not so sure, but I'd also like to hear what others think."

Nora could almost hear Helen laugh at the echo from the heir apparent, who Helen was always skewering for imitating her father. "If he stops without warning in the hallway, she's going halfway up his ass," Helen loved to say. "Plumb that," she would add with a smile.

One of Helen's favorite stories was about the time David Jepson sent a company-wide email expressing his displeasure that urine was routinely found on the floor beneath the urinals in the main lobby men's room, risking a bad impression with visiting clients. Miranda had replied all: "This must stop."

"First of all," Helen chortled, holding her wine glass in front of her, "this being Saugatuck, neither of them saw this as the humor gold mine that it was. Not a single line about being 'pissed off,' or the 'next dick who does it,' nothing. Crying shame. A crime against humanity, really. Second, the bitch has never been in the fucking men's room."

Nora's job was to keep Helen laughing by saying, "And then there was poor Juan."

The company's answer to David Jepson's concern was to hire a nice middle-aged Latino man to stand in the restroom all day watching the urinals and wiping up any spray that hit the floor. He didn't hand out towels, or mints. He didn't speak to the visitors, although that may have been his poor English. Instead, he stood and watched men pee. Which had the predictable effect of creating a double epidemic of stage fright and class guilt that soon made the main lobby restroom a ghost town. Juan stood alone for days, until he was quietly reassigned.

After Nora's usual line, Helen laughed loud enough to turn heads on the Artisan patio. "Juan stood alone against the yellow peril! Urine big trouble now! So wonderful. And all because nobody could tell David Jepson there's pee under every urinal in the entire fucking world. How perfectly Saugatuck is that?"

"I'll go next," said Jefferson Jepson. "I don't think we need to make a federal case out of this. I wouldn't suspend Nora. I'd just ask her to take vacation until this is sorted out. Or send her on one of those god-awful trips to Australia that Rob has to take. We keep it quiet and see what happens."

"But Jeffey," his father responded, "that's exactly the kind of thing that would happen at some other place. Misdirection, false labels, sweeping under the rug. That's not what we're about. It's not what we've built."

Before Jeffey could respond, Miranda jumped in. "I have to agree with David," she said, using her father's first name, as all three children did inside the business.

"Okay, whatever," Jeffey replied in a hurt tone. "It just seemed more fair to Nora."

David turned to Marcus Baum. "You've been quiet, Marcus."

"Just thinking," Marcus said. "I'd like to hear Nora on this."

"Yes, yes," David said, turning toward her. "Nora, please come to the table. I'm not sure why you're sitting over there. We've made no decisions."

Nora stood and moved to a chair down the table from Rob and Louis.

As she always did in MC meetings, Nora took a moment to quiet the noise in her head. "It's from all the things not being spoken," Helen had explained when Nora first confided in her about the vertiginous feeling. "You're about to speak in a room of geniuses with more layers than a piece of fucking baklava, but you have to pretend it's simple as a sheet cake. You'll get used to it."

Nora took a deep breath and spoke. "I think it's fair to say that I'm operating under something of a cloud here because there are facts that look bad for me. But I also think there are people in this room who had issues with Helen that will be of great interest to anyone looking to solve this case. To be honest, there are a lot of clouds in this room."

"What does that mean?" David asked.

Rob took that. "It means that Nora and I are aware of facts that create a serious conflict between Helen and other people in this room. And they are facts that could show us there's a killer in our midst—and it's not Nora."

He looked across at Arty. "And I do take your point about the reputational risk to Saugatuck. Which is why I think we should sort this out internally, here at the MC. We'll comply appropriately with all legal process from the government, but I think we would be best to do this in-house. Once we get to the truth, we can decide the best way to help the authorities."

Now he turned to David. "And I know how you feel about the government's ability to find truth."

David nodded. "They're well-meaning people, but they aren't as smart as we are. How do you propose we do this?"

"I think we use the MC," Rob said, "but we don't look to Nora to present it, or to any of us."

"You stay the RP," Rob added, using Saugatuck slang for the Responsible Party, or chair, of any meeting. "But we use Laslo and a guy Nora knows well—a Justice Department special agent on leave—to pull it together for us. Laslo and this guy Benny Dugan are both trained federal investigators. We have Dugan sign a nondisclosure agreement, then he and Laslo gather the facts and put them to us in a way we can then plumb. If we find useful stuff, we can share it with the government."

"Why an outsider like this Dugan?" Marcus Baum asked.

"Because Nora trusts him and this will be about her, at least a big part of it will be. Plus I worry Laslo's lost a little on his fastball after so long away from the FBI."

A chorus of voices started to speak, but David Jepson cut through it. "Okay, let's do it," he said loudly. "I'll be the RP, but Rob will be responsible for organizing it, and I agree in concept with using Laslo and this other fellow to gather and present the facts to us. Rob, you put it together and let us know. And I think that finishes our business." With that, David stood and walked quickly from the room, followed closely by Miranda Jepson.

Rob started to wheel away from the table, but paused and leaned back toward Louis Lambert, speaking in a whisper. "And you, gossiping motherfucker, should be here for all of it. Some major plumbing coming your way." With that, he spun the chair and rolled out.

CHAPTER THIRTY-TWO

"I don't need to prep for a meeting with some dude," Benny protested, "even if he's a billionaire. We're all born crappin' in our pants and we'll all go out that way."

Nora smiled and shook her head. "What a lovely way to capture the universality of human experience. Inspirational. Look, I can't speak about David Jepson's poop, but this isn't a normal place or a normal dude. When Rob takes you to see David, or any of them, especially when they are in a group, I want you to know some of their approaches."

"So there's a playbook?" Benny said.

"Early on, Helen taught me there are two main moves in an argument at Saugatuck—the 'overconfidence jab' and the 'emotion uppercut'—but they're a devastating combination if you aren't ready for them."

"Seriously?" Benny asked. "We really gotta do this?"

"Yes," Nora answered. "If you don't know this, these people—especially when they're together at the MC—can be very hard and they will undermine anything you have to say. It starts with someone, usually a smart younger person, calmly making a compelling point to an MC member. The MC member doesn't have an answer, but it doesn't matter because he just sets up the overconfidence jab.

"It goes like this:

"'Have you considered other possibilities?' the MC member asks.

"'Of course,' the kid says, 'but they don't make as much sense as what I just said.'

"'And so you're *certain* that you're right?'

"'I believe I am, for the reasons I said.'

"'Have you considered that you have a problem with overconfidence?'

"Bang!" Nora shouted. "The first jab. It rocks the kid, as the fight—which is not at all a fight and could never, ever, possibly be considered a fight and we would deny it was a fight of any kind—continues.

"The kid protests the punch in the face. He says, 'I don't think I have a problem with overconfidence.'

"So the MC member hits him again, a little harder this time: 'It's starting to sound like you're overconfident about your lack of overconfidence.'

"Bang!" Nora shouted again. "The kid's on his heels now, but trying not to look rattled.

"'I don't know what you mean,' he says.

"'You don't know what I mean?' comes the answer. 'Or you just don't want to acknowledge that you may be overconfident?'

"Bang! The third straight shot to the face. Now the kid is stumbling, dropping the gloves. Almost time for the uppercut."

"'I suppose I could be overconfident from time to time, but I think I've reached the right conclusion here, for the reasons I said.'

"'Exactly. You refuse to acknowledge other possibilities and your own blind spots, which is a known weakness of yours, am I right?'

"'I feel like you're avoiding the merits of my argument.'

"'And that feeling,' the MC member says calmly, 'is evident in the way you're approaching this. Your emotional reaction is not productive.'

"'I'm not emotional.'

"'Perhaps that's another example of your overconfidence. Your resort to feelings both reflects and feeds your overconfidence.'

"Now the kid's gloves are down at his side, his chin sticking out. 'I admit I'm starting to get angry about the way you're distorting what I'm saying.'

"The MC member is cold, clinical. It's almost over now. 'Your anger is unproductive and inconsistent with our values.'

"Boom!" Nora said. "The kid's on the mat."

"The MC member calls it. 'I suggest we pause this discussion to give you a chance to control your emotions so we can have a logic-based discussion, one in which you embrace the possibility that you could be wrong.'

"Ding ding ding!" Nora announced. "And then we never have that follow-up discussion. Good night everybody. Safe home."

Benny looked confused, so Nora went on.

"All Saugatuck veterans have watched the jab and the uppercut deployed with devastating effect. That's why all conversations here—especially at the MC level—are peppered with preambles—'I could be wrong' or 'I may not be seeing all the possibilities.' If you open with those, it's like lifting your gloves to your face as you move toward your opponent. The jabs can't reach you and, without them, the uppercut can't be thrown."

Nora beamed. She was a born teacher. "Now you get it?"

Benny shook his head. "Look, coach, I appreciate you, but somebody pulls that shit on me, they can just go fuck themselves. I'm not a member of this cult."

Nora laughed so hard it was difficult to catch her breath. It felt good. "I'm not sure Saugatuck knows what's coming," she managed to say.

CHAPTER THIRTY-THREE

B enny and Laslo were in the uncomfortable chairs facing David Jepson's enormous driftwood desk. Rob Arslan, sitting next to them in his wheelchair, began with the Saugatuck practice of announcing the purpose of the meeting.

"Our goal today is to introduce you to Benny, who has signed a nondisclosure agreement, and lay out the way he and Laslo are going to approach their assignment. I asked that we not record this because of the sensitivity of some of the things we may discuss."

Jepson nodded and reached for his tape dispenser, pulling off a small piece. "As you wish," he said.

After briefly explaining Benny's background as the lead organized crime investigator at the United States Attorney's Office for the Southern District of New York, now on leave to work with Nora, Rob paused. When David looked up from the tape on his fingertips, Rob continued.

"Helen kept files on people here at Saugatuck," he said.

"What files and what people?" David asked flatly.

"I can't speak to exactly what's in them, but Benny and Laslo have gone through them. They can say whatever they think is appropriate, but they appear to be 'dirt files'—evidence of personal misconduct or failings by key people, things she also didn't share with Laslo or the MC. These almost seem like they were blackmail files, to be honest, although we don't know yet exactly how she used them. And as for who: Everyone who was in that MC meeting, including Louis Lambert. And including you."

"Well, I'd like to know a lot more about that," David said, now looking at Benny and Laslo, his voice louder.

"Before you do that," Rob interrupted, "there's another piece I need to tell you about because it may be connected. For the last few years, we've had indications—echoes and shadows really—that somebody was front running us. Tiny moves here and there mostly, but some bigger moves from time to time when we were active in the markets."

David's eyes widened. "I'm sorry, did you say 'bigger moves'? All I recall Helen telling me was that she was working to mitigate any front-running risk—which is always an issue in this business. She didn't tell me there might be something of consequence actually going on. This is *my* company."

"I know, I know," Rob said. "Of course. That was Helen's call. Her view was that she didn't have enough to escalate it fully to you. She had Brad Holtzer working on it before he, uh, left."

David made a sour face, but didn't speak, so Rob continued.

"She brought me into it so I could get them the trading tech details they needed: how we were spreading our trades, who we were using to execute, where the holes might be in our systems or processes. And when Holtzer left, it was one of the reasons Helen wanted Nora, an experienced investigator and prosecutor."

Rob waited a beat but when David didn't react, he continued.

"The bottom line is that Nora made progress. Somebody's been trading just ahead of us, timing their purchases to come just before ours raise the price, their sales to come just before ours drive the price down, and in a way that would earn them millions because they knew where we were going."

David's voice had returned to its usual flatness. "Again I must ask you: Why wasn't I told the extent of this?"

"I'm not sure," Rob answered, "but I suspect Helen was about to tell you when she was killed. I don't know the details, but I think she was close enough to figuring it out that she was going to come to you."

"Bit tardy, in my view," David said, shaking his head, "but too late now to take that up with Helen."

He pulled another piece of tape off the dispenser and gestured with it to the men in the chairs in front of him. "And so how does this connect to what Laslo and Benny here are being asked to do?"

"We think whoever killed Helen—again, if it wasn't Nora, which we feel quite confident it was not—was close to her and likely motivated by either the front-running investigation or the dirt she was collecting, or both. To find the truth, these guys will need to press people on all of it."

The office was quiet for several seconds before David spoke. "I'd like to see those files," he said.

Benny spoke for the first time. "Not a good idea, if truth is the goal here."

"Why is that?" David asked.

"Because you gotta be a suspect. I'm not sayin' you did it, but I'm sayin' we can't credibly investigate if we start sharing information with witnesses, even if they own the place."

"You seem quite confident of that."

The motherfucking jab, Benny thought, suppressing a smile. *Oh, I see you.*

"I'm not confident of anything about this," he said, "except I know from thirty years of investigating that you need to avoid tellin' your witnesses stuff before you find out what they already know and what they might be hidin'."

Benny nodded at Rob. "Not gonna show him either. And gonna interview him as soon as we're done here."

"Okay," David said quietly. "What does being 'done here' look like?"

Benny looked at Laslo, who seemed frozen, so he continued. "It looks like Rob wheeling on out of here, so we can ask you some questions."

David nodded, so Rob turned and rolled himself out of the office, reaching back to pull the door closed behind him.

"Go ahead," David said when the door was shut.

Again Benny turned to Laslo, who was silent. "Okay," Benny said, turning back to David, "lemme hit it directly. What's the deal with your wife being in the British Virgin Islands with all these young dudes?"

David cocked his head to the side. "*That* was in Helen's files?"

"I'm not sayin' that," Benny answered. "I'm just asking questions. So what's the deal with that?" He sensed Laslo stiffening.

David paused and looked out the window toward the river, which was at low tide. Then he looked back at Benny. "I'll answer it. My wife and I have what they used to call an 'open' marriage. I've discovered there is a new term for people like her—polyamorous. She has a variety of relationships. I'm grateful that she keeps them, largely, to our BVI house so it doesn't generate embarrassing gossip. I've learned to accept it because she's the mother of my children. I still love her very much, and I believe she loves me. End of story."

David stopped again, staring at the water. Both Benny and Laslo had been trained to let silence work. So they let it. After twenty seconds, David turned back to look toward them. "No, that's not true," he said. "That's not the end of the story. The rest of it, if I'm being completely honest, which I have to be, is that my wife is a beautiful woman, so beautiful that people assume she's with me because of my money. And I get why they think that, because the money would be a big part of any relationship I tried to start now. But we met in school, when I had no money at all. I was a slightly strange math person and she was a strikingly pretty and normal girl with no interest in math. But somehow we came to be together and sort of grew up with each other. Maybe she outgrew me, in a way. And, honestly, I know my life is better with her in it than it ever could be without her."

He reached for more tape. "And that's the full story."

"Helen ever mention your wife's relationships?" Benny asked.

"Never."

"She ever hint at it in a way to make you know she knew?"

"No," David said, his face now flushed. "May I ask you a question?"

"Sure," Benny said.

"Helen was spying on my wife and keeping a record of her, well, affairs?"

"Look, I'm sure this is painful—" Benny began before Laslo cut him off.

"Yes, she was, boss," Laslo said quickly. "She had a private investigator following your wife, taking pictures, collecting records. It's all in the file."

Benny was staring at the side of Laslo's head when David responded. "Thank you for telling me that, Laslo. I don't know why Helen would do that."

Benny turned back to David. "As long as we're on the topic, where were you the night Helen was killed?"

David leaned and took another piece of tape, before sitting back in his chair.

"I pause only because I felt an emotional reaction coming as a result of the implicit accusation in your question," he said flatly. "But I realize it's one you must ask. It was a Sunday night, as I recall. I was in my new Manhattan apartment, entertaining some of our clients. It's in the Steinway Tower on Fifty-Seventh Street. Eightieth floor. Amazing views. You can speak to my household staff and, if it came to it, I would permit you to verify my whereabouts with those clients. But I'd prefer we do that thoughtfully."

"We'll get back to you on that," Benny said. "Meantime, Laslo and I are going to need a dedicated space here to work this."

"I'll have my assistants arrange it," David said. He paused before adding, "Is there anything else?"

"No," Benny said, standing. "We appreciate your time. And sorry for the questions."

"No, no," David replied. "I appreciate your commitment to truth. And you seem quite skilled at it."

"Thanks," Benny answered, "but I don't want to get a swelled head. You know, overconfident and all."

When David appeared not to realize he was joking, Benny shrugged and followed Laslo out the door.

Walking down the hall he whispered intensely to Laslo. "Dude, what the fuck? Thought we agreed we weren't gonna tell him what's in the files."

"Yeah, I know," Laslo answered, shaking his head. "I'm sorry, but I could see my boat sinking so I called an audible at the line. Sue me. Let's grab Rob now. And I promise not to tell him stuff. He can't fire me."

CHAPTER THIRTY-FOUR

They found Rob in his office, packing for his trip.

"Hey," Laslo said, "can we grab you for a few minutes? I know you're headed out of town tomorrow."

"Of course," Rob said, gesturing toward the empty visitor chairs. He wheeled himself behind the desk. "Shoot."

Laslo pointed at the microphone in the ceiling. "Are we on or off?"

"Oh, off," Rob said, before adding in a whisper, "I had it disconnected long ago. Purely decorative at this point."

"Got it," Laslo said, turning to Benny. "You want to start?"

"Sure," Benny said, "and obviously we don't wanna embarrass you, but Helen gathered some stuff about your health and family struggles. Were you aware of that?"

"No, I wasn't," Rob said, "although I think it would have been obvious to those closest to me that I was having a hard time a while back."

"Do you remember talking to her about it?"

"No."

"So I'm guessing she never brought it up in a way that felt like she was holding it over you."

"You're correct. She never brought it up and we never discussed it."

Rob paused, before adding, "Look, she was nothing but supportive of me. I have this charity, 'Dustoff Home'—named for the military term for a medical evacuation helicopter. It's about helping disabled vets make the transition to a healthy life back here. We raise money for training, housing, and medical support. We give them mentoring and connect them to jobs. Lots of our best people at Saugatuck came to us that way. Helen was one of our biggest supporters and not just with her money; she helped hire people here and made sure they succeeded. She was kind and really made a difference."

"So why do you think she kept those files?" Benny asked.

"I'm not sure," Rob said. "A reasonable guess would be that it was some kind of rainy-day fund, that she would draw on to protect herself or people close to her. Look, I'm not here to judge her or defend her, but the financial industry is particularly inhospitable to women, especially at senior levels. So it's not wrong to think she needed to have an edge to survive, and that this was her edge."

As Benny made notes, Rob added, "But I'm just speculating."

Benny looked up when he finished writing. "Okay, so tell us about this front-running investigation. What was it and where did it stand when Helen was killed?"

"We do periodic audits to be sure that we're getting what is called 'best execution' on our trades. That means that the brokers we use to buy or sell are doing it well—getting us the prices we expect, charging us the fees we agreed to, ensuring people can't tell it's us making the move."

"I'm sorry to interrupt," Benny said, "but can you explain front running in a simple way?"

"Sure. It's a very specific and hard-to-see type of insider trading where someone steals the knowledge of your trades. Easiest way to explain is by imagining an ordinary stock transaction. If Saugatuck plans to buy a bunch of shares of XYZ company, that's going to cause XYZ's stock price to rise after the purchase. Maybe just a little, but it will affect XYZ's price. If somebody knows we are about to make that purchase, they can buy XYZ just before we do and make money when our purchase moves the stock up. Then they can sell their XYZ and cash in."

"Got it," Benny said.

"And I'm using a simple example but there could be front running on all kinds of transactions. Knowing what a big player like us is about to do is valuable information."

"Copy that. So what was the investigation about?"

"Okay, back to the periodic audits of trade execution. Those reports showed that, in tiny ways, we didn't seem to be getting the best pricing. Just before some of our transactions, there were little market moves that were unfavorable to us. Maybe luck, maybe not, but we saw it happening enough that Helen wanted to look into it. Brad Holtzer started the investigation, then Nora picked it up after she got settled."

"And where was it this fall?"

"I'm not sure of the details, but Helen and Nora both believed it was happening and it could be an internal leak. 'The call was coming from inside the house,' as they say."

"Who?"

"I don't know. Seemed unlikely to be from our trading team because they're so closely monitored. Maybe from research or account management, but they only know the general moves we plan, not the details a front runner would need about when and where. So I don't know. One possibility they were considering was a penetration of systems done through our data center, but I don't think that panned out."

"Data center?" Benny asked.

"Okay, now you're gonna get more than you asked for," Rob said with a smile. "I'm a geek, so stop me when I give you too much. A company like ours has to have a backup for all our systems, in case the primary ones fail because of a storm or we get hit with some kind of ransomware attack that locks up the primaries. That's a fairly common thing, so companies rent space at data centers that serve as backups."

"With you so far," Benny said, although he had stopped trying to write it down.

"We need the data center to be far enough away so it doesn't face the same risks from stuff like hurricanes or earthquakes, but it can't be too far or we won't have synchronous replication with the computers in Westport."

"Okay, stop right there," Benny said. "Isn't that a song by The Police?"

"Hah," Rob laughed. "Excellent pop culture reference. That's *Synchronicity*. I don't know what the hell Sting meant by that."

"I do," Laslo said. "Bit of a fan, I have to admit. It was Carl Jung's term for things that seem causally connected but really aren't—coincidences, for example."

"Wow," Rob said. "I'm gonna use that. But 'synchronous replication' means the backup is close enough that the speed of light doesn't make a difference. You see, our client and trade information in the backup has to be identical in all respects to the primary; even a small time difference created by light having to travel on a fiber-optic cable more than fifty miles would defeat synchronous replication. If that happened and we had a failure in the primary, we actually wouldn't know whether a client's account in the backup was accurate. Real disaster. 'King of Pain,' if you will."

"Bam," Benny said. "Okay, my head hurts, but I'm hanging with you. And so?"

"And so, we found a data center—actually I found it—in New Milford, about thirty miles north of here. It's over the hills and far enough away that it doesn't share Westport's risks to stuff like storms, but it's close enough that we achieve the magical, uh, synchronicity."

"Got it. So why would the data center be a place somebody could steal trade info from?"

"Because it's in a remote place and lots of other companies rent space there too. The security at ours is really good—which is one reason I chose it—but you'd have to put it on the list of places where there might be a weak spot. But, like I said, I don't think Helen and Nora found any problems there."

"Where did things stand on the front running then, as far as you knew?"

"Although the outside firms had largely been eliminated, the suspect list was still big. We couldn't find anything to help narrow it down—it could be one person or a few people working together. We had no good leads, but the numbers revealed that something shady was still happening. I think they were about to go more overt with the investigation and start pulling camera footage, access logs, stuff like that. They had asked me to put together lists of people with broad enough access to be suspects. Up to that point, they had tried to avoid making that kind of noise, because even rumors about front running would hurt us with clients and damage our reputation."

Benny leaned in close and spoke quietly. "Come on, you guys musta had some suspects? Who's top of your list? No, actually who was top of Helen's? 'Cause that mighta gotten her killed."

Rob made a sour face. "I have been wracking my brain and wish I knew the answer to that question, but the potential list includes most of our company."

"Well, it's most likely someone in her files and when she got too close they found out and killed her," Benny continued. "Murder is almost always about love, money, or secrets—different kinds for different classes of people—but always comes down to the same shit."

"I hope you're wrong," Rob said, "because then it's my fault for not helping her and Nora find answers sooner. I hope it's about her files and not the trading thing." He looked down, then up at Benny, tears filling his eyes. "Helen was a complicated person, but a wonderful one. We all miss her."

"Hey," Benny said quietly, "I'm sorry to upset you. No doubt Saugatuck people loved Helen. We're just tryin' to figure out who the fuck killed her."

Benny paused as Rob wiped his palms down his face. "Okay, we're almost done here," he said, "I gotta go back to the files business. Did you pull anything out of Helen's files when Tracey left them in your office before she gave them to Nora?"

Rob shrugged. "Why do you ask that?"

"'Cause there was a lot more shit in your file than there is now and we know you had access to them before Nora got them. You got anything to do with that, this'd be a great time to tell us."

The room was quiet for five seconds before Rob answered. "I'm an asshole," he said, reaching for one of his desk drawers. "I did. When Tracey left them, I took a look at my file and"—he pulled out an inch-thick stack of paper—"she had all this nasty shit about my struggles. So I yanked it. I shouldn't have and I'm so sorry if I've caused you or Nora any heartburn."

He put the stack on the desk in front of Benny. "But when you look at it, I think maybe you'll understand why I pulled it."

"Why do you say that?" Benny asked.

"It's the medical records of my breakdowns, and details about me stealing drugs and being strapped to a bed in a diaper at the lowest point in my miserable life. What's she need that stuff for? What's anybody need to see that stuff for? But I'm sorry. I really shouldn't have."

"So you were lying when you said you didn't know anything about Helen's files?"

"Yes, although it's true I didn't know she kept them until Tracey told me. But I gave you a bullshit narrow answer, because I didn't want to tell you what I'd done. Again, I'm sorry."

"I appreciate that," Benny said. "You look at any other files?"

"I did not, although I'm not sure why you would believe me at this point."

"So where were you the night Helen was killed?"

"Home. I know there was the usual Sunday night gathering at Compo Beach. I remember an all-employee email saying that it was the last company-sponsored sunset of the season."

"Company sponsored?" Benny said. "Ya gotta love the private sector! So we're talkin' free food and drink for everybody?"

Laslo jumped in. "Yep. Pretty great spread. Pizza from Angelina's. Awesome wines. I try not to miss them."

"Yeah," Rob said as he slapped his palms down on the two wheelchair armrests. "Except *I* miss them all because beaches are not my thing, for obvious reasons. So I was home. Don't remember what I was doing; probably working or reading."

"Ya got somebody who can verify that?" Benny asked.

Rob paused. "I don't think so. I live alone and don't remember any calls that night. But maybe. I'll check if you need me to."

"Maybe when you get back," Laslo said. "We'll get out of your hair. I'm sure you have a lot to do before the trip."

He turned to Benny. "Let's roll." The moment he said it, Laslo blushed and turned to Rob. "Oh, dude, I'm sorry—"

Rob laughed. "Oh come on, man, if we can't talk about rolling around me, life will be dull as hell. You roll. I'll roll later. Life rolls on."

———

"That check out with what Nora told you?" Laslo asked as they walked down the hall.

"On the front-running investigation? Yup. That's exactly what she said."

"What do you make of his messin' with the files?"

"Concerning," Benny said, "but understandable, and he gave it up without too much pushing. So, 'I don't know' is the answer, but there's a whole lot of people on my list above his name, I'll tell you that."

"Yup, I'm afraid it's gonna get messy now."

Benny smiled. "Probably, but that's the fun part. Bad cop gets a lot of playing time."

CHAPTER THIRTY-FIVE

As they waited for the elevator, Captain Dunham turned in a circle to admire the two-story glass lobby overlooking the leafy front lawn of the enormous Stamford state courthouse. "Our building's a piece of shit," he said in Demi's direction. "But people in Westport don't give a damn about cops, so we'll be in it forever." That didn't appear to call for a response, so Demi just stared at the numbers above the elevators, trying to predict which one would come to take them to visit the State's Attorney. "No wonder we can't get these people off their ass to actually charge a case. They live in a frickin' palace."

Demi decided not to point out that the prosecutors didn't actually live here and that the Westport police building, while cramped, was mere steps from a Patagonia clothing store, a Tiffany & Co. jewelers, and a custom cake shop—not exactly Afghanistan, in her estimation. The elevator doors finally opened and they rode in silence to the sixth floor.

Aileen Shapiro swept into the glass-walled conference room with a broad smile, her long silver hair held back on top of her head by red reading glasses she never seemed to use. "Captain, Detective, nice to see you," she said, shaking hands. "Can I get you water or coffee?"

"No, we're good," Captain Dunham said. "Don't want to take a lot of your time, but wanted to see where we are on the Carmichael case and when you think you might be charging it."

Shapiro's smile disappeared, but her tone remained pleasant. "Please sit," she said, gesturing to chairs across the conference table. "Well, we're not much further along than the last time we spoke, on the phone. We've got the body in Nora Carleton's canoe, which the whole world had access to. We've got the dead woman's blood on Carleton's car, which is significant, and two of Carleton's hairs on the dead woman—or at least hairs that are a mitochondrial match, so they're hers or from a close female relative. We've put Carleton at Compo Beach earlier that evening, but too early for the time of the death. And we've got that anonymous video sent to you, which may mean Carleton and the dead woman had a thing, and the victim texted Carleton the night she died, saying: *Need to talk*."

Shapiro paused and looked at the file in front of her, reading without retrieving her glasses from her head. "Oh, and we now have the toxicology and a supplement from the ME. No drugs or alcohol, but a bump on the decedent's head that they had missed initially. ME's theory is that Ms. Carmichael suffered some kind of blow to the head rendering her unconscious before being placed in the canoe and having her throat cut. That may explain how the perpetrator was able to move her before the killing. Nothing yet from the knives or the devices you took out of Carleton's home."

She closed the file and looked up at Demi. "And so, you want to charge who?"

"Carleton, obviously," Captain Dunham said. "She whacked her in the head, probably over some lovers' quarrel, stuffed her in the back of her car, then dumped her in the canoe, killed her, and took it out to Seymour Rock. In the dark, she missed the blood on her hands and got it on the car."

Shapiro continued looking at Demi. "So charge on the car blood alone, then? Because the rest is crap, at least so far."

She finally turned to Dunham. "Look, I love it when the investigators are aggressive, but we don't have enough to move on Carleton. You bring me a murder weapon or, I don't know, some incriminating admissions, an actual motive, stuff like that, we can talk. But we are nowhere near a charging decision."

Dunham's face had reddened. "Where are you on getting the victim's comms from Saugatuck?"

"Close, I think," Aileen said. "They've been a pain in the ass on that and Nora Carleton's work emails, but they also know I'm about to seek a court order to compel them and they don't want that. Too noisy. So I expect something within the week."

"Good, good," Dunham said, nodding his head.

"Maybe," Shapiro said, "but I really want to manage expectations here. I'm not taking chances with this case. She's now got very aggressive defense counsel and we need to turn sharp corners on this or we'll all be in a bad place. There'll be no bluffing on our side. I's will be dotted. T's will be crossed. You get what I'm saying?"

Demi spoke for the first time. "I think so, thank you. We're grateful for your support. We'll keep working it hard." She turned to look at her captain.

After an awkward pause, Dunham spoke. "Yes, I'm grateful, too, but I'm also dealing with a community of rich people used to getting what they want. I've been getting calls. They want justice *sooner* rather than *later*, so everyone can sleep better in Westport."

As he stood, Dunham added, "Also, so I don't lose the job I love. Let's stay in touch, 'kay?"

They rode in silence until the elevator doors opened to the vista of the courthouse's front lawn. "Fuckin' palace," Dunham muttered. "See you at work. I got some stuff I gotta do on the way back."

CHAPTER THIRTY-SIX

"**B**enny!" Nora shouted down the basement stairs.

The big man leaned out from the guest bedroom in a T-shirt and shorts. "What? What's wrong?" he called.

"Rob Arslan's in Norwalk Hospital. Car crash in Westport. Laslo says it was pretty bad. Feel like I need to be there."

"Let me grab some pants and I'll take you. Gimme two seconds."

They drove in silence for ten minutes, until the hospital came into view.

"Can I ask what may be a politically incorrect question?" Benny asked.

"This late in life you're going to start worrying about that? What?"

"What's a handicapped dude doing behind the wheel of a car? How's that work?"

Nora smiled. "You really have to get out more. There are all kinds of ways. Because Rob can afford it, he has a special car that lets him wheel his chair in from the back, then lock the chair between the front seats and slide himself over into the driver's seat. He uses hand controls for the brake and gas. Once he's in there, you would never know."

"Cool," Benny said.

"And as long as you're on this new sensitivity journey, it's better to call him a 'person with a disability.' Rather than 'handicapped dude.'"

They drove for a few seconds before Benny answered. "But it's still handicapped parking though?"

"Not anymore. It's called 'accessible parking.'"

"Jesus, I really do need to get out more."

Benny waited in the lobby as Nora hurried to Rob's bed in the ER. She found him propped up, with a bandage covering his nose, which was bracketed by what appeared to be large burns under both eyes.

"Oh my God, Rob, I'm so sorry," Nora said.

"I'm okay. I'm going to be fine," Rob said. Gesturing to his face with his hand, he added, "This is all from the airbag. Docs think the nose may be busted and these burns will heal. What hurts the most is my ribs. Hit the seat belt pretty hard. But I've broken ribs in my past life; these feel bruised. Still hurts like hell."

"I'm so sorry." Nora said again.

"Hey, easier than landing without an open parachute," Rob said. "I'll live, but I actually don't think that was the other guy's intention."

"What do you mean?" Nora asked, noticing Laslo for the first time.

"I was just telling Laslo what I told the cops. I was headed home on North Avenue, which, as you know, is straight as an arrow for miles. Nobody on the road, then I see a set of headlights coming and the bastard crosses to my side and drives directly at me. I dive right to avoid the collision and smack a big-ass tree. And here I am."

"Wow. Did the other guy stop?"

"Nope, no sign of him," Rob said. "Cops are calling it a single-vehicle accident, which is true in the sense that only one vehicle was totaled. The other took off."

"And there's nothing along that stretch of North that will have a camera," Laslo added. "All woods or houses set way back from the road. Unless they get lucky, this will stay a single-vehicle accident."

"Well," Nora said, "I'm just glad you're going to be okay. Please take it easy, okay?"

Rob smiled. "Oh, definitely. I'm about to spend about a hundred hours on a plane to see our friends Down Under"—he said it with an Australian accent: *un-dah*—"so it'll be nothing but rest."

Nora frowned. "You're still going?"

"'Course I am," Rob said. "Every quarter. They count on it. Little scrape isn't going to get in the way."

"Zoom is a thing. Ever heard of it?"

Rob smiled. "Can't say I have. And good thing, because can't beat wheeling around Canberra and Wellington. Beautiful places. And they are blissfully unaware of your favorite old-time wheelchair detective show."

"Stubborn bastard, Ironside. When do you go and when'll you be back?"

"Head out tomorrow, back week after next. Just long enough to be hammered by jet lag in both directions."

"Good. That'll keep you out of trouble. And David will hold off on any MC meeting about this until you're back?"

"For sure. I told him the fact-gathering will take at least that long. So the timing works. Wouldn't miss it for the world."

"I'm counting on you coming back," Nora said. "It's hard enough without Helen but without you at work, I'm all alone in the *Twilight Zone*."

Nora extended her arm to bump fists with Rob. "You take good care of yourself down there, okay?"

"Of course," he said, returning the bump. "And you be good, too. Reach out if you need anything. Coverage can be spotty, but we'll connect eventually."

Nora flashed a thumbs-up as she pushed through the curtain.

—◦—

Nora filled Benny in as they drove back to Westport.

"I'm not a big believer in coincidences," Benny said when she finished. "You?"

"Me neither," Nora answered.

"Feels like somebody was comin' after your friend Rob. Now why would they be doin' that?"

"Not sure," Nora said, "but it makes me think this really does have something to do with the front-running investigation."

"You were two of the three people besides Helen who knew about the details on the front-running thing," Benny said. "Helen's dead. You're being framed. And it sure looks like somebody's trying to kill Rob. Only one not accounted for is your predecessor, Holtzer, who's in the wind. Makes me really want to have a chat with him."

They drove in silence before Benny spoke. "Your boy Rob better have his head on a swivel. And an alarm and cameras. How's he getting home, anyhow?"

"Laslo will take care of him. The good news is he's headed out of town for ten days."

"Very good," Benny said. "I'll check in with Laslo, see if he needs anything. We're gonna be together all day tomorrow."

CHAPTER THIRTY-SEVEN

Benny and Laslo were parked on Main Street in Brooklyn, backed in against the side of the West Elm furniture company building, staring at the front door of the exclusive Clocktower condominium building.

"Folks live in Brooklyn their whole life and don't know we have an actual Main Street and a neighborhood called DUMBO."

"Life with you is an endless classroom," Laslo said, chuckling. "Seriously, why's it called that? Circus connection or something?"

"They wish it was that romantic," Benny said. "Sits between the Brooklyn and Manhattan Bridges so it's Down Under the Manhattan Bridge Overpass. Literally named for the initials. DUMBO. Used to be all dopers and artists—groups with some overlap, I realize—but it's expensive as hell now. All kinds of tech dough."

"Yeah, no shit," Laslo said. "That I can tell from lookin' at the cars and all the froufrou shops. But DUMBO? Seems made up."

"Well, I—look, there he is!"

A tall, bearded man wearing a turban had emerged from the front of the Clocktower building, looking up and down from his phone as if waiting for a ride service. Benny jumped from the passenger door.

"Mr. Singh!" he called, waving. "Mr. Singh! Over here."

"You're supposed to pick me up in front," the man said, taking angry strides toward the car. "Not exactly a five-star experience," he said before stopping when he noticed Laslo behind the wheel. But it was too late. Benny grabbed his jacket, spinning him to face the side of the car before leaning heavily to crush him against the closed passenger door. "Why the fuck you don't return our calls?"

"I don't know what you're talking about," Singh protested.

Benny spun him back around and bunched the front of his jacket in one enormous grip. "Laslo Reiner? Benny Dugan? Saugatuck? *Those* fucking messages. Ring a bell? And don't give me some bullshit answer."

Singh had regained some composure. "Unless you're the police and you're going to arrest me, take your hands off me or I'll have *you* arrested."

Benny let go, but leaned in close, his nose almost touching Singh's as he whispered menacingly. "We aren't the police, dick-head, but I'm tellin' you we will be out here all day, every day makin' a scene each time you come out of your fancy digs until you talk to us. Capisce?"

Singh seemed confused by the Italian, so Benny added, "Clear?" as he leaned back.

Singh dropped his head, then looked back up. "Okay, okay. What do you want?"

"Helen Carmichael. You know somebody killed her, right? We're tryin' to find out who. You can help with that. We need a half hour."

Benny lifted his chin toward the Clocktower building. "How about now, upstairs?"

Benny whistled. "Holy shit, ol' DUMBO's got some views, amiright?"
He was standing at the enormous black-framed windows overlooking
the Brooklyn Bridge and, across New York Harbor, lower Manhattan.
Turning back, Benny swiveled his head to take in the towering ultra-
white ceiling and the walls covered in blond wood and chrome. "PI
business been good to you, huh, Jatinder? You could have some amazing
Diwali parties up here."

Singh, perched nervously on a counter stool, didn't know what to
make of Benny's reference to the South Asian festival celebrating the
triumph of good over evil so he said only, "I've done all right. This is
my office and my home."

"Ha," Benny laughed, "you should see *my* office and *my* home. Could
put it all in your bathroom."

"Okay, let's get to it," Laslo cut in, gesturing to a litigation bag at his
feet. "These are copies of Helen's files, most of which seem to be your
work. Take us through how you got this gig, what you did, why you
think she wanted all this dirt on her coworkers, and what we might
be missing."

For the next hour, Singh reconstructed the work he had done for
Helen, identifying his reports and photographs.

"We just have a couple more questions," Laslo said, lifting a file.
"You found all this information about Jeffey Jepson's Chinese girlfriend
likely being a Chinese intel asset. Did you give any of that to the FBI?"

Singh pointed to his own chest. "*I* didn't, but that's not my job. It's
up to the client to decide what to do with stuff like that."

Benny had a slim folder open on his lap. "I didn't ask you anything
about this Rob Arslan guy," he said. "I see why you gathered the shit
about his problem with pills and whatnot, but why the financial report
on his charity, this 'Dustoff Home' thing?"

Singh took the report from Benny. "I think just to get a sense of his assets and whether the charity was bogus or not. As you can see, it has a huge endowment—like fifty million—but it's legit, does a lot of stuff for vets, and there was no smoke that he was skimming from it. In fact, he's one of the biggest donors. Puts his money where his mouth is, unlike rich mouthpieces asking for everyone *else* to donate."

"Who's Jeremy Parker?" Laslo asked, holding up another report.

"I didn't do non-US travel," Singh said, "except I agreed to cover Mrs. Jepson in the British Virgin Islands because it's close and pretty great to visit. The rest of the out-of-country stuff was subbed out to Parker, who's based in Abu Dhabi. Former British intel guy. I found him, but Helen went direct so I don't know what he did. Good guy but a little squirrelly so you might have a hard time getting to him. I'll give you his info."

Pointing to the bag of folders, he added, "My recollection is that the big travelers in there were Arty Falcone, David Jepson, and Rob Arslan."

"Why was she having you do all this?" Laslo asked.

"No idea. I assumed it was a company security thing. You know, making sure your top people are trustworthy. That seems to be par for the course in the finance world, which attracts a lot of weasels, in my experience. I thought maybe Saugatuck would be different but, nah, you people sure got some knots in your string, if you take my meaning."

Benny didn't, but said only, "Well, we appreciate you helping with this."

"No problem," Singh said. "Better than having you out front crapping on my property values."

"Can't believe I didn't get a ticket," Laslo said as he unlocked the car.

"Well, you can thank the New York Fire Department for that," Benny said, grabbing a laminated placard from the front dashboard.

Laslo glanced at the placard as Benny returned it to his bag. "So we're on official Fire Department business?"

"Hard to say," Benny replied with a smile. "Little fires everywhere, as you may have heard. Let's focus on how we're gonna get to this Jeremy Parker. There's nothing from him in Jepson's file, or Arslan's, but plenty in Arty's. He may have seen Arty doing shit in some Bangkok alley that didn't make the reports. Be good to know."

CHAPTER THIRTY-EIGHT

Captain Dunham was shouting from down the hall. "We got her! We got her! Demi! Get in here!"

When Demi Kofatos reached his office doorway, he was red in the face and pointing at his desk phone. "Just got off with the lab. Dead lady's blood is on a fuckin' knife from Nora Carleton's house. Hah hah, we got the bit—" he began, but stopped. "We got her now."

Demi slid into a chair facing the captain's desk. "Which knife, sir?"

"I don't know," he answered, looking down at a note on his desk. "Lab guy said it was Exhibit A27, so you'll know where it was found. He said it was a kitchen-type carving knife, consistent with the victim's neck wound. Boom. That pain-in-the-ass hedge fund lawyer is goin' down."

Demi stood. "I'll look at the search reports right now."

"You don't seem excited, Detective," Dunham said. "Why is that?"

"Well I don't know exactly what this means yet, sir."

"I'll tell you what it means. It means this case is cleared and a cell door will be closing on, excuse my language, Ms. Rich-Bitch Carleton."

"Got it, sir," Demi said quietly as she turned to the doorway. "I'll follow up."

She was back in five minutes, gently rapping on the door frame. "Come in, come in," Dunham said, looking up. "Whataya got?"

"It was a carving knife, all right," Demi said, looking down and reading from a document in her hand. "A Wüsthof Classic nine-inch hollow-edge carving knife. And it was found with a bunch of other knives and serving forks and spoons in a drawer in the Carleton kitchen."

Demi flipped through the document's pages. "But there were no other Wüsthof knives recovered."

Dunham squinted at her. "Why're you telling me that?"

"Well," she answered, "I just looked it up. Hundred and seventy bucks for that one knife on Amazon. Why would it be thrown in a drawer with all kinds of other stuff? And when she already has one of those countertop knife holders with a whole set of other knives in it?"

"You're her lawyer now?"

"No, I'm just a detective and it seems very odd. Why the hell would she keep the murder weapon in her own kitchen? If this is the actual murder weapon, then it must've been out there on the Sound that night. So why doesn't the murderer just drop it in the water? Seems really dumb to me and Ms. Carleton may be a lot of things, but dumb isn't one of them."

"Look, I know you haven't done a lot of murder cases, but, believe me, people who've killed other people do all kinds of stupid shit. Something about taking a human life fogs the brain. So let's not get our own brains fogged here by overthinking it. This is great evidence for the case against our prime suspect. Murder weapon in the perp's house. Ka-boom."

Demi started to go, but stopped and turned back. "So is our theory, sir, that Nora Carleton brought her own knife to the killing and then returned it to her kitchen? Or that she used a knife she found someplace else and still brought it back to her kitchen?"

Dunham was beet red now, his voice loud. "This is the picky-ass shit I was worried about when you came on board, Detective. Overthinking, going with your gut feelings, and thinking you know better than the rest of us. Again, murderers do strange stuff. Now, get outta my office and reach out to the fuckin' State's Attorney and make sure they have this. Then tell them we're ready to slap the silver bracelets on Nora Carleton. Rich people can't be above the law in Westport, 'cause they're all rich." He chuckled at his own joke.

"Yes sir," Demi said quietly as she turned into the hallway.

An hour later, Demi turned into her office doorway to find Captain Dunham sitting at her desk. He was red again, the lines on his face branching vividly.

"Where've you been?" he asked sharply.

"Out checking something, sir."

"What?"

"I ran by the victim's house to see if she had Wüsthof knives. She does, or did, rather. She had a butcher block set of these fancy knives. One is missing. Looks to be the nine-inch knife we found in Nora Carleton's kitchen."

"Did you call Aileen Shapiro, as I ordered?" he asked coldly.

"I did, sir."

"When?"

"Just now as I drove back from Helen Carmichael's house."

"Unfuckingbelievable," Dunham said. "You know how close you are to an insubordination charge? When I told you to call her, I didn't mean an *hour* later, after you'd finished working for the defense."

"Sir, I'm not working for the defense. I had a hunch and played it out. Now we know the murder weapon, which was in Carleton's kitchen, came from the victim's house. That's important to developing our case."

Dunham was calming down. "Yeah, maybe," he said. "What did Shapiro say about arresting Carleton?"

"She said she's not ready for us to do that yet."

Dunham almost shouted. "What the fuck? We gotta make an arrest here."

"And I told her you would want to speak with her about that, sir, so I expect you'll hear from her shortly."

"Damn right," Durham snarled. Her desk chair squeaked loudly as he stood up and walked angrily down to his office, slamming the door behind him.

CHAPTER THIRTY-NINE

"Well, I'm sure glad you got this office, Aileen, after so long as the deputy. Won't be long before they give you the top job in Hartford. You deserve it, you know."

Carmen had to resist the temptation to turn and look at Porter Raleigh. She had never seen him be charming, but he had dialed it up to eleven now, looking at Aileen Shapiro across the glass surface of her office desk. Carmen froze her polite smile and stayed focused on the State's Attorney.

"I sure appreciate that, Porter, especially coming from you. But one job at a time. That was your mantra, as I recall."

"It was, it was," Porter said, stroking his goatee, "although I probably should have skipped some. But—water over the dam, as they say."

He gestured toward Carmen. "My colleague and I appreciate you taking the time to meet with us. We heard about this knife business and wanted to see where things stand with our client, before anything happened that everyone would regret."

"I'm not sure what you mean, Porter," Shapiro said.

"Well, as we understand it, the murder weapon, which came from the victim's house, was recovered thrown in a cutlery drawer in our client's kitchen."

"Yes, that's right," Shapiro answered.

"And, apparently, the Westport police theory—which I assume you, as a sensible person, don't share—is that our client murdered her friend in or on the Long Island Sound, left the body in her personal bright red canoe, and then was careful not to drop the murder weapon into deep murky water where it would disappear forever so she could instead bring it back and put it in a drawer in her own kitchen. Oh, and leave it there for days, knowing the police will come looking for it. Do I have that right?"

"That is a theory, although I wouldn't describe it so sarcastically, Porter."

"I hope you would, Aileen, because it makes no sense and I believe any reasonable juror would find it unbelievable."

"Well, Porter, you know people sometimes—"

"Yes," he interrupted, "do stupid things. But highly intelligent people, even those supposedly bent on murdering close friends, do not do completely idiotic, light-myself-on-fire things. At least in my experience. And I suspect yours."

"Well, O. J. did have a glove with his victims' blood on it at his house."

Porter exhaled sharply through his nose and smiled tightly. "So Nora Carlton is O. J. Simpson now? You do know he was *acquitted* and the prosecutors' careers ruined, right? And, unlike my client, Mr. Simpson was actually guilty. Give me a break."

Porter and the State's Attorney were now staring coldly at each other, so Carmen jumped in. "And we all remember," she said, "that somebody broke into Nora's house the day after the killing, right?"

Aileen Shapiro broke off her staring contest with Porter and turned to Carmen. "Yes, that's what your client told the police, none of whom saw the alleged intruder, and there was no forensic proof of an intruder's presence."

Porter breathed loudly as all signs of his previous charm melted away. "Yeah, other than the tape on her front-door lock. Okay, I'm just going to cut to the chase here, Aileen. Our client didn't do it. I'm as sure of that as I have been of anything in forty years of practice. If you let the Westport cops railroad you into charging her, you will rue the day. I will win this case and make sure every lawyer and judge and legislator in this state knows that you were warned that you were charging an innocent woman and you did it anyway."

Shapiro sat up straight in her desk chair, grabbing her red reading glasses from her hair and gesturing with them. "Don't threaten me, Porter. I remember what *you* were like as a prosecutor and your forty years won't change that."

"And I regret some of what I did, Aileen, and because of it, I now work alone in a tacky little office between a dry cleaner and a Subway. I don't want you to have the same regrets, even though the five-dollar foot-long is a lovely sandwich. I'd like to see you move up in the system. I could see you as Chief State's Attorney. I could see you on the bench. Or not."

Shapiro glared at him as she returned the glasses to her head.

"Okay," Carmen said, breaking the silence, "we appreciate the time and we'd also appreciate your commitment that our client will be allowed to surrender if you ever get to the point of charging her, which we very much hope you don't."

Shapiro turned her head slowly to Carmen. "You have my commitment. If we charge your client, I will call you and arrange her surrender. But no decisions have been made. And to be clear, I will not be pressured into making a bad decision either way in this case. We will follow the facts and the law to do the People's work for the state of Connecticut. Your time is up here."

Carmen and Porter stood and left in the awkward silence that followed.

—⁓⁓—

They rode several floors in the elevator before Carmen spoke.

"Wow, I knew you were going to brush her back up a bit, but I didn't expect you to throw at her head."

Porter continued staring at the closed elevator doors. "She needed a message. Something to help her stand up a bit here. Resist the easy headline and pressure from overeager cops."

"Welp," Carmen said, "she definitely got a message. You also pissed her off and where that makes her want to stand is another question. But, hey, at least they won't arrest Nora publicly and she'll be able to turn herself in to be processed. So that's a win."

The doors opened. "We'll see," Porter said as he stepped out. "This is a sophisticated state but a very small one. Aileen knows that. She knows from my experience that if she fucks this case up, she'll be in Stamford until she retires."

CHAPTER FORTY

"Hey," Nora said as she leaned into the basement war room.

Benny jerked his head up. "Give a guy a heart attack, why dontcha. What're you still doing here?"

"Oh, I'm here full-time as of this morning. Suspended. 'On the beach,' as they say."

"What happened?"

"I don't know for sure, because they didn't tape it," Nora said. "All I know is Louis waited until Rob was out of town and then asked the MC—in his words—to 'reconsider my employment status.'"

"How do you know all this?" Benny asked.

"Because fucking Louis called this morning and fucking told me."

Nora now shifted her tone to imitate Louis's flat way of speaking. "We at Saugatuck have not prejudged your case, of course, but the risks to the firm's reputation have now grown to the point where the MC decided it was prudent to not have a prime murder suspect on site until this issue is resolved."

"Louis? That you?" Benny asked with a smile.

Nora ignored his attempt at humor. "Sneaky bastard just trying to push me aside because he wants my job. I lose my one remaining ally on the MC, temporarily, so Louie makes his move. It's actually brilliant.

Keep me as an employee, but don't let me actually do any work, and he slides into my office and my job. Very un-Saugatuck, if you ask me."

"Wait," Benny said. "They're *paying* you?"

Nora nodded.

"To do nothing?"

"Yup, I'm not allowed to do any work."

"Holy shit, how do I get that gig?" he asked, smiling again.

"No, it's embarrassing, Benny. Everyone at work will know I'm not there and they'll assume I did something wrong, a narrative that sneaky Louie will encourage. It sucks."

"Okay, I get that. But maybe not as much as *not* being paid a ton of money to stay home would suck, right? And you told me you got a huge to-do list, right? All kinds of shit to fix or change here at the McMansion?"

Nora grinned. "You really are a ray of sunshine, aren't you? All right, I'll get to work. You got complaints about the basement?"

Benny smiled back. "Now that you mention it, yes. There's a bulb out in the hall by the bathroom door. I was just gonna hit you on the Airbnb rating, but be nice if you could replace it."

"Light bulb is now on my list," Nora said. "What's on yours today?"

"I'm gonna run around with Laslo and check some shit out. Call or text if you need anything. Where's your mom?"

Nora lifted one corner of her mouth in a half smile. "She went to Hoboken to visit some of her friends. I can't believe she's not keeping you posted on her movements."

"You just can't stop, can you?" Benny said as Nora walked away. "And put the alarm on when I'm gone," he called after her.

Nora was in Sophie's bathroom tightening the loose towel rack when she heard the driveway sensor chime and glanced at the app on her phone. An unmarked police car had pulled into the driveway. She went downstairs and was disarming the alarm keypad by the front door when the doorbell rang.

Demi Kofatos looked embarrassed. "Oh, Ms. Carleton, I'm sorry to bother you. I was looking for Benny. Is he around?"

"No, he's out and about. You can hit him on his cell. Do you have the number?"

"I do," Demi replied, taking a step backward on the front stoop. "Many thanks. And, again, I'm sorry to bother you."

"No bother," Nora said as the detective turned to leave. "Hey, do you want a cup of tea or coffee?"

Demi turned back and hesitated. "That's nice, but I'm not supposed to talk with you without your lawyers."

Nora suddenly found herself speaking quickly, her words spilling out. "Well we can't talk about the case. We could talk about other things, but that's okay, I understand. You're probably too busy."

Demi tilted her head before answering. "Yeah, I guess that's right. And I have a few minutes. Thanks."

Nora stepped aside, gesturing toward the kitchen. "Coffee or tea?"

"What're you having?" Demi asked.

"Tea."

"Perfect."

Demi slid into a seat at the kitchen table as Nora fixed two cups of tea. "How about I interview you?" Nora asked as she carried the cups to the table. "That way we stay completely away from the case."

"Sure," Demi replied. "Where does the interview start?"

"Tell me your story," Nora said. "I always like to begin that way. Open-ended. I can learn a lot just by where the subject starts and where they go."

Demi narrowed her eyes. "Okay, I guess. My story's pretty simple. Born and raised around here. Both my parents were cops, believe it or not. That's actually how they met, on the job in Norwalk. Both Greek—actually a lot of Greeks in Norwalk; not sure why. So I went to public school in Norwalk, then to college at UConn, like a good girl. Lived at home in college to save money. Worked as a police dispatcher in the evenings. After graduation, I applied to Westport PD because they paid more and I really didn't want to be working with my mom and dad. Started in patrol, did all the jobs and shifts. Twelve years in, I made detective. And that's my story."

"A good story," Nora said. "Siblings?"

"Five kids in the family. We are Greeks, after all. I'm the middle child and the only girl."

"Wow, that must have been something, growing up with four brothers. Are they in law enforcement too?"

"Actually, none of them went into the family business. They do all kinds of different things."

"So why did you become the only second-generation cop in the family?" Nora asked.

"I'm not sure," Demi answered. "Probably some combination of a desire to please my parents and my admiration for my mom. I'm sure you know, but it isn't easy for a woman in law enforcement in a lot of places, and she came up when it was not a common thing. I think her own parents were horrified."

"You have a family of your own?"

"Me? No. Thirty-five-year-old single White female, which would be devastating to my folks if my brothers weren't such prolific breeders. Luckily, I've got ten nieces and nephews. Enough so my parents don't have time to focus on what a disappointment I am, relationship-wise."

Nora laughed. "Maybe you're just a late bloomer. You'll find your person." She paused before nodding down at the table. "And can I ask what's up with the black nails?"

"Ha," Demi answered, extending the fingers on one hand. "A subtle attempt to let my flag fly, I guess." She paused and looked down into her mug. After a beat, she glanced up at Nora and added, "I'm not gonna ask your story because I don't want some lawyers jumping on me and I kinda already know it."

Nora chuckled. "Yeah, we don't need them mad. But can I ask how police officers afford to live around here?"

After chatting about housing prices, Demi used a pause in the conversation to push her chair back. "Listen, thanks for this," she said, standing. "Here's hoping we can talk again someday, in different circumstances. Never got the chance to drink the tea with all my talking. Sorry. Where should I put the mug?"

"Oh, just leave it," Nora said. "I'll take care of it."

"Right," Demi said stiffly, extending her hand. "I'll reach out to Benny."

Nora shook Demi's hand. "You do that. And thanks for telling me your story. It's a good one. And I'll bet it has a happy ending."

Demi chuckled as she broke the long handshake. "Not too soon, I hope. The ending I mean. But I appreciate the thought. Have a good day."

CHAPTER FORTY-ONE

"Oh my God," Porter Raleigh said as he walked back into Nora's kitchen holding his phone. "Aileen must have known this the entire time she was talking to us. This is a really clever move by our State's Attorney. I should have thought of it."

Nora looked up from the table where the team was gathered. "What?"

"She's gone with a one-person grand jury," he said, gesturing with his phone. "I just got the word from a friend in Hartford. Seems Aileen applied to a special panel of judges for the appointment of a grand jury, which we don't have in Connecticut anymore, except for this strange old thing called an investigative grand jury."

"You lost me," Nora said. "I spent a lot of time with federal grand juries, but I have no idea what you're talking about."

"Lost me too," Carmen added.

"For good reason," Porter answered. "The US Constitution requires that a grand jury—twenty-three citizens good and true—see evidence and vote in secret before anyone can be charged with a federal felony. That's why you two spent so much time with grand jurors in your old jobs. So did I. But the states don't have to do it that way. And, like a lot of them, Connecticut stopped using grand juries long ago. They start felony cases here by a prosecutor making a public accusation, and then providing evidence in open court at a preliminary hearing to establish that there's probable cause. If the judge agrees, a trial is next."

Carmen still seemed confused. "Okay, so the feds and New York and Jersey all still use grand juries. Connecticut doesn't. They go straight to a preliminary hearing. Got it. So what the hell are you talking about with this one-person grand jury thing?"

"There is a state law in Connecticut that's used very rarely. It allows for the appointment of a single judge to investigate something. The judge does it in secret, with the prosecutor's help, like a normal grand jury would, but it's him, or her, alone sitting there hearing evidence. And when all the evidence has been presented, that one judge makes a recommendation whether a person should be charged or not."

"A recommendation?" Nora asked.

"Yes," Porter answered. "The judge who is the grand jury can't charge anyone, but his recommendation really forces the prosecutor either to bring a case or drop it. No way any State's Attorney would go in another direction. And that's what makes it such a smart move in any case that's a flaming bag of crap like this one. The move is genius because it protects Aileen from any fallout over the decision in the case."

"Courageous," Carmen said, shaking her head.

"They used it years ago in the case of the Kennedy family cousin—Michael Skakel was his name—accused of killing a fifteen-year-old girl in Greenwich, when he was also fifteen. Poor victim was beaten to death with a golf club—really a savage crime. And there were rich, powerful people on both sides of the case. It was absolutely gonna be a no-win decision for the State's Attorney. Endless publicity, none of it good, and lots of emotion. So years after the killing, they threw it to an investigative grand jury. A judge was appointed to be that grand jury and he spent almost two years on it before recommending they charge the kid—by then a grown man—which they did and he was convicted, although the state Supreme Court eventually threw out his conviction for other reasons."

"Strangest damn thing," Carmen said, still shaking her head.

"You're right, it is strange, which is why only a couple states still have something like it—Wisconsin and Michigan, I think. Aileen has to tell the state court leadership that the normal investigative techniques won't be enough to solve the case so she needs to be able to subpoena records and force testimony, the way a grand jury can."

"Easy enough for her to say that here," Nora said.

"Exactly," Porter replied, "and she avoids any criticism for charging you or for not charging you. So smart. You have to hand it to Aileen. She saw it work in the Skakel case, which was in the Stamford courthouse when she was just starting out as a line prosecutor. Not only smart, but also confirms her ambitions to move up the ladder to bigger things."

Benny had been quiet until now. "Really, dude?" he said angrily. "Maybe you could tone down the celebration that Nora's nightmare is going to stretch out even longer."

Porter looked embarrassed. "Right, right, sorry about that. It's just a move I should've seen coming. No celebration intended. But this *does* mean she's trying to avoid the pressure from the cops. And a single-judge grand jury may be something we can use to our benefit."

The kitchen was quiet for a moment before Porter looked at Nora and spoke again. "Can I switch topics and ask where things stand with this bizarre Saugatuck 'search for truth'?"

Nora pointed to Benny. "He's got the ball on that. But I'll add that it's only bizarre if you don't know the culture of the place. It's the combination of Saugatuck's genuine commitment to finding out what is true, combined with a confidence—or arrogance, depending on your viewpoint—that they're better than anyone in the world at sorting through facts. It's hard to describe, but they've made billions doing it. You kinda need to live it."

"Hard pass," Porter said.

"Yeah, me too," Benny said. "But what Nora says—as weird as it sounds—is real. And it's the reason that the founder Jepson wasn't kidding when he said he wanted Laslo and me to really dig into it. Right off the bat, we asked *him*—personally, one of the world's richest dudes—some pretty brutal questions. It was clearly painful, but the man didn't flinch."

"And so where do things stand with that?" Carmen asked.

"We're marching our way through everybody Helen had a file on. Gonna do whatever we can to shake loose somebody who might've decided to hurt Helen."

"And blame me," Nora added.

"Yes, that," Benny said, pointing at Nora. "We've barely started. We began at the top and interviewed David Jepson already and then Rob Arslan before he left on a business trip. By the time he gets back in a couple weeks, we'll be done interviewin' everybody Helen had shit on. Then it'll be time to brief their bizarro Management Committee and my goal is to have a clear list of suspects or, even better, one prime suspect by then. What they'll do with it, I can't say, but if we can clear Nora, I will personally spill that shit to the police ASAP."

"What about the PI angle?" Carmen asked.

"We found Jatinder Singh, as you know. Nothing much new there, except he put us onto another PI, who did the international piece for Helen. Seems like that would be most interesting about Arty Falcone, the Saugatuck client relations guy, who comes across as slimy—and

I know slimy when I see it. The PI is a Brit expat based in the UAE. We're tryin' to track him down, but he seems like the kind who doesn't wanna be tracked down."

Benny paused and then rapped his knuckles on the table. "Oh, and speaking of tracking down, Laslo is still workin' to get a last known address on Nora's predecessor, Brad Holtzer, the strange duck from the funeral. Says he's close. Just waiting on info from Saugatuck's bank."

CHAPTER FORTY-TWO

Artemis Falcone knocked on the frame of the open door. "Hey guys, my assistant told me you needed to see me."

"Yeah, Arty," Laslo answered. "C'mon in. Welcome to our palace."

Benny and Laslo were working out of a small windowless storage room. After David Jepson's direction that they be given a private workspace, the room was quickly cleared out and furnished with three chairs and an old "partners" desk so Benny and Laslo faced each other over the large surface. They positioned the third chair at the midpoint of the enormous desk, looking across it to the wall.

"Weird spot for the interview subject," Laslo said as they set up.

"No, perfect," Benny answered. "Really fucks with people that they can't see both of us at the same time and gotta keep turning their head. And we intend to fuck with some of these mopes."

Arty Falcone slid into the chair facing across the desk's midline. "Never been down here before," he said, turning his head from Laslo to Benny and back to Laslo, the strong scent of cologne beginning to fill the space. "Didn't even know we had a basement."

"Well, you do," Benny said flatly. "So you like to fuck children, do I have that right?"

Arty's head snapped quickly to look at Benny, his hair swinging out of place. He brushed it back. "What'd you say?"

Benny recognized the classic delaying tactic and so hit him again quickly.

"You heard me. Bad enough the shit you do to actual grown women around here—which we'll get to—but fuckin' adolescents in Bangkok? You kidding me?"

The normally smooth, lightly tanned Falcone was now red, a mixture of anger and panic playing out across his face. As planned, Benny now gave him a focus for that emotion.

"Helen was holdin' all this shit over your head, wasn't she?"

Falcone needed time to think, so Benny gave it to him, dropping one open palm loudly on the file folder in front of him. "This is Helen's file on you. Pictures, reports, all the nasty bits. But we ain't the cops. Right now we don't give a shit what you were doin' on your own time. We wanna know what Helen was up to. She jam you or not?"

Arty almost seemed relieved. "Yes, yes, she did. She came to me, all concerned-like. 'Oh Arty, I'm worried about you and your family. You could put yourself in a position to be blackmailed, blah, blah, blah.' I told her I didn't know what she was talking about."

He paused and gestured toward the file under Benny's huge hand. "But she says, 'Don't bother,' and tells me she has it all documented—photos, the whole nine yards."

Arty turned his head to look at Laslo, his tone almost pleading. "And, look, I never did anything nonconsensual. Okay, maybe I didn't exactly have verbal consent before some of the grabbing and shit at parties here, but everybody was drunk and it was only kissing and stuff and we were just having some fun. But overseas—where you gotta realize things are different than they are here—I never forced any of those girls. Never raised a hand."

"I told you," Benny said, pulling Arty's attention back, "this ain't about us investigating that shit. This is about us trying to understand what Helen did to you."

"Yeah, yeah, okay," Arty said. "She said she was glad she was the one who knew about it all because she knew how to protect the company—and me. She said she needed to know I was on the Saugatuck team. I told her I was, I was."

He turned to Laslo and added, "I am, you know," before turning back to Benny. "She told me I would be okay so long as she didn't hear about me doing anything again. I told her I wouldn't. She said she'd be watching and there would be no second chance. She'd have no choice but to go to David, who would fucking fry me."

He swiveled his head back to Laslo. "He would, by the way. You know that."

When he turned back, Benny's eyebrows were arched. "And so?"

"And so, what?" Arty asked.

"You keep your promise to Helen?"

"Oh, I did," Arty said, moving his head back and forth quickly between the two men as he spoke. "I did. Kept it in my pants and my hands to myself since that moment, which was almost a year ago. Swear to God. She scared the shit out of me."

"You know Helen was also trying to figure out who was front running Saugatuck, right?" Benny asked.

"I have no idea what you're talking about."

"You know what front running is, of course?"

"I do," Arty said.

"That another of your kinks?"

"How the hell would I front run? You need information about particular trades, before they happen. I never had that. They wouldn't let me within a mile of our trades. I'm the client schmoozer."

Benny paused and brought one hand to his chin, as if thinking, and then dropped the hand. "So forget the front running. But on the sex front, where you have major expertise, if Helen goes away, your problems go away. Amiright?"

"Look, I get why you say that, but I didn't kill Helen. Sure I was pissed at first, but I actually think she saved me, in a way."

"Where were you the night she was killed?" Benny asked.

"Home, with my wife. I didn't go to the sunset party at Compo. After my little chat with Helen, I stopped going to company parties. Drinking and cute women are a bad combo for me. So I was home, probably watching TV. My wife can tell you."

He paused before quietly adding, "Look, I've done stuff I shouldn't have, but I'm not a killer."

Benny looked at Laslo and nodded slightly. "Okay Arty," Laslo said in a loud voice. "Thanks for coming down. We'll be in touch."

Arty put his hands on his thighs to push himself out of the chair but paused and inclined his head to look at the thick file, which was still covered by Benny's hand. "Hey, any chance I can have that?"

"None," Benny said softly.

Arty rose from the chair and moved toward the door before stopping to turn back and look at the ceiling. "Hey, you didn't tape that, right?"

"Why you ask that?" Benny replied.

"I don't know," Arty said. "It felt personal and I didn't give my consent to be recorded, is all."

Benny laughed, "Yeah, good to be reminded just how much you care about consent. Go on, get outta here. We're done with you, for now. And, Jesus man, can you take some of that cologne with you?"

"Thanks for coming down, Arty," Laslo said again.

CHAPTER FORTY-THREE

"All rise!" At the sound of the courtroom clerk's practiced announcement, Superior Court Judge Robert Robinson swept into the room and then stopped at the top of the three stairs up to the bench. He was a tall man with close-cropped salt-and-pepper hair—pleased he still had all of it as he approached sixty—although he wished his once trim frame didn't fill a judicial robe quite so much.

"It's just her," he said to the clerk, smiling and pointing across the empty courtroom at Aileen Shapiro. "Not sure we need to be that formal. And I'm also not sure why I'm wearing this robe. Habit, I suppose."

As he dropped into the big leather chair, he added, "Like a nun." But neither his clerk nor the State's Attorney appeared to get the joke, so he let it go, just another reminder that courtrooms were where real humor went to die.

"Ms. Shapiro," the judge said, "I've never been part of an investigative grand jury, so you'll have to excuse me."

"I haven't either, Judge," Aileen replied.

"We'll figure it out together, then. Honestly, before my happy life up in New Haven was interrupted last week by the Chief Justice, I had actually never even *heard* of a one-person grand jury. Maybe I saw it while studying for the bar, but that was a long, long time ago."

"I know how you feel, Your Honor. I am a little more familiar with it, because there was one here in Stamford when I was new. The Skakel case."

"Yes," the judge said, "that makes sense—another case involving the one percent and murder. One can't help wondering how often you prosecutors utilize this particular extra layer of care in cases involving people who are—"

"Judge," his clerk interrupted. "I just want all participants to know we've begun the audio recording."

"Right, right," Judge Robinson said quickly. "And of course, the identity of the participants will be irrelevant to this court, uh, grand jury."

"Of course, Judge," Aileen said.

—⁂—

Robbie Robinson had been on the bench in New Haven for seventeen years, after the state Judicial Selection Commission ended his career as a criminal defense lawyer—a job he had loved—by recommending him to the governor for appointment to his first eight-year term, which had been renewed ever since. Robbie knew the governor wanted to appoint a Black judge, but beneath the expected headlines about the governor's embrace of diversity, Robbie also knew there was an important reality: The people of Connecticut needed to have competent judges who were Black, both for the way they had experienced life and the way those in their courtrooms would experience the justice system.

Robbie had grown up poor in New Haven and excelled at the private Hopkins School—a familiar path to Yale—which he attended on a full academic scholarship. But he decided not to apply to Yale, despite the encouragement of a variety of Hopkins faculty members. Instead, he went to Howard University in Washington, DC, and stayed to attend Howard's law school. As he explained in a speech at Howard long after graduating, "There are many fine schools offering a fine education, but I wanted to know that whatever grade I got, good or bad—whatever they said about me, good or bad—was without regard to the color of my skin.

"And they kept that promise," he added with a smile. "I got both good and bad, which was what I deserved."

—⟨⟨∘⟩⟩—

"So what's our first step, Ms. Shapiro?" the judge asked.

"Your Honor, I think it makes sense for me to first call a police witness to outline all the evidence gathered so far in the case. And I have a variety of reports and photographs that we can make grand jury exhibits when that witness testifies. Once you have a sense of what we have so far, we can talk about further investigation, what records or people we should subpoena. Does that make sense?"

"Makes sense," the judge answered. "The floor is yours."

"Thank you, Your Honor. Let me just step out to make sure my first witness is set to go."

"Take your time," he replied. "I think this can be more informal than our normal proceedings."

Aileen smiled nervously as she walked past the empty jury box and out a side door of the modern dark-wood courtroom. She pushed open the door of the jury room. "Okay, Demi, he's all set. You ready?"

"Uh, I'm starting to think I'm not the best lead-off witness," the detective replied, not making eye contact.

"What?" Aileen asked just as a toilet flushed in the juror restroom. She turned to see Captain Dunham emerging from the bathroom, drying his hands on a paper towel.

"Hi, Aileen," he said. "Don't know whether Demi had a chance to tell you, but we've decided I should be the first witness."

"What do you mean? That's not your call."

"Well, I feel like it is," he replied. "I'm the supervisor on the case and Demi's never testified at a grand jury before. I did it a million times in New York. I also discussed it with my chief. We agree it should be me."

"First," Aileen replied, "this isn't like any grand jury you've seen. It's just a judge by himself. Second—"

"Testified to judges a million times too. You just gotta know what they want," Dunham said.

Aileen ignored the interruption. "Second, I'm working here as the lawyer for the investigative grand jury, so I'll decide who testifies and when."

"Isn't that the judge's job?" Dunham sneered.

"Technically, yes."

"Then shouldn't you ask him if I can be the first witness?"

"I'm not going to involve Judge Robinson in your unprofessional line cutting."

"Okay, then let's do it," Dunham said before running his hands over the front of his uniform. "That's why I got dressed up."

The State's Attorney stood silently for a long moment, then shrugged her shoulders. "Fine, you're up," she said as she turned and left the room.

Dunham winked at Demi. "Told you she'd be okay with the switch," he said and followed the prosecutor through the door.

CHAPTER FORTY-FOUR

C hip Jepson was next up in the basement interview room. "So what's the goal of this meeting?" he asked Laslo as he dropped into the chair at the partners desk midfield line. His tone was confident, bordering on arrogant. Turning his head to Benny, it became condescending as he translated Saugatuck-speak. "What I'm asking is: Why are we here?"

"Oh, I got it the first time, champ," Benny said. "We're here because *Daddy* wants us to find out if anybody in *Daddy's* company did something bad to Helen, who was an important person in *Daddy's* company. How's that, goal-wise?"

Chip didn't know what to make of this big stranger, so he just nodded. Benny let the silence sit for a bit and then began without warning.

"Helen knew you were a rapist, right?"

"I'm sorry?" Chip responded.

"Don't be sorry, just answer the question. Did Helen know you raped a girl in college?"

"I never raped anyone," Chip answered indignantly. "I believe I know what you are referring to and I had consensual sex with a girl I was actually dating at the time, who turned out to be a gold digger. Thing is, *she* practically raped *me*. She wanted sex and money and ended up with both."

Laslo had never seen Benny's angry face, until now. The big man slapped his hand on the file in front of him and almost threw it open, leaning down to loudly read from a piece of paper in the folder. "Labial tears and vaginal bruising consistent with nonconsensual intercourse. Abrasions consistent with attempted forced penetration of the anus."

Benny leaned his chest over the corner of the big desk toward Chip and lowered his voice, which now came out almost as a growl. "You can sit there and say you believe in the fucking Easter Bunny for all I care, but don't insult me by telling me some greedy girl was 'making love' with you. You may have been dating that poor young woman, but that just makes it a thing we call *date* rape. Lucky for you, we're not here to investigate what happened in college, but don't try to stick something up my ass, okay? Maybe that's your thing, but this ain't your moment."

Chip looked at his feet and didn't speak, so Benny went on.

"There was bad shit in college. Your mommy knew but Daddy never did. The plot twist is that Helen found out all about it, which is why it's in the file in front of me. My question is: How did she use this with you?"

When Chip looked up, his eyes were alive. "Yes, she knew, that evil bitch. And yes, she held it over me, telling me my dad would freak out if he knew, telling me I didn't have the character necessary to lead this company, telling me I should support Miranda in everything."

He turned to Laslo. "Helen Carmichael was an evil, controlling person. I'm no saint, but she was nothing like what they say, the bullshit you heard at her funeral. Vicious. Manipulative. She was never going to let me lead this place. Never. And you know what? I'm glad she's dead. My family's company is better off without her. Hell, the world's better off without Helen Carmichael."

He turned back to Benny. "But I didn't kill her. You think I'm an idiot? Kill somebody who was blackmailing me? How's that gonna work out?"

"You ever try to make money off Saugatuck's trades?" Benny asked.

"Never," Chip said. "Why would I do that?"

"I don't know," Benny said, looking at the ceiling, "maybe because Daddy's allowance wasn't big enough."

"Look," Chip said, "I've got issues with my father's approach to intergenerational wealth transfers. I don't get why he's so tight, never have. But I'm going to run this firm someday. Why the hell would I ruin it by abusing client information to trade for my own account? You can think whatever you want about me, but I'm not going to blow up the goose that's laying the golden egg."

Benny paused before saying, "Can't argue with that. Where were you the night Helen was killed?"

Chip answered without hesitation. "Manhattan. We had a reception at my dad's new apartment on Fifty-Seventh Street for all our New York state and city government investors. State comptroller was there. Even the governor. I was required to remain until it ended around nine."

"You come back here then?"

"No, I stayed overnight at my dad's place. It's big as a fricking house, except eighty stories in the air. I stayed in one of the guest bedrooms. Took a car back to Westport Monday morning after rush hour."

Laslo cleared his throat. "Hey, you ever read *Where the Crawdads Sing*, or see the movie?"

Chip turned and shook his head *no*.

"I don't want to be a spoiler," Laslo went on, "but basically it makes the case that a person could say they were far away in a city for a meeting or something, but actually take public transportation back and forth to kill someone and nobody would be the wiser."

"Haven't seen it," Chip said, "but I'm guessing that person wasn't staying in a building with security all over the place. If I left my dad's place, there'd be a record. Billionaires have a way of making it hard to sneak in and out of their hundred-million-dollar needle-skyscraper duplexes."

He turned back to Benny. "And, look, I'm sorry we got off to a bad start about the college thing. I'm a husband and a father now. I'm not proud of everything I've done, but I didn't kill Helen."

Benny was unmoved. "Appreciate your coming down. I haven't read that book, either, but we'll check out your dad's cameras that night. By the way, you didn't hire someone to kill Helen for you, did ya? Lots of books and movies out there about that kinda shit happening."

Chip ignored the question and walked out the door.

When he was gone, Benny turned to Laslo. "You better have a fuckin' nice boat to put up with workin' with this crowd."

Laslo smiled. "Better than the boat I'd have if I was still at the Bureau."

"Yeah, whatever," Benny said. "Still not sure it's worth it, for a fuckin' boat. Look where poor Nora's little red boat has gotten her so far. But to each his own. And I gotta call a time-out from this parade of awesomeness to grab some of Saugatuck's free food. Then we chat with Miranda."

CHAPTER FORTY-FIVE

"Please state your name for the record," Judge Robinson's clerk said after administering the oath.

"Thomas P. Dunham, Captain, Westport Police Department."

Aileen Shapiro's voice drew Dunham's attention toward the end of the empty jury box, where she was standing behind a small podium.

"Captain, you've been called before this investigative grand jury to provide testimony concerning your department's investigation of the murder of Helen Carmichael. At His Honor's request, I will direct the questioning, but Judge Robinson will also ask questions, as he wishes. Do you understand?"

"Yes ma'am, yes sir," Dunham said solemnly, turning his head to nod at the judge and then back to the prosecutor. He wore his dress uniform with his gray hair newly cut short, his ruddy face clean shaven.

The State's Attorney asked a series of questions to have Dunham lay out the basics of the case: the crime scene, including lab results, the blood on Nora's car, the murder weapon in Nora's kitchen drawer, the *Need to talk* text from Helen to Nora shortly before the murder, the cell phone video of the two women kissing on the sidewalk.

"Is what we have just reviewed a fair summary of the evidence gathered so far?" Aileen asked.

Dunham leaned back in his chair, interlacing his fingers across his midsection. "Yes ma'am, it is," he said with a faint smile.

Judge Robinson's voice made Dunham drop his hands and turn toward the judge's bench, which was slightly behind and to his right. "So you think that's enough?" the judge asked.

"Seems like plenty to me, Your Honor."

"I see," Judge Robinson replied. "Tell me more about your motive evidence?"

"Absolutely, Judge," Dunham said, now fully turned in the witness chair. "It's obvious to us that the victim and the suspect had a secret romantic thing between the two of them prior to the murder."

"And how is that obvious?"

Dunham's neck was turning pink. "Well sir, you saw the video. The secret kiss in the dark and everything. Also, the suspect is clearly the aggressor there."

Judge Robinson glanced toward Aileen. "Is there more to the video than what you showed here?"

"No, Judge," she answered.

He looked back at Dunham. "I see a kiss, singular. I see no 'everything,' although I have no idea what that means and nothing in that video looks like aggression to my eyes. Do you see something else, Captain?"

"Uh, no, Judge. I mean we all see the two women having some kind of physical contact of an intimate nature there and it must have been a secret because everyone questioned says they had no idea there was a romantic relationship between those two. That's all I meant."

"When was that video taken?"

"We don't know, Judge. As I said, it came to us anonymously and there's no metadata. But there's no doubt it's them."

The judge looked again toward Aileen. "And Ms. Shapiro, in the event this case were charged, what would be the prosecution's theory of admissibility for an anonymous video like that?"

"I'm not sure, Judge," she answered. "I suppose we could argue that it's self-authenticating because witnesses could identify the two women depicted."

Judge Robinson raised his voice. "No, no, not in an era of deep fakes you can't. Without someone saying they filmed this or someone saying they were there and this represents what they actually saw with their own eyes, there's no way you get that in as evidence at a trial."

He turned back to Dunham, who seemed confused. "But forget all that, Captain. Tell me again why this is proof of motive?"

"Again, Judge, sir, like I said. If they had a thing going on, love scorned is the oldest motive we have for murder."

The judge smiled tightly. "I'm not sure that's right. I think ol' Cain would deny he was in love with Abel. But tell me the evidence for the scorned part?"

Dunham hesitated, looking confused by the vaguely familiar biblical names. "Well, I'd need to check with the detective on the case, but this Carleton woman being involved with a victim found dead in her canoe supports a fair inference that they had a falling out. That's how we see it."

The judge's smile was gone. "So your belief that Carleton is guilty allows you to see that the relationship was a likely motive."

"Yeah, Judge, that sounds right."

"But isn't motive evidence something we look for to *determine* whether someone is guilty?"

"I'm not sure what you mean, Judge, sir."

"Well, we're trying to figure out who killed Helen Carmichael. As I hear your testimony, you believe it was Nora Carleton. When I ask you why she would do such a thing, you are essentially telling me that she did it because you know she did it."

"Oh, no, Your Honor, sir. I'm saying this is a slam dunk because of the canoe, the car blood, and the knife at her house."

"Got it," the judge replied with a pained look. "So tell me again, why should I believe that Ms. Carleton killed her friend and coworker? And 'Judge' will do, or 'Your Honor.' I don't need the 'sir' as well, Captain."

Dunham gestured toward the video screen. "Well, Your Honor—" He paused to stifle the "sir." "—there's gotta be some kind of passion related to their secret relationship. A secret lesbian relationship has its own complications in the real world, if you know what I mean."

"Actually, I don't know what you mean, Captain, this not being the 1950s. So what, exactly, is the evidence, beyond this anonymous inadmissible video, that these two people had a romantic relationship and that it generated enough passion to lead to murder?"

"We don't have that at this point, Your Honor, but given the strength of the physical evidence, it seems we are good to move forward with an arrest. With your permission, sir, I mean Judge."

Dunham paused, then added, "Oh, and the text the night of the murder is evidence that they were in contact the night of the murder and Ms. Carleton must be lying about that. That *Need to talk* thing makes it clear that the victim reached out specifically to our suspect to talk that very night."

"But didn't they work together, Captain?"

"They did."

"Have you ever told coworkers you needed to talk to them when it did *not* involve a potentially violent romantic falling out?"

Dunham's brow furrowed deeply. "I'm not sure what you mean, Your Honor. I'm a happily—"

Judge Robinson cut him off. "Never mind. Ms. Shapiro, do you have further questions for this witness? If not, perhaps he can be excused and you and I can confer."

"Certainly, Judge," she replied. "I have no further questions. Captain, you may step down."

———

When the door had closed behind Dunham, Judge Robinson cleared his throat. "Ms. Shapiro, as I understand Connecticut law, we are not obligated to transcribe conversations between myself, as the one-person grand jury, and you, as counsel for the grand jury. Is that your understanding?"

"It is, Your Honor."

He smiled at his clerk. "Well, then, that completes the audio recording for today and you can go, with the thanks of the grand jury."

When the clerk was gone, Judge Robinson came down from the bench and slumped into a chair in the jury box, putting his feet up on the railing. "Are you kidding me, Aileen? This thing has holes bigger than the Lincoln Tunnel."

He gestured toward the closed courtroom door. "And that moron is driving this bus?"

"No, no, no, he is not," she answered. "*You* are, with my assistance, and a very able detective from Westport. And, yes, we have some major holes in our case against Carleton, but there is strong physical evidence."

Judge Robinson tilted his head to one side. "And that physical evidence is so stupidly strong that it makes those gaps even larger. If I knew a bigger tunnel than the Lincoln, I'd go with that. I need to understand why a woman as smart and accomplished as Nora Carleton would do something like this and do it in the dumbest way imaginable. And please don't tell me your theory is that she implicated herself so she would not be implicated. I'm not up for an episode of frickin' *Murder, She Wrote.*"

"That is not my theory, Judge. I simply want to assist you in making an honest assessment of this case. Based only on the evidence."

He tapped the center of his chest, fingertips sinking into the black robe fabric. "So for *this* grand jury, let's talk about how you're going to get that kind of evidence of motive—or demonstrate its absence conclusively."

He paused and looked around the courtroom. "And speaking of this grand jury, we need to change it up in here so it feels less like a bench trial and more like I'm trying to investigate something, with your help. Next time, let's you and I just sit and face the witness. And I'm going to drop the robe business."

"Whatever you like, Judge. You *are* the grand jury."

CHAPTER FORTY-SIX

Miranda Jepson was never ruffled. Even her standard work outfit—quarter-zip black Saugatuck company-logo fleece, black skinny jeans, and brown Chelsea boots—was accessorized by a string of pearls. She didn't so much sit as glide into the chair Laslo indicated, smoothing her long center-parted blonde hair so it lay straight across her collarbones on either side. She sat up straight, pivoting her head from Laslo to Benny and back, as if at Wimbledon waiting to see who would serve first—and whether anyone would be polite enough to offer her a Pimm's Cup.

Laslo spoke first, as planned. "Miranda, you know why we're here. Would you start by telling us about your relationship with Helen Carmichael?"

"Of course," Miranda answered smoothly, her accentless American English the product of the best private education money could buy. "She was like a mother to me. Of course, I have an actual mother, but we've never been close. Helen was a mentor and close friend and a vital colleague. Her loss to this company and to me personally is beyond measure."

It was Benny's turn. "So you had problems with your mother?"

Miranda turned to him slowly, shifting her whole body to face him and smoothing her hair again with both hands. "Fairly typical for my demographic, I think. I was away at school and she was, well, *away* quite often. We were perfectly civil, but never developed, especially in adulthood, the kind of supportive relationship I had with Helen. And, for her part, Helen never had her own family, so I think she thought of me as a daughter in many ways—with the twenty years between us."

"You close with your father?" Benny asked.

"Oh yes," Miranda said, her face lighting up. "Very."

"Fair to say you have 'daddy issues,' then?"

The light disappeared. "Meaning what, exactly?" she asked coldly.

"Well, meaning that Marcus Baum is your dad's closest confidant, his alter ego, and you were fucking him. So meaning that."

Miranda turned so quickly to look at Laslo that one side of her hair swung over her shoulder. When he said nothing, she turned back to Benny without adjusting it.

"What exactly are you trying to do—" she began, before Benny cut her off.

"Look, I'm up to my ass in lies in this bastion of truth, so why don't we just cut the shit."

He tapped a thick finger on the file in front of him as he continued. "Helen knew you were banging Baum. She documented it in her file on you. I couldn't give a shit who you fuck, honestly. What I want to know is what Helen did with that information."

Miranda paused and looked down for a long moment. Then she looked up, retrieved the errant hairs, and smoothed them down.

"Yes," she began quietly, "I had a relationship with Marcus, who was unhappy in his marriage. Helen learned of it and talked to me. I agreed with her that it was a mistake. I remember her words: 'Don't crap in your own nest.' If it goes bad, she said, you will have hurt yourself. If it goes well and you end up married, you are now Marcus's wife and just moved down a peg. That's the way this world is for a woman, she said. If you want to run this company, you have to do it on your own. That's why Helen never married and I knew she was right."

"So what happened?" Benny asked.

"I broke it off with Marcus. He seemed to take it well. Helen even got me a therapist."

"Helen hold this over you? People 'round here say you always went her way in the MC."

"Certainly not," Miranda answered, "but it made me appreciate her judgment very much. I knew I could count on her to give me good advice and to make good decisions."

"Where were you the night she was killed?" Benny asked.

"Seriously?" Miranda replied, sounding offended. "You think maybe I killed her, loaded her in a canoe, and dragged her out to Seymour Rock? What, I blow up to the Hulk when I'm angry? I'm *smaller* than Helen, for God's sake. How am I going to do that?"

Benny sniffed. "Maybe your boy Marcus helped you move her, hoping that would get you two back in the sheets."

Miranda ignored that. "I went to the company party at Compo Beach, where I drank too much, to be honest. I took an Uber home."

"Why weren't you at the client thing at your father's place in the city?"

"He didn't ask me to come. I don't really know those clients anyway."

"Where's your house?" Benny asked.

"I have a place in the city, on Central Park West, but on work nights I almost always stay here in a house I have on Turkey Hill Road. I went directly there after the party and was there all night."

"And your private security cameras will back that up? Some of these fancy houses gotta have escape tunnels to sneak out through, amiright Laslo? We gotta check into that."

"I don't know about any tunnels, but her place used to be Martha Stewart's," Laslo said, prompting Miranda to turn and glare at him.

"No shit," Benny said. "My office locked her up some years back. Small world. Bet it's tasteful."

Miranda didn't answer. "Are we done here?" she asked coldly.

"Yes, we are," Benny said. "Thanks for comin' down."

Miranda didn't return his smile. With one final angry glance at Laslo, she left the little room.

"Whoa," Benny said, turning to Laslo. "If looks could kill."

"My mistake," Laslo said. "Probably just sunk my fucking boat. I was only trying to be nice. I didn't know she was sensitive about the Martha Stewart thing."

"See?" Benny answered with a smile. "Good cop ain't all it's cracked up to be. You wanna switch?"

"Not on your life. You're doing a fine job of ensuring you never work here."

Laslo looked at his notes before adding, "Hey, you didn't ask her about front running."

"Yeah, I know," Benny said. "Seems pointless. Like her brother, she's got a load of dough coming and, unlike him, she's probably gonna inherit the place. No way she front runs. And I didn't want to offend her."

Laslo laughed. "Too late, my man, too late. Baum's next. Want me to grab him?"

"Yeah, let's do him before those lovebirds have a chance to chat."

CHAPTER FORTY-SEVEN

Marcus Baum didn't turn his head. From the moment Laslo showed him to the chair at the center of the partners desk, Baum swung one foot under his butt and sat on it comfortably in his wrinkled jeans and gray hoodie while staring straight ahead at the blank wall. Whenever Benny or Laslo asked a question, he answered in the same flat, polite tone, looking at the wall, with nearly every answer preceded by the same movement of his arm: He lifted his right palm onto the top of his head and smoothed his short black hair from back to front, although the hair needed no smoothing and was too short to ever need it.

"I didn't like Helen very much," he said in response to Benny's question.

"Why?" Benny asked.

"Two reasons," he said, "one her, one me. First, she seemed culturally subversive, like the commitment to truth and transparency was a part-time thing for her, a bit of a lark. And she had that loyalty thing they have at other companies—my people, your people. Second, she was always being sarcastic, which I suppose is a manifestation of the first thing, but I listed it as a second item because I personally found it frustrating and a bit confusing."

"Can you say more about what you mean?"

"Sure," Marcus said, looking at the wall. "In a meeting, she might say, 'Oh, that's a *great* idea,' when she didn't mean that and, in fact, meant the opposite, which she was somehow attempting to convey by her emphasis on the word 'great.' I recognize that's sarcasm by definition, but saying words you don't mean to say something else that you *do* mean is a strange way to communicate, especially in a culture devoted to logic and transparency. When I would call her on it, she would invariably answer, 'It's just a joke, Marcus.' But was it? I'm not sure. Anyhow, I often found her frustrating."

"So truth and transparency are important to you?" Benny asked.

"The paramount values. This place is built on them."

"Helen's files have her helping you leak shit to *The Wall Street Journal* about David Jepson—how he's odd and over-the-hill and the company's a mess. Where's that in your values hierarchy?"

Marcus drew his mouth into a line before saying, "I shouldn't have done that. But I did. No excuse."

"Why'd you do it?"

"I was out for drinks one night with Helen and got to talking about some of my frustrations with David and the pace of his transition. She convinced me he needed a shove and that would be a good way to do it. So I told her she could do it for me. It was a mistake but it wasn't her fault."

"Got it," Benny answered. "And where on the hierarchy of values would I find incest?"

Marcus didn't turn. "I don't know what you mean. Incest?"

"Well," Benny explained, "you and David Jepson are like brothers, right?"

"I think that's accurate. Younger brother and older brother, but like brothers."

"So that makes his kids kinda like a nephew or niece to you."

"I suppose so."

"So whataya doin' fucking your niece, Miranda? That's what I mean by 'incest.'"

Marcus still didn't turn and his tone didn't change. "Oh, well, it wasn't incest because David and I aren't actually brothers."

"But you did have an affair with her, right?" Benny asked.

"I did," Marcus said, nodding.

"Did you care about her?"

"Yes, I cared very much. I still care about Miranda."

"Why did you two break it off?"

"I didn't. Miranda broke it off after Helen talked to her and told her she should."

"How did that make you feel?"

"That made me feel really bad. I loved Miranda. I thought we might be together forever. After I got divorced, of course."

"Of course," Benny echoed. "So Helen cost you this relationship?"

"In a sense she did, but I see her as merely a proximate cause. The root cause was Miranda's lack of adequate commitment to the relationship. She thought the potential costs to her outweighed the benefits. Helen merely helped illuminate the factors in the weighing. I would weigh them differently, but I wasn't the one doing the weighing."

"Did Helen ever speak to you about the relationship?"

"She did not."

"Did you ever get the sense she was going to use it against you, like telling your wife or David what you had done?"

"No. I told my wife, which is why I live alone now. And I would have told David if it was ever relevant. And now you are making me think I should."

"So you're telling us you had no hard feelings toward Helen over this?"

"I wish she hadn't done what she did, but it also allowed Miranda to make a fully informed decision, which is always optimal. I didn't like Helen for the reasons I said, but it wasn't about me and Miranda."

"You know she was trying to figure out who was front running the company?"

"I did not."

"Know anything about that?"

"No."

"Did you do it?"

"Of course not," Marcus said. "I know I look like I sleep in my car, Mr. Dugan, but I'm worth four billion dollars. I don't need to steal from my clients."

"Fair enough," Benny said. "Where were you the night she was killed?"

"I'm not sure. I know I was very drunk, because I usually drink a lot on Sunday nights. I remember watching a football game at a bar in downtown Westport and then I think I got an Uber home. But I don't recall it."

"So you didn't go to the Compo Beach party."

"I didn't. I don't enjoy those crowded things, with all the chatting."

"Did you know about Nora's canoe?"

"Of course, everyone does. I've been in it a time or two."

"Did you kill Helen?"

Now Marcus turned and looked Benny directly in the eye. "I did not."

"Do you know who did?"

He didn't break the stare. "I do not."

"Okay, Marcus," Benny said, "thanks for coming down."

When he was gone, Benny said, "Whoa, that was more than a little creepy. So much to say and so little emotion." Then he looked at his watch. "Shit, almost six. I gotta run, Laslo. We'll talk more about Robot Baum tomorrow. Right now I got my check-in with Detective Kofatos. I'll call you from the car after. Get a good night's sleep. I know how taxing good cop can be."

"Wiseass," Laslo replied. "Okay, lemme know how it goes. See you tomorrow."

CHAPTER FORTY-EIGHT

I t felt strange for Benny to be showing his driver's license and not his badge to the desk sergeant, but Carmen's words echoed in his ears: "We don't want to give anybody an excuse to say we abused government authority to help Nora." So he slipped the license through the teller slot in the bulletproof glass. "Here to see Demi Kofatos," he said into the speak-through vent in the window.

Special Agent Benny Dugan would be buzzed right in, but the officer behind the glass barely glanced at Benny's New York State driver's license before tossing it back through the slot. "Have a seat," he said without looking up. Benny did as instructed, feeling his badge push into his lower back as he sat on the hard plastic chair. *Sucks to be a civilian*, Benny thought, shifting in the small chair.

In less than a minute, the door buzzed open and Demi leaned out. "Special Agent Dugan," she said.

He jumped up. "No, no," he said in a stage whisper, "just Benny, at the moment. Trying to help a friend is all. Not government business."

"Got it," she replied, shaking his hand and directing him down the hallway and up the stairs toward her office.

Demi walked quickly ahead of Benny so she could enter her tiny office before he did, sliding around the desk and indicating a visitor chair for him. He moved into it carefully, knees tight against her desk.

"Thanks for giving me a few minutes of your time," Benny said as Demi sat behind the desk. "I really just wanted to check in, maybe give you a sense of how we're seeing this thing, without lawyers preventing normal human conversation."

Demi smiled. "Makes sense. So how're you seeing this thing?"

"Not for nothin', but it's a setup for sure."

Demi didn't react, so he went on. "And I'll talk about this the way I would see it in your shoes. No doubt Nora's big enough that she could move unconscious Helen to the canoe. She's also strong enough to get the canoe out to the rock and swim back. After that, the case goes to complete shit."

Demi had to suppress a smile. She found the big man strangely charming. "And how, exactly, does it go to shit after that?"

"Nothing else makes any kinda sense. She used *her own* canoe? Seriously? How fuckin' stupid is she? She goes to all the trouble of moving the canoe to S'more Rock or whatever—"

"Seymour Rock," Demi interjected.

"Right," Benny said, "that. Goes to all that trouble, but somehow wipes blood on the back of her own car?"

"And the hairs?" Demi asked.

"Helen and Nora were best friends. I'll bet there's Helen hairs on Nora's clothes. Tells you nothin'."

"The knife?"

"Yeah, that's the capper," Benny said. "Evil murderer Nora grabs a knife from the victim's house, takes it to the water to kill her, then takes it back to her own house and puts it in a drawer? You fuckin' kiddin' me? You'd know somebody put it there even if you didn't know some dickhead was in her house the day after the killing."

Demi was silent, so Benny went on. "Hey, anytime you wanna react to any of this, that'd be welcome. And we're off the record here. But you see this for the shit it is, right?"

Demi didn't answer that. Instead she said, "What do you make of the scorned lover motive?"

Benny rolled his eyes. "Ah, come on. We're in the evidence business. What's the evidence of that? That they kissed? Which Nora says happened about two years ago?"

Benny paused before adding, "Look, I'll go *way* off the record, 'cause I trust you, just on instinct. I don't trust your prick of a boss as far as I could throw him, so this is between us. We been goin' through Saugatuck with a fine-tooth comb, looking for motive. We got zip on Nora. But we got motive comin' out the ass for about half a dozen of her colleagues. Seems our girl Helen was collecting dirt on her colleagues and using it to squeeze 'em—gently, but squeezing nonetheless. We still got threads to pull, but Nora doesn't even make honorable mention in this league of motivated douchebags."

Demi studied the surface of her desk before responding. "Okay, look, I'm going to trust you, which I may live to regret. Off the record, right?"

Benny nodded.

"I see it like you do. It's just too good. Doesn't make any sense. People do dumb stuff in the heat of passion, but if Nora dropped that knife in her own kitchen drawer that night, she knew it was going to be there when we searched long afterward. Why would she do that?"

"She wouldn't," Benny answered. "And she didn't."

"I know that's probably right," Demi said quietly, "but I'm not driving this bus. I think the prosecutor has her head mostly screwed on straight, but my boss is pushing her hard and she's under a lot of pressure to charge something. I can't talk about details but I think she's using a special state procedure to give herself an excuse. I'm just not sure—an excuse to do what?"

"I appreciate you being straight with me," Benny said quietly. "You figure anything out on that video you got of Nora and Helen? I heard there was no metadata on it and nothing useful off the email account it came in from, but whoever sent you that is somebody I'd like to stare at."

"Still way off the record?"

"Totally."

"Yeah, we've had some movement there. My boss wasn't happy we didn't know more about that so there's been a lot of action on it. With the info we got from your team, we went to the restaurant, Artisan, and got a pretty good bead on when that must have been. We know the corner where it was filmed, so we're getting a warrant to geofence it with Google and find out every phone that was in the area at that time. The judge was a little concerned about being overinclusive, but we think it'll be a pretty tight fence. Can't be many phones near that corner around that time. Then we'll run them all down and see what we can see."

"God, I love actual police work. Nice to see it being practiced."

"If I get anything, I'll see if there's any way to give you a heads-up, under our usual rules. And I'd appreciate it if you'd share anything you got on who else might have done it."

Benny exhaled audibly. "I really wanna give you all that, Demi, because you've been great to me. But it's not my call, which is why I kept it way off the record. But I hear ya, I hear ya. And there might come a time when I spill it all to you—for Nora's sake—but it's too early now. I can't lose access to Sauga-fuck, I mean Saugatuck, until we get more answers."

Benny stood and extended his hand across the desk. "I appreciate you being a pro. Let's keep this channel open, okay?"

Demi nodded, then turned her head to look in the direction of her captain's office. "Carefully, though, right?"

"On my life," Benny said, before turning from the office.

CHAPTER FORTY-NINE

"What was the best part of your day, Nana?" Sophie asked, looking up from her plate.

Teresa put her fork down and beamed. "Can I have more than one best?"

"Mommy says no," Sophie replied, sounding very serious and looking toward Nora. "Right Mommy? There's only one best of something? Right?"

Nora nodded and smiled. "That's right, ladybug, but if Nana wants to tell us two great things about her day, we should let her, don't you think?"

Sophie smiled and nodded.

"Okay, then," Teresa said, "I have two. My first best is having dinner with the two most amazing girls in the world." She gestured toward a small lump of painted clay in the center of the table. "And my second best is the art Sophie made for us at school."

"It's not *art*, Nana, it's a *turkey*. And it's for Thanksgiving, which is coming soon, right?"

"That's exactly right," Nora said. "And speaking of Thanksgiving, you know Daddy and Vicki will be here for Thanksgiving, right?"

When the little girl nodded, Nora went on. "And you may hear people talking about something great that is happening with them."

"What, Mommy?"

"Well, Vicki is going to have a baby. Isn't that cool? And you know what's even cooler? That baby will be your brother or sister, depending on whether it's a boy or a girl."

Sophie's eyes were wide. "Wow!"

"I'm not sure of the exact date but after Christmas, closer to spring-time. I think the baby is due in April or May, so not right away. But the baby's in her tummy and you may be able to tell when you look at her."

"Oh, I hope it's a girl, I hope it's a girl. I really want a sister." She turned to her grandmother. "Girls are pretty great, right Nana?"

Teresa reached and gently squeezed Sophie's wrist. "They're the best," she said.

"Should we keep doing best-part-of-your-day?" Sophie asked. "I'll go. Best part of my day is *that*. I'm gonna have a sister, maybe."

Sophie looked at her mother. "Why do you look sad, Mommy?"

Nora perked up. "Oh, I'm not sad. Just tired. Can I go now? I'm going to take two like Nana. Best part of my day is this dinner with you two and my other best is that Vicki's going to have a baby." Nora looked down at her food. "Now let's finish eating so you can play for a little bit before bed."

"Hi, Benny!" Sophie called as the big man stepped into the kitchen.

"Hey Sophie!" Benny said, pausing briefly at the door to the base-ment. "Don't let me interrupt dinner. I'm headed down to do some work. And no rush, but maybe I can update Mommy on some stuff after dinner."

"Sure thing," Nora said. "Be down when the bug here gets her jammies on."

—⁘—

The top of Sophie's head was just visible above the back of the family room couch as she read to her dolls. Teresa reached from the sink and handed Nora a plate to put in the dishwasher. "Hey," she whispered in a voice almost lost in the running water, "so the baby is not really your best. Am I reading that right?"

"You are," Nora said quietly. She lifted her chin toward the family room. "It's not *really* her sibling—it's her *half* sibling—but I can't figure out a way to say that without looking like a jerk."

"I think you're talking about it just the right way," Teresa answered. "At the age of eight, she has to embrace this without any qualifiers. She'll figure all that out down the road."

"You're right," Nora said tiredly. "I know that. It's just the same old weirdness I feel about Nick—who I really, really don't want to be with—and some sadness around the fact that I may be single for the rest of my life. Also, this Helen nightmare is hanging over our lives. So I'm definitely feeling weird about the baby news and I know there's good reason for that. But I just want things to get back to normal and it feels like we'll never get there."

Teresa pulled her daughter into a hug, leaving wet handprints on the back of Nora's shirt. Then she pushed her away gently, slipping her hands to hold her shoulders. "It's going to be okay. You know that, right? All the sources of weirdness will work themselves out and we'll find a new normal and it'll be the best normal ever. Don't lose sight of that."

"I won't, Mom," Nora said, pulling her mother back into a brief hug. "You finish here while I take Soph up?"

"Of course," Teresa said. "And I may run a cup of tea down to our hardworking basement dweller."

Nora gave her mother a crooked smile. "You do that. Very kind of you. You're such a giver."

"Stop," Teresa protested, returning the smile. "How'd you like to be alone in the basement all the time?"

"Fine, Mom. But if Sophie wants you to read books to her, I'm coming down to get you. Don't let me walk in on anything that would land me in therapy."

"Your mind, sometimes," Teresa said, shaking her head. "My goodness. And I'd be happy to read books to Sophie tonight."

─────

"Coming down the basement stairs!" Nora shouted before adding, "Now walking toward the wine room!"

Benny and Teresa were sitting in the two war room chairs sipping tea. "You really are a comedian," Benny said as Nora entered.

Turning to her mother, Nora said, "This looks very civilized, but you're needed two flights up. Ladybug insists that Nana read tonight."

"I'm on it," Teresa said, standing. "Benny, a pleasure as always." Benny stood and smiled as she left the room.

"Jeez, you're getting all kinds of manners," Nora said when Teresa was gone.

Benny's face flushed as he sat back down. "Just tryin' to be polite."

"Forget it," Nora said. "Catch me up on the day."

Benny went to the whiteboard. "All kinds of strange shit today in the temple of truth and transparency," he said, using the knuckles of one hand to quickly knock on four photographs taped to the board. "Arty, Chip, Miranda, and Marcus. We did those four. Now just gotta do Jeffey Jepson and your boy Louis Lambert."

"Ick," Nora said.

"And, just so you don't think I was goofing off, I also went and saw Demi Kofatos today."

"You really are earning your money. Let me double your salary!" Nora said with a smile.

"Remind me again: What money?" Benny said.

"And that's exactly how we can afford to double it. On with the update," Nora replied, pointing to the whiteboard.

"Jesus, what a crew you work with," Benny said. He stepped back and pointed at the photographs this time, as if moving down a line of targets at the shooting range. "Arty's an evil piece of shit, Chip's just a douchebag frat boy, and Miranda's an ambitious stone-cold queen."

"Marcus?"

"That strange dude is actually the only one I like. I'm warming up to this unemotional but completely honest Vulcan shit. But lemme take you through what each of them said."

When he was done recounting the interviews, Nora chuckled. "Mr. Bad Cop got a lot of work done today."

Benny nodded and smiled back. "A lot."

"But it sounds to me as if you don't like any of them for the actual crime?" Nora said.

"That's right. They all had reason to not like Helen, but enough to kill her? Hard for me to see. And none of them were suspects in your front-running investigation, so even if they were doing it—and I see nothing that says they were—they didn't know they were being chased."

Benny paused before adding, "Strangely enough, the one I could most see offing Helen is Miranda. But she's right that I can't picture her getting it done physically. She's about Helen's size, maybe even smaller. Maybe under that smooth pearls-on-a-fleece shit, she secretly hated Helen with the heat of a thousand suns—and that motivated her to get it done."

"And you'll finish with Jeffey and Louis at the office tomorrow?" Nora asked.

"That's the plan. We got Jeffey at the office but Laslo and I decided to hit your boy Louis at his place in the city. Given what's in his file, I'd like to get into his house. And, like I told you, I also wanna talk to a bunch of the assistants."

"Tell me again why you want to meet with them?" Nora said.

He stood and walked to the whiteboard in their little war room at Nora's house. He tapped on the pictures of Saugatuck's leaders as he spoke.

"So you told me that all these people at the top have at least one of those 'assistants.' All those smart young worker bees are on the inside watching what goes on to kinda help and protect their boss right?"

"That's right," Nora said, "like I have Abe and Helen had Tracey."

"Good so far. When I wanted to know what was goin' on in a Cosa Nostra family, who would I try to flip? The guys near the top, around the boss—the underboss or the consigliere. They're on the inside. They see stuff, they hear stuff, they carry out orders."

Nora smiled. "That all makes perfect sense, but try not to lead with the Mafia informant comparisons if you actually meet with the assistants."

"Nah, that's just for you, but I wanna meet with the bunch of 'em. Those people know stuff. Hell, for all I know, one of 'em did Helen."

Nora arched her eyebrows at that.

"But not impossible, right?" Benny said.

"Not *impossible*," Nora agreed. "And I very much agree you could learn stuff from them, even if they aren't murderers. So how do you want to do it? One on one?"

"No, thought about that, but makes more sense to start with a free-for-all. Get 'em all in a room and let peer pressure work. As I understand the place, they'll wanna demonstrate their complete transparency and ruthless commitment to truth. If those kids believe that shit the way you say they do—even when a lot of the grownups clearly don't—it may help 'em open up. So let's get your young honest Abe to set me up to meet with the assistants ASAP."

"Okay," Nora answered. "I'll get him on it. Anything I should know from the Demi meeting?"

"Oh right," Benny said. "That was an interesting one. First, dickhead Porter was right; they're definitely using this one-person grand jury thing. She didn't say exactly, but she said, if you take my meaning. Second, I have a strong feeling she's on team Nora, but her boss is pushing hard to make an arrest. This whole thing doesn't feel right to her—which it shouldn't to anyone who's not a moron—and I get the sense she's draggin' her feet a bit. Could be wrong, but that's what I left with."

"Interesting," Nora said. "I like her."

"Yeah, I know. But maybe too early to book a weekend in the Hamptons or some shit. It's just a sense I got. Like I said, I could be wrong."

Nora smiled. "You really are getting all Saugatuck, aren't you? 'Could be wrong, could be wrong.' Next thing, you'll be wearing a fleece sweatshirt and sitting on your foot."

Benny laughed. "Not at fucking gunpoint. Now go kiss your angel goodnight."

CHAPTER FIFTY

Jefferson Jepson's eyes nervously swept the little basement room, settling on Laslo, who motioned with his hand to the chair at mid-desk. "Hey, Jeffey, come on in. Take a seat."

Jeffey sat, bouncing both feet nervously while looking at Laslo and stealing glances to his left at Benny. He was a thin man, his narrow face and prominent cheekbones framed by dark hair in a shag cut.

"Looks like fuckin' Mick Jagger," Benny had told Nora when he first taped Jeffey's picture to the war room whiteboard. "How the hell does one twin look like he fronts for the Stones and the other looks like one of those Australian actor brothers?"

"Hemsworth," Nora said with a smile. "They're fraternal twins, Benny, the kind that aren't identical but born together."

"Whatever."

The investigators had decided to change their approach for the skittish Jeffey, with Laslo doing the questioning and not introducing Benny, who simply lurked in Jeffey's peripheral vision.

"Thanks for coming in," Laslo said gently. "We wanted to ask you about Helen. Could you start by telling us what you thought of her?"

"Sure," Jeffey responded, pulling down on the sleeve hems of his fleece as if his wrists were cold. "She was the main source of joy in this place. Nora brings some and so does Rob, but Helen was our sun."

"What do you mean?" Laslo asked.

"She was genuinely funny, which we don't have a lot of because humor is rooted in absurdities and contradictions and we're not supposed to have those in logic-land, but she saw them and had the guts to call them out, which was hilarious. To be honest, though, I didn't let on that I saw her humor and I feel a little guilty about that."

"Why didn't you?" Laslo asked quietly.

"I get plumbed enough about my logic. It's selfish, but I didn't want to volunteer for more plumbing. Still, I liked her and am sorry she's gone."

"She ever talk to you about your Chinese girlfriend?"

When Jeffey hesitated, Benny cleared his throat and Jeffey turned quickly toward the sound. Benny didn't speak, but arched his eyebrows. Jeffey turned back to Laslo.

"Yes," he mumbled. "It was a clusterfuck, but I was so grateful it was Helen who handled it."

"What do you mean?" Laslo asked.

"She came to me and laid out what Fang had done and that she was working for Chinese intelligence. Really, what I had *let* her do, without knowing I was letting her. She stole so much shit from us, put stuff on our systems, and all because I was an idiot. But Helen said there was no need for my dad to get involved. She would handle it, with the tech people like Rob."

"Really nice," Laslo said.

Jeffey pulled on his sleeves. "I actually think 'kind' is the best word. She didn't beat on me and plumb the shit out of me the way my old man would've. She just said she knew I hadn't done anything on purpose and that she would take care of it. Kind."

"Makes sense," Laslo said. "You know anything about the front-running investigation Helen was doing?"

"I've heard that term but I have no idea what it means. So, no."

"You do any trading using information about the company's planned trades?"

"I would have absolutely no idea how to do that. So, again, 'no' is the answer. You know my portfolio is facilities, real estate, and catering, right?"

Laslo paused and added, "Got it. Where were you the night Helen was killed?"

"I went to the sunset thing at Compo, then I hit bartaco over here on the river. I'm kinda regular there. Got pretty shit-faced. Took an Uber home. Be easy for you to check out."

"Okay," Laslo said, extending his hand, "thanks for coming down, Jeffey."

Jeffey shook Laslo's hand as he stood. Stealing a final glance at Benny, he left the room.

Laslo closed the door and turned back to Benny. "Whataya think?" he asked.

Benny chuckled. "That putz didn't kill her. But Helen was some operator. Gotta hand it to her. She had this kid by the short hairs for the rest of his life. And the best part is, he thinks it's 'kind' that she's got a fistful of his pubes. Impressive shit."

"Yup," Laslo said, shaking his head. "Helen not only didn't tell David about a Chinese spy getting access to this company, but she didn't even tell *me* and I'm in charge of goddamn security. And she sure as hell didn't tell the New Haven FBI that a fucking MSS agent was ass-deep in the world's largest hedge fund. Helen just fixed things on her own. Then she put Singh's reports in her private file and held Jeffey tighter. What a world."

"Lemme ask you somethin' else," Benny said. "Why all the drinking?"

"What do you mean?"

"I mean I'm all for knocking back a few, but this is like the third MC member talking about getting blind drunk. What gives?"

"Ah," Laslo said, "good eye. Took me a while to understand it, but I think it's a product of the culture here. In most places, work and life are on a spectrum from dead serious at one end to falling-down drunk at the other. But in between serious and unconscious on that scale are all the ways most people have fun—puns, jokes, pranks, storytelling, karaoke, shit like that. Here, the culture crushes humor and fun, both with logic and the number of hours they work, so the only outlet for a lot of them is at the far end of the scale: They drink until they fall down. Then they work twelve hours the next day and do it again."

Benny was quiet for a moment. "Actually kinda sad," he said. "Was gonna ask if you wanna grab a beer at the Shoe on the way home from the city tonight, but don't feel like it anymore."

Laslo smiled. "Fuck you. I'll pay. Maybe that'll help you work through it."

Benny returned the smile. "It's a damn good start. Assistants, Louis, then free beer."

CHAPTER FIFTY-ONE

Abe had removed the tables from one side of a large training room, filling the space with a dozen chairs arranged in a semicircle, and one for Benny in the mouth of the U. Laslo sat off to the side, behind the group. Benny waited outside for the seats to fill, one for each MC member's assistant—including the extra two assigned to David Jepson and Marcus Baum—and one for Louis Lambert's assistant. Helen's assistant, Tracey, also joined the group. When the twelve were seated, the big man walked in the room and sat facing them, his sockless shins visible, including the one with the gun in an ankle holster.

Benny skipped any introductions. Surely they knew who he was and he didn't care much who each of them were. Laslo could tell him later if it mattered.

"So why do you work at this fucked up place?" he began.

"It's not fucked up," said Sally, who was Rob's assistant. "At least not compared to the rest of the world." She held up her prosthetic arm. "I've been in some fucked-up places and left pieces of myself there. I was with some fucked-up organizations, where people didn't even *try* to tell each other the truth. What makes this place different is that we try, we really do."

"And we work hard," Abe added, "but we get paid better than any place else and we get treated with more respect, especially compared to other places in finance."

Benny sniffed at that. "Yeah, I don't wanna be talkin' outta school here, and my apologies to whichever of you works for Arty, but do the women really get treated with respect? 'Cause I've heard some things."

One of Marcus Baum's assistants, a twenty-eight-year-old woman, raised her hand and Benny nodded to her. "What you heard was real," she said. "Some bad stuff has happened, but people like Helen worked to shut it down."

There were nods all around the circle as she went on, especially from the women. "She *fought* for us," the woman continued, "in ways a lot of our colleagues don't realize. But we're in positions where we get to see things, so we know. Helen stood up for us. Arty didn't get fired, but he was better, and the place got better because of it."

Tracey raised her hand. Knowing she couldn't see him, Benny spoke. "Tracey?"

"That's true about Helen," she said, "but it was broader than stopping physical stuff. She had been at other companies in finance. She knew how they treat young people: Like some kind of disposable tool, to be thrown out after a short time, except for the ones who were in the boss's fraternity or eating club. I know it probably sounds like bullshit from the outside, but all the talk about community and meritocracy here is real. They push us hard, and if we don't cut it, they cut *us*, but if you can keep up, they want you to make a life here, no matter whose fraternity you were in, or what you look like. We're a private company, so we don't talk about it much, but it really is like the places you've read about—a Chobani or a Winnebago—where they'll pay you fairly; more than that here, actually—and the higher-ups want you to own a piece and share in the profits from your own effort. On some level, that makes it feel like we're family."

Abe jumped back in. "I'm not just saying this because of who my boss is, but the talent here is incredible. Sure, we have weird aunts and uncles, like any family, but it *is* a family, except without a lot of the pathologies in other corporate families."

He looked in both directions at his colleagues before continuing. "And maybe one other thing that's hard to talk about: A lot of us are different, both physically and neurologically. We aren't typical, we aren't like other people. But here it's only about what we can do. That's pretty cool."

David Jepson's junior assistant, a thirty-year-old man, raised his hand. "I'm guessing in your investigation you've seen some warts on our senior leaders. And that's too bad. But, in a way, *they* aren't this place. *We* are this place. There are hundreds of us who work hard, don't lie to each other or motherfuck each other, and really want to do the right thing. Some of us will stay, some of us will go do other things, but all of us will be glad we were here and knew each other. And tried to live in a way most people don't."

"Tracey?" Benny said when he saw her hand again.

She pointed in the direction of the previous speaker. "You won't hear what Ben just said at other companies. It just doesn't exist. *That* is what makes this place special. That kind of people. Whether you leave here after three years or stay forever, you'll be glad you came."

Benny chuckled. "Okay, you guys are startin' to make me wish I was young and smart, and I'm neither. I'm here just tryin' to do my job, so I gotta ask you: Who killed Helen? You're tellin' me this is one big family and I'm tellin' *you* that murder happens in families all the time. Help me with your big brains. I need answers sooner rather than later."

There was a long silence before Abe spoke. "I think the reason we're quiet is that we don't guess and we don't gossip. I can tell you for sure that Nora didn't do it because I know her character and I would bet my life on it. But I don't have any facts that would let me tell you who I think did it. I'm guessing nobody else does, either."

Benny could see nods all around the semicircle. "So you don't know," he said, moving his head to look at each of them.

"That the truth?" he asked.

Every head nodded.

"Of course, if any of you did it, you wouldn't tell me because you would've decided the commitment to truth is bullshit. How's my logic?"

Nobody in the horseshoe answered, but a loud voice came from the side. "Impeccable," Laslo said. "You're smarter than you let on."

Benny stared at the silent group, then spoke, his voice loud and agitated. "Oh, c'mon people, do the right thing here. I'm not gonna hold you to anything but I need some thinking. Good police work starts with hunches or suspicions and then searches for facts to prove or disprove. Hunch with me."

Some of the assistants shifted in their seats, so Benny kept pushing and stayed loud. "Dirty Arty? Freaky Louie Lambert? What about the Jepson brats, especially Thing 1 and Thing 2? And don't tell me you don't call them that, even if it's in your own head."

He waited a beat and then gave his final push. "A woman is dead here, people! Throat cut ear to ear. You know Nora didn't do it. So who the fuck did? Give me something."

Tracey couldn't see how uncomfortable her colleagues were. "Tracey," Benny called, "think out loud with me."

She leaned forward on her chair. "Well, Helen wasn't a big woman, but it would take someone pretty strong to move her around the way they say she was moved. That's another reason I don't think Nora did it, in addition to not being stupid enough to do all the things they say she did. But Arty is strong enough. Lord knows he tried to grab enough of us before Helen shut him down. And Chip Jepson is damn strong too. Enough to do it on his own or maybe with his brother's help."

She paused before adding, "Again, I'd like to stress that my comments came in response to your request for speculation."

"Thank you, Tracey," Benny answered. "Yes, speculation, that's what I want. And that's part of why we aren't taping this. Who's next?"

Abe spoke. "As long as we're talking about strength, what about Louis? I know he thought Nora stole his job and that Helen engineered that. There was always a hell of a cold front between him and them."

With that, the floodgates opened. Suddenly Benny was refereeing a free-for-all of guesses and suspicions, some educated, some wild. The conversation went on for another hour before Benny called a halt. It was as hard to stop as it had been to start.

"Okay, whoa, whoa, whoa, thanks everybody. That's just great. You've given us a ton to think about. Appreciate the brainstorming. And, listen, let's keep this little session to ourselves for now, capisce?"

Every head nodded as the assistants stood and filed out of the training room. Laslo made his way toward Benny through the departing crowd, thanking each of them for their help. When the room cleared, he looked at Benny with wide eyes. "Wow, you got them going."

Benny smiled broadly. "Turns out the saints of Saugatuck love gossip as much as the rest of us."

Laslo returned the smile. "But you said it wasn't gossip. Brainstorming, you said."

"Right, right, I forgot," Benny chuckled. "Brainstorming. That's what it was."

Laslo got serious for a moment. "I was impressed how many of these folks think Louis might have done it."

"Yeah, me too," Benny replied. "And perfect timing 'cause we get to see the whites of that weirdo's eyes this fine evening, amiright?"

"You are correct," Laslo said. "Field trip into the big city."

"I'm drivin'," Benny said.

"Wouldn't dream of having it otherwise," Laslo said in a mock serious tone. "I live for another chance to hear you shout at your fellow New Yorkers."

CHAPTER FIFTY-TWO

Pomander Walk ran between Ninety-Fourth and Ninety-Fifth streets, midblock just west of Broadway on Manhattan's Upper West Side. The tiny make-believe–looking development of attached two-story Tudor-style homes was built one hundred years earlier to replicate a London theater set and had somehow survived the onslaught of high-rise apartment buildings. And although the occasional celebrity took up residence—including, most recently, a famous woman accused of murder—most of its life had been spent the way its residents intended—out of view.

After depositing his NYFD plaque on the front dash, Benny stood with Laslo on the dark sidewalk examining the intercom system next to the tight metal mesh of the street entrance. He ran his finger down the row of names. "There's our guy," he told Laslo, pointing to the name "L. Lambert" next to one of the little black buttons. He withdrew his hand.

"You gonna ring him?" Laslo asked.

"Nah, makes it too easy for him to ignore us. Rather get in there and bang on his door. So we wait."

About five minutes later, a well-dressed woman came toward the gate from the inside. Benny lifted his phone to his ear and began a loud and imaginary conversation as she reached the gate.

"Okay, Mr. Lambert, that's fine. One of your neighbors is coming out now. Got it. We'll meet you at your front door."

The woman glanced up at Benny and smiled, holding the gate's door open for him. "Thank you, ma'am," he said. "Have a great evening."

"Works every time," Benny whispered to Laslo as they walked casually up the paved path between the two rows of faux-Tudor town houses, stepping around the imitation London streetlamp as they looked for Lambert's door.

"There," Benny said, hopping up the three steps to the front stoop, where he began knocking on the blue arch-top door.

A voice came from inside. "Who is it?"

"Louis, it's Laslo and Benny from work," Benny said.

"Who?"

"Saugatuck? Working for David Jepson? Ring a bell? Don't wanna cause a scene here, Lou."

The door opened enough for Lambert to peek around it and Laslo noticed Benny slide a loafer-clad foot into the opening. "What do you want so late?" Louis asked.

"Mr. Jepson just wants us to ask you a few questions. Won't take but a minute."

"Can't we do it tomorrow?"

"Jepson strike you as somebody who takes 'later' for an answer?"

Lambert paused and then swung the door fully open. "Come in," he said in a morose voice.

As they followed Louis down the center hallway, Benny's head turned side to side, taking in the rooms they were passing. "Whoo-eee," he said loudly. "You got some amazing art here, Louis."

Louis stopped and turned back, a look of pleasure on his face. "You know art, Mister—"

"Dugan, but it's Benny. Only secondhand. I locked up a bunch of art thieves back in the day. Including one who was supposed to be the world's best. Learned a bit by osmosis."

"Oh," Louis said, turning to continue the walk to the back, "I was assuming you were a collector or student."

"That a Chagall?" Benny asked, pointing at a stained glass hanging in the hall.

Louis stopped again. "It is indeed," he said. "So you *do* know art."

"Well," Benny said, "again, just a little. But I've always appreciated the way he used his lead strips to connect so many different hues of the same primary color and in ways that seem chaotic, but really aren't, if you take the time to actually look."

"Well, do come in," Louis said brightly, gesturing toward the back room. "I don't get many visitors, but it's nice to have one who can see clearly and appreciates the complexity of true art."

Behind Louis's back, Laslo turned to Benny and bobbed his head side to side while miming a pretentious face. "Easy," Benny whispered. "I flipped a perp who loved Chagall, that's all."

"So you live in the city full-time?" Benny asked as he dropped onto the couch with Laslo. "Not just on weekends like the rest of the Westport crowd?"

"That's right," Louis said. "I don't mind the reverse commute and the suburbs are a wasteland in the visual arts."

Laslo reached into his bag, retrieved a file folder, and passed it to Benny. Louis's eyes tracked the file's journey, but he didn't speak.

Benny let the silence linger, opening the file on his lap, and flipping loudly through pages of paper. At last, he looked up. "Helen had a file on you, did you know that?"

"I did not."

"Had 'em on a lot of people at the company, know that?"

"I did not. And if you are speaking about Saugatuck company records that might be relevant to the matter of Helen's death, I should have been made aware of them and they should have been reviewed to see if they were pertinent to law enforcement requests."

"Yeah," Benny said, dismissively. "This is us making you aware, but these were personal with Helen, or so it seems."

"Well that's a determination that should be made by competent counsel and—"

Benny cut him off. "Helen had a thought about you," he began, swinging his arm to indicate the walls of Louis's home. "Her thought was that all of this was a fuckload more art than a man of your means could afford. She had a thought that you lived here in this very expensive little gated slice of old London so no Saugatuck types got a glimpse of your, uh, collection. She had a thought that you bought all this using money you stole by abusing Saugatuck's confidential trade information."

When Louis didn't react, Benny added, "So *you* got any thoughts? About her thoughts, I mean?"

"I do not," he said, flatly.

Benny flipped a page and began counting lines of text with his index finger. "She's got you in the market six, seven, *eight* times making the same moves Saugatuck is making, at right about the same time. Now, I'm no expert, but seems sensible for her to be thinking you were front running your employer, no?"

"It would not be sensible for her to think that," he said calmly, "for a variety of reasons. First, those records appear to be from my own trading account, in my own name, which I was required, like all employees, to provide to the company quarterly. I'd be a poor front runner to be doing it in my own name and then turning it over.

"Second, it's logical that my trades would occasionally mirror Saugatuck's because part of my job is to read the daily newsletter sent to all clients, in which Saugatuck offers its view of world events, asset classes, and various market segments. It's logical that, from time to time, my trades would line up with the company's because both were the product of that same worldview. Saugatuck's particular trades, of course, would be driven by its own algorithms, which I did not have access to, but if the company told clients the US energy sector was about to decline, it would make sense that both I and the company might sell the same oil stocks at the same time."

Louis sniffed and added, "Lastly, I would need far more than I ever made in the markets to purchase the art you see here."

"So you believe in coincidences?" Benny asked.

"Well," Louis replied, "it's logical that two similar events could coincide without being causally related, so, in that sense, yes, I do. And here there is a logical explanation for occasional similar trades."

"Did Helen tell you she thought you were front running and using the dough to buy all this art?"

"She did not."

"Where did you get the money?"

"I'd prefer not to say."

"Where were you the night Helen was killed?"

"I'd prefer not to say."

Benny's face flared red and his words came out rapid-fire. "You motherless fuck. A woman's dead and an innocent woman is being set up for a fucking murder and you think I'm gonna take that for an answer?"

Louis leaned slightly back in his chair, as if to get away from the angry big man. "I'm sorry Helen is dead. I did not kill her. I don't have a view on whether Nora did or not. And despite your evident emotion, I decline to discuss my personal finances or my whereabouts with you."

Benny stayed red. "You hate Nora Carleton, don't you?"

"I do not. She seems like a person of integrity, which I admire. I simply think she is not the best possible general counsel. She is merely the best we have. And those are different things, which I thought Saugatuck understood."

Laslo jumped in. "Who would be the best general counsel?"

"I believe I would be, for reasons I would be happy to detail."

Benny snorted. "Hard pass, pal."

Laslo leaned forward on the couch, speaking in a quiet voice. "So if hiring Nora was inconsistent with Saugatuck's commitment to always hire the best, how did that happen?"

"I believe Helen engineered it and then built some sort of alliance with Nora, and the two of them with Rob Arslan. That's another thing that should not happen at Saugatuck. Alliances are, by definition, based on considerations other than transparent facts."

Benny's face was returning to its normal color. "So you hated them all."

"No," Louis replied, "and I know it can be difficult for people not to project emotions onto relationships, but I bore them no ill will. I simply thought their conduct was inconsistent with our values. I wouldn't kill them or frame them. I would just prefer they not act that way and, were it up to me, they would not work at Saugatuck. But it is not up to me."

Benny slapped the folder closed and handed it to Laslo before standing. "Okay, this is a waste of time." He stepped toward Louis, who was still in his chair, and loomed over him. "But let me make you an unemotional promise here, Louis. I find out you're lyin', that you had any part of killin' Helen or jammin' Nora, I'm gonna smash that Chagall over your tiny head and then feed you the pieces. Put that in your fuckin' logic pipe and smoke it."

With that, Benny led Laslo through the house, calling over his shoulder, "We'll show ourselves out."

Laslo paused midway down the center hall to admire a landscape photograph, but Benny turned and tugged his jacket sleeve. "C'mon, we're wastin' our time," he growled.

When the sidewalk gate clanged shut behind them, Laslo laughed. "Jesus, Benny, you're supposed to play *bad cop*, not goddamn Thanos. Threatening to break his art over his head? Feed him pieces of stained glass? Whoa."

"Yeah," Benny said quietly, "I went too far. But something about talking to that computer dick just frosted my flakes." He shook his head and added, "I'll be a lamb at our next stop."

"What's next?" Laslo asked, walking to the front passenger door.

"Gotta see an old friend for some help on Daddy Jepson's fancy apartment building."

Benny steered to the curb on the north side of Fifty-Seventh Street near Sixth Avenue, just in front of the former Steinway piano store, which had somehow sprouted the world's thinnest skyscraper out of its roof. He rolled his window down and waved to an attractive, professionally dressed Black woman in her thirties who was standing in front of the entrance on Fifty-Seventh Street's "billionaires row."

The woman walked around to the driver's side and leaned toward the open window. "Hey big man, how's Nora holding up?"

"She's doin' okay, considering," Benny said before turning to his passenger. "Hey, Jessica, this is Laslo Reiner, working with me to help Nora. Laslo, this is FBI Special Agent Jessica Watson. Laslo is retired Bu and Saugatuck's head of security. And a friend to Nora."

Jessica reached across Benny to shake Laslo's hand. "Great to meet any friend of Nora. Where you retired out of?"

"New Haven," Laslo said. "Did first office here, then escaped to the burbs."

"Hah," Jessica replied. "I haven't escaped yet, but I just got moved to a terrorism squad."

"Seriously?" Benny asked. "We lost you in our battle against organized crime?"

"Unfortunately, you have," Jessica answered, "but now it's the battle against people who want to blow stuff up. So still seems like good work."

"It is, it is," Benny said. "Gonna miss you, though. I'll tell Nora you said hey. You get what we talked about?"

"Yup," Jessica said, pulling a thumb drive from her jacket pocket. "All cameras for the entire building for the Sunday you asked about, and the next day."

"Awesome," Benny said, taking the drive and handing it to Laslo before lifting his chin to the building. "I called Jessica to see if the New York office had any hooks that might help us here in zillionaire land. Turns out she had the mother of all connections: Her training agent retired when they opened this place, became head of security."

Laslo leaned forward so he could see Jessica. "Many thanks. We'll protect our source."

"Appreciate that," Jessica answered. She dropped her palm on the open car windowsill. "Stay in touch and thanks for keeping me on team Nora. Let me know if I can do anything else to help."

"Will do," Benny said, putting the car in gear and pulling away.

CHAPTER FIFTY-THREE

Benny yawned loudly and stretched, just as Nora stepped into the basement war room. "Keeping you up, Mr. Rough?" she asked.

"Listen, Ms. Smooth, it's been a long stretch of talking to strange Sauga-fuckites. Hope they pay you a shit ton of money to work with these geeks."

Nora smiled. "They do. Got a wine room, don't I?"

"Too tired to fight for my room name," Benny said.

"You can sleep as soon as you give me the report."

"Simple," Benny replied. "Jeffey is squirrelly as shit but confirmed he was banging a Chinese spy when she wasn't sticking thumb drives into his computers. Helen found out about it and demonstrated her kindness by not telling Daddy."

"Think he hurt her?"

"Hell no. Thought of her as the mother he never really had. I gather there was a lot to like about Helen, but that woman had ol' Jeffey in a squeeze and he never even felt it."

"The assistants?"

"Good group of young people. I got 'em goin' and they brainstormed with me for a long time, but we didn't solve nothin'. Still, was worth it to get their juices goin'."

"And my buddy Louis in the city?"

"Lucky I didn't punch his lights out."

"Do tell," Nora said with a grin. "It's not like you to have violent feelings."

Benny walked Nora through the visit to Pomander Walk. "So, end of the day," he finished, "I'm not sure what to make of him. Won't talk about money or alibi. Anybody else, that would be lighting yourself on fire. Him? Seems weirdly consistent with innocence, for reasons I can't fully explain."

"And you said you saw Jessica?"

"Yeah, she sends her love. They moved her to a counterterrorism squad. Not sure what terrorist groups she's working, but she seems good. And she did us a solid getting the feed from the cameras. Laslo and I already went through all of it."

"And?"

"Daddy Jepson and Chip both go to the client shindig at the eightieth floor duplex—which is frickin' enormous, by the way. David doesn't leave until the next morning, which checks out with what he told us."

"And Chip?"

"That's the strange one. Despite what the prick told us, he leaves after the guests do, about nine. Gets in what looks to be an Uber out front. He comes back at about one A.M., and then leaves again about eight A.M., an hour after his father does."

"What do you make of it?"

"Hard to say at this point, but he's sure as shit not at the duplex when Helen is killed. He's out and about. Now, whether he's out to Westport and then back like that *Crawdads* thing Laslo talked about—and I meant it when I said I would watch that even though it looks like a chick movie—we can't say at this point. But the little date-rapist piece of shit was lying when he said he spent the whole night at Daddy's fancy apartment house."

"How are you going to track it down?"

Benny smiled. "If I was workin' for the government, I would hit Uber with a subpoena and then get his phone pings and keep serving subpoenas until I have him nailed, but we're not here from the government, as they say, so I'm thinking we just bluff him. He don't know what we got, so I think Laslo and I take another run at him. See what he does."

Nora nodded. "Makes sense. What's your gut telling you?"

"Honestly?" Benny said. "I'm not trustin' the gut much on this. I don't think I have enough experience with Sauga-fuck rich people. If he was some guy in a tracksuit standin' in front of a social club in Brooklyn, I could tell you his next three moves and what hair gel he uses. These Richie Riches? No gut feelin' for them, so I'm just gonna keep hammerin' until something comes loose. Ya got a better idea?"

"Nope, I got nothing to add to that. Except you do realize that I'm employed by Saugatuck and you calling it Sauga-fuck is not hitting my funny bone tonight." Nora paused, then said, "But I'm just really tired. I'm grateful, Benny. I don't know what I'd do without you. I just—" She stopped, her voice choked off by emotion.

Benny looked in pain. "Hey, hey, none a that from the great Ms. Smooth. Everything's gonna be okay. You got a team. Me, Carmen, Jessica, we're always here for you. Even dickhead Porter. I can't imagine what it feels like to be you right now, but we're gonna set this right."

Nora nodded, her eyes filled with tears.

"Now go get some rest," he added. "Think those happy thoughts you're always tellin' your little girl to keep in her head at bedtime."

Nora stood and sniffled as she turned to the doorway. "Okay, I'll do that. You too—okay, Mr. Rough?"

"I'm on it, Ms. Smooth," he answered, pointing in the direction of the basement guest room. "Five more minutes here and then I'm in my fancy Connecticut bed over there.

"Oh, hey," he called after Nora. She stuck her head back in the doorway. "You sure you're okay with me hangin' around for Thanksgiving? I'll be with my boys at Christmas but I could also make the drive out to Long Island to eat turkey with Calvin and his wife and little Claire. She's old enough now to appreciate her grandfather's humor."

"Wow, she must be really mature," Nora said with a smile, "but we really want you here. Also, with Nick and Vicki coming, we'll have a crowd anyway. And you'll be a distraction from any awkwardness, you know, with Vicki's pregnancy and all. The three women of this house would miss you if you ditched us for Thanksgiving." She grinned and added, "Especially my mom."

"Okay, okay," Benny said. "Enough of that. I'll be here. Lookin' forward to it. Sleep well. I'll let you know how it goes with our boy Chip. And I'm also gonna pull Louis in again. After we left the city tonight, a little bird told me something that I want to shove up Spock's ass."

"Well that's quite the tease, Mr. Rough."

"Yeah, sorry 'bout that, but I need to protect my source so I can keep back channels open."

Nora shook her head with a smile. "I'm too tired to want to know about your channel and how it connects to Louis's butt. At the appropriate time, though?"

"Of course. Sleep tight."

CHAPTER FIFTY-FOUR

"**S**o where is he?" Benny asked.

"His assistant says he hasn't seen him and can't reach him," Laslo replied. "He already missed a couple meetings this morning."

"Son of a bitch. You think he got wind we have tape of him coming and going the night Helen was killed?"

"Maybe. He's gotta know that's why we want to chat."

"Okay," Benny said, "Let's grab Louis, then see what we can do about layin' hands on Chippy."

<hr/>

"Thanks for coming down, Louis," Benny said, staring at the awkward lawyer seated at the midline of the desk. "Just a quick follow-up for you."

Louis nodded but didn't speak.

"Somebody sent the cops a video of Nora and Helen kissing a couple years ago. That you?"

Louis didn't answer. Instead he seemed to shrink as he looked across the desk to the blank wall, letting out an audible sigh. The room was quiet—even for Saugatuck—but Benny filled the silence.

"You know what? Don't answer. Let me instead share my knowledge of the intersection of technology and the law of search and seizure.

Maybe not your specialty. Did you know that whenever your phone is on, Google is keeping track of it, whether they made the phone or even if you just have one of their apps? Even if you wouldn't dream of sending an email or surfin' the web, Google still knows exactly where it is and how fast it's moving. Amazing. You with me so far?"

Louis's expression did not change.

"Excellent. And here's the *really* cool part: A judge can order Google to produce a record of what phones were at a particular spot on a particular date in a particular time window. It's called geofencing. Questions to this point?"

Louis didn't react.

"Okay, good, good. Now we get closer to home, to coin a phrase. We know Nora and Helen kissed at the corner of Pequot Avenue and Westway Road two years ago, 'cause we've seen the film and talked to Nora. But, pretty vague time frame, right? Except we know from the magic of restaurant payment records the exact day they were at Artisan and what time they paid the check. And we know it's a fifteen-minute walk to the corner where they kissed. So we know the window in which to ask what phones were near that corner. We know when and where to look. Pretty exciting, dontcha think?"

Louis shifted in his seat.

"Contain yourself; we're almost there. And do you know whose phone was at the corner when the two women were, when a video of them was taken that was later sent to the cops? A place nowhere near his fucking home or work?"

Benny now leaned forward to stare at Louis, who still did not react.

"Your phone, motherfucker! Your phone was there, in your fucking stalker hands! Videotaping two women out for a walk! That's what this magical intersection of technology and law tells us. So what's your answer there, Louie? Are you the creep following two women around and takin' videos? And remember, this is the land of truth, so you better tell it like it is."

Louis paused, then said, "It was I who took that video, and I sent it to the police after Helen was murdered."

"Why'd you do that?"

"The recording or sending it to the police?" Louis asked.

"Both'd be swell," Benny replied.

"I made that video on my phone one night after seeing them having dinner in Southport. I was interested in the nature of their relationship—because I could not understand how Nora was hired over me on the merits. I made the video because it was relevant to that question. I seemed to be the only one who saw the inappropriateness of Helen's feelings toward Nora. I kept the recording as a reminder that things were not aboveboard with those two and ultimately decided to send it to the authorities because it seemed relevant to their investigation. Let's not forget that Helen was found murdered in a canoe belonging to Nora and, in my view, she remains the prime suspect."

Benny blew air out of his nose. "Well thanks for sharing, Louie, but I'm thinkin' maybe you were so angry that *you* killed Helen. And then *you* put her in Nora's canoe and then *you* sent your creepy spy video to the police to jam her. How'm I doin' so far?"

Now Louis's voice rose for the first time. He didn't answer Benny but instead turned to look at Laslo. "I did *not* kill Helen and I am offended by the accusation, especially in this setting, when I have been nothing but honest. Additionally, the police have my alibi and I am *not* a suspect no matter what this, this—outsider says."

The room was silent until Laslo spoke, looking at Benny. "I can see a variety of areas in which plumbing Louis would seem to make sense, don't you agree?"

Benny answered in his flattest Saugatuck monotone. "I very much agree further plumbing may be in order, but I'd prefer it take place at the MC."

"Logical," Laslo answered. He turned to Louis and arched both eyebrows. "To be continued. Thanks for coming down, Louis."

Louis looked genuinely confused, but didn't speak. Instead, he gently slid his chair back, stood to hitch up his belted jeans, and walked from the room.

When he was gone, Laslo lifted his feet onto his side of the desk. "Son of a bitch. That was a thing of beauty. And please tell me you weren't making up the geofence stuff?"

"Ha," Benny answered, "I protect my sources, but that juice was worth the squeeze, eh?"

Laslo whistled quietly. "Sure was. Now we gotta figure out what to do with it."

CHAPTER FIFTY-FIVE

Nora was up early to meet with her lawyers. "I think I should testify before this grand jury judge," she said, her eyes darting back and forth between Carmen and Porter Raleigh.

They both started to speak, but Nora raised her hand. "I know, I know, but hear me out."

She pointed at Porter. "You said Judge Robinson is a solid person who cares about getting it right."

"I did," he replied, "and he is."

Now she turned to Carmen. "And you've always said I make a good impression, which I took to mean you think my inner goodness is reflected outwardly, but if it's something more hurtful than that, please don't tell me."

"I have," Carmen said with a smile. "And it was what you thought."

"So he's a good person, with whom I can connect, and he doesn't have the power to charge me anyway, right? All he can do is recommend that I be charged or not be charged. What do I have to lose?"

"You have a lot to lose here," Porter said. "Whatever he recommends, the State's Attorney is going to do. That's the whole reason she went this route—so somebody else would take the hit, either way. She's going to do what he says."

"Agree you have a lot to lose," Carmen added, "like giving them a roadmap to testimony you might give at trial. Like making a false statement—without intending to—that they later say was evidence of your consciousness of guilt."

"I get all that," Nora responded, her eyes now moist. "I really do. But I didn't kill Helen and if I can get one on one with Judge Robinson, he's not going to recommend they indict me. I just know it. And I'd rather take my swing now, in secret. If I wait until I'm charged, I'm ruined and Sophie will never get over it. Even if I get acquitted at trial."

Both lawyers studied the kitchen table until Nora added, "Look, just think about it. I'm sitting here on indefinite leave from work doing home repair projects and am available whenever you decide to let me talk to Judge Robinson. In the meantime, I agree with your plan of trying to get some of the motive stuff from Helen's files in front of him."

"Oh, it'll definitely get to him," Porter said, "if we give it to the State's Attorney. The law requires her to provide the one-person grand jury with evidence that might tend to support innocence. Again, though, we'll be giving up stuff we might otherwise surprise them with during your trial if they indicted you."

"Got it," Nora answered sharply. "Again, I am really keen not to be indicted. Really, really keen."

"The trick," Carmen added, "is going to be getting Saugatuck's sign-off on doing the selective sharing. And we *will* need their consent. Benny signed a nondisclosure—and, of course, he would break it for you in a second—but we don't want to go there. We're gonna see if we can get David Jepson to green-light some sharing."

Nora arched her eyebrows. "Now *that* would surprise me. He's all about internal transparency but this is some mighty dirty laundry to be hanging on the line for the world to see."

"Well, not the world," Porter said, "just Judge Robinson and the State's Attorney. Remember, the same kind of secrecy rules apply to this that you're used to with the federal grand jury system. So it's more like letting a couple folks peek over the fence at your laundry."

"I still agree Jepson will be reluctant," Carmen said, "but I think if we start with your buddy Louis Lambert we may get somewhere."

Now Nora just looked confused. Carmen chuckled. "Seriously. Porter and I think there's a strong logical argument that the content of the files doesn't belong to the company. If he's as logic-driven as you say, I hope we may have some luck."

"So do I," Nora said, shaking her head. "So do I."

"I still don't understand your claim that Helen's files don't belong to the company," Louis said, his voice coming through the speaker in Porter's strip-mall office.

"Simple," Porter answered, "she didn't use Saugatuck resources to create them, she never mentioned their existence to anyone at Saugatuck, they were intended to further her own interests, not the company's, and they have not been in the company's possession since her death."

"Well that's not correct," he replied. "As I understand what you told me, they were locked in her office until her assistant removed them and took them home, after which she gave them to Nora."

"That's right," Carmen said, "but being physically on the premises doesn't, alone, make them Saugatuck's property. I'm sure there's lots of stuff around your office that is yours even though it's on company real estate. I understand you collect art. If you bring a piece to the office, it doesn't become Saugatuck's."

"No doubt," Louis said evenly, "but these files were about Saugatuck's employees and their conduct on company trips or at company events. It feels more like an Edward Hopper–type portrait of Saugatuck's interior that I painted in my office during business hours."

"Look, Louis," Carmen said, "we may not convince you, but I'm not sure what your remedy is here. We propose to tell the State's Attorney that Benny Dugan has exculpatory evidence, which will force her to call him as a witness. Of course, it's hearsay because Benny didn't write any of the reports and his knowledge is based on reading them and interviewing witnesses, but hearsay is admissible in the grand jury. She has to call him."

"And his nondisclosure agreement?"

"He's going to try to avoid saying anything he learned from interviewing Saugatuck employees. We will be transparent about that with Aileen Shapiro. Of course, if she wants to force him to, she can, because a grand jury subpoena beats an NDA."

"And when she subpoenas him for the actual files?"

"We'll turn them over," Carmen said.

The phone line was quiet for several beats before Porter spoke up. "Look, let me give you a peek at our strategy. All we want to do is show this grand jury—this judge—that there are a whole lot of other people with motives in this case, something Nora lacks. We think this will be enough to kill any accusations against her. If we're wrong, we can fight with you and Shapiro about what's admissible after indictment. We won't hold anything you do here against you at that stage, but we have to try to end it now."

"I see, "Louis said. "And the front-running investigation, which I also knew nothing about until an unpleasant visit to my home from Mr. Dugan?"

"Not going to touch it with Aileen or in Benny's testimony. That's clearly Saugatuck information, clearly covered by Benny's NDA. So it stays off the table until we talk about it down the road, if it ever gets that far. This is just about showing the judge there are a lot of other suspects."

There was another long delay before Louis spoke again. "And doesn't that include me?"

"It does," Porter answered forcefully. "Sorry, man, but if you're in the files, you're on the list." He paused before adding, "Look, we don't think you have any remedy to stop us from this limited disclosure to the grand jury, but we wanted to give you a heads-up so you, and your client, knew we were being surgical and so you, and your client, would know we're also being reasonable."

"I'll talk to David," Louis said and hung up.

Porter reached and pressed the button to end the call on his end just as Carmen got up and walked to the huge front window of his office space, looking up and down the sidewalk. "Wow. I thought you were kidding about being between a Subway and the cleaners. You hungry?"

CHAPTER FIFTY-SIX

Benny came up the basement stairs to a busy kitchen. "I'm so sorry," he said, not making clear whether he was apologizing to Nora, Sophie, or Teresa, who were each occupied doing something. "I had no idea things got started so early. I heard all the talk about the Macy's Parade last night and figured I needed to be up before that."

"Hi, Benny," Sophie said, holding up two hands covered in flour. "Nana says we have to get the pies started before we see the first balloon. You can help. Wanna try the new apple peeler?"

"If you'll show me what that is," he answered, grinning.

"Let Benny get a cup of coffee," Nora said. "We have time. And then you can show him the peeler."

"Morning, Benny," Teresa said. "No pressure at all. We're just glad you'll be joining us."

"Mornin', Teresa," he answered. "Glad to be here. Just let me know how to help. Low-skill positions only, please."

A marching band on Thirty-Fourth Street blared from the TV as Sophie led Benny to the corner of the big kitchen, where she scrambled up on a stool to reach the counter surface. Next to the toaster sat a foot-tall appliance that resembled a rocket launchpad, complete with service tower and two thin perpendicular swing arms.

"Watch this!" she said, jamming a large Granny Smith apple down on the spiked base before moving one of the arms onto the top of the apple, which was now securely in place. Next she swung the spring-loaded second arm so it pressed against the apple.

"Watch those fingers, little girl!" Nora called.

Sophie looked up at Benny and rolled her eyes, before glancing back down to press a button on the side of the launchpad. The apple began spinning and the spring arm, which was equipped with a sharp-tipped blade, began spitting a linguini-looking string of apple skin as it stripped the spinning fruit.

"Ta da!" Sophie announced, releasing the power button and freeing the newly peeled apple from the capturing arms.

Benny was genuinely amazed. "Are you fricking kidding me?" he said, scooping up the long continuous apple peel.

"We don't say 'frick,' Benny," Sophie answered.

As if to appeal, he looked quickly at Nora, who denied the challenge. "We don't. That's right, Sophie."

Benny smiled. "My bad," he said. "Can I do one?"

"Of course," Sophie answered, handing him a fresh apple. "Nana needs at least six for every pie. And we can do the potatoes with this too."

"You just rocked my world, Soph," Benny said. "I could do this all day."

As the eight-year-old and the enormous man set to work, Benny made conversation.

"So how do you feel about becoming a big sister?" he asked.

"I don't know, Benny. I'm a little nervous, I guess."

"You're gonna do great, Soph."

"I hope so," she answered, "but we won't have the same mom so it'll be different than a real sister."

Benny thought for a moment, then said, "Well, kiddo, this old guy's been around the block a few times and learned a lot about families and I think you're wrong there, Soph. World's got all kinds of families, in all shapes and sizes. Love is what makes a family and I've seen how much of that stuff you and your family got. Your little sis is a lucky kid and she's gonna learn a ton from you."

Sophie smiled. "You sound like Mom and Nana."

Benny grinned back at her. "Most important stuff I know I learned from your mom." He smiled and winked at Teresa. "And your nana."

The parade was over, the television was off, and the kitchen was almost clean when the driveway sensor chimed. "That'll be Nick and Vicki," Nora called, wiping her hands and heading for the front door.

Nick parked a new silver car in the driveway, jumped from the driver's door, and rushed around to open Vicki's door, offering her a hand to help her out.

She just started her second trimester for God's sake, Nora thought.

Vicki had her highlighted blonde hair pulled tightly back in a ponytail. She wore a soft gray wool shawl over a teal-blue knee-length maternity dress with tights and black boots.

She looks gorgeous, but a little early for a maternity dress, dontcha think? No, no, cut the shit and be nice. Vicki is Sophie's stepmother and that baby is her half sibling. We're gonna love our way through this.

"Range Rover!" Nora called. "Fancy stuff."

"Vicki's dad gave it to us as an early baby gift," Nick said, beaming. "Pretty sweet ride."

He still resembled Nora's high school boyfriend—and the father of her child—but somehow he seemed more grown-up as he crossed the driveway, one hand under his wife's forearm, helping her watch her step, the other holding a wine gift bag.

Maybe it's the hair or the outfit, Nora thought. His normally unruly black hair was combed and seemed to be parted with the assistance of gel or something. His familiar hoodie and jeans had been replaced with khakis and a button-down shirt and a leather jacket. He was wearing actual leather shoes instead of his usual Vans.

Nora couldn't help herself. "And look at you, dressing like an adult."

"Thanks," he said with a broad smile.

"Nick's a manager now," Vicki explained. "My dad says he's killing it. He'll probably be running the place in a few years. Maybe they'll be bigger than Saugatuck by then."

Vicki's father ran an investment management company that apparently had big dreams.

"Maybe," Nora said. "With Nick at the helm, who knows where they can go."

Vicki squinted, as if she just got a whiff of sarcasm. "That's right," she said, "sky's the limit."

Nora gave them each a quick hug and held the door open. "Happy Thanksgiving. We're so glad you're here. Mom and Sophie are finishing in the kitchen. Turkey's cooking. Oh, and my friend Benny Dugan is joining us. He just finished setting the table. Come on in."

Nick, Sophie, Teresa, and Benny were in the family room watching the
Dallas Cowboys beat the perennially hapless New York Giants. Nora
didn't care about football, but she loved watching her mother root for
the Giants, who played in New Jersey not far from the family's roots in
Hoboken. So she was mildly annoyed when Vicki steered her toward
the living room just as she headed for the empty spot on the sectional
facing the TV.

"I thought we could catch up," she said. "You know, mom talk."

*Seriously, woman, you are barely four months pregnant. I pushed that
little human over there out of my body while you were still in high school.
Maybe we wait on our "mom talk" until you catch up?*

"Sure," Nora said with a tight smile, turning away from the game
and heading for the living room. Vicki sat at one end of what Sophie
called "the nice couch" and patted the cushion next to her, but Nora
took the third cushion. Vicki quickly scooted over next to her, their
knees now almost touching.

"Thank you so much for having us here for Thanksgiving. It means
a lot to me. And I'm so excited—and more than a little nervous—that
Sophie's going to have a sister. I just hope I can do it."

Nora touched her knee. "You can definitely do it. You'll be great,
Vicki. I was nervous, too, but it'll be fine." She paused, then added,
"And I appreciate the way you talk about your baby and Sophie being
sisters. I think it's really important that Sophie never feels 'less-than'
when she's around her dad's new daughter."

"Oh my goodness," Vicki said with obvious feeling, "of course.
Absolutely."

Nora felt a wave of emotion. "I appreciate you saying that. And I
promise you the same for your little girl. I think it's up to the adults to
make sure the kids are all right."

Vicki dropped her hand on top of Nora's. "I couldn't agree more. I'm so glad you said that."

She paused and pulled her hand back before continuing. "And given that it's just us girls, can I ask you about having Sophie?"

"Sure," Nora said. "What about it?"

"Did you have a C-section?"

"No, I didn't need one, thank goodness. She actually came out much quicker than I expected."

"Oh," Vicki said. "My mother thinks I should just tell the doctor I want a C-section. She says it'll make the whole thing easier and while I'm numb, the plastic surgeon can join in to put everything back in place and tighten my tummy."

Nora's eyes widened. "They do that? They do elective C-sections? And plastic surgery at the same time?"

"I don't think it's something they broadcast, but Mother says the best doctors in Greenwich do it all the time. She also says I shouldn't breastfeed because of the way it will stretch me. I'll just need surgery on my boobs so much earlier than I will without it."

Nora didn't speak. Vicki looked at her without blinking, her eyes slowly filling with tears.

"Oh, Vicki," Nora said finally. "It's going to be okay. You, and your little girl, are going to be okay. I don't know anything about the stuff you said, but my advice is to figure out what's best for you *and* your baby. Pregnancy is going to change everything, including your body, but in wonderful ways. You're gonna have a beautiful baby to love and take care of, and you'll be her mom for the rest of your life. Don't let anyone tell you this is about your tummy or your boobs. It's about what will ensure your baby is healthy and happy."

"I know, but I'm still so nervous."

"My body changed a lot after Sophie was born and I loved breast-feeding and I'm kinda fine with where I am, but everyone has to do what works best for them. You've got this, Vicki. You'll figure it out."

Vicki was crying silently now, tears rolling down her cheeks.

"Everything all right in there?" Nick called from the family room. "You two are awfully quiet. And you're missing a great game. Giants are coming back."

"Yes," Nora and Vicki answered in unison, before smiling at their unintended harmony.

As the two women rose from the couch, Nora pulled Vicki into a hug. "You're going to do great and I'm here to talk whenever you want. Now go watch enormous grown men try to injure each other. I gotta go carve the turkey."

—◦◦◦—

Sophie fell asleep while Nora was reading to her. The house was quiet except for the sound of the faucet at the kitchen sink. It had been a wonderful day. Nora was thinking about Vicki as she walked down the stairs and turned toward the kitchen. Through the French doors, she could see Teresa and Benny standing side by side at the sink finishing the dishes. It made her smile to see them there—Teresa washing, Benny beside her with the towel. But they weren't passing dishes. They were frozen. One more step toward the glass doors and Nora could see over the kitchen island. They were holding hands and staring at each other.

Nora could retreat or advance, but she wasn't going to stand still and watch something she couldn't unsee. She loudly cleared her throat. They dropped hands and were staring into the sink as she came into the kitchen, speaking loudly.

"A Thanksgiving for the ages. What say you two?"

Teresa turned her head and smiled. "It sure was," she said as she glanced up at Benny, who hadn't moved. "And those apples and potatoes were extremely well peeled. Everyone noticed."

Benny was finally unstuck. Turning his slightly red face to Nora, he said, "Best Thanksgiving ever. And peeling was all Sophie. I was just the assistant peeler."

"Assistant to the peeler would be more accurate," Nora replied. "Next year you move up to assistant peeler."

"Fair enough," Benny said. "Lookin' forward to the promotion and I'll try not to embarrass the family."

CHAPTER FIFTY-SEVEN

Benny was seated as Carmen leaned on the witness room table with both hands. Even though she was standing, their heads were nearly level. "You clear on the scope, big man? You can talk about what you read in the files, but that's it. Nothing about the interviews."

"Even about that piece of shit Chip and him still being nowhere to be found?" Benny asked.

"No," Carmen answered. "I get why that's frustrating, but it's our deal with Saugatuck. We do nothing with that until the MC meets."

"Can I say we did interviews, if the judge asks?"

Carmen glanced at Porter. "Yes, but nothing about the substance," she said. "David Jepson is cool with this, but I really don't want you pushing your luck. Last thing you need is a billionaire coming after you for violating your NDA."

"Not much for him to take," Benny said, "but I also get it. Dude's been straight with us. I'll draw the line."

"And remember, all Aileen and the judge know is what we said in our letter: You have exculpatory information relevant to their inquiry."

Aileen Shapiro leaned in through the door. "We're ready for you, Mr. Dugan."

Benny pushed himself to his feet and buttoned his navy-blue blazer, smoothing his knit tie with the swipe of one hand. "Let's do it."

Benny was confused as Aileen steered him toward the witness box next to the judge's bench. There was no judge. In fact, the courtroom was empty except for a distinguished-looking Black man in a suit sitting at the counsel table closest to the jury box. After showing him to his seat, Aileen went and sat next to the man.

A woman entered the room, walked to a desk in front of the witness box, and pressed a button on what appeared to be a recording device. Then she pivoted to Benny.

"Please rise and raise your right hand. You solemnly swear or solemnly and sincerely affirm, as the case may be, that the evidence you shall give concerning this investigation into the commission of a crime or crimes, shall be the truth, the whole truth and nothing but the truth; so help you God or upon penalty of perjury?"

"I do," he answered.

"Please be seated and state your name for the record."

When Benny had done so, the woman turned and left the room.

The man spoke for the first time, his voice a smooth deep baritone. "Mr. Dugan, I'm Judge Robinson. I understand you have information you believe relevant to my grand jury. Let's have it."

Benny explained about Helen's files, how he came to see them, and what they said about Saugatuck employees. When he was finished, Judge Robinson took a breath and exhaled, the air coming out almost like a whistle. "So how was the deceased using this information, Mr. Dugan?"

Mindful of his instructions not to talk about his interviews, Benny still decided he could answer. "No doubt, Judge, that she was collectin' this stuff to use it—holdin' it over people whenever she needed to. But how she used it, when she used it, was gonna change with the person. Would depend on what Helen wanted."

"Nothing, really, on the Carleton woman," Judge Robinson said, his words more statement than question.

"That's right, Your Honor."

"Have you talked to the people that the dead woman had files on?"

"I have, Judge, but I'm not cleared to get into that."

"Why not?"

"Above my pay grade, Your Honor. Lawyers and all."

The judge paused and turned his head to Aileen. "We'll sort that out. You got anything?"

"No, Your Honor, except I want to confirm that Mr. Dugan will accept service of a subpoena calling for all the original files."

"Yeah, expected that," Benny answered. "The lawyers tell me I can give you the originals."

"Thank you, Mr. Dugan," Judge Robinson said. "Seems like we have ourselves an Agatha Christie thing going on up at Saugatuck, don't we?"

"Not sure what you mean, Judge. Not a big reader myself."

"All I mean is there are a whole lot of people in one company who may have had some hard feelings about Helen Carmichael."

"Agree, Judge," Benny said, "and the one with the least reason to kill her is the one in the trick bag right now."

"Ms. Carleton is not in any kind of bag at the moment," the judge answered. "The whole reason I'm down here doing this is to figure out what's what. I appreciate your help. You may be excused."

Benny stepped down from the witness stand and retraced his steps to the courtroom's side door. Once through the door, he headed down the little hallway to the witness room, but a voice to his left stopped him.

"Hey guy," called Captain Dunham, leaning out from what appeared to be the jury room. "Got a minute?"

"Sure," Benny answered as he turned toward Dunham.

"How'd it go in there?" Dunham asked.

"Fine," Benny said. "You want details, ask your prosecutor."

"Yeah, but I'm asking you—as a brother in arms."

Benny made a sour face. "Huh, don't remember Mom talking about you, *brother*. I'll take a rain check."

He started to walk again, but stopped when Dunham took a quick step toward him. The captain was several inches shorter, but he lifted himself so his face was inches from Benny's, whispering menacingly, "I don't know how you came up, Dugan, but I think you oughta reexamine your priorities."

Benny stepped one foot back so he could pivot and fully face Dunham. His words came out through clenched teeth. "You gonna throw hands, you best get to it. If not, you can get the fuck out of my face. And I know how *you* came up, *brother*."

The two men stood frozen, inches apart, until Benny spoke again. "We done here?"

Dunham took a step backward. "Just disappointed is all. Thought you were a stand-up guy."

Benny sniffed and walked off, adding, "Depends who's askin'. I like where I'm standing."

CHAPTER FIFTY-EIGHT

"Seriously?" Benny asked. "That ain't a bank."

"Sign says it is," Laslo answered, steering the car into the lot in front of the tiny one-story wood building. "Skowhegan Savings Bank of the metropolis of Kingfield, Maine."

Laslo cut the ignition and reached for the door handle. "And let me talk. We aren't in DUMBO anymore."

"Whatever," Benny said. "All yours."

Inside the little bank, Laslo was honest with the manager. They had driven six hours from Westport to the remote Carrabassett Valley of northwest Maine because they were conducting an internal investigation for their employer, Saugatuck Associates. As part of that work, they were trying to locate Brad Holtzer, the firm's former general counsel, whose last severance check had been deposited at this Skowhegan branch. Laslo didn't add that this was their last, best lead because they had none of the powers they once had as federal investigators.

The idea that the bank manager would recognize a photo of Holtzer struck Benny as absurd, but, as Laslo explained, Benny had "never lived where there were more critters than people and one of those people has a shitload of money."

The manager recognized Holtzer right away. "Good fella. Teaches up the road at the ski and snowboard school. Social studies and government, I think."

"The what?" Laslo asked.

"The Academy. Private school for young folks trying to make it big on the slopes at the Winter Olympics and all. They take classes there when they aren't skiing. Lotta champions came outta that place over the years."

He pointed out the front window. "Left outta here, fifteen miles up on your left. You'll know you've missed it if you see Canada."

"Thanks," Laslo said, turning to leave.

"Much obliged," Benny added.

When they were in the parking lot, Laslo smiled across the roof of the car. "'Much obliged'? You in a western or something? This is Maine, not Montana."

Benny blushed. "I don't fuckin' know. Just tryin' to be polite. Get in the fuckin' car."

<hr />

The Carrabassett Valley Academy sat just across the road from the river that gave the valley its name. The trees on the valley floor were bare and brown this time of year, with evergreens reaching up the sloped sides to the point where all plants surrendered to the stony peaks—a much lower tree line than in a place like the Rocky Mountains.

The school's L-shaped structure brought dormitories, classrooms, and indoor athletic training under one roof for the hundred or so students, who could look out their back windows to the bare summit of Sugarloaf Mountain.

"Thought this was a school," Benny said as they stepped into the silent entrance hall.

"It is," Laslo answered, "but I'm guessing by this time of day the kids are out skiing."

"In November?"

"Benny, did you look up? There's snow on the mountain."

"I don't look up when I'm outside. Nothing's gonna hurt me from up."

They wandered down the quiet hallway, peeking into classrooms until they saw him, grading papers at his desk in an empty room.

———

Holtzer seemed almost relieved to be talking with them, despite Benny fully embracing his bad cop role.

"Why you livin' off the grid up here?" he barked after Laslo introduced him.

"I'm not living off the grid," Holtzer protested. "I have a job, I pay taxes, I have health insurance, internet. All in my own name, by the way."

"But nothing on a credit check puts you here," Benny answered. "No real estate, no connection to an address. Seems to me like you're hiding from somethin'."

"Well, that's because I live in housing the school provides and I don't use credit. I'm sure you know this, but I have money."

"Maybe," Benny said, "but you're a fancy lawyer. What the hell you doin' teaching ski brats in Cummerbund Valley or whatever?"

"Carrabassett. They're not brats. And I'm here because I don't want to be a lawyer anymore. I got what I wanted from Saugatuck. I came up here when I was a kid, and it seemed like a great place to live. That's it."

"What were you doin' sneakin' into the funeral down in Southport?"

"I didn't want the Saugatuck crowd to see me, but I felt like I owed it to Helen to be there."

Laslo spoke more gently. "Why didn't you want anybody to see you?"

"Honestly? Couple different reasons: I still have a bad taste in my mouth from that experience and I also feel a little guilty about the way I played it to get out of there."

Holtzer explained that he had doubts when Saugatuck recruited him about whether he would be a good fit, but decided there was little risk, given the contract they agreed to—with the ten-million-dollar payout if he was fired for any reason in the first year. "I asked for that because I was giving up so much long-term comp at my other place. This way, I figured, if they cut me—as they do, you know—at least I walk away whole."

Holtzer said he concluded quickly that Saugatuck's aspirations were noble and embraced by most of the workforce. "But the top level was a snake pit," he said, "which surprised me. And it surprised me even more to learn that Helen was poisonous too."

"Why do you say that?" Laslo asked.

"I mean, she was great. Smart, funny, hardworking, and cared for her people. That was obvious right away. It took me longer to realize that she was also a hell of a climber, and collected dirt on anybody who might get in the way of her being David Jepson's successor. She had a plan and she put together what she needed to accomplish it."

"What does that mean?" Benny asked.

"We were working in her office on a Saturday and she left for a while, so I poked around her office. She had a drawer with a lock in her credenza—which was unlocked that day—so I took a look. There were a bunch of files with the names of Saugatuck's top people on the tabs."

"Wow, you're quite the poker," Benny said.

When Holtzer didn't react to that, Laslo asked, "Did you get the chance to look inside any of the files?"

"I did, yes, briefly. I don't remember all the names, but I remember looking at the thickest ones—Arty Falcone's in particular was packed with nasty sex stuff. Rob Arslan's seemed about the same size, although I didn't have time to go through it. I just pulled one photo from his, an eight by ten of him wheeling into a van in some tropic spot, water in the background, palm trees. I could hear Helen coming back and I didn't want to get caught, honestly. So I put everything back and closed it up."

"Where do you think the picture was taken?" Benny asked.

"Don't know," Holtzer answered. "I remember he went to Australia and New Zealand a lot—and maybe I don't know those places well enough—but it seemed like someplace else. Like a more rural beachy feel to it. I don't know."

"So what was she using this stuff for?" Laslo asked.

"I'm not sure," Holtzer said, "although not for anything related to legal or compliance. And if *you're* asking me about it, I'm guessing it wasn't about protecting Saugatuck's security. That was your thing, right?"

Laslo didn't answer, so Holtzer continued. "I don't know. Except it couldn't be about transparency and truth, now could it? Secret shit locked away in some drawer. You can see why I needed to get away from that place."

Benny chuckled. "Mister Principles. So you pissed off your boss until he fired your ass and handed you ten million?"

Holtzer shook his head slowly. "Look, I'm not proud of what I did, but I also knew I'd made a mistake going there. Should I quit and leave ten million on the table? The money means nothing to them, and they're the ones who lured me to that snake pit. Okay, I'm not teaching about what I did in some ethics class, but I still sleep at night."

"Hey bud," Benny said quietly, "we're not here to judge you. Just trying to help our friend. Appreciate you talking to us."

—⁂—

Laslo turned right out of the school parking lot to begin the long drive home. "You're quiet," he said to Benny.

"Just thinkin'," Benny replied. "We knew Falcone's file was thick and nasty because we've been through it. But this piece about Arslan's file doesn't make sense. Was there a picture in the stuff Rob gave us? I don't remember one. And if it's not there, why would that be and what happened to it?"

Laslo drove down Route 27 for a mile before asking, "Honestly, I don't remember a picture, but I suppose I could have missed it in the stack. Next steps, other than seeing if there's a photo in what he gave us?"

"We really gotta connect with this Jeremy Parker," Benny said. "He's gotta have something more on Falcone than we do and maybe he'll have insight into the Arslan file. You any closer to putting us together with Parker?"

"I reached out to my Quantico classmate, who's the legat in Riyadh. He said he knows the legat in Abu Dhabi well and would put in a call to him."

"Remind me: legat?"

"FBI legal attaché, the senior FBI rep in another country. Bureau's got them all over the world, something like a hundred countries. They're all special agents sitting in our US embassies. It was originally part of J. Edgar's plan to have the FBI be the CIA too. He lost that fight after World War Two. Now their job is to share information with the host country's law enforcement—especially on terrorism—and they don't do anything without telling the CIA chief of station. Hoover must be rolling over in his grave."

"You been gone a long time. How come you know a legat?"

"They're pretty great jobs—interesting work, lots of free food and drink, cool travel—so only senior people get them. Which is why people who went through Quantico with dinosaurs like me are in those jobs now."

Benny chuckled. "Just think where you might be if you didn't want a boat."

Laslo gripped the steering wheel and smiled. "But then I wouldn't be with you having so much fun. In the *Cummerbund* Valley—is that what you called it?"

"Somethin' like that," Benny said. "Hey, cut me some slack. I'm a city guy. Too many hills, too many trees."

CHAPTER FIFTY-NINE

Nora fidgeted in the chair. It had been a long time since she'd dressed like a prosecutor—navy-blue Brooks Brothers pantsuit, short gold chain on top of a white cotton dress shirt, her chin-length auburn hair brushed straight with a center part. What had once been her daily uniform now felt foreign and confining, but a quarter-zip fleece and a scrunchie wouldn't do for court. She crossed and then recrossed her black flats, keeping her feet tucked under the chair. Her heart was beating quickly, but she could still hear her mother's voice. *Sit up straight and show the world what you're made of.*

She shifted in the seat again just as the man at the table spoke in a deep voice.

"Ms. Carleton, you know you have an absolute right not to do this."

"I know that, Your Honor," Nora answered.

"And that your appearance here today is entirely voluntary?"

"It is, Judge."

"That you have a right to remain silent?"

"Absolutely."

"That anything you do say to this grand jury can be used against you?"

"Yes, sir."

"That your lawyer can't be in here with you but that I will give you a reasonable opportunity to step out and consult with your attorney at any time?"

"I appreciate that, Judge."

"You still want to be a witness today?"

"I do, Judge Robinson."

"Why?"

"Because I didn't hurt Helen Carmichael and if I were indicted it would ruin my life, and most importantly it would hurt my eight-year-old daughter, Sophie. And I'll do anything I can to avoid that. So here I am."

Judge Robinson looked down at some notes in front of him on the table, then quickly looked up, shaking his head slightly. "You know what? The rules of evidence don't apply in here and it's just me—and Aileen—trying to figure out what happened, so let me go a little out of order. Who do you think killed Helen Carmichael?"

"I honestly don't know, Judge," Nora answered. "Seems like it had to be somebody close to her, somebody strong enough to move her unconscious body around. And also somebody who knows me well enough to know my canoe, my car, where I live. I suppose I should add that it must be someone who hated both of us."

Nora exhaled. "So that's people she was keeping files on, although, to be honest, I find it hard to believe any of them disliked me that much, except maybe Louis Lambert. Which is why I really don't know who killed her, other than it wasn't me."

Judge Robinson continued looking at Nora. "Were you in love with Helen?"

"No, not in that sense, Judge. I loved her, like she was my big sister—although it seems I may not have seen her as clearly as I could have. It's true that, early on, I had a crush on her. Kissed her one night—and I'm guessing you've seen video of that—but it didn't become a thing. The two of us actually agreed it would be a mistake. So, no, I wasn't *in love* with her, but I thought the world of her."

"What do you make of the idea that you were some kind of scorned girlfriend and that's why you killed her?"

Nora grimaced before answering. "Doesn't make any sense to me, Judge, like so much of this: the knife in my drawer, blood on my car, Helen in my canoe."

"Have you given any thought to why someone would have it out for both of you?"

"Of course, Judge."

"And?"

"We were doing one thing together that might explain it. In fact, it was the reason she brought me to Westport. We were trying to figure out whether someone was stealing Saugatuck's trade information to get into the market just as the company was making a move, so they could make money off the impact the company's trades would have. It's called front running. Very hard to detect and a way for a crook to make a lot of money if they do it right."

"So where'd that stand?"

"We had done enough work to be reasonably confident the thief wasn't at one of our brokers or support companies. None of them knew enough to explain all the similar trades. It had to be coming from inside Saugatuck, somebody with a complete view of our trading."

"And?"

"And nothing, Judge. Could have been somebody she had a file on or somebody she didn't. Our suspects were anyone with access to our trades or, actually, anyone who might have access—authorized or not—to our IT systems. There was still a lot of work to be done. We had reached a point where the investigation was going to risk being revealed publicly, which could be bad for the company. But there was no other way to find the culprit or culprits. Our investigation had hit a wall."

"Why do you think Helen wanted to talk to you the night she was killed?"

"I don't know. If you go back through our texts, that was something she said a lot when something popped into her head. It was her way of telling me to remind her when we were next together that there was something she needed to discuss. I don't know what it was that night, but after receiving texts like that over a weekend, it was my habit to stop by her office on Monday mornings to ask about it."

Nora paused and looked down before continuing. "Of course, I'd give anything to go back so I could call her right away and ask. But I didn't think of it as anything different or urgent at the time."

Judge Robinson turned to Aileen Shapiro, who continued the questioning, but in a much more predictable pattern. She took Nora through her family and education, career as a federal prosecutor, path to Saugatuck and her work there, the party at Compo Beach the night Helen was killed, that she was alone at home later that night, the alleged intruder the next day, the knife drawer—all the expected questions. But it felt anticlimactic to Nora. Every time she looked at Aileen, she saw Judge Robinson sitting next to her, motionless, leaning back, his hands clasped across his middle, fingers interlocked as if in prayer, a hint of a smile on his face. She couldn't shake the feeling that he had already heard what he needed to hear.

CHAPTER SIXTY

"I like what you've done with the place," Rob said with a smile as he rolled into the windowless basement room at Saugatuck, parking his wheelchair facing the midpoint of the partners desk. "So what's new?"

"Thanks for meeting us early, Rob," Laslo said. "I'll bet the jet lag is a bitch."

"Actually, right now it's midnight in Sydney—and in my body—so I'm okay. I'm going to be hurting in about three hours."

Rob turned his head as Benny spoke. "Wanted to catch up with you on some stuff related to Helen's files."

"Sure," Rob said. "What can I help with?"

Laslo spoke again, so Rob turned. "We finally found Brad Holtzer. It's a long story, but we talked to him. He says he got a look at Helen's files before he left—well, before he got himself fired, which is another thing."

Benny continued the story, so Rob turned again. "He says your file was not only a hell of a lot thicker back then—which I know we've covered with you—but that he remembers seeing a photo of you that looked like it was taken on some tropical island, wheeling into some van. It's not in what you gave us. We're wonderin' what you make of that?"

"Huh," Rob said, frowning and lifting one hand to his chin. "No photos in what I saw. And I don't even know what he might be remembering. Could it be New Zealand? I go there a lot. And I get around in vans."

"Yeah, yeah, we know," Benny replied. "Which is why we asked him that very question. He says no. Says he knows New Zealand and that ain't it."

"Don't know what to tell you. Maybe Brad is mistaken about how well he knows New Zealand? They have some beautiful beaches, as does Australia. But to be honest, I don't go to beaches much."

"You been to any other beachy-type places recent years?"

"No," Rob said, putting his hands on the arms of his wheelchair. "It's really not my scene."

Benny stared at Rob for a beat, then said, "Yeah, that sounds about right. Appreciate you talking with us. We're runnin' some stuff down that may help us understand all the files, including yours. We'll let you know if we have follow-ups."

Rob nodded. "That makes sense. Please let me know how I can help. Nora doesn't deserve the treatment she's getting." He turned his wheelchair, adding, "I understand you guys are going to report at the MC this morning. I look forward to that and don't let them rattle you."

"No chance," Benny said. "See you in a few."

Rob wheeled out of the office.

"What do you make of that?" Laslo asked.

"I still like the dude," Benny answered, "but I have trust issues, and Holtzer's memory was pretty strong. I think we continue to push on all these people. How about we grab some free food before the lions' den?"

CHAPTER SIXTY-ONE

There were no assigned seats at Management Committee meetings but everyone was in the usual seats around the giant rectangular table of the conference room. David Jepson sat at the front of the room, flanked by Miranda and Marcus Baum, with Jeffey Jepson in the last seat along that edge. As usual, Arty Falcone sat along the river, his back to the water, next to the empty chair normally occupied by Chip Jepson. Across from Arty, facing the river, was Rob Arslan, in his wheelchair, sitting between Louis Lambert and Nora. The normally unoccupied fourth side of the table hosted two participants this morning: Benny and a deeply uncomfortable-looking Laslo.

"How was your trip?" Nora whispered to Rob, whose face still showed signs of the cuts and bruises from the car accident.

"Good," he answered before gesturing to his ribs and adding, "Still a little sore around the middle, but the flights didn't make it any worse. And our clients Down Under appreciated me playing hurt. How's it been without me?"

"Unbearable," Nora said with a smile. "But actually, I have a lot to update you on. Things could get real in here today, starting with me being here at all."

Nora stopped whispering as David began the meeting by waving the camera operator out of the room. "Due to the sensitivity of our discussion today, we won't be recording." Looking around the room, he added, "And I'd like to excuse our assistants this morning as well."

With that, the staff members along the wall stood and followed the camera guy toward the glass door. As Abe passed Nora, he leaned down and whispered, "Break a leg," prompting Rob to recoil in mock horror. "Wow, Abe, ableist much?"

Abe turned bright red. "I didn't—" he stammered.

"Just fuckin' with you man," Rob said with a broad smile, waving with the back of his hand. "Go, go, just a cripple joke."

When the staffers were gone, David looked toward Benny and Laslo. "As the MC knows, I authorized these two gentlemen to begin a search for truth around what happened to Helen. I realize the authorities are doing likewise, but I have little confidence in them. I've asked our investigators here this morning to give us an interim report on their work and to offer committee members the opportunities to plumb as they wish."

The moment David stopped speaking, Louis leaned forward. "Can I raise a procedural issue concerning Nora? As you know, to mitigate reputational harm, the MC suspended her, with pay. I'm wondering whether it is appropriate for her to be here, in the building."

"Are you fucking kidding—" Rob began, but David cut him off.

"No, no, this meeting directly concerns her, so it's appropriate that she's here. There is no need to revisit the suspension issue, but it makes sense to have her here now. Proceed."

By agreement, Laslo did the talking, which was fine by Benny. He took the committee through the discovery of Helen's files and then went person by person around the room, summarizing the derogatory information Helen had gathered on each and the results of his and Benny's interviews. It was shocking, even by the standards of hyper-transparent Saugatuck, but David had insisted. He even demanded they begin with him. So the meeting started with his unconventional marriage and his wife's polyamorous ways. Then Miranda and Marcus's affair and Marcus leaking to the *Journal* with Helen's help. Jeffey and the Chinese spy. Rob's history of painkiller abuse, domestic strife, and suicidal ideation, and his effort to hide some of the records. Arty's sexual misconduct at home and abroad. Louis's Met-level art collection and refusal to answer questions except his admission that he sent the video of Helen and Nora to the police.

Laslo finished the way he and Benny had planned: He reported that there really wasn't anything on Nora in Helen's files and then turned to the absent Chip Jepson, recounting the sexual assault information and the secret payoff engineered by his mother.

The room was silent when Laslo finished. After several seconds of quiet, Benny took over.

"Here's the thing," he began. "I know this is some ugly shit, but the point of this wasn't to make you feel bad. You should, but that's not the point. We looked at all this tryin' to understand why Helen collected all this garbage and who might have wanted to hurt her as a result. We talked to each of you about that, and our assessment is that you were mostly honest in the interviews."

He paused before adding, "With the notable exception of our buddy Chip, who is still in the wind. I know the rules, but we really should talk about him even though he's not present." He then laid out the security camera evidence of Chip's departure from his father's building the night Helen was murdered, consistent with him travelling to Westport, killing Helen, and returning to Fifty-Seventh Street.

When Benny finished, David's shoulders slumped. "It seems as though we have found a difficult truth," he said quietly. "What do you suggest as next steps, Mr. Dugan?"

"I'll talk to the cops, and share the video, if that's okay," Benny said. "They're gonna want to document Chip's trip that night. Then talk to him, if they can. And Laslo and I have a few other loose ends to tie up. Maybe we will do this again in a few days?"

David was already standing, looking shaken. "Yes, agreed. Meeting is adjourned." He hurried from the room, followed closely by his two other children, Miranda and Jeffey.

As the room began to empty in awkward silence, Nora came around to Benny and Laslo. She sat on the table, looking over her shoulder to be sure nobody could hear her. "David seems crushed by the idea that Chip may have done it."

"Don't blame him," Benny said, "and Chip sure looks good for it, what with all the sneakin' around that night and then ghosting us when we dug into it. Cops are gonna want to jump on him."

"Just depressing," Nora said. She turned to look at Laslo. "Why're you so quiet?"

"Not sure," Laslo answered. "Lots of stuff isn't adding up for me." He paused and shook his head, then added, "Let me sleep on it. How about you show me the famous wine room in the morning? Give me time to organize my thoughts."

"No problem," Benny said, with a chuckle, "but don't get too organized; would kill the team vibe. And while it's fresh in mind, you wanna pop by Chip's office?"

"Sure," Laslo answered.

Chip's assistant was angry, but trying not to show emotion. "I just don't understand why it's appropriate for you to be looking through Chip's stuff," he said calmly.

Laslo took it. "Because the MC has empowered us to investigate Helen's death. Chip has made himself unavailable to both the MC and to us and so the next logical step is to look for relevant evidence here."

Laslo paused, then added, "If there's additional plumbing you wish to do, I suggest you walk down to David's office and ask your questions."

Benny had not stopped going through Chip's desk while Laslo spoke and was now examining a thumb drive he found in the top desk drawer. "Can you log in here and open this?"

"Sure," Laslo said, putting his credentials into the desktop, "but if this is some Chinese intel shit, I'm gonna kill you."

He paused for a moment, staring at the computer monitor. "The good news is that it doesn't seem to be. Looks like a bunch of JPEG files, all encrypted."

"That's weird," Benny said. "Lemme see that again."

Laslo pulled the thumb drive and handed it to Benny, who turned it over again and again in his palm. "You know anything about this?" he asked the assistant.

"Never seen it before," he answered.

Benny held it up to Laslo. "See that little cursive 'D' on there? Bet that's some kinda brand. I'm gonna send it to some colleagues and see what they can tell me."

"Thought you were on leave."

"I am and did I say who I'm sending it to?"

"You did not."

CHAPTER SIXTY-TWO

"This is a huge moment," Benny said as he came into the war room carrying a spare chair. Never had a three-person meeting in here."

"Well, thanks for letting me come over—big honor," Laslo said, before turning to Nora. "And your mom seems really nice."

Benny and Nora exchanged glances. "Uh-oh," Laslo added, "What'd I do?"

"Nothing, nothing," Nora said quickly. "I just like to tease Benny about hitting on my mother."

"Here we go," Benny exhaled. "Okay, okay, let's not drag my partner here into all this. Down to business, people. So what were you chewing on all night, brother Laslo?"

"The art on Louis Lambert's walls."

"Say more," Benny replied.

"The night we were at his place, I noticed a photograph of some gigantic boulders in clear water. Stopped to look at it on the way out because I'd seen it before. It's of the famous Baths in the British Virgin Islands. I took a day trip there on my honeymoon."

"Great," Benny said. "So?"

"So I remembered that Helen's files have Katina Jepson in the BVI all the time, with her 'friends'—her being polyamorous or whatever.

What if all the weirdness with Louis isn't about Helen or isn't *just* about Helen? What if it's about something Helen never put in her files? That Louie and Mrs. J are a thing?"

Benny blew air out his nose. "Well knock me the hell over with a fuckin' feather. David Jepson's missus and Louis Spock as fuck buddies?"

"Yup, I suppose you could put it that way," Laslo said. "And what if? What if Louis is some sorta kept dude, part of her polyamory thing? What if it's *their* art, together, and that's why he won't talk about it? Do you think Helen figured it out and that got her killed? Classic jealous husband or the less classic protective female gigolo?"

"Whoa," Nora whispered.

Benny turned to look at Louis's picture on the whiteboard. "Holy shit," he said quietly.

"Holy shit is right," Laslo echoed.

The room was silent for several beats before Nora spoke. "And can I ask about a different thing? How are you guys thinking about the picture Holtzer told you he saw in Rob's file? It's been bugging me."

"As it should," Benny answered. "We don't know what to make of it. First, Holtzer could be remembering wrong. Or it could be Rob on a client visit to the Aussies or Kiwis. Or not. But whatever it is—or was—why is it not there anymore? There are zero photographs. So even if it's Rob doing Saugatuck's business, where'd it go?"

Nora exhaled audibly. "So Holtzer's wrong or lying or Rob's lying or wrong or somebody else took it or Helen pitched it for some reason."

Benny laughed. "Exactly. Totally nailed it. But seriously, if we find the guy who took photos for Helen overseas, we may narrow that list down. Stay tuned."

CHAPTER SIXTY-THREE

They were back in the uncomfortable chairs in front of David's enormous desk. For a few moments, no one spoke—the Saugatuck silence that Benny was increasingly comfortable with.

"You had follow-up questions?" Jepson asked.

"We did," Benny answered, willing himself to speak slowly and flatly. "Did you know your wife was sleepin' with Louis Lambert?"

"I did," David answered evenly.

"Know she was buyin' him all kinds of fancy art for their Manhattan love nest?"

"I did not know the particulars, but it would be consistent with my wife's character to be generous in that way."

David paused before adding, "Mr. Dugan, reading people is not my strength, but I sense that you are emphasizing salacious details in some kind of effort to elicit a reaction from me. I assure you, I long ago found a place of equipoise with my wife's life choices. Yes, I knew about her relationship with Louis. It is the reason he will never rise higher in the organization. I cannot trust him to be transparent. In fact, it may be that I have been too generous to him and I should fire him. I will think about that during calmer times."

"You know anything about your boy Chip's sex activities outside marriage?"

"I do not. Why do you ask?"

"We found a thumb drive in his desk with all kinds of encrypted photos. Comes back to some high-end sex club in the city—called 'D.' Ring any bells?"

"I am unfamiliar with that establishment, or any others like it. Nor do I know anything of Chip's activities in that regard, which I hope very much are confined to his own marriage."

The room was quiet except for the sound of crinkling tape until Benny and Laslo got up and walked out.

Nora was wide-eyed when Benny finished briefing her in the basement office he and Laslo used.

"What the hell?" she asked.

"Some wacky shit," Benny replied. "And I have no fuckin' idea what equipoise is."

"I think he means he is at peace with it."

Benny shrugged.

"So what's next?" Nora asked.

"On Louis, not sure," Benny said. "Not a crime to be banging the boss's wife, who is also banging lots of other dudes, and with her husband's permission, which is all totally fucked up. Need to think some more about all of that."

"And Laslo mentioned something about early tomorrow?" Nora asked.

"Runnin' out another lead from the dirt in Helen's secret files. Our man Laslo here found us a connection to the missing private investigator. Just gotta go to frickin' New Haven in the middle of the night to get it. Lucky to get out alive."

Nora looked confused.

"Ignore him," Laslo said. "My Bureau contacts are putting us together with the Abu Dhabi PI Helen used on foreign stuff. Because of time zones, the meeting is early, which is what our colleague here is complaining about. Don't know what'll come of it, but we'll let you know."

Nora grinned. "But you're done early today, which is shocking, given how much I'm paying you."

Benny chortled. "Oh no, my fearless leader, hardly. We are off to dark spaces under bridges in Gotham City, looking for our fugitive."

"Where?" Nora asked.

Laslo answered. "Not as fancy as he makes it sound. We're gonna run down the sex club lead we got out of Chip's office."

"Got it," Nora said. "Don't stay out too late."

Benny groaned. "Isn't that where this conversation started?"

CHAPTER SIXTY-FOUR

"When you worked in New York, this was still the Queensboro," Benny said, looking up at the early–twentieth–century bridge above them. "Can't get used to calling it the Ed Koch. I got nothin' against the guy—he was mayor forever when I was comin' up—but can't we just leave the bridges named for the places they connect? The Cuomo? Seriously? Still the Tappan Zee to me."

Laslo just nodded. "I thought it was the 59th Street Bridge, back in the day."

"It was. That and Queensboro at the same time. Both names of places, not dead dudes."

"Got it," Laslo said, gesturing with his head. "Speaking of places, here it is."

They were approaching the front of a nondescript black metal door in the wall of a gray stone building directly under the bridge. A formally dressed, enormous man with a shaved head and a sour expression stood in front of the door. Suddenly a huge smile cracked his face. "Benny Dugan? *Minchia*, as I live and breathe."

Benny threw his arms wide. "Anthony! What's good, my man?"

With that, the two giants merged in a full-on hug. Not some kind of dap-with-a-fist-to-the-back half hug, but a complete embrace. When they separated, Benny turned. "Anthony, this is Laslo. Laslo, Anthony. We did some stuff together, back in the day."

"I was picking up that you'd met," Laslo said dryly.

"So what can I do you for?" Anthony asked.

"Not here on the G dime," Benny said. "Private gig, but trying to understand somethin' about a dude who frequents the establishment."

"Place is tight as a tick," Anthony said, "but for you, anything." He pivoted and pulled the wide door open, shouting inside. "Gloria! Some close friends here. Be smart to give them what they need."

——————

Laslo witnessed a second gigantic hug on the way out.

"Get what you need?" Anthony asked.

"Yup. Appreciate you. How's your mom?"

"Hanging in there. Still grouchy as hell but it keeps her going. Never gonna get her out of Canarsie."

"Worse places to be," Benny said with a smile. "You be good."

"You too. And thanks for everything."

"Back at you, big man."

——————

"What the hell?" Laslo asked when the car door was closed.

Benny laughed loudly. "Locked him up some years back. He was a low-level wannabe Brooklyn gangster. I convinced my office to give him a break and he straightened out—in the sense that he's now a sex-club bouncer and not a more serious organized criminal. It's all about how you define success. But basically a good kid."

"Some freaky shit going on behind that door though."

"No doubt, no doubt. Is it weird for me to admit I'm disappointed Chip isn't a murderer but just a sex addict with some very strange tastes?"

"Yeah, that's weird to admit," Laslo said with a straight face. "We now know he comes here all the time, spends a ton of dough to have people do stuff that's gonna haunt my dreams, and they can prove he was here the night Helen got whacked because he charges the nasty to his Amex."

"And to be clear," Benny said, "I'm mostly disappointed that we haven't solved Helen's murder. Only a tiny piece of the disappointment is the fact that Chip's a piece of crap and I wish he was getting locked up."

"Helpful clarification," Laslo replied.

"Whatever," Benny said. "Bottom line, seems he's only hiding from us because he's shady as shit, not because he's a killer."

"And more likely, he's hiding from his father, because Chip *had* to know we have him coming and going that night and he was gonna have to say where."

Benny put the car in gear. "Home to bed for us, my man. We're in New Haven Dhabi in the middle of the night."

CHAPTER SIXTY-FIVE

The New Haven FBI building did not have a welcome mat. Built in the wake of the 1995 domestic terror attack on the Oklahoma City federal building, the five-story brick and glass building sat in the center of a square city block, buffered from the public by parking lots and black fencing on all sides. There were only a handful of cars in the lots before dawn as Laslo and Benny were admitted through the sidewalk screening center and began the short diagonal walk across the parking area to the building.

"Remind me why we're here in the frickin' dark?" Benny asked.

"UAE is nine hours ahead so we're doing this on his schedule. Plus fewer people will notice my guys here doing us a favor."

Ahead, a gray-haired man in a suit was holding the door open. "Hey Laslo," he called as he extended his hand. "Great to see you, brother."

"You, too, Pete," Laslo said before introducing Benny. "Appreciate you doing me a solid here. Won't forget it."

"Just put the new boat in my driveway," the agent said before turning quickly to Benny and adding, "Kidding, of course."

"No doubt," Benny replied as they stepped into the elevator.

"And it turns out," the agent said, "that this isn't much of a favor. Legat Abu Dhabi wanted to do it on civ-itts anyway. Seems your witness is a CHS."

Benny knew what CHS meant: Jeremy Parker, the private investigator they were about to interview, was apparently someone who supplied information to the FBI. As a result, he was listed in the Bureau's records as a Confidential Human Source, a broad category that included everyone from an Omaha businessperson sharing insights on local economic conditions to New York mobsters ratting out their friends in hopes of avoiding prison. There were all kinds of human sources, but to the FBI, the *C* for confidentiality was the most important part. The agency was maniacal—for good reason—about protecting the identities of people who shared information.

When they were seated and alone in front of a screen in the fourth-floor conference room, Benny turned to Laslo.

"Hey, not for nothin', but your buddy in Riyadh musta really gone to bat for you to get this. New York office fights me tooth and nail over acknowledging a CHS, even if it's somebody I fuckin' flipped in the first place."

"Yeah, we go way back," Laslo said. "But I also think they'd rather do this than have all kinds of motion in their backfield from us trying to flush Parker out. This way, it's quiet and controlled. And the Bureau knows what we're up to."

"Of course," Benny said, shaking his head. "I really am losing some of my cynical edge living in Westport. I gotta get back to dog crap on the sidewalk, people honking as soon as the light turns green. You know, the real world."

As Laslo laughed, the screen for the Secure Video Teleconference System—inexplicably pronounced inside the FBI as *civ-itts*—came to life. At the other end they could see three men at a table in a room with bare walls.

"Good afternoon," one of the men said. "I'm special agent Cary Armstrong, the legat here in Abu Dhabi. Are you reading me okay?"

"Five by five," Laslo said, using the universal government expression for a strong and clear connection. "I'm Laslo Reiner of Saugatuck Associates here in Connecticut and retired from the New Haven division. With me is Benny Dugan, who is currently a special agent with the US Attorney's office in Manhattan, but is on leave to work with me on the matter we wanted to discuss with Mr. Parker."

"Great," Armstrong replied, gesturing to the people beside him. "With me here at the embassy of course is Jeremy Parker, who is a friend of the Bureau. I'm also joined by my colleague Martin Shelton, OGA."

Benny scribbled a note as Armstrong continued talking. *OGA?*

Other Government Agency, Laslo wrote. *Never name the CIA.*

Dumb gov shit, Benny wrote back as Armstrong continued his introduction.

"—and so, given our productive relationship with Mr. Parker, we were happy to make our facilities available so you folks could have a conversation. And Mr. Shelton is here because, as you know, the Bureau does not maintain undisclosed source relationships OCONUS"—he pronounced it *oh-cone-us.*

Benny was scribbling again: *???*

Outside the Continental US, Laslo wrote.

"Jesus," Benny said out loud.

"I'm sorry?" Armstrong asked.

"Nothing," Benny said. "Stray voltage."

"Okay," Armstrong said, "so why don't you go ahead and ask your questions of Mr. Parker?"

"Sure," Benny replied. "I'll start. How come you been jerkin' us around until we called your FBI boy?"

Laslo didn't wait for an answer, pushing his left leg against Benny's right under the table as he spoke. "I think what Mr. Dugan means to say is that we recognize this has been a difficult connection to establish and we appreciate your time, Mr. Parker. So we won't waste it. Let me ask you this: Could you briefly describe how you came to perform investigative services for Helen Carmichael?"

In his British boarding school accent, Parker explained that Helen had hired him to follow three people during their international travels—Arty Falcone, David Jepson, and Rob Arslan. Ms. Carmichael asked that he photographically document everything he observed regarding all three targets and she paid him well for his efforts.

Jepson's travel was boring—"uneventful" was how Parker described it—except that Jepson's interest in climate change took him to challenging environments around the globe—"godawful places" in Parker's formulation—but some of the photographs from his trips were breathtakingly beautiful.

Falcone, he explained, was more traditional, staying at five-star hotels around the globe as he traveled to visit existing and prospective clients. "No doubt your man Falcone has a taste for young women, too young in my estimation, but who am I to judge the way you Americans act?"

It seems Parker had followed Arty to a variety of brothels known for the exploitation of girls. "No indication of rough stuff, but one might say the entire endeavor is the product of rough stuff, no?" Parker was forced to take some distasteful photos of Arty's escapades, but that was why he was paid so well.

He began to itemize Arty's visits when Benny cut him off. "Yeah, thanks, but what about Arslan?"

A look of annoyance crossed Parker's face, but he followed Benny's change of subject.

"That was an odd one. Fellow's in a wheelchair, as you surely know. But is there more than meets the eye?"

"Why do you say that?" Laslo asked.

"Well, it was the places he went. I followed him on three trips to Australia and New Zealand. On each one he did the expected, stopping in Canberra and Wellington. But on each trip, he also did the unexpected: he took the three-hour flight from Sydney to Port Vila, the capital of Vanuatu."

"I'm sorry," Benny cut in, "where?"

"Vanuatu," Parker said—repeating the name "*van-ooh-ah-too*"—and clearly relishing the chance to give the Americans lessons in both geography and pronunciation. "It's an island nation northeast of Australia, due north from New Zealand. Capital, Port Vila, which is pronounced *vee-lah*. Not far from Fiji. Anyhow, he took a side trip there every time. Rolled his wheelchair out the front door of Bauerfield International Airport and into a van, which took him to a fancy area outside Port Vila. Did my best to follow in a cab. I wasn't prepared on the first trip, but I had a car waiting for me the second time, although—"

Parker paused. He was accustomed to making interrogators work for it. "Although what?" Benny asked.

"I still couldn't follow him to the drop-off," Parker said before pausing again.

"Why not?" Benny asked, not trying to conceal the irritation in his voice.

"Because the final piece of his journey was down a long, narrow, dead-end road, then up a very steep path to a lovely home overlooking Mele Bay. It was a surveillance nightmare."

"Sounds like it," Benny said. "So what *were* you able to see?"

"Not very much. I would see the van stop at the bottom of the path before it made a three-point turn to retrace the route. I never got close enough to follow on foot. But it would have been quite taxing for me in any event and my approach would have been totally exposed, without cover of any sort."

"Wait," Benny said, "so how did a guy in a wheelchair make it? He have help?"

Parker paused yet again, then said, "That's just the thing. I don't know and I never got close enough to say."

"And the home?" Laslo asked.

"Yes, right. It was in the name of a woman without apparent connection to your man or to your firm. Except of course that your man went there three times on my watch, flying back and forth from Sydney. It should all be in the file. I sent everything to Ms. Carmichael—description of each trip, property owner's name, dates, flights, and photos of everything."

CHAPTER SIXTY-SIX

Benny and Laslo didn't speak until they were clear of the FBI fences and in Laslo's car.

"What the actual fuck?" Benny asked.

"I assume you mean on Arslan. So, so strange. How could he have someone—family, lover, I don't know—in this Vanuatu place and nobody at Saugatuck ever heard of it?"

"Well, 'nobody'?" Benny said. "I don't think that's right. Helen sure knew because that pompous prick Parker put it in his fancy illustrated reports."

"Which are not in Arslan's file," Laslo said.

"But that doesn't mean they *weren't*, at least at some point. Where's the photo our guy in Cummerbund Valley saw? We're supposed to believe Rob pulled all kinds of shit out of the file but not the photos? Or Parker's reports? Tough to swallow that."

"Yup," Laslo said. "I really liked him. But now I don't know what to think."

"Same for me, but somethin' doesn't smell right. Let's just run it straight up the middle and go talk to Rob. Agreed?"

"Agreed," Laslo said, steering away from the curb.

Benny pulled out his phone. "And lemme call Nora while we drive back."

She answered on the first ring, her groggy voice coming through the speaker.

"Hey, Benny, everything all right?"

"Yeah, yeah," Benny said, "sorry to wake you."

"I gotta get Sophie up for school anyway," Nora said. "What's going on?"

"We just did our video session with Jeremy Parker in Abu whatever."

"Dhabi," Nora said. "How'd it go?"

"Weird, which is why I called. We talked about Jepson, Falcone, and Arslan, the three he covered on travel. No biggie on the first two. Jepson's clean, but he spends a lot of time hugging baby seals or who the fuck knows. Falcone's a piece a shit, banging teenage girls all over the world. No shocker there. Laslo's gonna make sure the Bu follows up on that part. The weird one is actually your guy Rob."

"How so?" Nora asked, coming fully awake.

"Parker covered him on three trips to Australia and New Zealand. All fine, except each time Rob took a side trip to this little island country—and Laslo's gonna have to help me here—Vanna White or some shit."

"Vanuatu," Laslo said loudly, enunciating the syllables.

"Right," Benny said. "That. And every time he went to the same fancy house, middle of nowhere overlooking the ocean. House is owned by a woman Parker said has no connection to anything. You ever hear of Rob having a squeeze in Vanna whatever?"

"I've never even heard of that country."

"Well Rob sure has. He keeps goin' there and I'm thinkin' we need to know why ASAP."

"Why so urgent?"

"'Cause Parker says he wrote reports—including lots of photos—on all of Rob's trips there and none of them are in Helen's files. Put that together with your predecessor saying he saw a beachy picture in Rob's file and we're thinking somebody is tryin' to hide somethin.' If there was nothin' to Rob's little side trips, why'd Parker's reports go missing? Look, Nora, I know he's your friend, but I'm not feeling the love there anymore."

The line was quiet before Nora went on. "Rob's a good, good person and I really do trust him, Benny. Let's take a breath here and not jump to conclusions all right?"

"Hey, hey—" Benny began before Nora cut him off.

"Rob has been a loyal friend and someone I could always count on to have my back at Saugatuck. At this point, I don't know what to think."

"Hey look," Benny replied, "I'm not sayin' Rob is dirty here, but I *am* sayin' we need to put it to him directly. 'Cause either he's dirty, or somebody's fuckin' with him, too. So we're gonna go clear this up at the office right now. He's always in early. Let's meet up there."

"Okay," Nora said. "Let me know. I'll be in after I drop Soph at school."

"Roger that," Benny said.

———

Nora swung her legs over the side of her bed and sat up, staring at her phone. *This place is going to be the end of me. Rob's my friend, for God's sake.* She scrolled in her contacts and thumbed Rob's cell number. It went to voicemail. "Hey Ironside, Nora here. Just want to give you a heads up that Benny and Laslo want to meet up this morning—first thing. Some stuff has come up about you. I'm sure it's a nothing-burger, but let's all meet at the office ASAP to clear things up. Benny and Laslo are headed there now and I'll be there as soon as I drop Sophie off at school. It'd be good to not have any hanging chads on this thing. Talk soon."

Nora sat on the edge of her bed for a long time before finally pushing herself up to go wake Sophie.

CHAPTER SIXTY-SEVEN

As the line of fancy cars wound its way toward the school drop-off, Nora's racing mind was interrupted by a voice from the rear passenger seat. "Why can't I sit in the front seat, Mom?"

"Because you're eight, bug."

"Maddy's mom lets her sit in the front seat and she's eight."

"Her mother is eight?" Nora said, turning to show Sophie her smile.

"Mom! You know what I mean."

"Lemme do some research," Nora said, inching the car forward. "Gotta protect my ladybug. Safety is always first in this family." They were at the drop.

The receiving administrator opened the door for Sophie, welcoming her to Greens Farms Academy in the usual British accent.

"Love you, Mom!" Sophie called as she jumped onto the sidewalk.

"Love you back!" Nora answered, then quickly shouted, "Hey, hey, your backpack!"

With a pained smile, the woman who had been closing the door paused. Nora reached to the backseat and lifted Sophie's backpack to her. "She'd forget her head if it wasn't screwed on," Nora said.

With a look that was either confusion or concern, the woman from the school answered, "Perfectly lovely child."

Mortified, Nora glanced at Sophie, who already had the backpack on and was skipping into the building. She steered her Honda away from the curb, joining the parade of departing Range Rovers.

The friendly voice came from behind the cubicle wall. "Hey, boss, and, of course, I mean that in a nonhierarchical way. I'm so glad they ended that stupid suspension."

"Hey, Abe," Nora answered, peering over the privacy partition. "Yeah, me too. I don't even think there was a meeting about it now that I'm no longer the only murder suspect in the place. David just told Louis to have me come back to work."

Nora came around the corner of the partition and lowered her voice to a whisper. "Even with the way Louis talks, I could tell he hated calling to tell me that," she said, before adding in a normal tone, "But, I'm back! And tell me, how is excellence this morning?"

"Excellent and free," Abe said, holding up a plate covered in baked goods and fruit. "You gonna nourish?"

"Of course," Nora said, "but I really need to get hold of Rob. His cell keeps going to voicemail. Have you seen him?"

"Nope. Let me see where his assistant is. Maybe Sally knows."

Nora was in the kitchen filling her bowl with yogurt and granola when Abe leaned in. "Talked to Sally. Rob left a voicemail saying he was running late, but that was early this morning and still no sign of him. She doesn't know of any meetings out of the office and he hasn't checked back in with her, which is unusual. She's worried he may have been in another accident or something and wants to call Westport PD. I talked her into waiting a while longer."

"Yeah, that's really not like him," Nora answered. "Okay, thanks. Let me see if Laslo has a bead on him."

Nora set her food on her desk and walked down the hall to Laslo's office. He and Benny were sitting across from each other in front of the desk. "Rob?" she asked.

"No," Laslo replied. "Haven't gotten to him yet. No answer on the cell. Don't have him badging in through security either. So he's not in the building. We'll keep looking."

"Okay," Nora answered. "Let me know?"

"Will do," Benny said, studying her face. "You okay?"

"Yeah, I'm just a little thrown by the Rob thing."

Nora started to leave, then stopped in the doorway and turned back. "Uh-oh," Benny said, "I know that look. What's wrong?"

Nora shook her head. "I fucked up, guys. After we spoke this morning, I called Rob, left him a voicemail. Told him something came up about him and you two guys needed to talk to him right away."

Benny dropped his head.

"I know, I know," Nora said. "That's why I said I fucked up. But he's a friend of mine. A really good guy who's been through hell in his life. I just didn't want to treat him like a perp or something, getting hit with a cold interview. I should have thought it through. I'm sorry."

Benny looked up with a kind smile. "No worries, Ms. Smooth. You were always a sucker for the decent gesture. Character flaw. Can't be helped. So we march on and we find him. Laslo will get a ping if he badges, and in a bit we'll try his place. You stay here. Be in constant touch."

"Roger that," Nora said as she turned to leave.

"Hey," Benny called after her. Nora turned. "I meant it," he said. "No biggie. You've fucked up far worse than that. So have I. Let it go."

Nora smiled tightly. "I'll try. Let me know what you find out."

CHAPTER SIXTY-EIGHT

She could feel it the moment she heard her mother's voice on the phone.

"Nora?" Teresa asked.

"What's wrong, Mom?"

"I'm at the school, to get Sophie, as always. They say she's not here."

"What?" Nora answered.

"They say she was picked up already. Nice man in a Cadillac Escalade, the lady says. Says Sophie clearly knew the man and was excited he was picking her up."

"Where are you now, Mom?"

"Standing in front of the school."

"The school lady there?"

"Yeah."

"Put her on."

"Hell-ooh," came the woman's voice.

"Who is this?" Nora asked.

"Amelia Longwell, Ms. Carleton. It's good to speak with you."

"No, it's not," Nora said sharply. "You let my child get in a vehicle with someone who is not an authorized guardian. How the fuck did that happen?"

The line was silent before Ms. Longwell cleared her throat and answered in her loud headmistress voice, "Well, Ms. Carleton, and I would ask you to please use civil language, the vehicle was near the front of the line, the man very clearly said he was here to pick up Sophie, and she obviously knew him and trusted him as if he were family. I realize I should have verified that his name was on the list but—"

"Oh, you got his name?"

"I did not, regrettably," she answered.

Nora was almost shouting now. "Oh my fucking God. You need to go back inside and pull the video of the pickup. You just gave my child to a stranger."

"Well surely not a stranger, Ms. Carleton. As I said—"

Nora was actually shouting now. "Go! Go! I'm calling the police! Go!"

Teresa's voice returned. "You okay? Seems like it must have been Rob. Strange, but not bad, right?"

"I don't know, Mom. We've been trying all day to find him. I hope it's nothing, but maybe bad."

"What do you want me to do?"

"I need you to go home and check to see if Rob dropped Sophie off or maybe he's there with her. Call me and let me know and then please stay close to the phone in case they call or show up. I'm gonna get the cops and Benny."

"Okay, I'll call if she's there. She's gonna be okay, Nora. I'll hold down the fort for when she gets home. I love you."

Nora hung up and called Benny, who answered on the first ring. She quickly told him what had happened.

"Son of a bitch," he said. "I'm standing at his place. He still ain't here and no sign of him or the car. Why the fuck would he take Sophie?"

"Don't know, but I have a bad feeling, Benny."

"Okay, lemme grab hold of Demi Kofatos. Maybe Westport PD has some license plate readers or road cameras we can get a hit off. Talk soon."

He hung up.

CHAPTER SIXTY-NINE

Nora sat at her desk, her mind racing, trying to figure out how to get her daughter back, hoping this was just a huge misunderstanding. Suddenly a familiar wave of calm washed over her, one she had felt many times in courtrooms—a surprising sense of peace under great stress.

Her cell phone buzzed. No caller ID, but she answered it anyway.

"Hello?"

"Hey, it's Rob."

"Rob? What the hell are—"

"Listen, don't talk," he said, his voice low and serious. "I'm in a bit of a jam and I'm very sorry to worry you, but Sophie is okay."

"Rob, what's going on?"

"She's okay, but I need you to come to where I am and tell nobody. You'll see her when you get here. But if you tell anybody, we'll be gone."

"Rob, seriously, what're you doing?"

His voice rose in anger. "Nora, this is an emergency and I am not going to repeat myself. I'm about to give you directions. Write them down, then leave your phone in your office and drive here. I'll explain everything. But I meant what I said about not telling anyone. I will be able to tell if you aren't alone."

"I got it," Nora said quietly.

"Good, here are the directions."

⸻

"The drive should take just under an hour," Rob said when he was finished.

"Can I talk to her?"

"Sure. She's right here."

After a brief pause, Sophie's sunny voice came on the phone. "Hi Mommy! Rob has the coolest country place. You coming?"

Nora felt herself choking up and paused to suppress it.

"Mom? You there?"

"Yes, I'm here. Of course I'm coming, ladybug. You having fun?"

"A ton. He has a PS5 with headsets! It's so cool. You gotta try it."

"I will, I will. Be there soon. Love you, bug."

"Love you too, Mommy. Bye."

Rob's voice returned. "See you soon and remember what I said. No joke."

"Got it. See you soon."

Nora stared at her phone for a long time, her mind racing, trying to decide what to do. *Fuck, fuck, fuck. Benny's going to be so pissed, but what choice do I really have? This is about Sophie. I'm not taking chances with her. Deep breath, Carleton, you can handle Rob.*

She put the phone in her desk drawer and hurried to her car.

⸻

Nora followed Rob's directions north into the hills of Connecticut for almost an hour as the sun set. Her mind raced as she entered the little town of Bridgewater before the directions took her off the main road onto increasingly smaller routes.

Why would Rob take Sophie? And why here, this place, these hills?

She drove for several minutes, then suddenly slapped the steering well and shouted to the empty car. "Son of a bitch! He's the fucking front runner!"

She began nodding rapidly while staring at the road ahead.

I'm almost to Route 202. Over these hills is our goddamn data center—the one fucking Rob oversees. The one that our system tests every Sunday morning. The one that would be an all-you-can eat buffet for someone who wants to know the next week's trades and who has the right credentials. The one we asked Rob to check the accesses on to be sure it wasn't where the front runner was getting the information. How could I be so stupid?

Now she drummed on the steering with the fingers of both hands.

But how? How would he go there all the time without lighting himself on fire? The guards would know him. He's in a wheelchair, for Christ's sake, so who helped him? How?

Nora was so distracted that she almost missed the last turn, onto a dirt road that wound its way up a wooded hillside and ended in a clearing occupied by a log cabin set into the hill. Rob Arslan's custom Escalade was parked in the clearing. The cone of her headlights illuminated a wide set of stairs leading up to a broad porch where rocking chairs framed the entrance.

The door opened and a man came into the light, one hand resting on Sophie's shoulder as he limped to the edge of the porch. Sophie waved enthusiastically as they stood there. Rob just smiled.

CHAPTER SEVENTY

Benny shook his phone. "Can't reach Nora at all," he said to Laslo. "Calls, texts, nothing. Her mom's at the house. No sign of Sophie and she hasn't heard from Nora since they talked an hour ago. Says her location shows Nora's at work, but Abe says she left. What the fuck?"

Laslo was looking at his own phone as they sat in Benny's car outside Rob's Westport home. "Yeah, she's not at the office," Laslo said. "We got her pulling out of the garage an hour ago, but that's it."

"How can a town like this not have a single license plate reader up or cameras on the main roads? How the fuck you know who's comin' and goin'?"

"Blue state," Laslo said glumly. "Our elected leaders don't want to infringe or something."

"Unfuckingbelievable," Benny replied. "Cops won't even do a welfare check on Rob. Sayin' we don't have a basis and shit." He paused, then hammered his right palm into the top of his steering wheel. "That's it. Enough dickin' around. I'm goin' in. Don't give a shit anymore. Somethin' ain't right."

Benny jerked his car door open and walked quickly up the ramp toward Rob's front door. Several steps behind him, Laslo asked, "So how do you plan—" just as Benny kicked the front door in, triggering the sound of an alarm.

"Now I see the plan," Laslo said.

"Maybe that'll trigger a welfare check," Benny announced as he marched inside.

The two men split up and swept the one-story Craftsman-style home as the Klaxon security alarm rang around them.

"Laslo!" Benny shouted from the bedroom. "This don't make any fucking sense!"

"What doesn't?" Laslo said loudly as he entered the room.

Benny was holding a new pair of Hoka running shoes. "Nearly broke my neck tripping over these," he said. "Why's a disabled guy gettin' kicks like this?"

Laslo shrugged and Benny turned the shoes over to show the soles. The waffle pattern was studded with small stones jammed into the rubber bottoms. "And how the fuck he get pebbles stuck in there?"

CHAPTER SEVENTY-ONE

Nora was having trouble processing what she was seeing. She shook her head but the image didn't change.

"Hi Mommy!" Sophie called. She began to move toward Nora, but Rob squeezed down on her shoulder, holding her in place. "Ow, Rob, that hurts," Sophie complained.

"Mommy's coming up," Rob said in a sunny voice. "Aren't you, Mommy? Toss me the keys, would you?"

Nora lobbed the car keys up the stairs. Still gripping Sophie with one hand, Rob took an awkward step to the side and caught them with his free hand. He then turned and limped through the open front door, steering the little girl in front of him. "Come on, Nora," he called.

Nora climbed the stairs and followed them inside. As she stepped past Rob, she was struck by how tall he was. He pushed the heavy wood door closed behind her and locked it. Only then did he lift his hand from Sophie's shoulder. She rushed to her mother. "Mommy! I'm so glad you came. Isn't it amazing that Rob can walk now! I thought it was one of Nana's miracles, because we pray for him all the time, but he says it was special medicine."

She turned to him, adding, "Right, Rob?"

He nodded. "That's right, Sophie, and it *is* kind of a medical miracle."

"It does seem like quite a miracle, Rob," Nora added, staring hard at him.

"And this place is really cool," Sophie continued. "There's a whole 'nother house downstairs, underneath the ground. I'll show you!"

Sophie pounded off into the kitchen toward a set of carpeted cellar stairs. Rob silently gestured to Nora to follow. She narrowed her eyes at him, her mind racing. *Stay focused. Stay in the moment.* She said nothing as she gripped the railing and followed her little girl down the long steep stairs.

It was a doomsday prepper's paradise, but all Sophie could see was the enormous television screen, which was paused on one of her favorite games from Roblox. She plopped on the black leather couch in front of it, grabbed headphones, and began working the controller as the game sprang to life. Nora scanned the space. The walls were covered in white custom cabinets and shelving holding supplies—everything from foodstuffs to books. A set of bunk beds with soft-looking pillows and colorful comforters occupied one corner. The floor was covered with a plush blue and black carpet. The walls were poured concrete painted sky blue. The space was luxuriously outfitted for a long haul.

Never taking his eyes off Nora, Rob lifted one of Sophie's headphones and said, "Your mom and I are going upstairs to chat for a minute. You chill and we'll be right back."

"Okay," the little girl replied, "but hurry because I want to play you, Mommy."

"Be right back," Nora said quietly. She gave Sophie a quick side hug before turning to follow Rob back upstairs.

Rob climbed the stairs quickly, taking two at time with his good leg and dragging the other foot up as he pulled on the railing. He waited for her at the top, closing and latching the heavy metal door behind them.

"What the fuck are you doing?" she demanded. "You have three seconds to explain why this isn't a fucking kidnapping and why you shouldn't be in goddamn jail. And how the hell are you walking around?"

"All that's going to take more than three seconds," Rob said.

He took a deep breath before continuing. "Nora, I need you to stay calm and listen to me. I'm so sorry all this happened. But please understand that I had no choice. You know I'm a good person. I've made mistakes, but it's going to be okay. I promise."

He pointed to the armchairs by the fireplace. "Can we sit?" he asked.

"No, we cannot," Nora said sharply. She paused and looked down for a moment before continuing. "Okay, so you can walk. How long have you been faking it? Is this related to the medical research my mom said you talked about at your charity's fundraiser? She said you dreamed of getting your life back. You got her all teary. Is that what this is?"

Rob exhaled. "The technical term is 'dancing protein molecules' and they stimulate nerve and blood vessel regrowth. I got one leg fully back. The other is making progress."

"So the molecules thing, that's real?"

"It is," Rob said, "very much. Pioneered at Northwestern University."

"And I'm guessing you got some of it early because you put money in."

"I did," Rob said, "and there were risks. I was basically a human guinea pig, but as you can see, it was worth the risk."

Nora looked disgusted. "No doubt, and you were so grateful that, rather than share this wonderful news to give hope to others, you stayed in a wheelchair."

"There were lots of good reasons to not go public right away," Rob said quietly.

"I'm sure," Nora said. "Criminals can always convince themselves."

She gestured toward the back of the cabin. "So our data center is just over that hill, am I right?"

"Not far," Rob said quietly.

"Short walk?"

"Yes," Rob said.

"No wheelchair path, though, so a front runner's gotta walk the whole way, huh?"

Rob paused, then slowly said, "It takes me a long time."

Nora started shaking her head. "And you hobble in there as somebody with no connection to Saugatuck, probably in a fake mustache and glasses."

Rob didn't answer so Nora went on. "Son of a bitch. I can't fucking believe we had *you* check out whether the data center was the vector for front running. How stupid am I? Of course, it made sense because you're the tech guy, and I don't suppose we could have imagined you were *walking* over the fucking hill from your little Unabomber cabin here. But, then, that was the point of continuing the whole wheelchair thing, right?"

"You aren't stupid," Rob said, his voice barely audible.

"Yeah, and Helen wasn't either," Nora answered. "She was ahead of me. Which, I'm guessing, is why she's dead."

When Rob didn't respond, Nora went on. "That's what Benny and Laslo figured out this morning. Helen put a PI on your travels and he caught you diverting to some strange place in the Pacific. Vanna-something."

"Vanuatu," Rob answered.

"Never heard of it, but I'm guessing you were stashing your money there."

She stared at him, then said, "And here's another wild guess: It's one of those places you can buy citizenship and they never extradite."

"It's more complicated than that," Rob said.

"Always is," Nora said sharply, "but let's not get distracted with the South Pacific hideout. Let's get back to the part where you kill Helen and then try to frame me."

Rob dropped heavily onto a kitchen stool, using one hand to massage his thigh.

"She got the PI's report," Nora continued, "put it in her file, figured out you were the front runner, and then confronted you. Hell, I'll bet she was about to tell me. But never got to 'cause you cut her throat."

"She just wouldn't listen, Nora. You know what she was like."

Nora raised her voice. "Here's what I know, Rob: She's a *was* because you murdered her. All this crap about dreaming of getting a life back and you take hers."

Nora stayed standing, now looking down at Rob and dropping her voice into the sympathetic tone of an experienced interrogator. "You had to kill Helen, right? She gave you no choice."

Rob exhaled loudly. "I didn't plan to. I didn't want to. I almost had enough money and I was ready to stop on my own terms. Without her scheming, you and I would not be having this conversation. But you know how she was—at least *now* you know. Always had to have the dirt—on all of us. I don't know, maybe she thought I was doing drugs or banging sheep or something in New Zealand. She probably just thought it would be good to have even more dirt on me just in case she ever needed to control me like she did the others. Helen was always about the dirt. Fuck."

"Tell me what happened," Nora said quietly. "Exactly."

Rob took a deep breath. "That Sunday night she asked me to come to her place. So I did. I rolled up the ramp she'd put in because"—he raised his fingers in air quotes—"we were supposed to be friends. I knocked and let myself in. She's standing there on her phone. I bet she was texting you before her big reveal with me."

Nora blinked. *Need to talk.*

"She lays it all out and you know what? She was really enjoying herself. Says she knows I've been making side trips to Vanuatu. She was damn smart; I'll give her that. She accuses me of being the front runner. Says she hasn't figured out exactly how I did it, but that's just a detail. Then she gives me this big smile and tells me to just confess. She promises if I tell her now, it'll go easier for everyone."

"So what did you do?"

"I denied everything, but she kept saying 'facts are stubborn things,' like she was fucking John Adams or something. I finally gave up and begged her. Pathetic, but I still thought we were friends. She let me beg. I pleaded with her to not ruin me and explained how it would also ruin Saugatuck and hurt so many innocent people, including all the vets we'd helped through Dustoff Home. I told her why I did all this—things you don't know about my family, my kids—and I promised she would never see me again and she could handle the situation however she wanted once I was gone."

"What'd she say?"

"She laughed in my face. *Literally.* You're lucky you never saw Helen's cruel side."

Rob exhaled sharply and shook his head. "She made me beg and then laughed at me. I was a fraud, she said, a criminal. I had 'delusions of grandeur.' Then she turned away from me, still laughing like it was the funniest thing she ever heard. She said I was pitiful and an embarrassment and that I was not going to get away with it."

Rob bowed his head.

"Look, I know you hurt her," Nora whispered. "Tell me what happened."

He stared down at his hands on his lap as he spoke quietly, jaw clenched.

"You know they turn us into killing machines, right? The training they put us through and the missions they send us on are all about locking away emotions and doing what has to be done."

Rob was quiet again for several beats before he slowly lifted his head and looked up into her eyes.

"Helen started walking up the stairs as she taunted the cripple in the wheelchair. I had to protect my life and all the people who depend on me. Nothing else mattered. I was back in the fight. Helen was the enemy. When I jumped up, she looked shocked and tried to run up the stairs. Of course I don't move the way I once did, but I still caught her from behind. I applied a blood choke hold and she was out almost immediately. It was automatic. When I let go, she fell hard, hitting her head."

Nora didn't show any reaction, whispering, "But you can't stop there. She knows too much."

Rob was calmer now. "You're right; I had no choice. My original plan was to just disappear when I had the money I needed and I was almost there. A boating accident off the coast of Australia would do the trick. 'Poor Rob. He'll be missed. What a good guy. He left everything to his charity.' But Helen was going to ruin it all and I couldn't let that happen."

Nora's pressed on, her voice rising now. "And so help me understand why you framed me?"

He leaned back, studying his hands. "To buy time. That was really shitty, but I also knew you would be okay in the end and I was on auto-pilot at that point, figuring things out as I went. Swimming at night is something we're trained to do and it was one form of exercise I could do in secret after I started getting my legs back. Anyway, I drove Helen to Compo, set her in your canoe—she was light as a feather—and swam it out to Seymour Rock. She was out cold the whole time. Then I cut her throat. She felt no pain, which I hope brings you some comfort."

Nora narrowed her eyes and shook her head. "None."

"Look, Nora," he protested, "I'm just telling you what happened. Hoping you'll understand on some level. Anyway, I got the hell out of there. I swung by your house to put the blood on your car and came back the next day to put the knife in your kitchen. And I'm sorry."

"At that point, why didn't you just take off for your island getaway?"

"Again, it was about timing; I wasn't ready. I had to make one more trip to Vanuatu—to set up a final group of accounts—and one more set of trades back here to fund those accounts. *Then* I would be set forever, just like Dustoff Home is. That's a real charity, by the way, and does real good. And I bought the time—or I thought I did—because nobody suspected me of anything, especially after the car accident—"

"Which you also faked," Nora interrupted.

"I did, yes. I thought after all that, it would be easy to see this thing through because the guy in the wheelchair can't be the problem, right? And if the actual front runner tries to take me out in a car accident, then I can't be the bad guy, right? Everyone always underestimated me and I figured they always would. It was a huge mistake to come back, but I was only thinking about all the people who need my help."

Nora remained standing and crossed her arms, letting the silence work.

Rob lifted both hands, palms toward her. "Before you came to Saugatuck, I started helping injured vets, using my own money. I bought wheelchairs, paid out-of-pocket for prosthetics, helped with housing, job training, whatever I could do."

"You're a hero," Nora said sarcastically.

Rob's hands were still in the air. "No, listen, I'm not trying to get a medal. I'm trying to explain how this whole thing started and what it grew into."

Nora just stared at him. He dropped his hands and went on.

"I felt like I wasn't doing enough, and I was pretty pissed off at Saugatuck. I busted my ass for this company, working for billionaires who don't work as hard as I do. They paid me good money, compared to the rest of the world, but not compared to what they rake in. And, honestly, they treated me like some kind of pet, a public service they perform, as if I didn't get enough of that shit from the government and politicians."

He changed his voice, doing an imitation of flat-affect Saugatuck-speak. "Rob's smart, but a bit of a low-level thinker, not conceptual the way we are. Of course, the clients love him and it's so good for our image to have a decorated veteran in a wheelchair working here. Let's even put him on the MC, but don't give him real responsibility."

He returned to his own voice. "And I could tolerate the condescension, I really could. But Jepson fucking lied to me. Ten years ago, he looked me in the eye, probably with tape on his fucking fingers, and told me he saw me as his successor, that he thought I had the integrity and the ability to run Saugatuck. I believed him. Then I watched him—Mr. Truth—make it a lie as he got ready to give it all to Miranda or fucking Baum. He just wanted a Delta Team guy in a wheelchair. Like art in the goddamn lobby. Fuck him."

His breath was ragged and his eyes were welling up. "My wife and I know from personal experience that no one really cares about veterans. She was a PT nurse for vets. That's actually how we met. I fell in love with my nurse—the cliché. But we connected on every level and we both saw the neglect and rejection suffered by too many veterans trying to return to a normal life. No one really helps them. The normal people aren't the problem. It's the fat cats in their luxury boxes at football games getting all misty-eyed at some military flyover, then screaming bloody murder when their taxes might be raised to fund veteran services or cover our healthcare. Well, fuck them. Maybe what I did forced them to pay a little of their share."

"Got it," Nora said flatly, "good speech. So what *did* you do, exactly?"

"At the beginning, I traded using whatever data about Saugatuck's positions I could pick up at work. I was careful and could only do so much with the information I had, but I made money and put it into helping vets. That's how it started."

"And so it all went to charity? Bullshit."

"Well, that's complicated. At first it did, and in a big way. Dustoff Home has done a lot of good—housing, equipment, training, follow-up care, and even the medical research that helped me walk again—and it'll go on forever with the endowment it has now."

"Lovely," Nora mumbled. "And? I know that can't be the end of this little story of yours—the one where you kidnap a little girl to cover up your achievements for humanity."

"It's not the end," Rob responded, "because things changed three years ago when I started using the data center to make extra money. Julie got pregnant and I realized it was time to start looking out for my family. I knew all along that Julie and I would eventually have to get out of here after what I'd done. Stealing for charity is still stealing.

So we made a plan and I started transferring some of what I made to accounts in Vanuatu. When I told everyone we got divorced, Julie had actually moved ahead to have our baby and get our new home compound set up. I visit whenever I can, especially when seeing Saugatuck clients on that side of the world. Julie got pregnant again and now we have two. They're waiting for me to join them and to finally stay there to live in Vanuatu full time."

Nora shook her head. "Happily ever after."

He looked confused, as if he couldn't tell whether she was being sarcastic. "I hope so. The kids were born in Vanuatu, but they also sell citizenship—like you said—and in return our money helps their economy. And that means we'll be able to stay. I don't know whether you've ever checked, but there really aren't many places like it—that don't extradite to the United States. It's a beautiful country, though getting fucked by climate change. We're gonna live there, raise our family, and find ways to be helpful. But that's for another day."

He stopped and shrugged, adding, "And that's my story."

Nora was unmoved. "But you know that's all just one big crime, right?"

Suddenly Rob was irritated. "Of course I know, I knew. I just said that."

He paused and then lowered his voice to a tense whisper. "I have two kids and my wife waiting for me, Nora. I just want to go to them and you'll never hear from me again."

Nora turned away from him and then spun back. "So what're we doing here, Rob? What's Sophie doing here? You're not really going to hurt an innocent little girl, who adores you by the way."

His breathing quickened again. "It's all I could think of when things fell apart. I need two days, then I'll be in Vanuatu and it'll be over. I need you to tell your friend Benny—and Laslo—to stand down for a couple days. That's it."

He nodded toward the cellar door. "You two'll be fine down there. Plenty of supplies. In forty-eight hours, I'll get a message to them about where you are. Then we live our lives."

Nora could feel her heart beating in her chest, but she nodded calmly.

CHAPTER SEVENTY-TWO

Rob stood and pulled a flip phone from his pocket, handing it to Nora. "Burner phone. Call your boy Benny."

"Why would I do that?"

Rob narrowed his eyes. His cold tone surprised Nora. "Because you have no choice, Nora. I am going to see my wife and kids and we *will* have our happily ever after, to use your words. And you're going to help me so you can get back to *your* happy life with Sophie."

She dialed the phone.

"On speaker," Rob said.

Benny's voice came through the little device. "Who's this?"

Nora kept her voice normal. "Mr. Smooth, it's Ms. Rough, can you hear me okay?"

"Five by five," Benny said.

"Hey, I just wanted to tell you and Laslo that Sophie and I are fine but we're going to be on a little trip for a bit. We'll get a message to you as to where we are and you can come pick us up. But I need you to stand down on the investigation until then, capisce?"

"How long you think it'll be?"

"Two days, tops."

"So no more trying to track Rob down, shit like that?"

"Correct. Stand down. Really important, okay? Laslo too."

"Okay. Weird, but I'll do what you say."

"Thanks Mr. Smooth. Bye." Nora clapped the phone shut and handed it back to Rob.

"Okay, good," Rob said. "I really hope he listens to you. But even if he doesn't, they'll never find this place."

Nora sighed heavily. "Sophie needs to eat, Rob. She has to have dinner."

"Sure," he answered. "That's fine. I have lots of food. How about some pasta with sauce, maybe some peas, and apple slices."

"Fine," Nora answered. "Let's make enough for us, too, because I'm hungry."

"I'm going to need you in the bunker while I fix it."

"Really? So I'm going to run away into the woods and leave my daughter? Or I'm going to overpower you? Come on."

Rob paused for a moment before saying, "Okay, but if you try anything, I'm going to have to lock you down there."

He gestured toward the back wall. "Sit there in the corner while I cook. Then we'll eat downstairs when it's ready."

"Sure," Nora said, trying to keep her voice level. She slid a wood dining chair into the corner.

Rob opened a drawer and clumped quickly toward her. "Let me have your wrist," he ordered, producing handcuffs. Nora raised her hand and Rob manacled her to a cupboard handle. With his prisoner secure, he began moving about the kitchen preparing the food.

"You know I don't care if you get away, right?" Nora said. "I only care about Sophie. I don't care about Saugatuck's money or reputation. I'm glad you've done good with a lot of the money. I'm glad you can walk again. I also hope you'll be happy in Van-whatever with your wife and kids."

"Vanuatu. It's so beautiful, Nora. I know it can never happen, but I truly wish you and Sophie could visit us and see it."

"Uh, sure. Anyway, I'd love to hear about your wife and kids—which is amazing, by the way."

Rob tilted his head as if considering the prospect. "I really can't tell if you mean that, but I'd like to tell you about it anyway." Then he began talking as he turned to the stove.

"Julie was a nurse at Walter Reed. I met her when I was in bad shape, physically. She helped me through all that, and then I put her through hell when I got hooked on the pills and lost it mentally. That stuff in Helen's files about how messed up I was after I left the hospital was all true. I was a case and a half, and Julie carried it all."

"So she was never your ex?"

"Not officially, although we were estranged for a long while. My addiction and PTSD pushed her away. But when I quit using and got counseling and started to get my shit together, she came back. Julie helped me get my upper body strong and helped me learn to live a productive life in a wheelchair. We started the charity together and then I figured out how to get more money for that and it was a very slippery slope from there to where we find ourselves now."

He pulled a knife from a drawer and began cutting apples as he talked. "We both knew we had to get away from all this—a clean break. Like I told you, when I decided to use the data center to make big money, we also knew the risk of being caught increased. So we made our escape plan and she moved to Vanuatu and set up our life there, and thank God for Zoom. We spent as much time together as we could on my client visits—which, by the way, is how I originally learned of Vanuatu."

Rob looked up and smiled at Nora. "My visits were 'productive,' as they say. We have two boys, almost three and nine months."

"Can I ask their names?"

"Sure," Rob said. "Osman is the oldest—good, strong Turkish name. Irwin is the little guy, after her dad. Wouldn't be my pick, but relationships are about compromise, right?"

Nora smiled and nodded. "They sure are."

Rob turned back to the stove but kept talking. "I love those little boys more than I can describe. People who've never been parents can't understand what those little ones mean to us, how we would do anything for them, to protect them. I know you feel that way about Sophie and you've done a great job."

Nora managed to feign good humor. "Yeah," she said with a smile, "right up to the point where she's locked in a bunker at some desperate criminal's hideout."

"Hey," Rob replied, turning to face her, "nothing about this situation is a reflection on you as a parent. That little girl is not going to be harmed by this. Two days of TV and video games is all this is."

"I hope so," Nora said sharply, before adding in a gentle voice, "You do know that both Sophie and I actually care about you, right?"

"I know that," Rob said. "I wouldn't do this if I had any other choice. But I don't."

He poured the cooked pasta into a colander in the sink, speaking through the steam. "I've done some stuff I wish I hadn't, Nora. But I've also done a lot of good for people who needed me, both on the battlefield and here at home. I'm nowhere near a perfect guy and I'm so, so sorry for what I had to do to Helen. And to you."

He kept talking as he turned to the stove to stir the peas. "But there are no uncomplicated people. And when it came down to it, Helen was not a good person, Nora. If she had shown the tiniest bit of empathy, things would have gone down differently. Anyway, I can't relive the past. But I *can* keep my promises to the wonderful woman who helped me find life again and literally gave life to our two little boys, who aren't to blame for any of the mistakes I've made."

Nora studied him as he moved around the kitchen. Despite the limp, he was an imposing figure. *And a highly trained one,* she thought. *It can't be about tackling him. I've got to connect.*

"How about a glass of wine?" she asked. "I can drink with one hand shackled. And I'm sure you have good wine here, even in your hideout."

"I do, I do," Rob said, as a slow smile came to his face. "You know me too well. And I suppose a glass wouldn't hurt. I'm off in the morning and there isn't a lot of Willamette Valley pinot noir in Vanuatu. Although I gotta say they have all the good New Zealand stuff."

He opened a weathered-looking kitchen cabinet to reveal a wine refrigerator, retrieving and opening a screw-top bottle. "I know this hurts the cork business in Portugal," he said, examining the cap, "but it works." He poured glasses, handing one to Nora.

"To you," Rob said, raising his glass. "I faked a lot of stuff, but my admiration for you was real. Still is. I realize our association ends tonight, but I'm better for having known you."

"Back at you," Nora said, lifting her glass. "I'll miss you, your wit, and your kindness, especially to my little girl."

Rob took a drink of wine and sighed, before walking to Nora and unlocking the handcuffs. "I'm sorry I did that. Just need to be sure I get to my family. You gotta understand that."

"I do," Nora said quietly, rubbing her wrist. "Let's get Sophie her food. I promise not to attack you with the peas."

CHAPTER SEVENTY-THREE

Rob and Nora were back in the kitchen, washing the dinner dishes side by side at the double farm sink. He seemed completely relaxed now, chatting away about his two little boys as she reached into the soapy water to retrieve dishes for him to rinse next to her. Nora's heart pounded on each dip into the water as she tried to feel for the knife he had used to slice the apples.

She was so distracted that she thought she might be imagining the faint colored light. But then it came again, the red and blue blinking inside the cabin. With each turn up the wooded entry road, the strobing grew more intense. Rob grabbed Nora by the arm and shuffled quickly to the wall. He turned off the lights and yanked her to the floor with him.

"Goddammit," he said angrily. "What'd you do?"

"I didn't do anything. And that hurts."

Rob shook his head. "So fucking close," he muttered.

A voice outside called over a loudspeaker. "Robert Arslan, this is the Connecticut State Police. Come out with your hands in the air."

There was a crackling sound and then a different voice boomed, a thick Brooklyn accent filling the clearing in the woods. "Rob, it's Benny. You motherless fuck, it ends here. You're a man of honor? Show it. Let Nora and Sophie go."

Inside, Rob kept a firm grip on Nora's arm and stared out the window for a long minute. Then he calmly whispered, "Time for you and Sophie to play video games."

Nora tried to reason with him. "Rob, at least let Sophie go. You can keep me as your hostage, whatever it takes, but please, please let my little girl go."

"Just stop talking, Nora, and don't upset Sophie. That's all I'm asking you to do right now."

He rose on one leg without letting go of Nora and pushed her ahead of him down into the bunker. Sophie was oblivious, headphones on, lost again in the world of Roblox. He put Nora on the couch next to her little girl and stood looking at them as the Connecticut State Police voice returned, its demand for surrender echoing down the basement stairs.

Rob glanced at the stairs and back to the couch, his hands on his hips. Then he spun quickly and entered a code on a keypad and opened a tall metal locker, withdrawing an AR-15–style weapon.

He twisted his head toward Nora. "I'm proud of the good I did. Please don't let them hurt my family."

With that, he turned abruptly and began limping rapidly up the stairs, the gun in one hand while the other pulled on the railing.

He didn't load it. There's no magazine in that gun.

Nora jumped up after him. "Rob, stop, stop!" she called, chasing him on the stairs.

Rob paused several steps above her and turned, a glassy look in his eyes. "I'm sorry Nora, I can't go in some cage."

Nora found herself struggling for breath. "Think of Julie and your boys, think of Osman, Irwin," she gasped.

Rob's reply was flat and calm. "I'll never stop thinking of them, or Julie. Goodbye, Nora."

Then he surprised her with how quickly he got to the top, slamming and latching the bunker door, leaving Nora shouting into the heavy steel door. "Rob, please. You don't have to do this!"

CHAPTER SEVENTY-FOUR

A tall, muscular man holding a weapon and dragging one foot emerged from the front door and into the state police spotlights, like an actor making his entrance onto an elevated stage. As the cops began yelling, "Drop the gun!" Rob shouldered the weapon and pointed it at them. Instantly, his body was jolted by the impact of bullets, his shoulders spasming and twisting. He fell where he stood, the unloaded rifle clattering to the porch.

Benny ran forward, trailed closely by a short, dark-haired female officer in plain clothes. They raced up the stairs and past Rob's body. Demi turned left into a bedroom as Benny moved right into what looked to be an office.

"Nora!" he shouted, ripping open a closet door.

He sprinted back to the entryway as Demi emerged from the bedroom, silently shaking her head. She turned into a bathroom as Benny ran into the kitchen yelling, "Nora! Nora!"—his voice almost obscuring a distant thumping. He picked up the faint sound and unlatched the door, nearly tearing it from its hinges as he pulled it open to find Nora.

"Demi, I got her!" Benny called as he yanked Nora up the top two stairs, pushing her toward the safety of the kitchen. Then he started down, holding his gun in front of him, calling, "Sophie?" as he went.

Nora went after him. "She's okay, Benny. Nobody else is down there. She's okay."

Benny took no chances. He crept down the stairs in combat position, Nora leaning on his broad back. The little girl was on the couch, mesmerized by her video game, its music filling the headphones.

The movement caught Sophie's eye and she turned to Benny, her face lighting up just as he slipped his gun hand behind him.

"Benny!" she shouted. "This is the coolest game. You wanna play? Maybe me and you against Mom and Rob?"

Nora rushed past Bennie and scooped Sophie. "Why're you crying, Mommy?" the little girl asked.

"Oh, I'm just so happy to have us all together," Nora said, holding the hug.

"Benny," Demi called from the stairs, "a word?"

He turned and walked halfway up the stairs, stopping when he and Demi were at eye level. "Gotta get Sophie out of here without more trauma," she said quietly. "This isn't my crime scene, but I know the state people and they're good guys. They don't need Sophie here to interview her—and given that the perp is down hard, I doubt they'll ever need to talk to her. I'm gonna ask them to cut the lights and cover the body. Then you and Nora take her out to my car. She sees nothing and we're gone. I can bring Nora back if they want to talk to her here tonight."

Benny was impressed and it showed on his face. "Outstanding. We'll wait here for your signal."

Demi turned and then stopped. "Did you fire outside? I didn't."

"No," Benny said. "Figured the troopers had it. Didn't make sense for me to be throwing rounds in the Connecticut woods and whatnot."

"Good," she answered, "they'll have less of a problem with us leaving."

Five minutes later, Demi's voice carried down into the bunker. "All squared away. Let's roll."

"Sophie, it's time to stop the game," Nora said calmly as she gently lifted the earphone from one of her daughter's ears. "We're going home now. Nana's waiting for us."

"Okay, Mommy. I can't wait to tell Nana about Rob's cool place."

Nora lifted Sophie into a blanket, cradling her head against her chest as she followed Benny up the stairs. They walked through the cabin, across the porch—where they passed a lumpy drop cloth—and out into what appeared to be a dark parking lot. Weaving through the cars, they found Demi's. Nora and Sophie sat in the back for the drive to Westport. Sophie was asleep before they reached the main road out of the woods, her head on her mother's lap.

Nora spoke just loud enough to be heard above the reassuring hum of the tires on asphalt. "How did you find us?"

Benny turned, checked Sophie, and then whispered his answer. "First, your duress signal was solid. 'Mr. Smooth'? In my dreams. Second, your mother is the hero of this story. She put some kinda doohickey—"

"Apple AirTag," Demi whispered.

"Right, AirTag," Benny echoed quietly. "Somebody gave it to her as a present last Christmas and she didn't want anybody tracking her. But, rather than pitch it, she put it in one of the little zipper pockets inside Sophie's backpack. Actually forgot she'd done it, until she remembered in the middle of this shitstorm. Amazing woman. She remembered, got us up on it, and Demi and me and half the state of Connecticut were on the way."

Teresa was standing on the front steps in Westport, clasping and unclasping her hands.

As Demi's car came to a slow stop in the driveway, Nora gently slid from under Sophie's sleeping head and leaped from the car. She ran into her mother's arms and buried her face in her shoulder. Neither could speak for a few moments until Nora whispered, "You did it. You saved us."

Teresa Carleton lifted her tear-streaked face to the parked car. "*They* saved you. All I did was remember the darn AirTag that I didn't want in the first place. But I heard something on NPR about them being good for finding stuff like kid's backpacks, so I thought, 'Why not?' Then I forgot about it, until I remembered and called Benny."

"Oh, Mom," Nora cried into her mother's sweater. "I'm so grateful for you, for Benny, Demi, everyone."

Nora gently pushed back from her mother and smiled. "And NPR. Can't forget them. Come on, let's get our girl."

Demi and Benny were out of the car, standing awkwardly on either side. Nora mouthed, *Thank you,* to Demi across the roof and leaned in the passenger side to gently lift Sophie into her arms. "We're home, ladybug," she said quietly. "We're home."

"I'm so tired, Mommy," Sophie answered. "Can we skip books tonight?"

Nora smiled. "Of course."

As she walked to the front stairs carrying Sophie, Nora glanced back to see her mother hugging Benny. Teresa's cheek was pressed into his sternum, his chin rested on her head, his thick arms were folded around her. Their eyes were closed. She noticed Demi standing to the side, smiling as she watched Nora and Sophie. Nora smiled back and carried her little girl to bed.

EPILOGUE

The big moving company truck was leaving ruts in the pebbles as it slowly beeped its way backward toward the front door.

"It's not coming up on the sidewalk, right?" Sophie asked as they watched the truck creep closer to where they were sitting on the front stairs.

"They'll stop and put out a ramp," Nora explained, immediately regretting the reminder of Rob Arslan's SUV.

"And everything will fit in there?" Sophie asked, her eyes wide, apparently not having the same unpleasant memory.

"I hope so," Nora said. "Don't want to pay for another truck."

Teresa's voice came from behind them. "The Carleton girls are off on another adventure. The excitement never ends."

"But I love it here, Nana," Sophie answered.

Teresa slid between them onto the top stair. "I know, bug, I know. I do too. But you're going to love our new place in the city. The park, museums, shops, restaurants. A cool new school. It's going to be amazing."

They all looked up at the sound of a car pulling in the driveway and stopping beside the moving truck.

"Daddy!" Sophie shouted as she sprinted toward the silver Range Rover.

Nick lifted Sophie in his arms and carried her back to the stairs. "Hi ladies," he said, setting Sophie down.

"Hey Nick," Nora said.

"Hi Nick, how's baby Amelia? And Vicki?" Teresa asked.

"Both happy and healthy, thank God," Nick replied. "That little girl is eating up a storm."

He put his hand on Sophie's head and added, "Just like her big sister did when she was a baby."

Sophie reached up and grabbed his hand with both of hers. "You wanna go on the swing, Daddy?"

"Maybe a little later, Soph," he answered. "Mommy and I are going to take a walk."

"Can I come?" Sophie asked cheerfully.

Nick made an exaggerated serious face. "Not on this one. Mommy and Daddy stuff."

Nora nodded and stood. "Be back in a few minutes, bug. You and Nana make sure the movers don't need anything."

"This just feels like it's happening fast," Nick said as they approached Southport beach.

"Well, it is, sort of," Nora answered. "I didn't expect Carmen to be confirmed so quickly as Manhattan US Attorney. And I also didn't expect her to ask me to be her deputy, but it's one of those offers you can't refuse."

"Look, nothing against Carmen," he said. "She'll be an awesome US Attorney and you always said she was a great boss. I just wish it could wait until fall. It'll be so much easier to bring Sophie back and forth when Amelia is a little older and Vicki is feeling better. And, honestly, it's going to kill me not to have her for a full week each time."

"Look, I get that. And I'm grateful to you for working it out. She'll be here in Westport at least every other weekend, like we agreed, and holidays and longer in the summer, which starts now. My mom says you don't need to worry about getting her back and forth. She'll bring her or I will."

Nick grinned. "And I hear rumors you might have someone to stay with in Westport."

"Ha!" she answered. "You're tapped into the gossip these days?"

"No, but Sophie is," he said with a chuckle.

Nora's tone became serious as she turned her head toward him. "Hey, you know we're going to make this work. We *will* make Sophie happy and the good news is it makes her happy to be with both of us."

"I know that, and I'll do my part," he replied. "Vicki's parents have a place in the city, too, just across the park from where you'll be. Maybe we can use that some weekends to make it easier."

"Great," Nora said. She paused before adding, "And with school out, you know this is the best time to move Sophie, right?"

"Yeah, I know," Nick said glumly.

Neither spoke as they walked along the broad gray beach, staring at the rippled sandbars exposed by low tide. When they reached the jetty, the beach disappeared. Their route turned inland toward home and Nick broke the silence.

"Is this whole Helen thing going to cause you any problems going back into the government? Clearance-wise and all?"

"I don't think so," Nora replied, "especially after Judge Robinson issued his grand jury report saying I didn't do it and Rob did. All the surveillance videos from the data center and the financial records on the front running lined up with everything he told me."

"That's good," Nick said, kicking a rock ahead of him on the road. "But aren't you also leaving a lot on the table at Saugatuck by quitting in the middle of the year?"

"Actually, they've been great," Nora said. "With David stepping away and leaving Miranda in charge, it's the perfect time. She wants her own general counsel, which makes sense, so they're taking good care of me, money-wise—more than fair, as they say."

Nick booted the rock again. "And what did they decide to do about what happened with Rob Arslan?"

"You know I can't talk about that," Nora said sharply.

He gave the rock a hard kick. "Come on, Nora, it involved our daughter's life, which is why you told me about it six months ago. And I've never said a word about the details, as I promised, and I never will. But seriously, what happened with all that money and with his family?"

Nora stopped walking and turned to face him. "Okay, you deserve to know, but not a word to anyone, okay?" Nick nodded and Nora continued, "Believe it or not, they decided to let it go. David's view is that most of it went to a good charity anyway. And the piece Rob's wife gets to keep in the South Pacific is not that much in the great scheme of things—or at least in Saugatuck's world—and this way they limit the reputational hit. One of our executives killed another, but there's a good chance the front running doesn't come out. And going after Rob's widow seems pointless and cruel at this point. They're going to generously estimate what impact it had on client accounts and credit them the money, so only Saugatuck will take a financial hit over the whole thing. Then they can present it to our regulators privately as a problem found and problem solved."

"Wow," Nick said, "smart move, but still a lot of money."

"Ha. Surely you've been in hedge fund–land long enough to know that in a world of billions, tens of millions is a rounding error."

Nick shook his head and continued walking, abandoning his kicking rock. "Yup, you're right. Strange world."

With a smile, he added, "You sure you want to leave all this behind?"

"Very," Nora said, grinning back. "Although, as I said, I *will* make it work so you see Sophie a lot. This family will stay a family."

"Thank you," Nick replied. He took a few more strides and then added, "Honestly, Nora, it's because of you and your mom that I'm any kind of dad to Sophie. I appreciate what you've done and I know you'll do the right thing."

"Thanks for that, Nick," she said, reaching over to give his arm a quick squeeze before shoving her hands into her jacket pockets.

They walked on in comfortable silence.

—————

When Nora and Nick reached the front stairs, Sophie and her grandmother were deep in conversation.

"I'm just going to miss my friends here, that's all," Sophie was saying.

"You're going to see them a lot," Teresa answered. "And you'll make so many new friends. Here's the thing, bug: You're going to have twice as many friends as other kids have."

Sophie was thinking about that one when an unmarked police car pulled in the driveway. It stopped next to the Range Rover and the driver's door opened. "Speaking of friends," Teresa said with a smile.

"Hi Demi!" Sophie shouted as she jumped to her feet.

Demi swept the little girl up in her arms. "How's Super Sophie doing today?" Demi asked as they embraced.

"Okay, I guess," Sophie said, "just a little sad."

"We were talking about new friends and old friends," Teresa explained.

"Oh, it's great to have both, Soph," Demi said. "And you'll be close enough that you can see all your friends, whenever you want." She turned to Nora and added with a smile, "At least that's what I've been promised."

She smiled at Nick and extended her hand. "You must be Sophie's dad. I've heard so much about you. Demi Kofatos."

"Oh, I'm so sorry," Nora said. "Yes, this is Nick. This is Demi. She's with Westport PD and helped us a lot last year."

"I remember," Nick said. "It's nice to finally meet you. Thank you for all you did for our family." He paused and added, "Now, I have to run home. Soph, a hug for your dad? And tomorrow we'll hit the swing, I promise."

Sophie hugged her father and then stood on the stairs waving with the others as they watched the Range Rover navigate out between the truck and Demi's car. "Bye, Dad. Love you!" she shouted.

As Nick's car drove up the street, Nora's phone rang with the theme to *The Godfather*. She pulled it from her pocket and smiled.

"Mr. Rough, what a pleasure! I have you on speaker. I'm here with Mom, Sophie, and Demi."

"Hi all," Benny said. "Everybody doin' okay?"

"We are," Nora answered. "And you?"

"All is well," Benny said, "I'm about to go into a meeting with the US Attorney—Carmen says hi by the way—and it's in a SCIF so I won't have my phone. Jessica's gonna be there, too, because it involves her squad. I'm kinda a big deal now, doing secret stuff, as you know. Just needed to ask Teresa something but she wasn't answering, so I tried you."

"Oh, that's a little hurtful," Nora said, looking at Sophie and Demi. "Don't you think, girls? Benny using us like that to get to Nana?"

"Such a comedian," Teresa said, extending her hand. Nora gave her the phone, which Teresa took off speaker, holding the device to her ear as she walked away from the others. "Hey, you" was the last they could hear.

Demi looked at Nora and raised her eyebrows. "'Hey, you'? More here than meets the eye?"

"Oh," Sophie said, "Nana and Benny are dating. At least that's what she says. They talk on the phone all the time."

Nora smiled and shrugged. "Out of the mouths of babes, as they say."

"And a skiff or whatever?" Demi asked.

"Sensitive Compartmented Information Facility," Nora said. "Secure place where you can talk about classified material. No phones. Big part of the US Attorney's job is national security stuff—terrorism, espionage. That's one of the reasons I'm excited to be back."

Demi frowned. "Important work. Hope you don't forget a lowly local cop."

Nora laughed. "Yeah, 'lowly' *Captain* Kofatos. You pretty much run the place now that Dunham got fired for lying about his shady employment record. I still can't believe Westport PD didn't know he was chased out by the NYPD until Benny told them. But I'm sure the new leadership will be more thorough."

"Yep, that's actually gonna be top priority. In fact, we're already double-checking several background checks, especially the Dunham hires." She smiled and added, "Anyway, I'm just putting in my time until Laslo hires me and I can get a boat."

Nora smiled back. "Maybe you should consider becoming a fed at some point. No boats. But plenty of action. New York City is an exciting place and you could work with friends."

"Doesn't sound too bad," Demi replied. "At some point, I'd love to—"

"You're it!" Sophie interrupted, tapping Demi on the shoulder before jumping to her feet and disappearing into the maze of boxes crowding the front hall, Demi close behind yelling, "Look out, I'm fast and I'm gonna catch you!" Nora smiled as their laughter echoed through the empty house.

ACKNOWLEDGEMENTS

My writing would not be possible without Patrice, and without our kids, who helped at every turn. I'm also very grateful to my friend-readers—for their friendship even more than their valuable feedback —and especially to Westport's own Jack Menz, whose warmth and integrity were a gift that his family and friends lost far too soon.

As usual, my awesome agent, Kirby Kim at Janklow & Nesbit, and literary assistant Eloi Bleifuss made the book better, as did the team at Mysterious Press. Otto Penzler and Luisa Cruz Smith remain the dream team, but now I know and deeply appreciate the rest of the team, including Charles Perry, Julia O'Connell, Will Luckman, and their partners at Norton. I'm grateful to them all for making this possible—and fun. And last, but not least, special thanks to Aileen Boyle of Audere Media for great advice, hard work, and unshakeable good humor.